Three Times the Lady

Anna Chant

Copyright © 2016 Anna Chant

Anna Chant asserts the moral right to be identified as the author of this work. No part of this publication may be reproduced, distributed, or transmitted in any form or by any means, including photocopying, recording, or other electronic or mechanical methods, without the prior written permission of the author, except in the case of brief quotations embodied in critical reviews and certain other non-commercial uses permitted by copyright law.

Standard Copyright Notice
All rights reserved

Cover image from: CoverTemplates.com

*For my grandmother, Margaret
And in the loving memory of my grandfather, Roy*

Part One: The Year of our Lord 856

Princess of West Francia

Chapter one

Judith knelt before the high altar in the abbey church, knowing the prayers she should be making would not come. Cold from the stone floor seeped through the rough cloth of her habit, but did nothing to numb the ache in her knees. Peeping upwards all she could see was the white covered heads of the nuns, bent in devotion. Quickly she lowered her eyes again, before the priest noticed her inattention.

She shifted slightly, which eased the stiffness in her limbs, but left her mind as restless as ever. It was not that this life was terrible or that anyone was unkind to her. On the contrary, the nuns from the Abbess downwards treated her with the respect due to her rank, but the life was a tedious one. She longed for the chance to escape, although she knew it was hopeless. Her father had sent her to the Abbey of Hasnon two years before with the intention that she would make her vows and remain there or in a similar institution for the rest of her life. As the oldest daughter of King Charles of West Francia, it was considered unwise for her to marry. Such a marriage could give a man ideas beyond his station, making him a threat to her brothers. In an abbey she would not only receive an education, but would be likely to rise quickly to the position of abbess. There she could wield the power necessary to support her father and brothers and would, no doubt, one day welcome her as yet unborn nieces for their own incarceration.

"Heavenly Father, teach me to be content with this life," she prayed. "Forgive me for my desire for a life beyond these walls." Judith sighed. Her next confession would need to be a lengthy one, but at least it would give the priest something to do. She couldn't imagine many of the nuns having much to confess.

"Benedictus. Go in peace my children," the priest intoned.

Judith rose from her knees in relief. Terce was over. She would not have to wear out her knees on this stone floor again until noon. Noon, just a few hours away. Judith felt like screaming every time she heard the bell which ruled their lives. She looked around at the serene faces of the other nuns. They hurried to their morning work appearing contented with their lot. Giving no sign of her own resentment, Judith made her way to the workroom where she would spend the morning embroidering altar cloths. She watched the lower born nuns heading out to their tasks in the fields, feeling almost envious. She had heard it was back-breaking work, but at least it would be something different.

"My lady," a soft voice called.

Judith turned to see one of the nuns approaching her.

"The Abbess wishes to see you, my lady."

Judith's mood lifted at this slight variety to her routine. She made her way along the cloister, her mind running through all the possibilities for this summons. As she arrived at the sacristy she straightened her mantle, wishing that a mirror was not considered vain, so she could check her appearance was appropriate. Judith had taken to studying her appearance in the reflection of the washing bowl, although this gave her little pleasure. She supposed the plain leather belt did at least accentuate her slender waist and nothing could hide the beauty of her dark brown eyes, but the grey robe and white mantle concealing her hair did nothing to flatter her. Determined to appear regal, even if she could not look beautiful, Judith stood up straight as befitted a Princess of West Francia and knocked firmly on the door. Presumably she looked acceptable or the nun would have warned her.

"Enter."

She pushed open the door and entered a small chamber. A tiny window allowed some light, but for the most part, the room was cast into shadows brightened only in patches by flickering candles. The sacristy was almost completely taken up by a table covered in manuscripts. Behind the table sat a diminutive woman, wearing the fine jewelled cross of the Abbess.

"Ah, Lady Judith. Sit down, my child."

Judith sat on the stool indicated to her, feeling slightly surprised. Evidently this was to be a long talk.

"Lady Judith, you have been here now for two years. Are you ready yet to take your vows?"

Judith's heart sank. Nervously she shook her head.

"You are fourteen now, Lady Judith, no longer a child. It is time."

"I have no calling, Reverend Mother," Judith replied in a small voice.

"Why not?"

"I… I don't know," she said, her regal manner dissipating.

The Abbess looked stern. "Do you lust for the touch of a man?"

"No!" Judith was shocked. She would certainly prefer marriage to life in the abbey, but had given no thought to the marriage bed.

"Are you sure, child? Lust is a sin which should be purged."

"No, Reverend Mother. I swear I have felt no such desires."

"So what draws you beyond these walls?"

Judith thought quickly. She could not complain of the monotony of her existence. She doubted very much if the Abbess would be pleased to hear that Judith yearned for fine clothes, feasting and all the other trappings of a secular life.

"I always hoped to bear a child, Reverend Mother," Judith said, thinking surely this was an understandable desire. It wasn't a lie either. When she had resided with her siblings she had helped to care for each new brother and sister who arrived. Since arriving at the abbey she missed them intensely.

It seemed to work. The Abbess relaxed slightly. "The urge to become a mother is a powerful one. I too once felt it. But it will pass. Why, we often have young girls arrive here, who miss their own mothers. When you take your vows you could help care for them."

Judith shook her head, her heart sinking once again.

"Motherhood is full of risks, Lady Judith. If you wed, you may not live to care for your own child. Caring for the young novices could prove to be far more satisfying." The Abbess' voice had a hard edge. "Are you sure it is not a man you want? Look into your heart, child."

Reluctantly Judith realised she could not completely deny this. Yet it was not lust she felt. Her mind drifted back to the happy days of her childhood, listening to the musicians and storytellers as they told their tales of dragons and heroes. Although she knew such dreams to be childish, she too had dreamt of meeting and marrying such a hero. She looked the Abbess firmly in the eye. "I swear to you I have felt no lustful desires for any man."

"I am glad to hear that, but I do not understand what is holding you back from your vows. Lady Judith, you are a clever young woman. I am not certain that in a marriage you would be allowed to use your mind as you can here."

"I know."

"Indeed life outside of these walls may not be so different. Your days would be spent in sewing, weaving and ordering the household just as they are here."

"I realise that," Judith said. Yet in a way the Abbess was wrong. At court she could sew fine clothes and weave beautiful tapestries. It was nothing like the plain stitching and endless altar cloths which were her tasks there. There would still be regular prayers, but the bell would no longer rule her life.

The Abbess shook her head. "Why will you not take your vows? It is foolish to resist. Your father will never let you marry, but if you make your vows he will appoint you abbess. You will rule over your abbey's lands as surely as any empress."

Judith knew that everything the Abbess said was true, but she shook her head resolutely. She might have to stay there, but until she took her vows she had hope. Hope she might one day preside over a fine household and wear beautiful clothes. Hope she might bear and raise a child of her own.

The Abbess sighed. "Very well, Lady Judith. I shall have to write to your father and inform him you are still resisting your fate. Go now."

As Judith left the sacristy in relief, she wondered what her father's reaction might be. She had not seen him in the two years she'd been at the abbey and had only occasionally met him before. He was unlikely to be moved by her plight. Her mother, Ermentrude, would be even less bothered. No doubt she was with child again or have recently given birth. As Judith arrived in the workroom to continue stitching the altar cloth, she blinked back tears at how little hope she had.

For some weeks Judith's life continued as normal. The toll of the bell summoned her to prayers several times a day and she endured the simple meals, the dull tasks and nights on her uncomfortable straw pallet, until one summer's day she was again summoned to the sacristy.

The Abbess looked up, frowning. "I have heard from your father, Lady Judith."

Judith had not been asked to sit down, so stood, anxiously waiting to hear her father's will.

"He wishes you to join him at the Palace of Verberie."

Judith's surprise was so great she was unable to fully restrain a joyous smile at this announcement.

The Abbess continued to frown. "Do not hope for too much, Lady Judith. His message makes clear that he still wishes you to adopt a religious life. This will undoubtedly be a short visit."

Judith bowed her head, trying harder to hide her excitement.

"When am I to go, Reverend Mother?"

"He will send an escort for you when he wishes you to depart. Be prepared to leave as soon as they arrive."

Judith nodded, thinking she would be prepared to leave that very day.

"What am I to wear?" she asked. "Am I to be at court dressed as a nun?"

"Do not be insolent, my lady," the Abbess snapped. "You will dress as your father commands. If he wishes you to wear anything other than your habit, he will provide it."

"Forgive me, Reverend Mother," Judith murmured.

"Lady Judith, you will be representing our order at court. I trust you will behave accordingly."

"Yes, Reverend Mother."

"And I also trust that when you return, you will have cast off all childish dreams. It will be time to take your vows."

Judith hardly heard any more of what the Abbess was saying. She was too busy trying to keep her face composed. The moment she was dismissed and the door had shut behind her, she gave up. A huge smile of triumph lit up her face. She was leaving and was determined never to return.

Chapter two

A week later the entourage arrived. Judith was impressed by the glossy horses and the fine red and black tunics of the eight men who had come to escort her. A riding tunic had been found for her, but it was of a dull brown. She could not help feeling most unworthy of the grandeur of her escort.

"Now remember what I have said, Lady Judith," the Abbess said, as they left the abbey. "I expect to hear that your manner at court has done us credit."

Judith curtseyed to the Abbess, giving no sign of impatience. "Farewell, Reverend Mother. I shall endeavour to always be a credit to your guidance."

The Abbess relaxed into a smile as she made the sign of the cross in blessing. Judith smiled back, before taking the hand of the man who stood by her horse. She nodded graciously to him as he bowed over it, knowing that from this moment she must always display the dignity of her rank. She was the daughter of King Charles, who was the grandson of another Charles – Charles the Great, the first in her family to be crowned Emperor of the Romans. Judith the nun-in-waiting was no more. It was time to take her place as a true princess of West Francia. As the horses trotted away she did not look back.

Fortunately the weather was warm as it took four days' riding to reach Verberie, stopping each night at small abbeys and churches along the way.

"It is not too much further, my lady," the leader of the

entourage told her just after noon on the fourth day of riding.

Judith nodded to him, her mind quickly going over everything she wanted to say to her father.

"Once we are through the forest we will be able to see the palace," the man added.

All she could see before her was endless trees. No doubt her father and his men hunted in these forests. Judith thought longingly of fine venison and roasted boar. It would be good to eat such things again after the two years of simple meals she had endured. She looked ahead, eager to get her first glimpse of the palace. She could not recall being there before, having been raised with her brothers and sisters in a much smaller residence. Eventually the trees thinned and they came out onto a tract of meadow land.

"There," the man pointed.

Judith reined her horse in to stare at it. This palace was bigger than ever she had dreamed. A huge stone edifice was towering over the surrounding walls. She tore her eyes away from the main building to see a myriad of outbuildings. Judith's escorts smiled at each other as they took in the wonder flickering across the Princess's face.

They rode through several gateways and a paved courtyard before dismounting in a smaller courtyard close to the palace entrance. Boys ran forwards to take the horses and Judith gave an admiring look at her surroundings. Up close the palace was even more magnificent. Rows of stone and wooden buildings lined the courtyard walls, but she barely glanced at those. All her attention was on the facade, lined with columns stretching from two lofty towers at one end to the church at the other. This was truly a residence for a mighty king.

"Come, my lady." Her escort gestured towards the doorway.

A man in flowing white robes encrusted with gems was coming down the steps. The golden cross on his chest and the finely wrought ring on the hand raised to them in blessing, proclaimed him to be a bishop. The men bowed deeply to him and Judith too dropped into a curtsey.

"Welcome to Verberie, my lady," the man said. "I am Father Hincmar, Archbishop of Rheims."

"I thank you for your welcome, Father," Judith replied.

Hincmar looked at the men. "I will escort the Princess from here. Come, my lady, your mother is awaiting you."

Judith followed him into the palace. "Is my father here?"

"No, my lady. He has been in Burgundy this last month. He will return soon, we believe."

Judith felt a touch of relief that she would have some time to accustom herself to the palace, before having to discuss her future with her formidable father. Chambers and passageways followed on from each other. She smiled as she admired the intricate tapestries lining the walls, many telling stories she remembered from her childhood. Already she felt at home.

"I understand you have reservations about taking religious vows, my lady," the Archbishop interrupted her thoughts.

"A religious life is a noble one, Father," Judith replied calmly. "I would not wish to dishonour it by taking vows with doubts in my heart."

Hincmar nodded, his face expressionless. "We will talk more of this while you are here, my lady. Perhaps I can help you see your path with more clarity."

Judith screamed an inward denial as she smiled at the holy man. "I will appreciate your guidance, Father."

Hincmar knocked at a stout oak door and a voice invited them in.

"Your daughter is here, my lady," Hincmar said and left Judith in the doorway.

Judith stared at the woman who had risen to her feet. Remembering her manners, she bent her knees into a low curtsey.

"My dear child, please rise and come to me."

Judith took the hands of her mother, Queen Ermentrude. They had not met in the past two years and she thought the queen looked thin and pale. Ermentrude was dressed in a green dress, sweeping over a red tunic. The hems and sleeves were exquisitely embroidered and Judith looked resentfully at the plainness of her own tunic.

"You have grown so much, my child." Ermentrude smiled. "Come, sit down. Refresh yourself."

Judith took the chair indicated and sipped the goblet of wine handed to her. Compared to the watery ale she was used to, the wine was strong and full of flavour. Ermentrude dismissed the serving woman, fixing her blue eyes on her daughter.

"How are my brothers and sisters, Mother?" Judith asked, as her mother's scrutiny became uncomfortable.

"Mostly well, except... perhaps you have not heard about your sister, Hildegarde? She was born earlier this year, but we lost her in March."

Realising now why her mother looked so drawn, Judith reached out to take her hand. "Oh, Mother, I am so sorry."

Ermentrude squeezed Judith's hands. "These things happen. I have been fortunate the rest of you are well so far," she said with a smile that trembled. "I must confess I worry about Louis every time he is ill, but, God be praised, he keeps throwing off his illnesses."

Louis was Judith's next oldest sibling and the two had been firm friends throughout their childhood. Of all her family, he was the one she had missed most when she had been sent to Hasnon. "I wish I could see him while I am here."

Ermentrude's smile grew wider. "We hope you will. He is at Saint Dennis at the moment, but if he is well enough your father will bring him here. It will be good to have my two oldest children with me again."

Judith relaxed, pleased she seemed to be getting onto good terms with her mother. But her relief was to be short-lived.

"My daughter, why are you resisting your vows?"

"Why is it so terrible to want marriage and my own household?" Judith begged. "I want children. I am not cut out for a religious life."

"Oh, Judith, you know nothing of marriage. Look at me. I have been wed nearly fifteen years and I have had a pregnancy almost every year. You have no idea how tiring it is to be always with child. And within a few months of the birth of each one, your father returns to my bed and expects me to bear another."

Judith stared at her mother, shocked at the note of bitterness in her voice.

"And I so rarely even get to enjoy those children. What do you see in my life to envy? I have no power, if that is what you desire. An abbess has much more."

"Do you regret your children?" Judith asked.

"No, my dear child, of course I do not. I see you here, so beautifully mannered and assured. How can I be anything other than proud? But do you truly want my life?"

"I do not want a religious life."

Ermentrude sighed. "Well, it is your father's decision."

After an awkward silence Judith changed the subject. "Mother, what am I to wear while I am at court? Apart from this riding tunic, all I have are nun's robes. It would be good to wear something finer even if it is just for a short time."

A faint spark came to Ermentrude's eyes and she knelt on the floor next to her daughter, removing Judith's mantle and unfastening her hair. She smoothed out the dark locks which fell almost to her waist and stroked the soft skin of her cheek, still slightly flushed from her ride. "Oh, Judith, you have grown so pretty. Yes, I shall find some fine clothes for you. You should look like a princess while you are here."

So it was that when King Charles arrived a few days later, Judith was garbed as she had always hoped. Her mother had given her an embroidered pink tunic, with an over-dress of fine blue linen. Her dark hair fell over her shoulders and golden jewellery glinted around her neck and waist.

As her father strode into the hall, the women sank into deep curtsies and Judith did the same. He looked much the same as she remembered, tall and powerfully built. His hair was even darker than Judith's, with eyes just a shade lighter. Charles gave Ermentrude a polite, but perfunctory bow, before turning to Judith. He took her by the hand and studied her.

"Well, well, little Judith." His eyes shone. "You have grown into quite the young lady, have you not?"

"Welcome back, Father," Judith said demurely.

"So, what is all this I hear about you not wanting to be a nun?" he asked. To Judith's relief, his tone was good humoured.

"I do not think such a life is for me, Father."

Charles' eyes swept over her once again and he stroked his beard speculatively. "Perhaps you would be wasted in such a life."

Judith's heart leapt with joy. She had not expected such easy acquiescence. Ermentrude too looked surprised.

"You agree with her, my lord husband?" she asked.

"Perhaps." Charles frowned. "The Norsemen are proving troublesome. A king can never have too many allies in such times. A marriageable daughter could have its advantages."

Judith was aware her smile was a touch too triumphant as she looked around the hall, dominated by the huge table. Black and red banners emblazoned with golden lilies and crosses hung from the ceiling, while rich tapestries and weaponry brightened the walls. Perhaps soon she would be presiding over a hall similar to this one.

"I trust you have no romantic notions, Judith." Charles looked with irritation at Judith's smile. "You will wed where I command or you will return to the abbey. If you are a dutiful and obedient wife, your husband may come to regard you with affection."

"Of course I understand that, Father," Judith replied. "Naturally I will wed where the advantage to us lies."

"Good," Charles said, taking a cup of wine from a serving boy. "We will discuss this another day. Tonight is for reunions." He pulled a boy forward. "This lad has been looking forward to seeing you."

"Louis!" Judith cried, throwing her arms around the boy.

The boy returned the embrace, grinning from ear to ear. When he released her, Judith cast an apprehensive glance at her father, realising her behaviour had been too frivolous for a princess of West Francia. He gave her a disapproving look, but made no comment as he greeted Archbishop Hincmar. Judith looked back at her brother. Last time she had seen him he had been such a little boy. Now he was almost as tall as she was although very thin. A stranger would be unlikely to recognise them as siblings, but with his lighter hair and blue eyes, Louis strongly resembled his mother. He had recently been named as King of Neustria, but next to his powerful father, Judith had to admit he did not look the part.

"I scarce recognise you," Judith said, as Louis bowed before his mother.

"Y...You have ch...changed too," Louis replied.

Judith continued to smile, although she was sorry he had not yet outgrown his stammer. She had hoped it would improve as he grew older.

An impatient shake of the head was the only sign Charles gave that the stammer annoyed him as he took the hands of both his children. "It is good you two are here. I shall be able to present you to our guests."

"What guests are these, my lord?" Ermentrude asked.

"Do you remember King Athelwulf of Wessex? He bided with us a while last year on his way to Rome."

Ermentrude nodded.

"He is again passing through my realm on his return. I have ridden on ahead to be here to welcome him."

Judith sighed happily at the thought of helping to entertain foreign royalty. This was why she had wanted to escape the religious life. Already planning fine clothes for such an occasion, she missed the speculative look Charles gave her.

"We shall have some grand feasts during his stay," Charles said. "We must prepare. King Athelwulf will be here in a few days."

Chapter three

A few days later the sounds of foreign voices shouting instructions in the courtyard told Judith that the Wessex party had arrived. In the palace Charles had insisted no effort be spared to provide a magnificent welcome for the West Saxon King. There had been some muttering as to whether it was really necessary to go to quite such lengths to impress the visitors, but Charles pointed out that having just come from the papal splendour of Rome, King Athelwulf would be used to the finest hospitality.

Since his first night at Verberie, Charles had spoken little to Louis and even less to Judith, but the night before their guests arrived he took the time to ensure they understood the necessity of making a good impression.

"They are suffering from heathen raids in Wessex just as we are here. I want nothing more than to drive those barbarians away for good. The co-operation of Wessex would be most useful."

"I w...w...will t...try to i...impress K...King Athelwulf," Louis said, an anxious look creasing his face.

Knowing how the stammer angered her father, Judith quickly murmured her own assurances.

"Excellent," Charles said, directing a rare smile at his daughter. Almost as an afterthought he added, "King Athelwulf's young son is also travelling with him. Apparently he is a sickly boy. Make sure he too is welcomed." Charles looked with distaste at Louis. "I believe he is younger than you, but it seems you will have much in common."

∞∞∞

"Welcome to Verberie, my lord," Charles called jovially as the King of Wessex entered the hall for the welcome feast.

Judith watched as the two kings bowed to each other. King Athelwulf was of medium height with greying hair receding from a thin, serious face. The hair was longer than the Frankish fashion, falling almost to his shoulders and adorned with a golden circlet which glinted in the candlelight. He was richly dressed in a green linen tunic edged in fine gold threads, over dark breeches.

Athelwulf bowed deeply before Ermentrude and kissed her hand. "My lord, my lady allow me to present my youngest son, Prince Alfred."

At those words, a child stepped forward. He knelt to kiss the hand of both Charles and Ermentrude, bowing his fair head. Judith couldn't help but smile at the handsome little boy's accent as he spoke the words of greeting, his grey eyes looking earnestly at her father.

"Welcome, Prince Alfred. It is an honour to meet you." Charles patted the boy on the head, before turning back to Athelwulf. "My lord, please meet my eldest son, King Louis of Neustria."

Louis greeted their visitor formally, stammering more than ever with the solemnity of the occasion. A scowl flickered over Charles' face and Judith felt grateful to Athelwulf that he displayed no reaction other than to return the greeting with respect.

Charles took Judith by the hand. "And may I also present my firstborn, Lady Judith, Princess of West Francia."

Taking a deep breath, Judith swept into a low curtsey before the Wessex king. As she rose Athelwulf took her hand and bowed over it.

"I am honoured to meet you, my lady," he said, looking impressed.

Judith smiled back, knowing she was looking her best. Her pink overdress perfectly set off her dark hair and eyes, while a golden belt, studded with gems helped draw attention to her slender waist.

"We are delighted to welcome you to Verberie, my Lord King," she said, as Athelwulf raised her hand to his lips. "And you too, Prince Alfred."

"Thank you for your greeting, my lady. It is most pleasant for my son and I to be so warmly welcomed here after our long journey."

"I hear you have been in Rome, my lord. Your realm must be well ordered indeed that you have been able to leave it for so long."

"My realm is safe in the hands of my two oldest sons, my lady."

Judith did not let her face change by so much as a flicker, but her skin tingled at the mention of older sons. Her father's insistence that she dress her best for this meeting had not escaped her. She was certain his plans might include one of King Athelwulf's sons. She glanced at Charles, wondering if she had commanded the attention of their important guest for too long, but he was watching them with a satisfied expression.

Cheerfully, Charles invited his guests to be seated and Judith was unsurprised to find herself sitting next to the Wessex king. Determined to show herself worthy, she made sure to be charming to Athelwulf and Alfred. Despite their strong Wessex accents, both father and son had a good command of the Frankish language and she found Alfred to be an engaging child, very happy to talk of his time in Rome.

"There had been a huge fire in the Saxon Quarter," Alfred told her. "It was almost completely destroyed, but Father restored it all."

"It is important to me that the West Saxons have a place

to stay when on pilgrimage in Rome, my lady," Athelwulf explained.

"You are very wise, my lord. The men of Wessex are most fortunate." Judith hoped he might go on to talk more of Wessex and in particular his other sons, but instead both he and Alfred continued to discuss Rome and their long journey over the mountains. Judith was enthralled by their tales and the evening passed far too swiftly. It felt like she had scarcely sat down before it was time for the women and children to retire.

"Do not disturb yourself, my lord," Charles called when Athelwulf rose with Alfred. "Judith, my child, you can escort Prince Alfred to his chamber can you not?"

"Of course, Father," Judith replied, smiling sweetly at Athelwulf. "Please stay to enjoy the feast, my Lord King. I shall be pleased to look after Prince Alfred this night."

Athelwulf kissed Judith's hand. "Thank you, my lady. You have a daughter who is as kind as she is fair, my lord," he said to Charles.

Judith smiled to herself as she led Alfred from the hall. While they made their way along the passageways, she asked him the names of his brothers. She had a feeling she might be getting to know at least one of them very soon.

The next morning Judith and Louis were left to entertain Alfred while their fathers talked. It seemed odd to be showing him around the palace, given they were scarcely more familiar with the place than Alfred. The three were just returning from the gardens when a serving boy came towards them.

"My lady, the Lord King requests your presence in the Queen's chamber."

"Th...that's strange," Louis commented. "H...he cannot be f...finished with his talks already."

Judith smiled knowingly although she was surprised to hear

the talks had reached her already. "I must see what he wants. Please excuse me, my lords."

Judith walked briskly along the passageway. Athelbald or Ethelbert, she wondered. Athelbald, the elder, might be a more worthy alliance, but Alfred had told her that since the death of their mother, his relationship with his father had become increasingly volatile. If he fell out of favour, such a match might not be so good. However both sons had proved themselves to be fine guardians of their father's realm. Either would make an acceptable husband for a princess of West Francia.

Chapter four

As she neared the Queen's chamber, Judith was surprised to hear the sound of raised voices.

"She's only fourteen, Charles. How can you do this?" came her mother's voice. Ermentrude sounded distressed.

"It is a fine alliance," Charles snapped back. "She has no cause for complaint."

"No cause? How can you say such a thing?"

Judith hesitated before knocking. She had not imagined her parents would ever argue. The impression she had was that her father's word was law. She was puzzled too by her mother's anguish. It was obvious they were discussing her and Ermentrude knew full well Judith wanted to make a prestigious marriage. She brought the argument to an abrupt halt with a knock on the door.

"Enter," Charles called. "Ah, Judith. Come in."

Judith curtseyed. "You asked to see me, Father?" She looked around, but nobody else was present. Her mother sank down into a chair and bowed her head, but not before Judith had witnessed the distress on it.

"Sit down," Charles said, although he remained standing. "It seems you made an excellent impression on our guest last night. King Athelwulf has praised your manner and beauty to me."

Judith inclined her head, waiting for her father to get to the point.

"He has made an offer of marriage."

"That is most flattering of him," Judith said as calmly as she could. "To whom?"

"Don't be coy, Judith. I know you are no fool. To you, of course."

"I know that, Father." Judith gave a laugh. "Who does he intend me to wed? King Athelbald is his oldest son, I believe."

Ermentrude let out a low moan and Charles frowned. "No, my child. He wishes to marry you himself."

"But…" Judith's mouth dropped open. This was a possibility she had not considered. He was so old.

"You see, Charles, how ridiculous this is," Ermentrude burst in. "Judith is right. What of his sons?"

"From what I hear, his sons are a rebellious lot," Charles said. "He would be a fool to give either of his older sons so high ranking a wife."

"He is too old for her," Ermentrude protested. "He is far older than you, even. He is old enough to be her grandfather. If she were to wed a man of thirty or more I would not object. But King Athelwulf, although I am sure he is a good man, has seen more than fifty years."

"I care nothing for his age," Charles replied. "He has proved effective against the Norsemen in his realm. Such an alliance would be valuable indeed."

Ermentrude shook her head. "Does the thought of her marriage bed not disgust you? Look at her, Charles. How can you want her to give her maidenhood to an old man?"

Charles glanced at Judith, a flicker of guilt crossing his features as he met her wide eyes. He scowled at Ermentrude. "I will not be defied on this. If such a marriage is not to Judith's liking, she need not marry him. She can return to Hasnon and take her vows as I originally intended."

Judith heard no more of the angry words between her parents. Her thoughts raced. When she had spoken to Athelwulf the previous night, she had liked him very much but had considered him as a possible father-in-law. Now she needed to think of him in the light of a husband. He was very far from the romantic figure she had dreamt of, but that was of no matter. She had always known such a man was unlikely. Physically he had no doubt once been handsome. Those looks had faded, but there was nothing to disgust her.

Many of the Franks considered the West Saxons to be little more than barbarians, but Judith did not agree. Athelwulf had been finely dressed in the manner befitting a wealthy ruler. From everything Alfred had told her, it was clear he had been held in high regard in Rome. At the feast the previous night he had proved to be a learned man, yet there was no arrogance in his bearing. Quite the opposite. His manner towards her had been ever deferential. He was old, but he was intelligent and kindly. It could very easily have been worse.

"Father," Judith said, interrupting the argument. "I would be honoured to accept King Athelwulf's offer."

"No, no, Judith. Do not," Ermentrude begged.

"You want me to return to the Abbey, Mother?" Judith asked. "You know it is a life I have no liking for."

"Better than waste your beauty on an old man. My poor child, do you even know what marriage entails?"

Judith gave a short laugh. "Yes, Mother. There were widows at Hasnon. It was not all holy virgins."

"Then how can you agree to this?"

"Marriage to a young man is no guarantee of happiness. Such a man could be harsh or ungodly. King Athelwulf is older than I would have liked, but I detected no cruelty in him."

Charles laughed. "I don't know why I worried about Judith having romantic ideas, Ermentrude. Such foolishness is all in your own head." Charles turned his back on his wife to smile on Judith. "My dearest child, I am so proud of you. I can see you will be a most noble queen."

Queen. She liked the sound of that. Buoyed up by her father's approval, Judith smiled back.

"Queen?" Ermentrude spat. "Judith will not be a queen. Those Wessex men do not grant such a title to the King's wife. She will be a nobody."

"I am aware of the Wessex customs, my dear wife," Charles snapped back. "If Athelwulf wishes to wed my daughter, he will make an exception for her. If Judith is not crowned, there will be no marriage. Come, let us go to your future husband. I am sure he will agree our terms."

Judith laid her hand on her father's arm and in the ultimate insult to Ermentrude, they left her to trail behind them. They walked in silence to the hall, where Athelwulf and several of his men waited. All bowed politely as she entered. Judith kept her face expressionless as she dropped into a curtsey, ignoring the considerable curiosity on the faces of the Wessex men. She cast her eyes down, very aware of Athelwulf's steady gaze.

"My Lord King of Wessex, we are most flattered by your proposal," Charles said, getting straight to the point. "My daughter will be honoured to accept." Charles laid his hand on her shoulder and squeezed it slightly. Judith remained silent, feeling overwhelmed by all this.

Athelwulf bowed again to her. "The honour is mine."

"However, I do have some concerns," Charles continued. "I would need your assurance that my daughter will be treated with the highest respect in your land."

"You have that assurance," Athelwulf replied.

"Forgive me, my lord, but I require more than your word. I wish to see my daughter crowned Queen of Wessex."

There was a startled pause as Athelwulf glanced at his men. "That is not the normal custom in Wessex. Our ladies are treated with the utmost respect, but a crowning is for the king only."

"I mean no offence to the fair ladies of Wessex," said Charles. "But they are not normally descended from an Emperor. As you know, my grandfather and namesake was Charles the Great, the first Emperor of the Romans for many a century. My father, Lady Judith's grandfather, was the Emperor Louis. My daughter is worthy of the highest honour, or do you not think so?"

Athelwulf dropped his gaze, unable to meet Charles'

challenge. "My Lord King, please be assured that I hold Lady Judith in the very highest esteem. Grant me some time to consult with my advisors as to whether we can confer such rank upon her."

"Of course," Charles replied. "But be aware I will not allow Lady Judith to leave West Francia, unless she leaves as a queen."

Athelwulf bowed and withdrew with his men to a corner of the hall. Judith raised her eyes now Athelwulf was no longer looking at her. She watched him in conversation, trying to see beyond the grey hair and lined face to the intelligence in his eyes and the kindness of his manner.

Ermentrude sniffed. "Perhaps his men will advise against this," she said hopefully.

Charles shook his head. "Athelwulf will not allow a princess of West Francia to slip from his grasp. My daughter, you will be a queen before the summer is out."

Charles was right. Athelwulf soon re-joined them, his face all smiles. "We are in agreement, my lord. Your daughter is worthy of the highest honour we can bestow upon her. On the day Lady Judith becomes my wife, she will also become the Queen of Wessex."

"You do me a great honour, my lord," Judith said, plucking up the courage to meet Athelwulf's grey eyes. She smiled gravely at him, relieved to see only kindness in his gaze.

Athelwulf took her hand and kissed it. "I and Wessex are honoured by your acceptance, my lady."

Despite her bewilderment at how quickly events were proceeding, she continued to smile, pleased he was showing the proper respect due to her rank.

"Father Hincmar," Charles called. "With your blessing, we will solemnise the betrothal this day."

Ermentrude wiped away a few tears as she watched the Archbishop stand before Judith and Athelwulf. She found it almost impossible to watch as her innocent, young daughter was betrothed to the grey-haired man. Her expression was mirrored on many others who stood around. Age gaps were not uncommon in marriages, but one of forty years was extreme even for them. However, Judith felt no regret as she placed her hand in Athelwulf's. She had made her decision quickly, but with the option of being a nun or a queen, she did not see how she could have chosen differently.

"I, Athelwulf, King of Wessex most solemnly plight my troth to you, Lady Judith, Princess of West Francia."

"Repeat the words, Lady Judith," Hincmar said.

"I, Judith, Princess of West Francia," Judith said in a clear voice. "Most solemnly plight my troth to you, Lord Athelwulf, King of Wessex."

Athelwulf slipped a finely wrought gold ring set with a garnet over her finger. Charles handed one of his own rings to Judith, so she could bestow it on Athelwulf.

"You are now bound together as surely as husband and wife," Hincmar said. "May God bless your union."

Athelwulf hesitated before bringing his lips briefly to Judith's. His beard prickled her face, but Judith did not recoil. She smiled at him as he looked a trifle anxiously at her. With a twinge of amusement, she realised he was puzzled by her docility, but the concern in his face was touching

"We still have much to discuss on the Norse raids, my lord," Charles said. "But I am sure all our discussions will be as amicable as this one."

Athelwulf nodded. "Such an alliance will be useful to us both. God willing, the heathens will not stand a chance."

"You can go, Judith," Charles said. "We shall see you when we dine this night."

Judith bowed her head, dropping into a curtsey. She was relieved she would soon be alone to gather her thoughts. "I shall look forward to that, my lords."

Athelwulf kissed her hand once again. "So shall I, my dear lady."

Charles was clearly pleased with the proceedings as he smiled with more favour on his daughter than he ever had before. He clapped Athelwulf on the shoulders. "And I suggest we proceed with the marriage as soon as it can be arranged."

Part Two: The Year of our Lord 856 – 858

Athelwulf's Lady, Queen of Wessex

Chapter one

News of the betrothal soon spread and the shock at court was immense. Most were amazed the King was permitting his daughter to marry anyone, but a foreign man four times her age was even more peculiar.

Louis was the most outspoken. "H…how can you be married to that old m…man?" he demanded. "Y…you sh…should not s…stand for it."

"Hush, Louis." Judith frowned. "That is Prince Alfred's father you are talking about, as well as my betrothed."

"Y…you cannot want this," Louis said. "I m…mean n…no offence, Alfred."

Judith shrugged and lowered her voice. "I am not overjoyed at marrying a man old enough to be my grandfather," she said. "But the alternative is far worse. If I wed him, I become a queen. I will, I hope, have children. I will have a fine household. If I do not, I become a nun and my life might as well be over."

"Is there n…no alternative?"

Judith shook her head. "His age aside, I consider it a good match. From what I have heard, he is a noble king and a kind man. He is a loving father, is he not, Alfred?"

Alfred nodded, but he looked confused. "Are you going to be my mother?"

Judith almost laughed. Alfred was just seven years younger than her. Some of her other stepsons would be considerably older. "I suppose I will be," she said. "Is that so bad? We could become good friends, I feel."

Alfred smiled. "I am pleased you are coming back to Wessex with us."

"So am I." Judith smiled warmly back. She had given little thought to the family she was about to enter, but she realised at that moment that gaining a stepson as friendly and intelligent as Alfred, would be an unexpected benefit of the marriage.

But that summer did not see Judith as a bride or bring her a journey to Wessex. Just a few weeks after the betrothal accounts reached them of a Norse raid on the Frankish coast. Charles summoned his men and Athelwulf took the opportunity to prove his alliance and went with his own men in support of his future father-in-law.

Since the betrothal Judith had been seated next to Athelwulf at every meal. He was always courteous, but Judith had struggled to get to know him better. However, he sought her out before leaving to take a proper farewell.

"I shall pray for your victory, my lord," Judith said as he took her hand. "And shall await your safe return."

"Thank you, my lady. May I commend Alfred to your care?"

"Of course. You may rest easy, my lord. I shall be glad to give him my very best care."

Athelwulf bowed and kissed her hand. "You are most kind. Farewell, my lady."

Charles' farewell to both Judith and Louis was equally proper and stood in stark contrast to the fervent embrace between Athelwulf and Alfred. As the two kings rode away, Alfred looked close to tears.

Judith was unsure if she was feeling relieved or deflated by the postponement of the marriage plans, but the anxiety on Alfred's face reminded her of her promise. "Come, Alfred, we must occupy ourselves as best we can while our fathers are away. I would like you to teach me your language. It is not right that a queen cannot speak the language of her own people. Will you help me with this?"

Alfred's face brightened, and the two strolled around the

gardens, Alfred telling Judith the West Saxon words for everything they saw.

Over the summer Judith's friendship with her stepson grew. It was clear he was gifted with an intelligence way beyond his years. One day he showed her his most treasured possession. It was a book of tales from the land of the West Saxons. Judith, who had always loved stories, was fascinated to see such a thing.

"My mother gave it to me," he told Judith. "She used to read me and my brother, Ethelred, stories from it."

Judith, who had spent so little of her childhood in the company of her parents, was surprised at this. She could see how saddened Alfred still was at the death of his mother when she was not sure she would have even noticed if she had lost her mother at a similar age.

"Would you like to read some of the stories to me?" she asked Alfred gently.

"I can't read yet," Alfred replied, running his fingers reverently over the decorated letters. "But I can tell you some of the stories. I memorised them long ago."

Judith looked thoughtfully at Alfred, surprised he could not read. In West Francia a boy of his intelligence would have spent time in a monastery or in the company of a priest and would be able to read at least a little by the age of seven. Judith resolved to look into the matter of Alfred's education once they were in Wessex. It was clear these West Saxons could learn a lot about raising children from the Franks. But as Alfred chattered on about his childhood, laughing at memories of days spent with his parents, Judith couldn't help but feel wistful. Perhaps the West Saxons could teach the Franks a thing or two as well.

Charles and Athelwulf returned in jubilant spirits in the autumn, having seen off the Norse raiders. Ermentrude was unwell, so Judith welcomed the men back, glad for the chance to prove herself in the role of a queen. She waited formally next to Charles' throne as the two kings entered the hall together, Charles in the Frankish red and black and Athelwulf in a tunic emblazoned with the golden dragon of Wessex.

"Your betrothed has proved himself a most able warrior," Charles cheerfully told Judith.

Judith smiled as she stretched out her hand to him. "I never doubted it," she said warmly. "Welcome back, my lord. Prince Alfred will be pleased by your safe return."

"Thank you, my lady. I am most appreciative of the care you have given him."

"It has been no hardship," Judith replied. "He is a son to be proud of."

Athelwulf nodded, not hiding his pride at Judith's words. Charles looked approvingly on them as Athelwulf kept Judith's hand in his. "I am resolved that the wedding should take place with all haste," he said. "I don't doubt you are eager to receive your bride."

"I am indeed. I shall be the most fortunate of men."

The wedding was fixed for the Feast of Saint Nicetius, just two weeks after the army's return. On the morning of the wedding Judith awoke before dawn. She was in her mother's chamber and lay staring into the darkness, fear and excitement mingling in her.

"Are you awake, Judith?" her mother's voice came.

Judith lit a candle and turned to her mother. "I can't sleep," she said.

"Come here, my child."

Pleased by the unexpected instruction, Judith climbed into bed with her mother. Ermentrude put her arms tightly around her, surprising Judith with the intensity of her embrace. She looked up to see tears on her cheeks.

"Oh, Mother, this is my wedding, not my funeral."

"I know, my child, but this day is hard. I was older than you when I was wed, but I was still afraid. I think you are a braver spirit than I."

Judith sank her head against her mother's shoulder wondering whether that was true. She had revelled in the respect accorded to her since her betrothal, but the reality of her marriage and her new life over the seas was now before her. She could conceal her fear from all, but could not deny it to herself.

∞∞∞

That morning Judith was dressed in a creamy tunic of the finest wool and an even finer overdress of pink silk with elaborate draping sleeves. Judith had never before owned a silk garment and could not resist stroking the shimmering fabric in wonder. Gold and sapphire jewellery, a gift from her father, was clasped around her neck and wrists and a jewelled belt was fastened around her waist. One of the women spent an age combing her long dark hair until it flowed down her back, shining as much as the silk.

Charles' gaze proud when he arrived at the Queen's chamber to escort Judith to her wedding.

"You are the most beautiful daughter any man was ever blessed with," he said. "Wessex is fortunate to be gaining so fair a queen."

Judith was glad of the light cloak the women had wrapped around her shoulders, as she walked with her father to the church. She said nothing and nor did Charles give any further words of encouragement. The church was lit with hundreds of candles and reeked of incense. Franks and West Saxons alike had crammed into the church out of loyalty and curiosity to witness the spectacle, but Judith did not look at them. Her gaze went directly to the altar, where Athelwulf and Archbishop Hincmar waited.

Athelwulf turned as Judith and Charles entered. He was magnificently attired in a fine red tunic, lavishly edged in silk thread. A golden circlet was on his head and jewelled chains around his neck. An ornate sword hung at his side, proclaiming his warrior status, but all this magnificence could not conceal his age and as Judith took his outstretched hand, Ermentrude was not the only person in the church to shed a tear at the contrast they presented.

"I, Athelwulf, King of Wessex, do take Judith, Princess of West Francia as my wife with the full consent of her father, the most noble King Charles of West Francia."

Athelwulf slipped a gold ring studded with gems over her finger and looked expectantly at Judith.

Judith took a deep breath, but her voice still wavered. "I, Judith, Princess of West Francia, with the consent of my father, King Charles of West Francia, do take King Athelwulf of Wessex as my husband."

"In the name of our heavenly Father and our lord Jesus Christ, I pronounce Athelwulf, King of Wessex and Judith, Princess of West Francia, wed." Hincmar proclaimed.

Judith looked up at her new husband and he smiled reassuringly at her, before pressing his lips gently against hers. Judith had no time to absorb the reality of her marriage before Father Hincmar spoke again. "Lady Judith, wife of King Athelwulf of Wessex, I command you to kneel before the high altar."

Athelwulf stood aside as Judith did as she was bidden, feeling Hincmar's hand rest on her head. "May your marriage be blessed by Heaven, ever free from adultery committed by either body or heart. Permit not your eyes to look with desire upon another. You have been married to this man as a chaste virgin as Our Father commanded. May your union be blessed with many off-spring."

After further prayers for the fertility of her marriage, the

Archbishop looked over the assembled people. "This woman, Lady Judith, wife of King Athelwulf of Wessex has come to the altar in youth and beauty, as once did Queen Esther come to the people of Persia to ascend her rightful role as queen. Lady Judith, may you accept that role as she did, with wisdom and mercy. I anoint you as Queen of Wessex, just as Esther was anointed Queen of the Persians." Judith looked up into Archbishop Hincmar's solemn face as he marked a cross from chrism on her forehead. "Almighty Father, may she who is now anointed by your holy oil reign long over the fair land of Wessex with the courage, humility and virtue of her namesake, Judith of Bethuliah."

With the sacred oil still wet on her skin, Judith bowed her head in a fervent prayer of both gratitude that she had been granted this role and hope she could fulfil it. Faint gasps from the assembled people made her look up to see Hincmar holding aloft a golden diadem. Even those who had witnessed a crowning before, had never seen it performed on a woman. Everyone held their breath as he lowered it onto Judith's head.

"May you shine in your role of Queen as these gold and gems also shine, bringing the blessing of the sacred rite to the fair land of Wessex. I command you to rise, Queen Judith of Wessex."

Judith turned to look out at the people. Her appearance had already attracted much admiration, but now she looked regal.

"All hail Queen Judith of Wessex," Athelwulf pronounced, with a proud look at his queen.

His call was picked up by the people and graciously Judith inclined her head. Athelwulf took her by the hand and led her to a throne, draped in the banner of Wessex. They sat on it as a procession of Wessex men, led by Prince Alfred, came to kneel before her and swear an oath of loyalty. As the last one backed away from her presence, Judith looked after him, the realisation that those men were her subjects dawning on her. Athelwulf rose to escort her to the wedding feast, but Judith allowed herself a few moments longer on the throne, her bewilderment at her new role giving way to a surge of triumph.

Chapter two

On the morning after her wedding, Judith awoke alone. Athelwulf had already risen without disturbing her. Judith smiled slightly at this further sign of his consideration. She was surprised to see it was already full daylight and she smiled even more as she savoured the thought that the cloister bell no longer ruled her life. She was relieved her wedding night was over. When she had been brought to the bed the previous night, her mother had made her concerns obvious and remembering some of the tales of marriage she had heard from widows at the abbey, Judith too had grown anxious. But there had been no need to fear. It was already clear that the nights of pain of which she had heard so much, would not be her fate. She muttered a quick prayer of gratitude that her husband had proved to be a kind man. Less than a full day since her marriage, Judith was hopeful her new life would agree with her.

Judith wrapped the fur covers around her shoulders, glad she could now forever forget the coarse, itchy blankets of the abbey. Feeling overwhelmed by the events of the last day, she considered remaining in bed a while, but decided such an act lacked the dignity a queen should show. Resolutely she pulled a robe around her and pushed open the door to an ante-chamber.

"The poor, sweet girl," one of her women was saying. "Having to submit to an old man."

"And her not much more than a child," another replied. "Such a marriage is not right."

"Of whom are you talking?" Judith asked icily.

The two women gaped at her. Even in a loose robe with her hair tousled, Judith managed to be every inch the queen.

"If I find you are speaking of myself and my husband, I shall have you both beaten. I trust this is not the case."

"No, no, my Lady Judith," the first woman stammered.

"My Lady Queen is the correct way to address me," Judith informed the woman. Normally she would not worry about such details, but she was determined to stop any gossip in its tracks.

"Yes, my Lady Queen." The second woman cast her eyes down.

"One of you fetch my clothes, the other some food. You are not here to chatter. Is that clear?"

"Yes, my Lady Queen," both women said as they scurried to do her bidding.

Judith smiled to herself. Marriage was not so bad, while being a queen was proving to be everything she had hoped for.

∞∞∞

When Athelwulf returned to the chamber that morning, he found Judith seated on a bench by the window, a platter of bread and meat before her. She was dressed in a green tunic of the finest wool, her hair still loose around her shoulders.

He bowed to her. "Is all well with you this morning, my lady wife?"

Judith hid her smile at the note of genuine worry in his question. Athelwulf, like her mother, seemed far more concerned with her wellbeing than Judith was herself. "Of course, my lord. Will you join me?" She indicated the food and ale.

"I thank you, my lady, but I have already broken my fast. I came to present you with this." He gestured towards two men, who had been standing in the doorway. They carried in a chest and placed it on the floor in front of Judith.

"It is the custom in my land for a man to present his bride with a gift on the morning after their wedding," Athelwulf replied in answer to his wife's inquiring look.

He opened the chest and Judith gasped. The box was stuffed with fine cloths, coins and gem-studded jewellery. Never had Judith seen such an array of treasures. She knelt on the floor, lifting piece after piece in wonder.

"My lord, your generosity leaves me speechless," she said at last.

"I shall bestow some lands on you once we are in Wessex," Athelwulf said, as Judith continued to look at the marvels in the chest. "I hope that will sweeten the deal for you, my lady. I know you must think this a poor bargain."

Judith looked up, surprised by the awkward expression on his face. He was an intelligent man and she realised he must be aware of everything being said about them. Judith felt a sudden rush of affection which had nothing to do with her gratitude for his generosity.

She gestured to the bench. "My lord, will you not join me in a drink at least?" She handed him a cup of ale as he sat down hesitantly beside her. "My lord, may I speak freely with you?"

"Of course. My lady, we are not a formal bunch in Wessex. I would be pleased for you to use my name when we are alone."

"If you will do the same." She smiled. "Are you aware that before you proposed marriage, I was bound for a religious life?"

"When your father and I were discussing the possibility of a marriage, he told me you were intending to take your vows."

Judith couldn't help laughing, bringing a look of at first surprise and then pleasure to her husband's face. "I never intended to make my vows, but there was considerable pressure on me to do so. I do not know how much longer I could have withstood it, if you had not honoured me with your proposal." Judith paused, not certain she was making the right impression. She knew Athelwulf was a deeply religious man. "A religious life is an honourable one indeed, but it is not one I have any inclination for."

"I think you were born to adorn a court," Athelwulf replied. "Your beauty should not be concealed in a nun's habit."

Judith smiled shyly at the sincerity in his voice. She was also pleased that finally someone understood her point of view.

"Your offer freed me from that. You have conferred upon me a high position. I am accorded respect and honour beyond my expectations. I have fine clothes and riches. While there is still much for me to become accustomed to, please believe me, that even before your generous gift, I did not consider this a poor bargain." She stretched out her hand to him. "I only hope you never do."

Athelwulf took it. "My dear Judith, all I hoped for from this marriage was an ally in my struggles against the Heathen Army. To gain so gracious and beautiful a queen is beyond anything I expected. I am pleased with this deal beyond all measure."

"Then we are both content," Judith said. Taking another mouthful of ale, she summoned up the courage to switch language. "While you were away, I asked Alfred to teach me your language. Is he not a fine teacher?"

Athelwulf smiled back, continuing to hold her hand in his. Judith had spoken slowly and the accent made her hard to understand, but her words were perfect. "He is indeed a fine teacher and you a most able student."

"Athelwulf, I would like you to always use this language with me now. If you have the time, please tell me more of Wessex."

Athelwulf looked more delighted than ever with his new wife. "Very well, but you must tell me if there is anything you do not understand." Speaking slowly, Athelwulf told Judith of his four sons and his daughter who he had given in marriage to the Mercian king a few years before and who he still missed very much.

"Judith?" Ermentrude's voice came from the doorway. She stopped in surprise at seeing them seated together, Judith smiling attentively up at her husband. "Forgive me, my lord. I did not realise you were still here. I shall return later.

Athelwulf got to his feet, quickly draining his cup. "No, please do not, my lady. I stopped here for just a moment." He kissed Judith gently on the cheek. "I shall leave you ladies to your visit."

Judith watched him as he left, concealing a smile at his awkward manner, before pouring a cup of ale for her mother. Ermentrude was still staring at her. She had come, expecting to find her daughter in need of comfort. She was shocked to see her already on comfortable terms with her husband. In fact of the two newlyweds, Judith seemed to be the one more at ease.

"Mother?" Judith was holding a cup out to her, a bland smile on her face.

Ermentrude sat down. "Judith, are you happy?" she asked.

"Why should I not be?" she asked. "I have a gentle and kind husband. He is generous too." Judith indicated the open chest. She pulled out a golden bangle inlaid with green glass and fastened it around her wrist, making a show of admiring how well it went with her tunic.

Ermentrude shook her head. "It is easy to see the blood of Charles the Great runs in your veins. You are so different from how I expected a daughter of mine to be."

Judith raised her eyebrows at the hint of criticism in her mother's voice. It seemed Ermentrude would have been almost relieved if she had found her bewailing her fate in being married to an old man and sent away to a barbarian land. "He has treated me only with kindness and deference. I think he is more respectful of me than Father is of you."

"He treats you with respect now in your own land. You may find his manner changes towards you, once you are in his."

Judith considered this. "Perhaps," she said. "But I do not think so. Such courtesy seems to be a natural part of his character."

"I hope so, my child. I do want you to be happy. Perhaps as he already has so many sons, he will not be too demanding of you." Ermentrude sighed. "I am with child again."

"I thought you were," Judith said. "Perhaps we will both have a child next year. Please do not worry about me, Mother. Truly this marriage is not bad. I am proud to be Queen Judith of Wessex."

∞ ∞ ∞

Just two weeks after the wedding, Athelwulf, Judith and the Wessex men departed Verberie. The days before had been full of feasts and celebrations. For the most part Judith had enjoyed those weeks. It had given her enormous pride to attend the feasts at Athelwulf's side, taking her place as an equal of her parents, although privately Judith believed she now outranked her mother. Ermentrude held the title of queen merely as a courtesy. She had never been crowned. At the farewell feast Charles lavished her with gifts, making it plain his daughter was in high favour.

As the horses and entourage gathered in the courtyard, Ermentrude gave her daughter a last embrace. "Stay well, my child. Send us word whenever you can. You are in my prayers."

"And you will be in mine," Judith replied.

"F...fare well, Judith," Louis said and as he hugged her, Judith felt a single flicker of regret wondering if she would ever see her brother again.

Charles was sharing a last joke with Athelwulf, but he too took his daughter in his arms for a rare display of affection. "Farewell, my dearest child. You have made me most proud." He turned to Athelwulf. "I know you will take good care of my daughter. Remember, you bear a rare Frankish treasure with you this day."

"I do indeed. You may rest easy. Your daughter's well-being will remain ever a priority with me."

"And I hope soon to hear that a young Wessex prince is my grandson."

Judith smiled, hoping too that would soon be the case.

Athelwulf helped her onto her horse, before mounting his own and Alfred brought his horse to ride on her other side. Athelwulf and Judith smiled at each other, her excitement about seeing Wessex, easily overcoming any nerves.

"Let us head for home," Athelwulf said.

"Yes," said Judith, catching Alfred's eye. "Let us go home."

∞∞∞

It took four days to reach Calais where they were further delayed by poor weather. Ermentrude's fears that Athelwulf might become less respectful once they were away from her family, proved to be unfounded. His manner towards Judith remained ever deferential and he insisted that all treated her with the utmost respect.

"We should be able to make the crossing tomorrow," Athelwulf announced as he entered their chamber one evening. "The signs are that the weather will be fine in the morn."

Judith was sat on a low stool, staring at the candles. "That is good news," she replied, glancing up.

Athelwulf was shocked to see traces of tears on her face. Since leaving Verberie her spirits had been high and not once in their marriage had he seen her cry. He knelt down, putting his arms around her. "Oh, Judith, I am so sorry. I forget in my eagerness to be home, how hard it must be for you to leave your own land."

Judith gave a half smile. "I do not weep to leave my land," she replied. "I am looking forward to seeing Wessex."

"Then what has ailed you? Do not deny it, Judith. I can see you are upset."

Judith nodded. "My monthly bleeding has come upon me. I have not yet conceived."

Athelwulf tightened his arm around her. "Do not be distressed, my sweet girl. I had no expectations you would conceive so quickly. I would not reproach you."

Gratefully Judith leant her head against his shoulder, as he gently he stroked her hair. "Indeed I would not reproach you if you never conceive. It is far more likely the fault would lie with me."

"I do not think so," Judith said. "You sired a fine son little more than seven years ago. There is no reason why you should not sire another."

"Well, I hope I will. We shall pray to be blessed, but you must not worry yourself on this matter."

Fleetingly Judith wondered how her father reacted each month her mother failed to conceive and how he had reacted to her own birth, when surely it was a son he had wanted. Feeling gladder than ever for such an indulgent husband, she smiled to alleviate Athelwulf's concern and hoped she would quickly be able to repay his kindness with a son.

Chapter three

As the sailors had foretold, the next day was breezy but bright. The clear day meant it was already possible to see the faint outline of a coast on the far side of the sea.

"Is that Wessex?" Judith asked as they waited to board the ship.

"That is Kent," Athelwulf replied. "But it is part of my realm."

Judith had recovered from her disappointment of the previous night and felt most foolish for her tears. Even her mother, a woman who had spent most of the last fifteen years with child, had not conceived in the first month of marriage.

As she boarded the boat, Judith took one last look back at her native land. But once Athelwulf had settled her on a bench in the centre of the boat, she turned her eyes to the opposite coast. Alfred had run to the stern, pointing excitedly and shouting over his shoulder to his father about everything he could see. Athelwulf called back to him, but sat next to Judith, putting his arm around her shoulders.

"If there is anything I can do to make your life happier in my realm, you must tell me," he said.

Since he had witnessed her tears, he had been more solicitous than ever. Judith smiled as the sailors cast off and oarsmen manoeuvred the boat toward the harbour mouth. She reached up to take his hand. "I am most undeserving of such kindness," she said. "But I thank you. I feel sure I will be happy there."

The crossing was choppy but fast, as the wind skipped

their flotilla over the waves. Judith looked up at the standard fluttering from the mast. It bore the dragon of Wessex, a wyvern as Athelwulf had called it. It was her standard now and she could not help but feel proud. The day was cool and she pulled her cloak tightly around herself, glad Athelwulf had continued to sit with her. As the boat came into harbour, Alfred came to lean against his father's other side. Athelwulf ruffled his son's hair and they stared up at the white cliffs towering over them, emotion flickering over both their faces.

"We are home at last, my son."

As soon as the boat was secured, Athelwulf disembarked. Instantly the men who had gathered to welcome them, fell to their knees. Athelwulf smiled benevolently at them, waving them up.

"Welcome home, my Lord King," one the men said.

"I thank you. It is good to be back," Athelwulf said, extending his hand to Judith. She hesitated, savouring the moment of making her first step onto her new land. "My people," Athelwulf continued. "Please welcome Queen Judith of Wessex."

The men looked somewhat startled, but fell quickly back to their knees. Judith smiled, pleased to see that even in his land, Athelwulf was insisting she was treated with deference. "Thank you for your welcome, men of Kent," she said, taking care with the West Saxon words. "Please rise."

Behind her Alfred leapt to the shore, a broad smile on his face. Athelwulf put an arm around both of them. "Welcome to my realm, Judith. Come, Alfred, let us bring your new mother somewhere she can rest awhile after the journey."

They made a brief ride to a small residence in a commanding position on the cliff top.

"It is not the finest residence," Athelwulf warned her. "Canterbury and Winchester are much finer, although perhaps we have nowhere to match the splendour of Verberie."

Judith laughed. "You forget I was not long at Verberie. Before that I was at the Abbey of Hasnon. As long as I do not have to sleep on a lumpy pallet, I shall be most content wherever we reside."

Athelwulf took her by the hand to lead her into the hall. "I am sure we can offer you better than a lumpy pallet."

∞∞∞

The dwelling did indeed lack the elegance of the Frankish palaces, but nonetheless it was comfortable. Athelwulf planned to rest there a few days before continuing their journey to Winchester, the most prominent city of Wessex. A feast was hastily organised for that evening attended by many from the surrounding area and Judith was formally presented as their queen.

The day after their arrival Judith was resting in her chamber when a serving boy informed her that Athelwulf was requesting her presence in the hall.

"Prince Ethelbert has arrived," the boy said.

Judith took a moment to fasten up her hair before hurrying to meet another of her stepsons. She found Athelwulf standing by the fire, his arm resting on the shoulders of a tall, fair-haired man. So this was Ethelbert, the man appointed to govern Kent while Athelwulf was away.

Athelwulf turned as she entered. "Judith, my dear, please meet my second son, Ethelbert."

Ethelbert stared at Judith, obviously shocked by what he saw. Judith stretched her hand out to the thin young man, thinking privately that she was finding these Wessex men an awkward lot. "I am honoured to meet you, Prince Ethelbert."

"My son, as I am sure you are aware, this lady is my wife and the Queen of Wessex," Athelwulf said with a slight edge to his voice, as Ethelbert continued to stare.

Ethelbert's fair skin flushed and he dropped to one knee, taking Judith's hand. "It is an honour to meet you, my Lady Queen," he said, raising it to his lips. "Welcome to the Kingdom of Kent."

Judith bowed her head in a gracious acknowledgement, but before she could say anything, Alfred darted into the hall.

"Ethelbert!" he cried with a grin.

Ethelbert rose to his feet, catching Alfred up in an embrace. "Little Alfred, I would hardly have known you, you have grown so much."

Judith smiled as she watched them. These Wessex men might be awkward, yet their hearts seemed to be big. She noticed Athelwulf smile too at the reunion of his sons. Remembering her father's disapproval when Louis had greeted her with a similar exuberance, she was taken aback by his reaction.

"What are your plans now, Father?" Ethelbert asked. "Will you come to Canterbury?"

"I intend to remain a few days here before we start our journey to Winchester," Athelwulf replied.

Ethelbert frowned. "That might not be so easy."

"Why ever not?" Athelwulf demanded. "I had not heard there was trouble in Wessex. Is it the heathen army?"

"No, Father. It is Athelbald."

"What of him?"

Ethelbert glanced awkwardly at Judith again. "He was not happy to hear of your marriage."

"I did not think I needed my son's permission to wed," Athelwulf said sharply. "I do not care if he is happy about it. It is not his decision."

"I know, Father, but he does not want you to return to Wessex. His message was that you should stay here or-"

"Or what? Tell me exactly what he said, my son."

"Or better yet, return to West Francia."

"I will not. The boy will not stop me bringing Wessex's queen to Winchester."

"It is not just him," Ethelbert said, looking miserable at being the bearer of such news. "Bishop Eahlstan of Sherborne and Lord Eanwulf are backing him."

Athelwulf frowned, clearly disheartened by this news. "My plans remain unchanged. In fact, I shall bring them forward. Judith, Alfred, can you be ready to ride in the morn?"

∞∞∞

Athelwulf was agitated when he came to their chamber that night, the news of his son's rebellion visibly taking its toll. Judith watched him as he paced around, unsure how to comfort him, particularly as she appeared to be the cause of the upset.

"Bishop Eahlstan and Eanwulf too," he muttered. "I thought I could at least trust them. How did the boy turn those two against me?"

"I am sorry," Judith said suddenly.

Athelwulf stopped pacing and stared at her. "Why?"

"This is my fault. Your son is rebelling because of me." Judith attempted a smile. "I fear it is you who got a very poor bargain in this marriage."

Athelwulf sat beside her on the bed. "No, Judith, this is not your fault. I have often had trouble with Athelbald. Even as a boy he continually defied me. Our marriage is simply an excuse. Perhaps it was foolish of me to leave Wessex in his hands. I should have known he would be reluctant to relinquish it."

"But our marriage is making matters worse."

"No, it is not. An alliance with West Francia could never make matters worse." Athelwulf sighed. "But I do not want a fight with my son. We should be conserving our energies for the struggles against the Norsemen."

"Tell me more of Athelbald. I believe he is your eldest son?"

"He is my eldest surviving son. He was always a lively boy, far stronger than Athelstan, my eldest son. The proudest day of my life was when Athelbald fought at my side against the heathens at Aclea. It was a glorious victory and one I am not certain I would have secured without him. In the grievous days after Athelstan died, I took comfort in having so great a warrior as my heir. But Athelbald became difficult, resenting his younger brothers. I think he would have preferred to have had more sisters."

"Was there trouble between you before you left for Rome?"

"We argued sometimes. It got worse after his mother died. She was ever the peacemaker between us. I hoped giving him the responsibility of Wessex would improve matters, but I think it has made things worse. Judith, if you need to rest here longer, please tell me."

"Are you heading for Winchester?"

"I must."

"Then I am coming too. I think we should stand together," Judith said firmly. "Unless my presence could make matters worse."

Athelwulf's careworn face lightened. "No. Reminding the people of my alliance with West Francia can only be an advantage to me. They will want a king who can make such alliances against the heathens. Thank you, Judith." He kissed her hand before standing. "I have disturbed you long enough. Get some sleep now. I want to cover as much ground as we can tomorrow."

∞∞∞

It was a hurried departure from Dover, yet the sight was a splendid one. Athelwulf and Judith took their place at the head of an entourage of Wessex men all in red tunics. A scarlet standard, emblazoned with the wyvern fluttered over them. Athelwulf seemed calm that morning, with no sign of the distress he had shown the night before. Ethelbert rode at his father's other side, while Alfred drew his horse up beside Judith.

She glanced at him, detecting the excitement under his calm

expression. She smiled, understanding his emotion. She felt it too. This was the life she had longed for in the days when she had been shut up in an abbey.

But she felt ashamed at her excitement as Athelwulf looked solemnly at them. "I never thought to march against my own son."

"I hope it will not come to that," Ethelbert said quickly. "I do not wish to fight my brother. We have agreed well enough this last year."

Athelwulf frowned at him. "I trust you are with me. It is bad enough that one of my sons is defying me."

Ethelbert looked down at his horse's head and refused to comment.

"I am with you, Father," Alfred cried.

"And so am I, although I would be of no use in battle," Judith added, pleased to see his face brighten once again.

Athelwulf laughed. "I do not want to see Alfred in battle just yet either," he said. "But the support of you both will inspire me. Come, let us ride!"

They set a brisk pace, riding along the coast with Judith eagerly taking in everything they passed. The countryside was lush and green, although the year was advanced. She could see that once the trees were in leaf again, the land would be a fair one.

Three days later Athelwulf announced they were in striking distance of Winchester. He set up a base at an abbey and it was there that an envoy from Athelbald arrived. The news was not good. Athelbald was in residence at Winchester and he did not want his father coming near.

∞∞∞

Athelwulf was furious. "Winchester is mine. That boy will not keep me out."

Judith tried in vain to soothe him. She had never seen him

in such temper. His manner to her had always been so kindly, she had forgotten that under his gentle, scholarly exterior was a warrior of some repute.

"Father, I will not fight my brother," Ethelbert said.

"Then perhaps you should go to him," Athelwulf snapped. "I will have no traitors in my camp."

"Would you fight your father?" Judith demanded.

Ethelbert fixed his cold blue eyes on her. "It does not concern you, my lady."

"Anything which concerns your father, concerns me."

"I have no intention of discussing such matters with a woman, even if she does claim to be Queen of Wessex."

"Be silent, Ethelbert," Athelwulf roared. "You will not address Judith in that manner. Apologise immediately."

"We had no problems here before she came," Ethelbert said rather sulkily.

"No problems? There has always been trouble with Athelbald. And I suppose you do not consider the Norsemen a problem? Judith's presence here is a symbol of a powerful alliance that could rid us of those heathens once and for all. Apologise to her and accord her the respect due to the Queen of Wessex."

Ethelbert backed down at the anger in his father's eyes. "Forgive me, my Lady Queen," he muttered.

Judith looked at Athelwulf with increased respect. She had often thought his manner too mild to be an effective king and was impressed he could be so commanding when the occasion demanded it. "What will you do now?"

"Attack Winchester if I must," he replied with obvious reluctance.

"But, Father, you love Winchester," Alfred put in.

Athelwulf smiled at Alfred, the affection clear in his eyes. "I know, my son. It will pain me greatly to cause any destruction, but I cannot leave my city in the hands of my enemy." He shook his head. "My enemy. I can scarce believe I am using such words to describe my own son."

"Father, let me go to Athelbald," Ethelbert said, appearing moved by his father's emotion. "Not to join him against you, but to try to bring you together."

Athelwulf's shoulders slumped. "Can I trust you, my son? If you have to choose sides, who will you choose?"

Ethelbert's eyes dropped. "I don't know, Father. This is why I would bring you together. Fathers and sons should not fight and nor should brothers. I swear, by any oath you wish me to swear, that I will do my utmost to bring a resolution to please you both."

"Very well, my son. I will trust you. I would prefer not to fight, but there are some things I will not compromise on. My alliance with West Francia brings us great prestige and allies we desperately need. Judith will be treated with the highest respect here. She sits beside me on the throne and that is not up for discussion."

∞∞∞

It was with some sadness that they saw Ethelbert depart the next day. "I feel I am losing another son," Athelwulf said soberly.

Alfred looked bewildered as he stood beside his father. Athelwulf pulled the boy close to him and put his other arm around Judith.

"I thank God I have you two with me," he said.

"Perhaps soon you will have another son," Judith said, smiling, although somewhat surprised he was so grateful for her presence. She supposed it was more that he was glad for the Frankish alliance, given he had known her for less than half a year.

"I hope so. Your son would be most fine."

For several days they heard nothing. Many of the West Saxon nobility came to Athelwulf and urged him to attack. Athelwulf was cheered by the loyalty of these men, but insisted Ethelbert be given more time to bring a peaceful resolution. One visitor who was greeted with particular pleasure was the Bishop of Winchester.

"Father Swithun, it is good to see you. Does my son know you have come to me?"

"He does, my lord. He knows I do not condone his actions." The Bishop turned to Judith. "I fear you must have a poor impression of the diocese of Winchester, my Lady Queen, but even so, I bid you welcome."

Judith thanked him, taking an immediate liking to the kindly, grey-haired man.

"Father Swithun was my teacher when I was a boy," Athelwulf added. "And has remained my very great friend and advisor. Father, many are advising me to attack Winchester. Do you agree?"

Swithun looked solemn. "I would be grieved indeed to see Winchester under attack."

"And I do not want to draw arms on two of my sons," Athelwulf replied, smiling at his old friend.

"You have another son, do you not? Where is he?" Judith asked.

"Young Ethelred is also at Winchester," Swithun said. "He is in good health and spirits, although eager to see you."

"That is another reason not to attack Winchester." Athelwulf shook his head. "What of Athelbald? Have you spoken to him?"

Swithun nodded. "King Athelbald is concerned that if you should sire a son on the Queen, such a boy might have a greater claim to the throne of Wessex than he."

"A son of Judith's would certainly have a claim, but why would it be a greater one? The likelihood is that any further children I sire would be too young to reign upon my death."

"That may be true," Swithun replied. "But the Lady Osburh, although your much honoured wife and mother of your children, was not a consecrated queen. He fears Queen Judith's offspring would have a greater claim, particularly if such a boy was backed by West Francia. If you could find a way to assure him he remains your heir, I believe he would be more amenable. He has ruled well this last year."

Athelwulf's brow creased in thought. "I would be glad to leave him in command of a portion of my realm, if I could be certain of his loyalty. But I do not have that assurance at present."

A few days later a messenger came from Ethelbert, stating that Athelbald was willing to talk. Athelwulf sent his agreement with a mixture of anger and relief.

"What is Athelbald really like?" Judith asked Alfred that evening, when Athelwulf was busy elsewhere.

"Loud," said Alfred. "Whether angry or happy, he is always loud."

Judith was surprised. She began to see that compared to his father and brothers, Athelbald must feel very different.

"Let us sort that fool out," Athelwulf said as they mounted their horses the next morning.

An entourage, made up of countless Wessex nobles and clergy accompanied them as they rode in the crisp morning air to Winchester. Athelwulf was not enjoying the fine morning and he spoke little as they rode. Alfred was in better spirits, particularly as they got closer to Winchester and he recognised places from his childhood. Athelwulf reined in his horse as they came to the walls of the city and looked up at them, the emotion evident on his face.

"This is my home," he told Judith soberly. "My father is buried here. I'll not let the boy keep us out."

Chapter four

The gates swung open to admit them and Athelwulf brightened at the greetings called to him. Judith was greeted with open curiosity, but she kept her head high, smiling graciously at all, determined to display her quality as a Princess of West Francia and a Queen of Wessex. Before them, rising over all other buildings, were the Palace and the Minster of Winchester.

At the palace Judith straightened her clothes as she prepared to meet her eldest stepson. "Are you sure my presence will not make matters worse?" she asked.

Athelwulf looked proudly at her. Even in a plain blue riding tunic, Judith managed to appear effortlessly elegant. "No. It is right for you to take your place at my side as your father's representative as well as my queen."

She rested her hand on his arm as they entered the grand hall. The hall was huge, perhaps a little smaller than the one at Verberie, but as magnificent. Judith would have liked to have looked around more, but that would have to wait. They stood just inside the doorway, Athelwulf glaring at the group of men at the other end of the room. Judith recognised Ethelbert, so she guessed the dark-haired man standing next to him was Athelbald. Her eyes widened slightly as she looked at him. He was very different in appearance to his brothers. She could see a faint resemblance in his features to Athelwulf, but his body was far more powerfully built than either Athelwulf or Ethelbert. He stared insolently at his father out of piercing blue eyes, a smirk twisting what should have been a handsome face.

For a long time father and son glared at each other. Athelwulf waited for his son to greet him as befitted a king and a father, while Athelbald was determined not to show him any such courtesy. It was impossible to say how long the two would have stayed at this impasse, had not a boy slightly older than Alfred ran forward.

"Father!" he cried.

"Ethelred, stand back here, now," Athelbald yelled.

The child ignored him, flinging himself into Athelwulf's arms. His face broke into an unusually wide smile of delight at greeting the son he had not seen in over a year. After his father released him, Ethelred embraced Alfred. Athelwulf glanced at Judith, opening his mouth to chide his son for not greeting her next, but Judith smiled and shook her head, fascinated by the lack of formality in the family.

As Ethelred and Alfred drew apart, Athelwulf took his son by the shoulders to present him to Judith. She smiled warmly, eager to gain another friendly stepson. The boy bowed politely to her, but she could see from his expression that Athelbald had already given his own opinions.

However, Ethelred's interruption had done some good. With the encouragement of Ethelbert, Athelbald began to move down the hall. Looking relieved that the standoff was over, Athelwulf took Judith's arm and moved to meet his oldest son in the centre of the hall. Ethelbert bowed to his father, but Athelbald continued to look insolently at him. His message was clear – he considered himself to be of equal rank with his father.

"My dear Athelbald, I know we have much to discuss," Athelwulf pronounced. "But I am most heartily glad to see you."

Athelbald raised his eyebrows at that, but his lips curved into a smile. "And I, you, Father."

The two men embraced and a ripple of relief went around the room. It did not look like they would have to pick sides, at least not that day.

"My son, allow me to present my wife, Queen Judith of Wessex."

Judith nodded her head at the young man. His eyes swept rudely over her, before he burst out laughing. "I see why you were so long away, Father. You were waiting for her to be born!"

Judith flushed with rage and embarrassment, as a few muffled snorts were heard from the watchers. Athelwulf's eyes narrowed.

"Do not speak to my wife in that manner, Boy," he snapped. "I insist she is treated with proper respect."

Athelbald grinned, amused by his father's rebuke. He gave an exaggerated bow. "Please forgive me, Lady Judith. I bid you welcome to Winchester."

"My wife is a consecrated queen of Wessex," Athelwulf replied, not looking remotely appeased by Athelbald's words.

"Wessex does not have consecrated queens," Athelbald said. "I do not recognise her rank. I wonder what she did to make you grant her this honour. Oh well, no fool like an old fool."

Judith itched to slap his arrogant face, although she had a feeling this was exactly what he wanted. She extended her hand, her eyes narrowing. "I am pleased to meet you, Lord Athelbald," she said with icy politeness. "I thank you for your… welcome."

Athelbald grinned as if delighted by the fury in her eyes, as he took her hand and raised it to his lips. Judith kept her face in its mask of contempt, but the touch of his lips on her hand shocked her. Even after she pulled her hand away, she could still feel the pressure on her.

"The honour is mine, my lady," he said, turning back to his father. "Why was Mother not honoured with such a rank?"

"Your mother was the finest of women," Athelwulf said slowly and Judith could hear the grief in his voice. She had heard he had cared deeply for his first wife. "But her birth cannot be compared to the Lady Queen's. She is descended from the great Emperor Charles."

Athelbald shrugged. "I still do not recognise her rank, although I will endeavour to respect the fact that she is a Princess of West Francia."

"I may agree to compromise with you on much, my son, but not on this matter. My wife is worthy of the highest rank and the alliance she brings us with King Charles of West Francia is too valuable to be destroyed by your attitude."

Athelbald shrugged again as he turned his back on them to greet Alfred. The boy smiled at his brother, but Judith could see the conflict was upsetting him.

"Do not let him upset you, Judith," Athelwulf whispered to her. "I will ensure he recognises you."

"But this is not the only matter for you to discuss and I think my presence here is a distraction," Judith said, longing to escape the hall. "Allow me to take Alfred elsewhere. Is there a chamber we can use?"

"Go to the King's Chamber," Athelwulf replied. "I shall have some refreshment sent to you there."

"I am not certain I should allow you to use the King's Chamber," Athelbald said. "I have not returned Wessex to you and I may never do so."

"The King's Chamber is the most comfortable in the palace. Are you denying this to a lady?"

Athelbald's grin slipped for the first time and it was clear he felt at a disadvantage. "Very well. Make use of the King's Chamber for now."

Athelbald swept her another arrogant bow as Athelwulf led her and Alfred towards a doorway, where a curving staircase wound its way upwards. A serving boy was instructed to show them the way and Judith had to restrain herself from taking the steps two at a time, so eager was she to be away from her eldest stepson.

∞∞∞

Athelwulf joined her there much later in a furious mood. Judith was relieved she had sent Alfred away to join his brothers, so he would not have to witness this.

"Do you know what that boy is insisting on?" he raged. "He wants me to go back to Kent and leave Wessex to him. He wants to be the over-king. He wants me to guarantee that he will be my heir. And he will not accept you as queen. He says if he sees you on the throne, he will declare war. I'll not stand for this. It will be war in any case."

Judith tried to soothe him. "He is your eldest son. Surely it is right for you to name him your heir."

"Of course he is my heir," Athelwulf almost shouted at her. "But if I guarantee it, he will probably want to kill me."

Judith recoiled at his anger, but at that, some of the rage in him faded. "Oh Judith, forgive me. I am not angry at you."

"I thought it would be a compromise. If you agree to that, he may be willing to agree to your demands." Judith wondered whether she should relinquish her right to sit on the throne. It might make matters easier for Athelwulf, but even the thought of allowing that arrogant man to beat her was unbearable.

"He also wants an assurance that your children will not inherit from me. What do you think of that?"

"I have never asked you what your intentions are for any children I bear you."

"I intend to remove land from my realm into my booklands. I can leave such land as I please. As matters stand, Athelbald is to have Wessex and Ethelbert, Kent. But my booklands will be divided among Ethelred, Alfred and any sons you bear."

"Can Athelbald object to that? He must know you will make provision for your younger sons."

"He is not being reasonable." Athelwulf sank down onto a chair and put his head in his hands. Judith was concerned. This stress could not be good for him. She knelt down and hesitantly put an arm around him. He raised his head to look at her. "This is not the welcome I wished to give you."

"Do not worry about me and for now do not worry about our

children. We do not yet know if I will be blessed. Or we may be blessed with daughters."

"I am the King and you are the Queen. I'll not compromise on that."

"And nor should you," Judith replied, pleased this matter was not up for discussion. "What do the nobles have to say? It seemed to me they were most pleased to get their King back."

"That is true, at least from Kent and the east of Wessex. Athelbald has more supporters in the west."

"But surely none want conflict in the realm?"

"No, all want a speedy resolution." Athelwulf gave a wry smile. "They just need to agree on what the resolution should be."

"Well, you must not worry anymore this night," Judith said, feeling more concerned than ever by the drawn look of his face. "Have you dined? Shall I send for some sustenance?"

"I have eaten and if you have too, I think we should go to our rest. God help me, I shall have to enter further discussions in the morn."

∞∞∞

The next morning Judith slipped from the bed as quietly as she could. Athelwulf had been agitated and had slept little in the night. Now he was asleep at last, she did not want to disturb him. Holding the long green skirt of her tunic carefully to avoid tripping, she descended the staircase and to her dismay ran into Athelbald at the bottom.

"Well, well, if it isn't the little Frankish bride. And how are you faring this bright morn?"

Judith drew herself up to her full height as she glared at him. "I do not wish to talk to you, my lord. I have seen how you defy your father."

"And you think I should meekly let him disinherit me?" he asked with a sneer.

"Why do you think he would disinherit you?" Judith asked. "I do not think he has any such intention."

"Really? And what do you know about it? He has never cared for me. It is always the younger ones he favours. He dotes on Alfred now, but no doubt he will dote on your sons even more."

Judith stared at him. For a moment the sneer had slipped and she caught a glimpse of some very real hurt on his face. Athelwulf's closeness to Alfred was undeniable, as the two were so similar. Small wonder that Athelbald should feel left out.

"He and Alfred decide to gallivant off to Rome and I am considered good enough to manage his realm, but the moment he returns, I am to be cast aside," Athelbald continued, unaware of the Judith's sympathy. "Well, I will not stand for it. The old man can go back to Kent. You can be Queen of Kent for all I care."

"You cannot expect your father to be content with that," Judith said pleadingly. "Could you not make some compromise? Perhaps share Wessex? Allow him to remain high king, while you rule your portion."

"And have him continually interfere? I think not."

"He praised your abilities to me," Judith said. "I think he would respect your rule."

"If I suggest such a thing, will you urge your husband to accept it?"

"I might," Judith replied. "If I felt your demands were reasonable."

Athelbald began to scowl again. He took a step towards Judith, forcing her to back into the wall. She looked up at him in considerable alarm.

"I'll not grovel to you, my lady," he said.

He was standing so close to her that Judith caught her breath. She was very aware of his body just a hairsbreadth from hers. Athelbald caught the look in her eye and sneered some more.

"Do not be afraid, my lady," he said, running a finger down

her cheek. Judith was shocked at the feelings it caused. "You are too young for my tastes."

Judith pushed hard at him. "Do not touch me. I expect to be treated with respect. If you do not, I will not urge my husband to do anything other than fight you."

"Ah, such devotion. Do you love your husband?"

"I hold my lord in the very highest esteem and affection," Judith replied with dignity.

"That was not what I asked," Athelbald said. "Are you in love with him?"

Judith wanted to stamp her foot in irritation. "You know not what you ask," she replied. "Such a thing would never happen to you. You would never be sent away from your land in the company of strangers. You would not go alone to a land where you do not even speak the language. My husband does not have to treat me with such respect. I am at the mercy of his whims, yet he has ever treated me with deference and tenderness. I am grateful and regard him as the very best of men."

Athelbald looked stunned. "Forgive me. My mother would be ashamed of the way I have spoken to you this morn."

Judith swallowed, unprepared for the sudden change in mood. "I sincerely want you to reach an agreement with your father," she said. "Now, if you will excuse me, my lord…" Judith brushed past him to return to the stairs, forcing herself to take them at a dignified speed.

"My lady, you speak the language excellently," Athelbald called and she turned in surprise at hearing him address her in this more complimentary fashion.

Judith's heart beat faster as he smiled charmingly at her. Without the sneer, he appeared younger and most appealing. She bowed her head, not trusting herself to speak as she returned to the King's chamber.

∞∞∞

She found Athelwulf fully dressed and fastening his belt. He turned to her in some irritation as she entered.

"I have missed matins," he said. "I never miss matins. You should have woken me."

Judith's eyes filled with tears at the querulous tone of his voice. As she looked at him, it was impossible not to make comparisons with the arrogant, but vital young man she had just left. "Forgive me. I knew you had not slept well. I did not mean to displease you."

"I am not displeased with you, Judith," he said. He smiled as he met her anxious eyes. "No, truly I am not displeased. Have you broken your fast yet this morning?"

"No, I was intending to, but I met Athelbald," she said.

Athelwulf studied her flushed face. "If that boy insulted you…"

"He did not," Judith said quickly. The last thing she wanted was more trouble.

"Are you sure?"

Judith gave a mirthless laugh. "Well, perhaps a little. But a princess of West Francia knows how to deal with insults."

"Put him in his place, did you?" Athelwulf said, his lips twitching. "I wish I had seen it."

Judith was devoutly glad he had not seen it, but she smiled at him as he took her arm. "I think he may be in a more agreeable mood this morning. Perhaps your deliberations will go better."

Chapter five

Athelwulf decided that Judith should join the negotiations that day. They entered formally, accompanied by Bishop Swithun and took their places at the head of the table, although the throne on the dais remained empty while the matter was still in dispute. Athelbald and Ethelbert made their entrance in a noisier fashion. Among their companions were Bishop Eahlstan and Lord Eanwulf. Judith greeted them with icy politeness, determined to show the two men, who had turned traitor to their king that they were beneath her contempt.

Athelbald greeted her with a deference which was sufficiently exaggerated to afford him much amusement, but not so much that Athelwulf could complain. Judith had braced herself for meeting him and so was able to regard his smile with nothing more than a polite nod of her head.

Although Judith relished the importance at being asked to attend, it was to be a tedious occasion. She could speak the West Saxon language well enough for everyday matters, but the legal talk of that day was beyond her. It seemed most were in favour of Athelwulf taking back his throne, but Judith was not sure how many supported her right to share it. She found her attention often wandered now she was finally able to inspect the hall. It was a fine one with intricate wall-paintings, but as many of the tapestries were faded or blackened with soot, her thoughts drifted to the new ones she would make to replace them. She could not fault the huge tables stretching down either side of the room or the bright banners emblazoned with wyverns which hung from the ceiling. It would be a fitting location for the feasts she would organise and the musicians who would be summoned for their entertainment. All those days of dreaming she had endured at the Abbey of Hasnon were finally paying off.

Raised voices startled her from her daydream. The anger and the speed at which the men were shouting at each other made it even harder to follow, but Judith's heart sank. She didn't need to understand the words to realise the men seemed as far away from agreement as ever.

"Be silent," Athelwulf roared, rising to his feet. The hall immediately stilled causing Judith to feel proud as Athelwulf suddenly appeared a commanding figure. It was obvious to all who was the King. "I would remind you all, my lords, that we have a lady present. You will all watch your words."

"Perhaps we should not have a lady present," Athelbald shouted. "I do not see what right she has to be here."

"The Queen of Wessex has every right to be here."

"Stop calling her that," Athelbald snapped back. "Do I have to remind you why Wessex does not have queens?"

Athelwulf gave a slight laugh. "Just because Queen Eadburh, several generations back, misused her office, should not mean no lady can ever grace the title. Why, if we had a greedy and murderous king, would we do away with the office of Kingship?"

Athelbald scowled, but the question was unanswerable. Judith hid her smirk at seeing Athelbald at a disadvantage.

Athelwulf gave a grave smile at everyone and laid his hand on Judith's shoulder. "My lords, I ask you, if we bring back the office of Queen, who better to bear the title than one who has the blood of the Emperor of the Romans in her veins? Wessex should be honoured to receive so gracious a lady in its midst."

Judith cast what she hoped was a queenly look at the assembled nobles, pleased to see heads nodding and mutters of agreement.

"What does this mean?" Athelbald attempted to regain control. "Will she have lands?"

"Naturally I shall bestow some lands on my wife," Athelwulf said. "Do you begrudge her an income?"

Athelbald looked discomfited once again, but he did not give up. "And what of her children? Will they take precedence over myself and my brothers?"

"Any sons Queen Judith bears me will be Athelings. They will have the right to ascend the throne, but they will not gain precedence. As matters stand I intend you, Athelbald, to rule Wessex after me and Ethelbert to rule Kent. All other sons will receive lands, but will only ascend the throne if it is God's will."

"As matters stand?" Athelbald sneered. "I think you have some reservations on this."

"I do," Athelwulf replied. "To leave my realm to so traitorous a son seems foolish. Perhaps Ethelbert should have Wessex and Ethelred, Kent."

Judith was unable to keep the smile off her face at this. It was clear Athelwulf had struck a blow. He strode to the throne, pulling Judith with him. She felt him relax as he sat next to her, but there was no sign of relief on his stern face.

"I trust there are no further objections to seeing my wife as Queen," Athelwulf said. "I command all to show their loyalty."

Athelwulf rose up from his throne to leave Judith sitting there alone. He stood by her side as one by one the Wessex men came forward to kneel and kiss her hand.

"Athelbald, you too," he said, as Athelbald stood back.

Athelbald came forwards slowly, an expression of intense dislike on his face. Judith glanced up uncertainly at Athelwulf. He gave a reassuring smile and placed his hand on her shoulder. Athelbald did as he was commanded, bestowing the most perfunctory of kisses on her hand.

"Is there anything you can do to appease him? I do not think the trouble is truly over," she whispered, as Athelbald backed away still looking furious. "What of the idea you discussed with Father Swithun, where he would keep a part of Wessex?"

Athelwulf sat back down, putting his arm protectively around her. He shrugged. "Ethelbert, stand before me. My son, you did well while I was away. I would ask that you continue to govern Kent for me."

"Yes, Father," Ethelbert replied, but not without a concerned glance at his brother.

Athelbald was crimson with rage. Kicking back his chair, he stormed towards the door. Lord Eanwulf started to follow him with many another man too rising to their feet. Athelbald's followers were numerous and Judith knew Athelwulf was still some way from reclaiming his throne.

"This will mean war," he shouted.

"Wait, Athelbald," Athelwulf called before he reached the door. "I have not finished. Come here." Athelbald returned reluctantly, the look of hatred on his face making Judith shiver. His hand was curled around the knife at his belt. But Athelwulf was unfazed. "My son, I have just returned from a long journey. I have no wish to make another any time soon and Wessex is a large realm. Nor do I want any quarrel between us. Such a thing is not good for either Wessex or ourselves. I would be willing for you to continue to rule the area west of Selwood."

There was a faint gasp around the room. Everyone had assumed Athelwulf would be keen to punish his son if he got the chance but instead he was giving away half his realm, and the half which many considered to be the finer. Athelbald continued to look suspiciously at his father. He did not appear to consider this a gesture of peace.

"Will I rule independently? What assurances can you give me that you will not interfere?"

The nobles muttered to themselves, shocked at Athelbald's hostility. Even his supporters shook their heads, but Athelwulf maintained his smile at his eldest son. "You need no assurances," he said. "I am not a foolish man. I would never interfere unnecessarily. Your assurances are your own abilities. You have managed well this last year and have clearly inspired much loyalty in the west of Wessex. I accept that you are more able than I to govern that part of the realm. I am proud of you, my son."

Athelbald was left speechless as he fell to his knees, kissing his father's hand. Judith blinked back tears at the sight and she could see Athelwulf too appeared overcome with emotion. As Athelbald rose up again, the two kings embraced.

Athelwulf took the hands of each of his older sons. "My boys, I am glad to compromise. We must not fight each other. Our fight must be against the Great Heathen Army. We have now a new ally in King Charles of West Francia, whose daughter sits beside me on the throne. Together we can keep the heathen scum at bay."

Athelbald glanced at Judith during this speech, but the hostility in his face had faded. For her part, Judith was impressed with how Athelwulf had reconciled with his sons, wholeheartedly and without reservations, the loss of part of his realm seemingly irrelevant. Her own family seemed to be continually squabbling over territories and suspicion between her father and his brothers was intense.

"My lords, may I say something?" Judith asked, determined to follow Athelwulf's example of reconciliation.

"Oh, what commands does the great queen have?" Ethelbert muttered.

Athelwulf frowned, while Athelbald dug his brother in the ribs. "Be quiet. We should listen to our dear mother."

"Athelbald," cautioned his father.

"How can you object to that, Father?" Athelbald said, a look of malicious amusement on his face.

"Well, I object to it," Judith said with a smile. "Any woman would object to a title which must make her many years older than she is! But I know you are not formal here in Wessex. If my husband does not object, I would be pleased for you to use my name."

Athelbald smiled, still a touch maliciously. "What did you wish to say, my dear Judith?"

Judith barely repressed a shiver at hearing her name on his

lips. She smiled brightly. "I know you must both be eager to head to your realms, but Christmas tide is nearly upon us. I wish you will stay here until then, so we may celebrate together."

"That is an excellent idea, Judith," Athelwulf said. "I would be glad indeed to have my family all together."

Athelbald and Ethelbert looked at each other and nodded. "I will be happy to stay a while," Athelbald said. "Will this not be a sad Christmas for you, so far from your family?"

Judith shook her head with a laugh. "It has been an age since I celebrated with my family. My last few Christmas tides were spent in prayer and contemplation at an abbey."

She looked around the hall, imagining the great tables laden with food and wine, musicians playing and everyone dressed in their finest. This year would be different.

Chapter six

Christmas was a great success, in part thanks to the quantities of wine which Judith brought from West Francia. Her relations with her stepsons gradually improved, although none were as loving as Alfred. Ethelred had become quite friendly, while Ethelbert was distant, but unfailingly polite. Athelbald was the one who continued to bother her. In public he treated her with exaggerated courtesy, while in private his smile was teasing. It took every inch of Judith's Frankish breeding to remain in control. Judith knew she should avoid him altogether, yet inevitably she found herself drawn into his company.

As soon as Judith knew for certain they would be residing a while at Winchester, she threw herself into activity. Now the hall boasted several new and very fine tapestries while fresh cloths lined the thrones. The men at court had completely accepted their Frankish queen, while the women began to copy her elegant style of dress. For the most part, Judith was happy

The only blot on her happiness was that she had still failed to conceive. Athelwulf, as he had promised, never reproached her when each month she had to confess her failure. Inevitably he simply patted her on the shoulder and assured her they might be more fortunate the next month. Judith suspected that, although he would welcome a son who was descended from the Emperor, siring more children was not very important to him. Night after night she lay beside him, but most nights he simply kissed her and bade her good night, leaving Judith torn between relief and irritation.

She knew he was tired. Since their return he had been in continual demand by his people. It seemed every day there had been petitioners to greet, demands to settle and charters to sign. Judith smiled as she watched him that Christmas night, laughing with his elder sons, a wine cup in his hand. He looked relaxed and younger than she had ever seen him. Perhaps over this festive period he would have time to be more attentive to her and next Christmas she would be sitting at this table nursing a child.

She took the wine jug over to the three men. Athelwulf rose to his feet as she drew near and kissed her cheek. "My dearest Judith, I cannot thank you enough for arranging this. We are agreed that this has been the finest of festivities."

Judith flushed with pleasure. She knew how pretty she looked that night in a richly embroidered red overdress and a dark blue tunic. Golden jewellery glinted around her wrists and neck. She smiled at the three men, blushing even more at the flicker of admiration in Athelbald's eyes. She wondered if he still considered her too young for his tastes.

∞∞∞

As soon as the Christmas festivities drew to a close, Ethelbert departed for Canterbury. Athelbald lingered a little longer, but it was not long before he too took his leave.

"We must meet again in the summer to discuss matters and plan our strategy against the Heathen Army," Athelwulf said after embracing his son.

"Agreed, Father. I shall look forward to it, especially if I am to be treated to such hospitality again." He bowed to Judith. "Many thanks to you, my lady. Farewell."

Judith extended her hand, relieved this arrogant young man was departing. "A safe journey to you, my lord."

Athelbald kissed her hand with a smirk. "Why Judith, I

almost believe you are starting to like me."

Judith raised her eyebrows. "I endeavour to remember you are my dear husband's son and are therefore worthy of my esteem."

Athelbald laughed, ruffling his younger brothers' hair. "Farewell, boys. Come visit me at Sherborne in the spring if Father allows it."

Judith was surprised by the distress she could see on Alfred's face, as Athelbald and his entourage rode away. She had not got the impression he was at all close to his oldest brother. Athelbald and Ethelred were far closer. For herself, Judith was glad he was gone. She had found his company most unsettling over the past months. Now she could concentrate on her husband and the two younger stepsons who had need of her care.

"Race you back to the hall, Alfred," Ethelred called, running across the courtyard.

It seemed to Judith that Alfred was concealing his distress with an effort as he chased after his brother. Athelwulf put his arms around Judith as he watched his sons scamper away and kissed the top of her head.

"After my dear lady, Osburh, died I did not think I would ever again celebrate such a festivity with all my sons. Thank you, my sweet girl, for your efforts this Christmas. You have made me very happy."

Judith smiled back. "Then I too am happy."

Athelwulf had business with Swithun at the Minster, so Judith returned to the palace alone. But her thoughts on further improvements were dashed when she saw Alfred lying on the floor of the hall, Ethelred crouching beside him. Alfred was moaning and clutching his stomach. Judith ran to him, kneeling down on the stone floor.

"What happened?" she asked. "Did he fall?"

"No," said Ethelred, looking close to tears. "He just stopped and then sank down. What is happening?"

"I don't know," whispered Judith, feeling Alfred's forehead. It was hot and clammy. The boy cried out in pain.

"Where does it hurt?" Judith asked.

"My stomach," Alfred moaned, a spasm going through him. Suddenly he vomited on the floor, his body trembling with the effort.

Helplessly Judith stroked his hair until the retching stopped. His face was white.

"Can you stand?" Judith asked, gently putting her arms around him.

Alfred got shakily to his feet, but slumped against her, his body trembling. He cried out sharply in pain and doubled over once again. Judith struggled to support him as his legs gave way. She turned to the group of serving men and women who had gathered around. "Carry Prince Alfred to his chamber," she ordered.

Judith followed them anxiously as Alfred was lain on his bed, groaning again. Frantically she tried to remember what the nuns had done in similar circumstances.

"Take off his tunic. Let us at least make him comfortable," Judith said. "Send someone to the Minster for the Infirmarian."

Judith sat down on the bed, covering his naked, shivering body with a blanket. "What about some hot ale? Do you think you could drink a little?"

Alfred shook his head, his face creasing up in pain once again.

"Perhaps we should wait for the Infirmarian, my lady," Alfred's nurse said.

Judith nodded. "Stay with him. I must inform the King."

To her dismay Alfred was only half conscious, appearing to be suffering from no ordinary sickness. Athelwulf had told her how delicate Alfred's health was, but this was the first time she had witnessed it herself. She ran through the Minster, muttering a prayer for Alfred as she went and burst into the Bishop's chamber without knocking. He and Athelwulf both looked up from their manuscripts in surprise.

"My Lady Queen?" Swithun said.

"Judith?" Athelwulf said at the same time.

Judith caught her breath, knowing what a sight she must look with her cheeks flushed and her dress strained.

"Forgive me for the interruption, Father. My lord, Alfred has been taken ill."

Athelwulf got to his feet. "What ails him?" he asked.

"He has been vomiting and seems in such pain," Judith replied. "I have sent for the Infirmarian, but I thought you should know."

"You were right. Father, we must finish our talk another day. I must see to my son," Athelwulf said. "He has been so strong these last months, I had hoped he had outgrown his sickness."

"I shall accompany you," Swithun said. "I have some knowledge, although the Infirmarian is most fine. You were right to summon him, my Lady Queen."

"Yes, yes, thank you, Judith," Athelwulf said distractedly.

Judith was unable to feel any pleasure in the words of praise as she took Athelwulf's arm. The frown creasing his forehead as he strode towards the palace had completely driven away the relaxed look he had worn over Christmas.

"I knew he was not himself this morn," he muttered. "But I thought he was just sad to bid farewell to Athelbald."

In the hall, Athelwulf looked around in bewilderment, taking in the groups of anxious looking serving men.

"This is where he was taken ill," Judith said gently. "But I had them carry him to his chamber."

"I think Alfred was most fortunate you were with him, my Lady Queen," Swithun said, coming to Athelwulf's aid. "Come, my Lord King. Let us go to him."

"I shall join you presently," Judith said. "I must change."

Judith changed into one of her plainest tunics before returning to Alfred. She took with her a jug of hot ale. She didn't know if it would do Alfred any good, but they might all need some sustenance.

In Alfred's chamber she found Athelwulf standing at the foot of the bed, looking on anxiously as the Infirmarian tried to give Alfred a herbal concoction. Judith put her arm around her husband and he glanced down at her.

"His old problem has returned. The last time he was so ill, we were in Rome. The Infirmarian of the Papal Basilica treated him and His Holiness himself led the prayers for Alfred's recovery. He was most concerned for he considered Alfred his spiritual son."

"Alfred has always recovered," Judith said. "Surely he will this time."

"I pray he will." Athelwulf shook his head sadly. "Athelstan, my eldest son, was the same. He threw off the sickness countless times, but it claimed him in the end."

"I shall have prayers said in the Minster." Swithun rested a hand on the King's shoulder. "Your generosity to God's church is well known. I am sure He will listen to your prayers."

"Why has this sickness struck him again?" Athelwulf said. "He has been so well."

"Perhaps the rich foods he ate over Christmas played their part," Swithun replied.

Judith's face fell as she thought of the lavish feasts she had organised. "I am sorry," she whispered.

Athelwulf did not seem to hear her, but Swithun gave her a kindly smile. "Do not blame yourself, my lady. We always have great feasts at this time and I have found it is almost impossible to stop small boys indulging themselves."

The infusion the Infirmarian was giving Alfred did not appear to be helping. Alfred cried out in pain and Judith felt Athelwulf flinch at the sound. Again Alfred retched, bringing up whatever the Infirmarian had got into him. The monk shook his head.

Judith darted forward, snatching up a soft cloth. Dipping it in some water, she gently sponged Alfred's face and he became calmer.

The Infirmarian set down some more of the drink on the table. "It seems he cannot cope with such quantities. He should be given only small sips whenever he can."

"Will that help?" Athelwulf asked anxiously,

"I hope so, my Lord King." He looked back at the bed where Judith was still soothing the boy. "Perhaps a mother's attention too will do him good."

Chapter seven

But Alfred got worse, not better. For several days Judith remained in almost constant attendance, trying to fulfil the role of a loving mother. Yet barely could she get enough of the herbal infusion into him. Eventually she gave up and fed him on sips of mead instead, hoping the honeyed drink would give him the strength to survive. Often the boy became delirious and screamed for his mother. At other times, despite his delirium, he was almost calm and Judith was never sure if he felt soothed by her presence or whether he thought she was his mother.

Athelwulf too was often with them. Some days he only left his son's side to pray in the church. When Alfred was still, he and Judith simply sat side by side in silence, watching Alfred as he slept. Athelwulf's face became grey and drawn, causing Judith to fear she might soon have another invalid on her hands.

"You must eat," she said to him. "Just a little."

"No, Judith. I have no stomach for it. You go dine."

"Let me bring you something," Judith begged.

Athelwulf shook his head, staring sadly at his son.

Judith's heart went out to him and she put her arms around him. "Please, Athelwulf. Just eat a little. When Alfred recovers he will need his father to be well and strong."

"When Alfred recovers?" Athelwulf looked at Judith, a bitter smile on his lips.

"Yes, when," Judith said firmly. "I truly believe that."

Athelwulf couldn't help but smile at the determined girl. "I pray you are right. Very well. Bring me some bread and meat. Thank you."

Judith returned with food not only for Athelwulf, but a bowl of watery gruel. "Alfred seems calmer this night," she said. "Perhaps he can cope with food."

She slipped an arm under him, lifting up his head. He opened his eyes rather blearily. "Hush, Alfred," Judith said, as she spooned a single spoonful of the gruel into his mouth. She watched anxiously as he swallowed, before laying him back down. "Let us see how he tolerates that before giving him more."

Athelwulf was watching her, a tender smile on his face. "You are so good to my son," he said, taking a bite of the bread she had brought him.

Judith smiled back, suddenly feeling very weary. "Why should I not be? He was my first friend in this realm and has remained the greatest."

Judith leant her head against him and they sat in silence late into the night. On every occasion Alfred stirred, Judith gave him another spoonful of gruel. By the time they made their way to the King's chamber to dose uneasily for a few hours, there was a touch of hope in their hearts.

The next morning they returned to Alfred fearing, as they did every morning, they would find he had died in the night. The door opened just before they got there and his nurse came out. There were tears on her cheeks.

Judith's heart crashed, her arm automatically going round Athelwulf as she tried to think how he would cope with losing this beloved son. Athelwulf was staring at the woman, whose face, to Judith's amazement, had suddenly broken into a beaming smile.

"Oh, my Lord King," she said, barely able to get the words out.

Athelwulf did not wait for her to finish. He strode past her into the bedchamber, pulling Judith with him. There was Alfred, looking weak and wan, but sitting up in the bed.

"He has had five spoons of that gruel the Lady Queen left for him," the nurse said, still wiping her eyes.

Athelwulf was unable to speak, as he took Alfred in his arms. Judith blinked back her own tears. She planted a quick kiss on Alfred's head.

"Oh, Alfred, you did give us a scare," she said, as she left the father and son together.

Judith made her way to the hall, having little energy for any work that day. She took up some stitching, but for the most part it lay unimproved on her lap and it was quickly cast aside when Athelwulf joined her.

"How is he?" she asked.

"He is sleeping now, but he is so much better," Athelwulf said taking her hands. "I have ordered prayers of thanksgiving to be said in the Minster."

"I shall go to him when he awakes," Judith said. "God be praised that he is recovering."

"I have much to do," Athelwulf commented. "I have neglected all my duties these past days."

"Might I say something before you go?" Judith asked. "There is a matter which has concerned me for some time."

"Of course, my dear. What concerns you?"

"Alfred is a fine and intelligent boy," Judith said. "It has always surprised me that he cannot read or write. In West Francia the royal sons are sent to a monastery to learn such things. I wondered if such an education could not be arranged for Alfred."

Athelwulf stared at Judith. "You want to send him away?"

"He should learn such things," Judith replied, slightly surprised by his reaction.

"My God, my son warned me about this." Athelwulf dropped her hands, looking stunned. "He said you would try to come between me and my sons. Fool that I am, I did not believe him."

"My lord, I do not-" Judith started to say.

"Be silent, Judith," Athelwulf snapped. "My son is right. I am an old fool to have been taken in by a sweet face and charming manner. I truly believed you cared for him, but you have just been waiting for your chance to put some distance between us."

"No, no, my lord. This is not so," Judith cried.

"I will allow no one to come between me and my sons," Athelwulf continued, his voice still raised. "I trust that is clear to you, my lady. Now you must excuse me." He started to leave, but turned back, his face marred by a rage he had never previously directed at her. "And stay away from Alfred. I do not want you near him."

Athelwulf strode from the hall, slamming the door behind him. There was silence in the room, as the people gathered there stared at Judith. It was rare to see their mild king in such a temper, but to hear him raise his voice against the queen he had always been so determined should be regarded with deference, was almost unbelievable.

Judith blinked back the tears which had come to her eyes and looked wearily around. There was suspicion on the faces of all in the room. Despite the brightly burning fires, Judith shivered. She had never before realised how precarious her place was. She had been raised up to be queen, but at a word from her husband she would be cast down. She ran from the room before the tears could escape.

The draught in the stone passageway made the torches flicker wildly. Judith sank down to the floor, allowing the cold to seep through her tunic, cursing herself for raising the matter in this way. She was so accustomed to the Frankish way she had not stopped to consider how it must seem to the West Saxons. She thought of Alfred running to receive his father's embrace every evening. The relationship they had was so different from the one her father had with Louis. She knew she had been a fool to even consider sending him away to be educated, whatever the benefits to him.

But fresh on this remorse came anger that Athelwulf had so easily forgotten the care she had given Alfred and had not hesitated to expose her to the censure of the people.

It was poor treatment from this Saxon king towards the granddaughter of an emperor.

Resolutely she got to her feet and made her way to the chamber where she knew Athelwulf would be working. She did not knock before pushing open the door. He had been looking over some manuscripts with his scribe, but both looked up in surprise as she entered.

Athelwulf frowned. "I am busy, Judith. I do not have time to talk to you. Leave now."

"No," Judith said.

The scribe's mouth dropped open and Athelwulf's face darkened. "A wife must obey her husband. I should not have to remind you of that."

Judith quailed, but allowed no sign of that to appear in her still face and regal bearing. "My lord, before we left West Francia you told me that if there was anything you could do to make me happy, I should just ask. I have never yet asked you for anything and even now I am only asking for a little of your time. Are you not a man of your word?"

The anger building on Athelwulf's face suggested to Judith that her efforts to make up the quarrel were not going well, but he dismissed the scribe.

"I am now seeing your true character," Athelwulf commented. "I was taken in for too long by your sweet manner."

Judith tried frantically to think of something to say which would not make matters worse. Swiftly she swapped her arrogant manner for a humbler attitude. "Please forgive me, my lord, for my manner and my disobedience. I cannot bear that you are angry at me."

Judith's brown eyes gazed pleadingly at him, but he regarded her from eyes narrowed in suspicion. She swallowed and ploughed desperately on. "Please also forgive me for my suggestion that Alfred should be sent away. I spoke without thinking. In my land it is normal for the royal sons to spend time at a monastery to learn and in any case, my siblings and

I were not raised at court. I have never before questioned my upbringing and did not stop to think how unsuitable it would be for Alfred."

Athelwulf's face softened and he patted Judith on the shoulder. "Very well, I accept your apology. We will speak no further on this matter."

But Judith did not give in to the temptation to let the matter rest. "My lord, I beg you allow me to make one more suggestion. If it is a foolish one, please disregard it."

Athelwulf nodded, starting to look suspicious again.

"I know my suggestion was foolish, but I made it out of my very sincere regard for Alfred and my admiration for his intelligence. I truly feel he should learn to read and write."

"You think I have neglected his education?" Athelwulf asked with a raised eyebrow which did not conceal his annoyance.

"Most certainly not," Judith said quickly. "You took him to Rome. He has been in some of the greatest courts in Christendom. It is undoubtedly this which has caused him to be so wise beyond his years."

"Perhaps." Athelwulf nodded. "His Holiness himself praised Alfred's intelligence to me."

"That does not surprise me," Judith said. "But this is why he should learn to read and write. Is there any reason he could not be taught this here in Winchester? I know Bishop Swithun was your tutor. Of course he is busier now he is the bishop, but might he not find the time to work with Alfred?"

"He might," Athelwulf said thoughtfully.

"And are there no other knowledgeable men at the Minster? Or could some be brought here from other abbeys? They too could work with Alfred and such learned conversation would benefit us all."

To Judith's relief, Athelwulf smiled. "Are you finding us Wessex men a dull lot?"

"No, indeed. Dull is not the word," Judith said. "I have often regretted I could not send some Wessex men to my father's court to enliven it a little."

Athelwulf laughed at that and took Judith's hands. "Your suggestions are wise, Judith. When Alfred is recovered I shall speak to Bishop Swithun on this matter. But, my dear, I truly do have much to attend to. I must ask that you leave me now."

Judith nodded. "Of course. I heartily apologise for the interruption." She turned as she reached the door. "Might I see Alfred when he awakes?"

Athelwulf looked embarrassed. "Of course you can. That was a most cruel and uncalled for comment that I made. Alfred would not be happy if I kept you away."

∞∞∞

Judith remained shaken by the events of that day and when Athelwulf came to their chamber that night she did not greet him with her usual smile, wanting to make plain that a princess of West Francia was not to be treated with contempt.

"I can see I have displeased you," he said, as he got under the covers.

"You were very quick to believe wrong of me this day."

"I have admitted that you were right," Athelwulf said, a sharp edge to his voice.

Judith felt nervous. She did not want to start another argument, but she needed to make her point. She was determined not to become as downtrodden as her mother often appeared to be. "Was it Athelbald who said I would try to come between you and your sons?"

"No."

So it was Ethelbert. Although Athelbald had been the more openly hostile, Judith was not surprised. If Athelbald had suspected such a thing, he would undoubtedly have said it to her face. "His comments were misguided, but he is to be commended for his concern for his brothers," Judith said quickly. "My lord, I am aware you must listen to your sons."

Athelwulf looked irritated, but he put an arm around her.

"Judith, I thought we were beyond this formality. Please say what you want."

"I have ever tried to give Alfred the best of care, yet at a word from your son, you condemned me without allowing me the chance to justify myself. I am a stranger in this land. If you turn against me, I am nothing." In spite of her determination to remain dignified, tears filled Judith's eyes. She pressed her lips together, angered by her own weakness.

But as one tear escaped, the irritation vanished from Athelwulf's face. "Oh, Judith, I see you in the court behaving with such grace and assurance that I forget how young you are. I have not considered how frightening it must be for you to leave behind all that is familiar."

Judith blinked back the tears, shocked her emotion had this effect. "I am not usually frightened as I have your protection, but today I feared I would lose it. I am accepted here in Winchester because of your approval. Everything I have done will count for nothing if I lose that. I saw today how easily they would turn against me."

Athelwulf's heart had completely melted. "I behaved most poorly today," he said. "You are right. I should not have condemned you without allowing you to defend yourself. And whatever my concerns, it was very wrong of me to berate you in public. Please forgive me."

Judith nodded, surprised how easily she had brought him to her point of view. It occurred to her that Ethelbert could easily have been right to be concerned for his father.

"Judith, I most sincerely want you to be happy here. Are you?"

To Judith's disgust the exhaustion, anxiety and fear of the previous days caught up with her and she burst into tears. She tensed, certain she would infuriate him, but Athelwulf's arms tightened around her and he pulled her against his chest as she sobbed. When she calmed herself, she saw he was looking at her sadly.

"I think I have my answer. You poor girl, your father did you a very wrong turn in giving you in marriage to an old man such as myself."

"No, please do not think that," Judith begged, genuinely upset he was thinking such a thing after the comfort he had shown her. "It is true these last days have not been happy for us, but before that I was most happy and I am sure we will be again. These are foolish tears. Alfred is recovering and all is well between us. I am content."

"You are right. These have been difficult days. I have never seen Alfred so ill and I prepared myself for his death." He gave Judith a pained smile. "It seems I was so prepared to lose him, I saw threats to him where there are none. I am truly not normally so quick to poor judgement. You have my word I will never condemn you simply on the word of another. And if I am ever displeased, we shall speak of it in private. You will always have my protection. Never doubt this. Now, please assure me I am forgiven. I cannot bear that I have distressed you."

"Of course." Judith felt touched by his explanation. "I am not as hard-hearted as that."

A spark of humour returned to Athelwulf's face and he kissed Judith on the cheek. "Get some sleep now, my dear. All will be well."

Chapter eight

Athelwulf did not refer to their argument again, but over the next weeks he went to considerable effort to reaffirm Judith's position. He transferred more property into her name and publically presented her with some fine jewels to thank her for the devoted care she had given Alfred. No one at Winchester was in any doubt that Judith's status was high.

Alfred grew in strength and was able to leave his bed. Soon he was riding around the countryside as an eight-year-old boy should. Swithun started lessons with him and was delighted to receive so diligent a student.

"The last time I met with such a keen, young mind was when I taught you, my Lord King," he told Athelwulf.

Ethelred too started some lessons, but did not excel as Alfred did. In any case he left Winchester in the spring to visit his oldest brother at Sherborne. Athelwulf also was briefly away, when he journeyed to Kent to see Ethelbert. Judith did not accompany him, saying she thought she should stay with Alfred who was still too delicate to travel. The truth was she had no wish to see Ethelbert, knowing now that his polite manner concealed a deep suspicion of her.

Judith and Athelwulf welcomed increased numbers of learned visitors at Winchester from other parts of Wessex and beyond. To Judith's delight, the court began to achieve a more intellectual atmosphere. It was still some way from the levels of sophistication of Verberie, but it was also unhindered by the

THREE TIMES THE LADY

rigid formality of the Frankish courts.

As the months passed Judith learnt for the most part not to be disappointed by her continued failure to conceive. But she found it hard to conceal her emotion when news came from West Francia that her mother had been safely delivered of a baby girl named Gisela. Knowing her sister would be likely to spend her life in a nunnery, Judith couldn't help but shed a tear. It seemed so unfair that her parents had yet again been blessed, while she, who longed for a child to be raised with them at Winchester, seemed destined to remain childless.

∞∞∞

The peace of Winchester was disrupted in the early summer by the return of Athelbald, who swept in with a fine entourage on the back of a spirited black horse, accompanied by Ethelred. He gave his father and Alfred an exuberant embrace and bowed in an exaggerated fashion to Judith.

"Greetings to you, my Lady Queen," he said, his eyes sweeping over her.

Judith, who had managed to put Athelbald from her mind during his absence, felt flustered. She was very aware of how her figure had ripened since she had last seen him. His blue eyes looked on her appreciatively, but as this contrasted with a cynical twist of his lips, Judith could not be certain if his admiration was genuine. Athelwulf greeted Athelbald with delight. He had not once interfered in his son's reign, so it was an amicable reunion and many a feast was given in welcome.

Judith watched Alfred anxiously during this festive time, but although he suffered a few minor ailments there was no return of the sickness they had feared would kill him in the winter.

Soon Athelwulf and Athelbald started planning how best to secure the coast. Frequent messengers departed from Winchester bound for Kent or West Francia, as the various kings tried to agree how to deal with the Norsemen. Judith,

87

who had decided to see as little of Athelbald as possible, mostly left them to it. But occasionally she was asked to join them, to put her own name to the charters as befitted a queen of Wessex. On such occasions she sat beside Athelwulf, saying little, but struggling to hide the shiver of excitement coursing through her as Athelbald handed the quill to her and their fingers brushed.

Athelwulf did not appear to notice anything amiss with her manner, but Judith was not so sure about Athelbald. She suspected there was very little he missed. Athelwulf and Athelbald were on excellent terms, even if they did not always agree. Judith tried to leave them to sort out their disputes and only on one occasion dared to get involved.

"You have moved even more land into your booklands," Athelbald complained. "It is all very well assuring me I will be King of Wessex one day, but there will not be much left of it at this rate."

"You exaggerate, Athelbald. Wessex remains undiminished. But I must have sufficient land to leave my younger sons."

Athelbald's eyes swept over Judith. "Are you with child? When is this happy event to take place?"

Judith tried to hide her pain. "No, I am not."

"Still not? I had thought you such a dutiful wife."

Judith flushed, but Athelwulf put his hand on her arm before she could retort. "Judith is the most dutiful wife any man could ask for," he said. "It is not her fault we have not been blessed and I will not allow any man to cast such aspersions on her. Even you, Athelbald."

Athelbald shrugged. "Forgive me, I had not realised how sensitive a subject this was."

Judith bowed her head to hide the tears which had sprung to her eyes. She wished more than ever that she was with child. It would undoubtedly have kept her thoughts away from this detestable man.

"Well, if she is not with child, why are you taking so much land?"

"I must provide for Ethelred and Alfred. And I would like to leave something to your sister as well."

"I hear Alfred is studying with the Bishop. Is he bound for the church?"

"It is possible," Athelwulf replied. "His mind is certainly keen enough, but he is too young to make such a decision."

"It might be for the best. I think he is too sickly to make much of a warrior. He would make an excellent bishop." Athelbald's eyes gleamed mischievously. "He could even become pope one day. Would that not be fine?"

"You can mock," Judith said in an icy tone. "But I think Alfred could indeed aspire to greatness in whatever field he wishes."

Athelbald grinned. "Very well. I won't argue with you taking lands out of the realm. It would not do to offend the future pope, would it? But what of all this other money?"

"That is for the poor," Athelwulf said. "It pains me that any man in my realm should go hungry."

"But you have already taken so much from your realm. You gave a tenth to the church before you went to Rome. Am I to inherit an impoverished realm?"

"Certainly not. Wessex continues wealthy. Shall I ask Bishop Swithun to guide you through the accounts? You will see all is well."

Athelbald grimaced. "No, thank you. Spending time with a bishop is not the most pleasant way to spend a day. I can think of far pleasanter ones." His eyes rested speculatively for a moment on Judith. "Hunting, for example. We have not hunted together for an age, Father. Could we not arrange such a thing while I am here?"

Athelwulf brightened. "Certainly we can, my son. Once our business is concluded, that is what we must do."

Further conversation was halted at that moment by the entrance of a messenger. As Athelwulf rose to speak to him, Athelbald leant closer to Judith. "Always the business first. What harm would it be to take a break and hunt on this fine day?"

"A good king will always put the business of the realm before their pleasures," Judith said. "That is why your father is a finer king than you will ever be." She smiled, pleased to have finally said something to wipe the smirk from Athelbald's face.

But Athelbald's face lit up and he leant even closer to Judith to whisper, "But if he put his pleasure first, you might be with child by now."

Judith was speechless with rage as Athelbald leant back. He took a drink of wine, his faint smile mocking her as Judith longed to throw the entire jug over him. Athelwulf turned back to them, not noticing that anything was wrong.

"There is news from Ethelbert," he said.

Judith pushed her chair back. "If this does not concern me, can I ask you both to excuse me?"

"Of course, Judith. Is all well with you?"

Judith forced a smile. "Naturally, but I have much to do."

Both men rose to their feet. "Thank you for your time, my dear," Athelwulf said, kissing her cheek.

Athelbald bowed, still with that gleam of malice in his eyes. Judith escaped from the room, her composure only breaking as the door closed behind her. Athelbald's mocking words rang in her ears. She was considered by all to be a fair queen, yet it had become obvious her own husband had no desire for her. His manner remained affectionate and he complimented her often on her beauty, yet it seemed that Athelwulf had come to prefer the nights when he would casually put an arm around her shoulders and they would simply talk a while before lying down to sleep. Judith too enjoyed the easy conversation, but her longing for a child was as strong as ever and she could only regret that her chances of conceiving had become rare.

∞∞∞

Even Athelbald seemed to have realised he had gone too far in his comments, for his manner became polite and friendly.

Judith did her best to keep a distance from him, having assured herself she would never be able to like him.

It was only on his final evening that she saw him alone. As ever he took her off guard when he encountered her as she was leaving the hall.

"I know I have offended you, Judith," he said with a smile free of malice. "Please forgive me. I am leaving in the morn."

"I will not be sorry to see you go," Judith replied, for once not caring about remaining dignified. "Winchester is pleasanter without you."

The anger flared up in his eyes. "Yes, I know I am not good enough for this rarefied court you have created."

"That is not true. It is your manner towards me that I do not care for."

Athelbald arched an eyebrow. "I don't think that's true. I think your problem is that you care for me more than you would like."

Athelbald took hold of her hand and raised it slowly to his lips, his eyes fixed on her face. Judith's heart beat faster and she started to back away, but Athelbald clasped her waist to prevent her escape.

"Get your hands off me," she hissed.

"Is that really what you want?" Athelbald smiled. "What if I were to kiss you?"

In her heart Judith knew there was nothing she wanted more, but under no circumstances could she allow it. To betray her husband with anyone was unforgivable, but with his own son would cause unimaginable hurt. "Do not."

"Why not? You want to."

"Would you really hurt your father like this? What do you get from it? I am young and foolish and easily led astray. I think your betrayal would hurt him far more than mine." Judith's eyes narrowed as she drew strength from her anger. "I saw how hurt he was when you tried to take his realm. Now you want to take his wife. Is this what you have to do to prove yourself a man?"

Athelbald's face darkened with rage, but he released her. Judith allowed herself a brief smirk at her revenge and tried to ignore the feelings he had aroused in her. She fled along the passageway, hoping it would be a long time before she saw him again.

Chapter nine

After Athelbald departed, life slipped back into its routine. Judith continued to bring musicians and storytellers to the court and the learned men continued to visit. Ethelred rebelled against his lessons and spent his time in falconry and weapons skills, much as he had at Sherborne, but Alfred's education was progressing well. Bishop Swithun gave excellent reports, causing Athelwulf's pride in his son to increase.

But although her days were busy, Judith felt restless. It was not dissimilar to the feelings she had once felt in the abbey, when she had longed for something more from life. At the abbey she had been able to honestly tell the Abbess she did not lust for the touch of the man, but now she was relieved no one would ask her that. Often the words Father Hincmar had spoken at her coronation rang in her ears, as he commanded her not to look with desire on another. As the autumn came, marking a year since her marriage, Judith realised she seemed unlikely to have a child and she could not help wondering if this was God's punishment for her unchaste thoughts.

Athelwulf noticed how downcast she was and it was a relief for Judith to confess how she feared she would not bear a child since she could not admit how her dreams were often full of a dark-haired man with piercing blue eyes. Judith didn't even know why her thoughts drifted so frequently to him. She didn't like him, feeling only contempt for his wildness and his failure to share her more sophisticated interests. She was unable to talk to him in the way she found so easy with Athelwulf and Alfred, yet it was Athelbald who occupied far too many of her thoughts.

"I wish I could give you a child, my dear," Athelwulf said, when Judith confessed her fears. "Perhaps it may yet happen, but at my age we must not be surprised if it does not."

Judith shook her head. "You have sired many a fine son. The fault may well lie with me."

"I don't like to talk of faults," Athelwulf said, patting her hand. "You must not blame yourself. We shall keep praying to be blessed."

As her second Christmas in Wessex approached, Judith did not suggest that Athelbald and Ethelbert be invited, although she prepared herself for Athelwulf to choose to invite them. However he did not mention it and Judith planned a quieter celebration.

Just over a month before Christmas Athelwulf had some matters to attend to at a small settlement named Steyning, a couple of days' ride from Winchester. Judith accompanied him, welcoming the chance to see more of the realm. They had planned a short visit, but while they were away Athelwulf developed a cough and a slight fever.

"I think we should say here," Judith said, convinced that several days' ride in the cool air would not be good for her husband. "We can celebrate Christmas here as well as at Winchester."

"I think you are right, Judith," Athelwulf replied.

The first flicker of alarm stirred in Judith's heart. She had expected him to protest and insist on returning to Winchester. His easy acquiescence was strange, but she smiled brightly. "I shall send for Alfred and Ethelred. Shall I also summon Bishop Swithun here to celebrate the mass?"

Athelwulf coughed. It was a harsh, racking sound. "If you wish, my dear."

Suddenly more seriously concerned, Judith knelt down next to him. She touched his brow, shocked by how clammy his forehead felt. "You must rest, Athelwulf. We must have you well for Christmas."

Judith's worries increased when he took to his bed, but the arrival of Ethelred and Alfred a few days later raised his spirits and he seemed much improved. By the time Bishop Swithun arrived, he was sat in the hall and received his old friend with pleasure. Judith breathed a sigh of relief and planned an even quieter celebration.

That Christmas Athelwulf tired easily and there was no repeat of the merry manner he had displayed the previous year. He left the celebrations early, but he was not yet sleeping when Judith came to their chambers. They had been sleeping apart while he was ill as Athelwulf said he did not want to disturb her, but she looked in on him before retiring herself.

"I had thought you would be asleep by now." She smiled as she saw him propped up on the pillows.

"I am sorry we did not have the celebration you envisaged."

"Do not be foolish," Judith said, taking his hand. "This day has been most enjoyable. We shall have a more lavish celebration next year."

Athelwulf smiled a touch sadly. "Perhaps, my dear."

All the alarm Judith had felt before Christmas came flooding back. Despite his age, Athelwulf had always been a strong man, but suddenly he looked smaller and frail. In the candlelight it seemed to Judith his face had a grey tinge. "Of course we will," she said briskly. "You are recovering well now. A little more rest and you will be yourself again."

Athelwulf nodded. "I am sure you are right. Go to your rest and I shall do the same." He lay back against the pillows.

Judith kissed him on the cheek, shocked by how cold it felt. As he shut his eyes, she pulled the covers up around his shoulders. Reluctantly Judith went to the adjoining chamber, casting many backwards glances towards her ailing husband.

∞∞∞

The next morning Athelwulf did not get out of bed and this continued for several more days. Yet the rest did nothing to improve his strength. Judith brought food and drink to him herself, but it was rare for him to even pick at the food.

"You must eat. How are you going to get stronger if you do not?" Judith begged.

"I have no appetite. Perhaps I shall eat it later."

With a heavy heart Judith set the food on a table near his bed, knowing it would remain untouched. A bout of coughing tore through his body, bringing a hint of colour to his pale cheeks. She wiped his mouth with a soft cloth, but stopped, terrified as she saw the red smear on it.

"Is that blood?" she asked in a small voice.

Athelwulf was trying to soothe his throat with sips of mead. His hand shook as he held the cup. "It is not the first time."

Judith's heart thudded. "Why did you not tell me?"

"I did not want to alarm you, my dear."

"I am your wife. I should be concerned for your wellbeing."

"Your care is appreciated, but you must not worry yourself."

Before Judith could reply, the door opened to admit Alfred. "Shall I read to you, Father?" he asked.

Athelwulf's face lit up and Judith managed to smile at the affection between them. "What a good idea, Alfred," she said. "Bishop Swithun has praised your progress. I know your father will be pleased to hear it."

Athelwulf settled himself back on his pillows, a slight smile on his face as Alfred began to read from his precious book in a halting manner. Judith blinked back tears at the sight, as she left the two of them together.

She made her way slowly to the church which lay next to their residence and was relieved to find Bishop Swithun kneeling before the altar. Judith sat down at the back of the church, reluctant to interrupt his devotions. But he realised she was there for he quickly turned to her.

"How may I be of service, my Lady Queen?" he asked.

"I wish to speak to you of my lord husband," Judith said in a faltering tone.

Swithun's face was grave as he pulled up a chair next to her. "The King is not well."

Judith looked pleadingly at him. "I thought he was recovering, but he will not rise from his bed or eat. And, Father, this day I have learnt he is coughing blood." In her heart Judith knew these signs were not good, but she hoped the Bishop would say something reassuring.

"I fear he is becoming frailer, my lady," Swithun said, looking saddened.

"Is there nothing we can do?" Judith asked. She hated feeling so helpless.

"Prayers shall be said for him, my lady," Swithun replied, adding gently, "He has seen nearly sixty years. No man lives forever."

Judith bowed her head, a few tears escaping her eyes. "I must be able to do something."

"You are already doing more than you realise, my daughter," the Bishop said in a voice filled with emotion. "Such wifely devotion is serving him well. His fate is in God's hands. But whether the King remains on this earth for just a little while longer or many years, his life is more comfortable for your attentions."

Judith made herself smile at these words of praise, although they were bringing no comfort.

"There is perhaps one thing you should do," Swithun said.

"What is it?" Judith asked.

"Send for King Athelbald and Prince Ethelbert. They should be at their father's side at this time. And, my lady, I think you should do this urgently."

Judith froze. "Is it as bad as that?" she whispered.

"I cannot see into the future, my lady," Swithun said, taking Judith's hands between his. "But I think it would be wise. If it is a false call and they arrive to find their father recovering well, no harm is done."

Judith nodded. She rose to her feet, the pain filling her breast making this action an effort. "I shall need to talk to Ethelred and Alfred," she said, her heart breaking at the thought of the misery this would cause those boys. "Father, will you be present when I do this?"

"Of course, my daughter. I shall be here to assist in whatever way I can. Shall I also talk to the Lord King?"

"I know he will be glad to talk to you." Judith's face crumbled as she remembered how he had spoken to her on Christmas night. "But I think he already knows."

Chapter ten

Judith sent messengers to Canterbury and Sherborne that very day informing Athelbald and Ethelbert that their father was gravely ill and requesting they come to Steyning with all haste. Later she asked Alfred and Ethelred to come to the church, where Swithun welcomed them into a small chamber.

"Sit down, my sons," Swithun said.

Both boys looked nervous as they did so. Judith sat between them, taking a hand of each. Ethelred was only eleven and Alfred not quite nine. She looked helplessly at Swithun, having no idea of how to break the news.

"My sons, you know your father is most unwell," Swithun said.

The boys looked even more frightened and Judith realised they already knew matters were serious.

"He is receiving the very best care we can give," Judith said. "But he is not recovering as I had hoped. Indeed he seems to be worsening."

"Is Father dying?" Alfred asked, tears appearing in his eyes.

Judith longed to deny it, but false hope would be the cruellest of all. She put her arms around her two stepsons. "We fear so."

"My sons, your father has led a long life and has received many blessings." Swithun placed his hands on the boys' shoulders. "His life has also been a noble one. He is assured of God's salvation."

"Is there nothing we can do?" Ethelred said, stilling his

trembling lips enough to let him speak.

"Sit with him and talk to him whenever he feels able," Judith said. "Your chatter brings him great pleasure."

"Does Father know he is dying?" Alfred asked.

"I have spoken at great length with your father," Swithun said, with a kindly smile. "I cannot tell you what passed between us, for it was for God's ears alone. But I can assure you, his soul is untroubled. And I agree with what your dear mother has said. Speak with him or simply sit with him. Your presence will ease his mind still further."

The two boys looked at each other, their composure breaking. Judith pulled them closer to her, tears streaming down her own face. For a long time the three wept. Eventually Judith wiped her eyes.

"Forgive us, Father," she said.

"Not at all, my Lady Queen. You are young to be facing widowhood. And for you boys to be losing a father who has always been the kindest and most affectionate parent is grievous indeed. Remember you were blessed to have so loving a father. I shall keep you all in my prayers."

∞∞∞

Judith longed more than anything to be proved wrong, that Athelwulf would eat again and the blood would turn out to be merely from a loose tooth or some such trivial matter. But each time she saw him, her hopes were further dashed. He became thinner and weaker each day. However, the Bishop was right. He was at peace and seemed contented to see them, even if joining in the talk became too much for him.

One afternoon she sat beside him as he slept, looking at his still, pale face. His hair and beard were neat, for he liked her to comb it. To the end he was determined to look a king. Judith began to feel frightened. Although she had never loved him, her affection and respect had been deep and genuine. But more than that, she depended on him. Since the moment of their marriage, he had been her protector. He had raised her up to be a queen and had insisted she be revered by all. Even weak as he was now, his aura of protection was still around her. She felt bitterly afraid of what would happen after he died.

Athelwulf's eyes flickered open and he gave a faint smile to see her sitting beside him. Judith quickly forced the trouble from her face to smile back. As he tried to sit, she moved some pillows behind him.

"There, is that more comfortable?" she asked, keeping her tone light.

"Yes, my dear. Thank you."

"Will you eat a little?" Judith asked automatically, indicating a bowl of porridge.

"No, thank you. Just a little ale."

Judith held the cup to his lips. "I have had a message from Canterbury. Ethelbert is on his way. He should be here in the next few days. I have not yet heard from Athelbald, but the weather is poor. It is likely the messenger has been delayed."

"I hope to see them again," Athelwulf said, leaning back against the pillows and closing his eyes.

Judith took his hand, saying nothing.

Athelwulf opened his eyes again. "Judith, once they are here, we may not have so much time alone."

Judith nodded, surprised to hear his voice sounding stronger.

"Come closer, my sweet girl."

Judith sat on the bed, keeping his hand in hers. He smiled gently up at her. "Will you return to West Francia when I am gone?"

Judith felt a lump swell in her throat. "I have not thought of it."

"You must think," he urged.

"My father may expect me to become a nun," Judith whispered. "I have even less liking for that prospect now than before our marriage."

"You will have money," Athelwulf said. "The lands I bestowed on you, remain yours. If you wish to remain in Wessex, I shall command Athelbald to allow it."

Judith blinked back the tears. Even dying he remained determined to protect her and thanks to his generosity she would be a wealthy widow.

"Do not grieve for me, Judith. I lived my life before you were born. Marriage to an old man is no prospect for such a pretty, young girl as you. I hope your father finds a younger, finer husband for you after I am gone."

"He can find a younger man," Judith choked. "But he could not find a finer one."

Athelwulf smiled again. "After Osburh died I did not look for happiness, but you, my sweet Judith, have been a bright star, lighting up my last years. I have been proud to call you my wife."

"I have been proud to be your wife," Judith said, pressing his hand against her cheek.

The talk was obviously tiring him and he shut his eyes, coughs shaking his body. Judith was hardly able to see his face through her tears as she gently wiped away the blood trickling from his mouth.

For a long time she looked at him as he drifted off to sleep. Knowing it would likely be the last time she would ever do this, Judith lay down next to him, putting her arms around him. His body felt so thin and frail. It was dark before he woke again, but even in the gloom she could see the slight smile on his face. A cough racked through him once again, but she continued to hold him and he quickly soothed.

"Thank you, my dearest girl," he whispered.

Judith managed to smile brightly at him, before gently kissing him. "Thank you, my dearest husband."

∞ ∞ ∞

Ethelbert arrived the next day, shortly before a blizzard blew in. He was as distantly polite as ever towards Judith, but even so, she was relieved he was there. Alfred and Ethelred were both glad to see him and she felt the burden of caring for those two as well as her husband ease slightly. Athelwulf slept more and more. It became rarer for him to sit up in bed, but apart from the coughs tearing through him, he appeared to be comfortable enough.

As the weather worsened she feared Athelbald would not get to them in time. She had heard nothing since the messenger had departed and she wondered if he had befallen some accident. In such terrible weather she could not dispatch another, but she found it unbearable that Athelbald might still be unaware of his father's illness. She mentioned her concerns to Ethelbert, but he dismissed them.

"There is nothing you can do, so why worry?"

Judith sighed. "Your father so longs to see him one last time."

Ethelbert simply shrugged and returned to his father's side. The chamber was often crowded with many paying their last respects to their king. Swithun was in almost constant attendance. Judith and the three sons too often sat there, ensuring at least one of them was always with him.

"He is very weak now, my lady," Swithun whispered to Judith one evening. "I do not think he can last much more than another day or two. Perhaps not even that."

Judith nodded bleakly. It was another day of snow, but despite the cold Judith went out into the courtyard, a thick cloak wrapped around her, as she tried to prepare herself for these final hours. She stared into the white stillness, unable to believe she was so soon to be widowed. The moon was bright in a sky scattered with stars, lighting up the snow in an otherworldly gleam. As she looked up at it, a nearby neigh of a horse made her start. The thick snow had muffled the sound of a rider arriving. Judith stared at the black horse, standing out so starkly against the white ground, wondering who would possibly be riding in this weather. A cloaked figure dismounted and looked around him. Even in the darkness Judith recognised the figure.

"Athelbald!" she cried, lurching over the snow towards him, tears of relief falling from her eyes.

Athelbald caught her as she skidded in front of him and took her hands, both forgetting the anger in which they had previously parted. He studied her face anxiously, noticing the tears on it.

"Am I too late? The weather has been terrible. When the messenger told me how long ago you had sent him… My God, I have never ridden so fast or in such conditions."

"No, no, you are not too late. Your father is failing fast, but he will be so pleased to see you. Come!" Judith tugged on his hand, pulling him into the hall and calling for a servant to take the horse to the stable.

Athelbald glanced around the hall, his hood falling back from his head. His body drooped in exhaustion and his hands were like ice.

"Do you want some refreshment first?" Judith asked.

Athelbald shook his head. "No, I must see my father."

Judith took his arm to lead him up a narrow staircase. "Perhaps I should have sent for you sooner. He was unwell before Christmas, but he seemed to recover. It was only in the days after that I began to truly fear for him."

"That was less than three weeks ago," Athelbald said. "You have acted as quickly as you could."

As they reached the chamber door, Athelbald took a deep breath, preparing himself to bid a farewell to his father. They entered to a gasp of surprise and relief.

"Brother!" Ethelbert said, taking his hands.

Athelbald called a few greetings, but his eyes were fixed on the bed. Judith hurried forward, taking Athelwulf's hand in hers. "My dearest husband, your son is here. Athelbald has come."

Athelwulf's eyes flickered open. It seemed he barely had the strength now for even that small action, but as they focused on the handsome figure of his eldest son, they widened and a slight smile even curved his lips. Athelbald knelt down next to Judith, taking his other hand.

"My son," he whispered.

"I am here, Father," Athelbald said, the emotion evident in his voice.

Judith felt a wave of sympathy at his solemn expression, forgetting the sneer which so frequently dominated Athelbald's face.

Athelwulf's eyes flickered to Judith, a plea appearing in them and Judith knew what it meant. She nodded, kissing his cold forehead before turning to address the others in the room.

"The King wishes for some time alone with Athelbald. Let us retire to the hall a while."

She poured Athelbald some hot ale. "A serving lad will wait outside if you need anything."

Athelbald nodded. "Thank you. I shall call you all back once we have spoken."

∞∞∞

The hall was a silent place that evening. There was food on the table, but few had the appetite to do more than nibble a little. Ethelbert and Ethelred sat quietly side by side, Ethelbert's arm around the younger boy. Alfred sat next to Bishop Swithun, looking dazed. Judith sat on his other side, wishing she had some words of comfort.

But the only comfort was that Athelwulf was able to take leave of his eldest son. Judith knew he had spent some time alone with each of his sons. It would have been cruel not to have had some final words for the eldest. She glanced at Alfred, wondering what Athelwulf had said to him. No doubt he had expressed his great pride and given some last words of advice. She put her arm around him and he sank his fair head against her shoulder, a sigh of grief and exhaustion escaping his lips.

The hour got later, but no one suggested retiring. The serving men kept the fires and torches burning brightly. Judith was lost in her own thoughts when a serving man bade them return.

"But King Athelbald commands just the family and Bishop Swithun are present."

Judith nodded her agreement, placing her hand into Alfred's and leading them back to the death chamber. Athelwulf was lying flat, his eyes closed and his breath shallow. Judith doubted his eyes would ever again open, but she did not begrudge Athelbald those last moments of consciousness. He was sat beside his father, still holding his hand with traces of tears on his cheeks which he made no attempt to disguise. She knelt down at her husband's side, her hand still in Alfred's. As Alfred pressed his lips against his father's cheek, Judith was sure she saw a faint ripple pass over Athelwulf's face and she was certain he knew they were all with him. Trying to take comfort from this, she laid her head on the bed and waited.

The fire crackled slightly, but other than that, the only sound was the voice of Swithun as he chanted prayers. For the rest of the night they waited, the breaths becoming ever shallower, while the gaps between them grew longer. Several times Judith thought the moment of death had come.

It was still some hours before dawn when the curious choking noise came from Athelwulf's throat. Alfred shrank even closer to her as it stopped in one long sigh. Judith glanced at Athelbald, noticing the emotion on his face. She looked back again at the still figure of her husband on the bed. She would not turn sixteen years for more than a month and already she was a widow.

Chapter eleven

The rest of that night was a blur. Athelbald had taken charge and ordered everyone to get some sleep. Judith dozed intermittently in the hastily made up chamber, away from the spot where her husband lay. It was nearly noon before she joined her stepsons and Bishop Swithun. Athelbald had been proclaimed King of Wessex and Ethelbert, King of Kent, but both men were subdued.

"The funeral shall be soon," Athelbald announced. "He can be buried before the altar here in the church."

"Father would want to lie at Winchester," Alfred protested.

Athelbald gave Alfred a sad smile. "I know, Alfred, but look at the weather. We won't be able to make the journey to Winchester for some time. It wouldn't be right to leave his body unburied. He should have the proper rites as soon as possible, but we can move his body to Winchester at a later date."

Alfred gulped back the sob rising to his throat and Judith's heart ached to see the young boy behaving with such bravery.

Swithun patted him on the shoulder. "Your father's soul is safe with God. It matters not where he lies. For myself, I shall not care where they lay my body, as long as it is somewhere the rain can fall on it and ordinary folk can walk by."

"Does this matter meet your approval, Judith?" Athelbald asked.

Judith felt touched at the courtesy he was showing her and she nodded, the tears she had been holding back starting to trickle down her face.

"Oh, spare us the false tears, my lady," Ethelbert snapped. "You don't need to maintain your devoted act now."

Judith gaped at him, but before she could say anything, Athelbald glared at him. "Be quiet, Brother."

Ethelbert raised his eyebrows. "Are you as fooled by her act as Father was?"

"My Lord King," Swithun put in. "Your father's rites should not be marred by such accusations."

"No, they should not," Athelbald said. "And Father was not the fool you thought he was, Ethelbert. He never expected Judith to love him as a woman loves a man. And to tell the truth, I do not think he loved her as a man loves a woman. But in spite of that, an affection grew between them that was ever true and it brought Father much happiness in his last months. You will not mock her grief."

Judith looked at Athelbald in considerable amazement. He was the last person she expected to leap so wholeheartedly to her defence. He met her eyes, a hint of mischief appearing in them as he acknowledged her surprise. "Most of what Father said to me last night will remain between us, but I will tell you this. He asked that I protect Judith for as long as she wishes to remain in Wessex and that she continue to be accorded the respect due to her rank. His wishes will be honoured." He gave a faint smile. "Do not take this to mean I like you, my lady."

Judith managed to return the smile, but bowed her head to hide the tears which flowed even faster. The pain in her heart increased as she realised Athelwulf was continuing to protect her from beyond death.

"I think you should apologise to the Queen, my Lord King," Swithun said to Ethelbert. "You have not been at Winchester, as I have, to witness the Queen's devotion to both your father and your brothers."

Ethelbert scowled but he muttered his apologies and Athelbald quickly moved the discussion on until the rites had been planned. Afterwards Judith felt exhausted and excused herself to her chamber. She lay on the bed staring at the ceiling, not accustomed to being so idle but not having the strength to do anything more. Her future gaped ahead of her, but she had no idea what it could hold.

∞∞∞

The funeral rites were carried out with a ceremony and dignity that was a fitting tribute to a King who had reigned as long and as well as Athelwulf. Beneath the dignity, there was an undercurrent of genuine sorrow and not just from the family. Athelwulf's gentle manner had made him well loved by the people and it was obvious he would be much missed. In the days after the funeral Judith found a new role in caring for Alfred and Ethelred, who were both grieving deeply. She kept out of the way of her older stepsons, not wanting anything to damage the fragile truce between them.

∞∞∞

The snow remained on the ground for some weeks, but eventually it thawed enough for them to return to Winchester. It was a sombre ride with many backwards glances.

"I wish we weren't leaving him there," Alfred whispered.

"I know," Judith said. "But remember his soul is with God. We are not really leaving him at Steyning."

Alfred blinked furiously, trying to dislodge the tears as Athelbald urged his horse towards them.

"One day Father shall have a grand tomb at Winchester," he said. "And we shall have a ceremony to move his body there. Perhaps, Alfred, you will be one of the riders to accompany him on that journey."

Alfred nodded, appearing slightly brighter. Judith looked at Athelbald with a respect she had never felt before. Since his father's death he seemed to have grown up considerably. She hoped Athelwulf had realised that and known his beloved youngest son would be safe in Athelbald's care.

Arriving back at Winchester felt strange. Judith walked into the hall she had presided over, not knowing what her place was anymore. She sipped at a cup of wine wondering what she should do next.

"Judith," Athelbald said in a low voice as he saw her stand alone. "I shall be writing to your father to inform him of my father's death. Obviously I shall assure him that, as far as I am concerned, the alliance between Wessex and West Francia remains as strong as ever. Shall I say you intend to remain in Wessex, at least for the mourning period?"

Judith nodded. "I would prefer to be here for now. For the future, I just don't know."

She guessed it would not be long before Athelbald married, which could cause all kinds of complications. If Athelbald's wife was not a consecrated queen, it would be impossible to say who held the highest rank.

"I promised Father you would always have a home here," Athelbald said gently. "And of course you have lands in Wessex, but your father may have other ideas."

"A nunnery probably," Judith said. "Thank you. I shall be glad to stay here. What chamber should I use?"

Athelbald looked shocked. "I'd not take your chamber from you, Judith. Remain where you are."

Judith smiled but shook her head. "It is called the King's chamber for a reason and it is yours now. There are many comfortable chambers at Winchester."

A gleam of amusement lit up Athelbald's eyes and he leant closer to Judith. "You could share it with me."

Judith took a step back. "Shame on you, Athelbald," she hissed, hoping no one else would hear. "Your father is scarce cold in his grave. Do not speak to me like that."

Athelbald gave a malicious grin. "I think you would enjoy it," he said as he moved away from her.

Judith sighed, giving a weary shake of her head. Athelbald, it seemed, had not changed as much as she had hoped.

∞∞∞

A few weeks later Athelbald summoned Judith to his council chamber, where he was making plans for his crowning. He bowed courteously to her as she entered and invited her to be seated.

"Judith, I am sorry to have to ask you this, but is there any possibility you could be with child?"

Judith looked down, smoothing over the long grey skirt of her mourning clothes. "No. Your father has been gone more than two months and was ill for nearly two months before that."

Athelbald frowned, sorting among some manuscripts for a thick vellum scroll. Judith recognised the seal of West Francia at the bottom. "I have heard from your father."

Judith's heart sank. "What does he say?"

"He expressed his condolences and his hopes that we might remain in alliance against the heathen army, but he wants you to return to him."

Judith shook her head.

"He says, I will be grateful if you could arrange for the safe passage of my daughter, Queen Judith of Wessex at the earliest opportunity, unless she bears a Wessex prince in her body. It is right for her to receive the comfort of her mother at such a time and to be guided in her future in the appropriate manner."

"He means me to become a nun," Judith said.

"What a waste," Athelbald replied with a grin.

Judith narrowed her eyes at him in dislike. "What of your promise to your father to protect me and grant me a home in Wessex?"

"I wish to keep it, but I can't go to war with West Francia over this."

Judith's eyes widened. "Would it really come to that?"

"I don't know. What do you think would happen if I refused to return you? He would be likely to consider you imprisoned here."

Judith looked down in despair, tears filling her eyes, wishing more than anything that Athelwulf was still there. She looked up at Athelbald beseechingly. "Is there nothing you can do?"

Athelbald got to his feet and looked at her with a smirk. He knelt at Judith's side, putting his arm around her and gently running his fingers down her face. Judith froze for an instant before scrambling to her feet.

"What are you doing?" she gasped.

Athelbald caught her around the waist. "Do you want my protection?"

Judith backed away from him, colliding with the wall. "What sort of man are you?" she cried. "You expect me to buy your protection with my honour!"

Athelbald moved closer to her, his body pressing lightly against hers. "Are you tempted?" he asked, bringing his face so close his lips almost touched her cheek. He moved his hands to the neck of her tunic, looking down teasingly at her.

Judith gulped, angry with herself for feeling excited by his touch. She pushed against his chest. "I was your father's wife. How can you even suggest dishonouring me?"

"Such loyalty," Athelbald sneered, pulling away from her. "If you wish to remain ever true to his memory, I think a nunnery would suit you very well."

Judith shook her head. "You are leaving me no choice. It is clear I am not safe in Wessex. I shall be grateful if you can arrange my return to West Francia."

Judith held her head high, looking angrily into his handsome, arrogant face. "Is that really what you want?" he asked, laying his hand on her shoulder. He slid it gently down her arm to take her hand in his.

"Please leave me alone, Athelbald," Judith whispered, tears filling her eyes. "Yes, it is what I want. I am not strong enough to stay here."

Athelbald laughed out loud and he raised her hand to his lips. "You little fool, how can you think I would dishonour a woman of your rank? Do you think I want your father to kill me? There is a way you can remain here under my protection." He cupped her face in his other hand. "Will you marry me?"

"What?" As always in conversation with Athelbald, Judith could never guess what he would say next or in which direction his mood would turn.

Athelbald grinned. "Marry me."

"Are you mocking me?" Judith asked, trying in vain to see if there was trickery in his gaze.

"Why would you think that?" he asked, rubbing his thumb gently down her cheek. Judith tossed her head to rid herself of his hand. It was impossible to think clearly with him so close.

"I don't know what to think," Judith said. "Please be honest with me."

Athelbald backed away, gesturing at the chair. Judith sat down trying to calm her trembling body as Athelbald pulled his own chair next to hers and took her hand once again.

"Listen, sweetheart, I am being honest. The alliance my father made with West Francia was damned useful. I want to keep it. I suppose I could make an offer for one of your sisters, but they're all a bit young for marriage at the moment."

Judith stared at him, irritated by the jealousy flooding through her at the thought of him marrying one of her sisters. He grinned. "Anyway, why bring another Frankish princess over here when I already have one? Come on, Judith, marry me and remain Queen of Wessex. You're a very good one. Not to mention a very pretty one."

Judith smiled reluctantly. "But I was your father's wife. Would it even be allowed?"

Athelbald shrugged. "I would prefer us to say the words in front of a priest, but I can find one easily enough. An ambitious one, eager to serve the new king. How do you think your father will react?"

"I don't know, but the reasons for marrying me to Wessex remain. Once we were married I don't suppose there's much he would do. He wouldn't want to lose the alliance."

Athelbald grinned. "So, does this mean you're accepting me?"

"I would need to think about it," Judith said, trying to reclaim some control of the conversation. "But I will consider it."

"Don't act the princess with me, Judith. You know you want me. I'll satisfy you far better than the old man ever did."

Judith got to her feet. "If I marry you, it will be on the condition that you never say a word against your father. He was forced to anoint me queen by my father, but once in Wessex he did not have to honour me as he did. I could have been just a young, unimportant second wife, but he insisted that I be accorded the highest respect. He will always hold a place in my heart."

Athelbald looked taken aback. "Very well. He was my father and I loved him too. But marriage to me will be different and you know it. Not necessarily better, but different."

Judith laughed. "We do nothing but argue. It will certainly not be better."

Athelbald put his arms around her and Judith gave up the pretence, resting her head against him. She felt his lips in her hair. "So, will you marry me?"

"Yes," Judith said. "Yes, I will."

Part Three: Year of our Lord 858 - 860

Athelbald's lady – Queen of Wessex

Chapter one

"The wedding will need to be soon," Athelbald said.

"It seems so disrespectful," Judith replied.

"I wish I could give you a year, but I think your father would demand your return long before then. There would also be many in Wessex to make their opinions known if we delay. Far better to do this quickly and present it as a done deed."

Judith nodded. "Very well. Just tell me when."

Athelbald pulled a ring from his finger and slipped it over Judith's. "There, we are betrothed," he said. She smiled up at him expectantly. "You can go now. I'll send word when I have a priest."

Judith looked at him in exasperation. "We are betrothed. You can kiss me now."

"What makes you think I want to?" Athelbald asked, sounding surprised.

"Very well. A good day to you, my lord."

She turned to leave, but was unsurprised when Athelbald pulled her back. Her arms went around him and their lips met. Feelings Judith had never believed possible shot through her as he kissed her. He slipped one arm around her waist, the other cupping her neck in a gentle caress. Judith reached up to run her fingers through his dark hair, trying to pull his head even closer to hers.

Athelbald brought the kiss to an abrupt halt. "That will do, you little hussy. We're not wed yet." He pinched her cheek playfully and left the room.

Judith shook her head in bewilderment, wondering what she had just let herself in for.

∞∞∞

It was an effort for Judith to move through the next few days with the gravity and decorum appropriate for a widow. It was not that she needed to pretend her grief. That was still there and very real, but alongside it she was bubbling with excitement. Finally, a serving man brought her the message she had been waiting for.

"My Lady Queen, the Lord King asks that you attend the Minster after Vespers."

Judith calmly nodded her thanks as she looked into the man's face and wondered if he knew why she was being summoned.

That evening she carefully combed her hair and changed her tunic, feeling rather dissatisfied with her appearance. The dark colours she was required to wear for mourning did not suit her. She glanced at the pretty silk overdress she had worn for her wedding to Athelwulf and wished she could wear it again.

Although the spring evening was warm she wore a cloak and pulled up the hood so none would see her entering the Minster. The last of the monks had left, but the Minster was still filled with brightly burning candles. It seemed strange to be entering such an empty building for her wedding, particularly when she remembered the numbers of people summoned to witness her first.

She walked swiftly through the Minster searching for her betrothed, finding him in one of the side chapels with a dark robed man. Athelbald smiled when he saw her.

"I was starting to think you weren't coming," he said, stretching out his hands.

Judith took them, smiling shyly at him. The priest cleared his throat. "My lord, my lady, perhaps we could begin."

Athelbald nodded, pulling Judith up to kneel before the altar. It was draped in a cloth encrusted with gold threads, which Judith had stitched herself and presented to the Minster the previous Easter. Judith looked at the finely wrought gold and silver cross that adorned the altar and bowed her head in a brief prayer, before looking into the eyes of her betrothed.

"I Athelbald, King of Wessex, bind myself most honourably to you, Judith, Queen of Wessex for the rest of my days."

Judith smiled as she repeated the words. Athelbald smiled back. His face, for once free of arrogance, looked more handsome than ever.

"King Athelbald, Queen Judith, I declare you wed in the name of our lord, God and his blessed son, Jesus Christ."

Triumph came into Athelbald's face as he kissed Judith. She smiled back in delight. Yet again she had managed to escape a nun's vows and this time it was with a man she truly desired.

∞∞∞

They left the Minster hand in hand and once out in the courtyard, Athelbald pulled Judith into his arms to kiss her more passionately.

"Perhaps we should miss the meal," he said.

Judith laughed. "Don't be foolish. We cannot spend the night together until everyone has been informed." She felt slightly nervous about the reaction of the people.

Athelbald kissed her again and Judith felt dizzy with joy, confident this marriage would be even happier than her first. Certainly all the passion missing in that one, was more than being made up for now.

Other than the usual bows, no one took much notice of them as they entered the hall. It was, after all, not particularly strange for Athelbald to escort his widowed stepmother to the evening meal. But Judith was overjoyed to be entering the hall again as a reigning queen. She had missed presiding over the table. She glanced around, relieved to see Bishop Swithun was not dining with them that night, but Ethelbert was sitting near the top of the table, talking with Alfred and Ethelred.

The first looks of surprise came when Athelbald led Judith past the place of the widowed queen to the throne on the dais at the head of the table. A silence descended on the people as they tried to work out what this meant.

Athelbald smiled out at everyone. "My people," he announced. "I have happy news this night. Our fair Queen, Lady Judith, daughter of King Charles of West Francia has done me the honour of becoming my wife and queen."

Judith smiled graciously at everyone, trying to ignore the shocked murmurs. Her heart ached at the stricken look on Alfred's face as he looked down at his platter. But before Judith could say anything there was a crash when Ethelbert kicked back his chair.

"By God, Brother, what have you done?" Ethelbert's pale face was crimson with rage, his icy blue eyes narrowed.

"I have got married, Brother. Why do you find that so surprising? A king should make the effort to acquire an heir," Athelbald replied.

"Why her?" Ethelbert demanded. "You have ascended our father's throne and now want to take over his marriage bed as well?"

Athelbald grinned insolently at his brother. "I have not yet had the pleasure of taking over his marriage bed. It is why I am particularly keen to get on with our meal this night."

"Don't say that," Judith muttered under her breath, but Athelbald took no notice.

"You are as taken in by her as our father was," Ethelbert spat. "You are as big a fool as he was."

"How dare you, Ethelbert," Alfred cried, sounding distressed. "Father was not a fool."

Everyone was surprised to hear Alfred raise his voice. The boy was usually so quiet. Judith stepped towards him and put her arm around his shoulder, but Alfred shook her away.

"I thought you cared for Father," Alfred said, tears in his eyes. "How can you be married again already?"

"I cared very much for your father," Judith said. "But as a widow, I would have to return to West Francia and would probably be expected to enter a nunnery. Married to your brother, I can stay here with the people I now consider my family? I shall be your sister, Alfred. Is that really so bad?"

Alfred shrugged. He did not object when Judith embraced him, but his body was stiff.

"Is this marriage even legal?" Ethelbert demanded. "She is your stepmother."

"We were married in the presence of a priest in the Minster," Athelbald replied. "How can you question this?"

"I have the right to question it. If I am to be displaced in the succession, I would want assurances that such a child is legitimate."

"Of course it would be. Do you really think I would dishonour the daughter of the King of West Francia? Listen, Brother, Father was not a fool. He made a shrewd move in marrying Judith. You know how valuable an ally her father is. This makes Wessex powerful, not just here on our island, but across Christendom. If I keep Judith at my side, I keep that power."

Ethelbert shook his head as he picked up his chair, but he said nothing more.

"Let us dine," Athelbald said, sitting down himself. "My people, I command you to drink to the health of your queen, Queen Judith."

Everyone obeyed in a subdued fashion and the meal began. It was far from a merry affair. People spoke in low voices and Judith guessed many were whispering about her. Athelbald was in great spirits, but his jovial conversation was met only with strained replies from his brothers, particularly Alfred who merely nibbled at his food and excused himself early from the table. Judith kept her eyes cast down, knowing there would be time enough in the future to stamp her authority back on their evenings.

As the women and children began to leave the table, Athelbald turned expectantly to Judith, slipping his arm around her waist and running his hand down her thigh. Judith could not repress her shiver of excitement. Athelbald grinned and planted a kiss on her cheek.

"Get yourself to the King's chamber, sweetheart," he said. "Make yourself ready and hurry. I shall retire shortly."

Judith flushed and left the hall in as dignified manner as she could manage.

∞∞∞

In the King's chamber she quickly sent away her serving woman and got into bed. She looked around her. It was strange to be back. Almost she expected Athelwulf to enter at any moment. But when it was Athelwulf she was waiting for, she had never been in this state of excitement. She dismissed thoughts of him from her mind as the door opened and Athelbald came in. He didn't say a word to her while he kicked off his shoes and removed his breeches. Judith's heart pounded as he cast off his tunic to reveal a muscular chest dusted with dark hair. She was unable to take her eyes off his powerful body. He grinned arrogantly as he saw the look in her eyes and sat down on the bed.

"Just so we are clear, Athelbald, I may be married to you, but I am still not sure whether I like you," Judith said, pushing her robe from her shoulders. She didn't attempt to hide her own smile of triumph as the desire flared in his eyes. She was no longer the mere pretty girl who had arrived in Wessex, but had matured into an alluring young woman.

Athelbald laughed as he took her in his arms. "I'm not sure whether I like you either," he said, as he kissed her on her face and neck. His hands were slowly moving down her body causing waves of delight to run through her. He smiled teasingly at her again. "But we're going to have a lot of fun while we find out."

Judith slid down into the bed, pulling him with her. She ran her hands across his chest and shoulders, more aware than ever of the strength in his arms, before slipping her arms around his back, welcoming the feel of his body against her.

As he moved his body on top of hers, Judith gazed into his eyes, which had darkened with passion. Her lips sought his once again and the only thought in her mind was one of agreement. They certainly would have a lot of fun.

Chapter two

Unsurprisingly neither of them made it to Matins the next day. Judith awoke to find light already streaming through the chamber windows. She rolled over, propping herself up on her elbow to look at her husband. He smiled lazily up at her and she leant over him to plant a kiss on his lips.

"So, do you like me yet?" he asked.

"You're improving on acquaintance," Judith replied airily.

Athelbald laughed. "I suppose I shall have to keep trying," he said, as he seized her in his arms and pushed her onto her back.

Judith wound her arms around his neck, as his kisses rained down on her. The sensations that morning were even more intense than they had been the night before.

The morning was well advanced before Athelbald rose from the bed. "Get up, you lazy slattern," he called, pulling on his breeches. "You must have some work to do today."

Judith threw a pillow at him for that, but reluctantly pushed back the covers and dressed. Their high spirits were dashed when they arrived hand in hand at the hall to find Bishop Swithun waiting for them.

"My Lord King, I would like a private word with you and the Lady Queen."

Athelbald shrugged. "I might spare the time after we have broken our fast, Father."

"The matter is urgent, my lord," Swithun said, looking distressed.

Judith bit her lip. She had always liked the Bishop. "Let us talk with Father Swithun first."

Athelbald frowned. "No, Judith. I am hungry. Any business can wait."

Without another word he strode away and sat down at the table, filling up a cup with weak ale and grabbing a chunk of bread. Judith glanced at Swithun, dismayed to see he was looking sternly at her.

"Judith!" Athelbald called. "Come take some ale at least."

"Excuse me, Father," Judith murmured, taking a seat beside Athelbald.

She sipped uncomfortably at her drink, acutely aware of the Bishop still waiting to talk. But Athelbald continued to ignore him, pointedly laughing and jesting with his men.

"My lord, let us get this over with," Judith whispered, unable to bear it any longer.

Athelbald glanced down at her and sighed. "Oh, very well."

They made their way silently to the council chamber, where Athelbald flung himself into a chair. He looked insolently at the Bishop. "Say what you need to say, Father."

"I cannot condone this marriage," Swithun stated.

"I am not asking you to," Athelbald replied. "That is why we made our vows in the presence of another priest."

"My son, this marriage is not valid."

Judith gasped, her worst fears coming true but Athelbald grinned. "Are you implying that last night I dishonoured the daughter of the King of West Francia? That is a most serious allegation."

Swithun looked sternly at him. "I do not speak in jest, my son. I am aware of how serious this matter is, but I must state this. Such an incestuous marriage cannot be valid."

"Incest?" scoffed Athelbald.

"My son, you have married your mother."

Athelbald laughed out loud. "My mother? How can she possibly be my mother? She's more than ten years younger than me."

"In the eyes of God, she is your mother."

Athelbald shook his head. "Then I think God is not as all seeing as I used to think he was."

"Don't say that," Judith whispered, seeing the distress on Swithun's face deepen.

"What would your poor father say of this? You were ever a concern to him."

Athelbald leant forward, his eyes narrowed. "Some of the last words my father spoke to me, were to place Judith under my protection. I promised I would do this and in marrying her I have fulfilled that promise."

"You force a young girl, unprotected in this land, into incest and you consider that protection?"

"I was not forced, Father," Judith said quietly. "I agreed to the marriage."

"You are young and foolish, my Lady Queen," Swithun said. "He took full advantage of your defenceless state."

"Regardless of your opinions, Father, we are married. We were wed in the Minster in the eyes of God," Athelbald maintained. "And the marriage has been consummated."

"I guessed as much, but I am sorry to hear it," Swithun said. "I shall be discussing this matter with the other bishops in this realm. We shall make a decision as to whether this marriage is valid."

Judith bowed her head, seeing herself already ruined, but Athelbald was not to be defeated. He got to his feet. "Do as you will, Father, but let me remind you that the church occupied a privileged position during my father's reign and became most wealthy and influential. It does not have to continue that way in mine. I shall be informing King Charles of West Francia of the marriage and asking for the blessing of the bishops in his realm. My marriage and the alliance it brings me with West Francia will remain."

The three returned to the hall without further talk. The people there looked curiously at them, sensing the tense atmosphere. Alfred too was present, waiting for his lessons with the Bishop.

"Please grant me a little time, Prince Alfred," Swithun said. "I must pray for guidance."

Athelbald took Judith into his arms. "Don't look so concerned, sweetheart," he said. "He can splutter all he likes, but we are wed and nothing will change that." He gave her a long kiss, before heading from the hall.

Judith looked at Alfred, who was regarding her gravely out of grey eyes which bore an uncomfortable resemblance to his father's. "Father Swithun says you have committed a most grievous sin."

"No, Alfred. Of course, we are all sinners and we are most grateful for Father Swithun's guidance, but I have committed no grievous sin. Your brother and I were wed in the Minster under the eyes of God."

"Father has only been gone two months," Alfred said, his eyes filling with tears.

"I know." Guilt surged in her. "If I had the choice I would have waited. Please believe me, I cared very much for your father and continue to mourn his death, but my father was demanding I return to West Francia. Marrying Athelbald so quickly was the only way I could stay. I think your father would be glad that I am still here to care for you. And if I bear Athelbald a child, the union of Wessex and West Francia your father envisaged will be complete."

Judith was not sure if it was the boy she was trying to convince or herself. Athelwulf would certainly have been happy for Judith to remarry, but she suspected this undignified scramble to marriage so soon after his death would have deeply offended the ever decorous king. However Alfred seemed somewhat mollified.

"It will take me some time to accustom myself to this," Alfred said. "But I am glad you're staying here."

Judith hugged him. "Thank you, Alfred. Your friendship has always been important to me. I would be grieved indeed to lose it."

∞ ∞ ∞

Judith and Athelbald had their first public argument that night, just a single day after their marriage. Determined to keep some decorum, Judith dressed in a pale grey dress, over a dark tunic. Athelwulf had been gone such a short time, that it seemed appropriate for Judith to continue to display her mourning.

She walked into the hall, smiling with her usual assurance, to curtsey politely before her husband and king. He rose to his feet, but did not bow as she expected him to. His eyes swept over her.

"What are you wearing?" he demanded.

Judith glanced down in surprise.

"Why are you still in mourning?"

"Your father died just two months ago," Judith stammered.

"You're not a widow now," Athelbald snapped. "You are my wife."

"I still wish to show my respect."

"Would that be the same respect which sent you into a new marriage after little more than two months?" Ethelbert asked.

"Be quiet, Brother," Athelbald said. "That is not the issue. It is inappropriate for you to continue to wear mourning. Go change your attire."

Judith tossed back her head. "No," she said.

Athelbald's handsome face twisted in rage. "Do as you have been told."

"I will not."

"Damn it, Judith," Athelbald shouted. "A wife must obey her husband. Go to your chamber immediately and do not return until you are correctly attired."

"I am correctly attired," Judith said. "I will continue to display my mourning for my late husband. I will obey you in all other matters."

Athelbald thumped the table, causing jugs of ale to spill. "Change your attire or I will tear it off you."

Judith was outraged by his threats, but she arched her eyebrows and folded her arms. "That is no way to dissuade me from dressing this way."

For a moment Judith thought he might follow through with his threat. He grabbed her around the waist and his other hand went to the neck of her overdress. He looked at her mockingly, but Judith did not flinch before his gaze and looked directly back. Athelbald laughed and gave her a hearty kiss.

"Oh, sit down, you disobedient brat. We shall dine." He pushed Judith towards their throne. "I shall tear that dress off you later."

Judith sat down, smiling triumphantly, only to see everyone staring open-mouthed at her. This court was accustomed to the tranquil and benevolent Athelwulf with his Frankish queen sitting graciously at his side. Never had they been treated to such a spectacle.

Chapter three

A few weeks after their wedding the court moved to Kingston for Athelbald's crowning. His mood was high and Judith too was excited to be part of such an event. Her relationship with Athelbald had continued to be stormy. He started arguments in front of everybody over the most trivial of matters and it seemed to Judith it was only in their marriage bed that she managed to please him. If she was honest with herself, it was only in bed that he truly managed to please her. Often she wished she did not have to rise from those long and passionate nights, to a day where he was determined to find fault.

"Judith, will you at least come out of mourning for my crowning?" Athelbald asked her.

Judith considered this and assented. She was not unwilling to be out of the colours that did not favour her. "What should I wear?" she asked.

"I don't care," Athelbald said. "Just not mourning colours. This is supposed to be a celebration. I shall be in red."

Judith nodded. "I think it would be appropriate for me to wear the same."

When Judith presented herself to Athelbald before the crowning, he took a long look at her. She was dressed in a dark red overdress, lavishly embroidered with golden threads. The heavy gold diadem of a Wessex queen stood out dramatically against her dark hair, while costly jewellery studded with gems was fastened around her wrists and neck. Her attendants had all been most complimentary, but as Athelbald continued to stare, Judith wondered if he had found some fault. She looked back at him. His own tunic was of a similar shade and a cloak edged with fur swept around his shoulders. A gold chain hung from his neck and another formed a belt around his waist. Nothing could have done more to enhance his powerful, good looks.

"You look most fine, my lord husband," she said. "The people of Wessex are fortunate to be gaining so strong and handsome a king."

Athelbald smiled and took her hands. "Then it is indeed fitting I have at my side the most beautiful of queens."

Judith beamed, relieved he had found no fault with her that day.

"I have received a message from your father," he told her. "I suspect he sent it deliberately to arrive on the day of my crowning."

Judith reflected that this was indeed her father's style. "What did he say?"

"He congratulates me on my accession to the Wessex throne," Athelbald replied.

"What did he say about our marriage?" Judith asked impatiently.

"He expresses his shock and disappointment that his permission was not sought," Athelbald said solemnly. "But he trusts the alliance will remain strong and you are treated as you deserve."

"What does that mean?" Judith asked.

A gleam of mischief entered Athelbald's eyes. "I agree that treating you as you deserve is open to interpretation," he said. "But I think he is pleased the alliance will remain, although as we did not await his permission he cannot fully express his pleasure. I assume he wishes you to continue to share the Wessex throne."

Judith arched her eyebrows. "And is that not your intention?"

Athelbald grinned and pretended to consider the matter. "If you behave yourself."

∞∞∞

"My grandfather had this church built," Athelbald told her as they arrived at the Church of Saint Mary. "He summoned the bishops and nobles here and demanded they accept my father as his undisputed heir."

"They made a sensible choice." Judith smiled. "Not only did they gain a wise king in your father, but it led the way to you too ascending the throne."

"That is true," Athelbald said, looking pleased by her words. "And I hope our son will follow me, although that is not the way my father has left matters. He intended for Ethelbert to ascend the throne after me."

"Is such a will binding?" Judith asked in alarm. She too intended for a son of theirs to one day rule Wessex.

"No, although it is not a foolish idea. If I should die without a child or if our son is too young to rule, it is for the best that the realm passes into the hands of a strong man. But assuming I live as long as my father, our son will likely be fully grown and with the blood of the Emperors of the Romans in his veins, I think there would be few to contest such a succession."

Judith nodded her understanding.

"Now all that remains is for you to present me with a son," he said.

"We have only been wed a few weeks," Judith protested.

"Yes, I know I am being impatient." Athelbald gave a rueful grin. "But much as I am enjoying conceiving our child, I hope it will not take too long. Proof of God's blessing on our union will help quiet the bishops.

Judith smiled up at him, relieved they had managed so amicable a discussion. Perhaps as Athelbald assumed the dignity of a king, their lives would become calmer.

∞∞∞

Father Swithun had refused to perform the crowning, so Athelbald had sent for Bishop Eahlstan of Sherborne. This was not a man Judith cared for, as she had never forgiven him for his rebellion against Athelwulf. She wasn't certain she had completely forgiven Athelbald, although she knew Athelwulf had forgiven them both. But she nodded graciously to him when he came to their side. "It is time, my Lord King," he said

Athelbald straightened himself proudly and stretched out his arm to Judith. She laid her hand on it. There had been much discussion on her role in the ceremony. It was unusual for a queen to be already consecrated before her husband and she suspected it thoroughly irritated Athelbald. Eventually it had been decided she would accompany him into the church, ready to take her place next to him on the throne once he had been anointed.

There was a murmur of appreciation as they entered. Judith and Athelbald made a striking pair, both dark-haired and good-looking. Opinions among the Wessex nobles on their marriage had been mixed. To some it seemed a sign of their new King's good judgement that he was determined to continue such a prestigious alliance. While others, who had known Judith at Winchester, had always felt a little sorry for her being married to such an old man, however kindly he might be. They were pleased to see her with a young and handsome husband. But there were still many who were influenced by the bishops. None voiced their thoughts that day, but Judith knew those men considered their union incestuous and that behind some of the loyal smiles, lay bitter condemnation.

Athelbald knelt before the altar, while Judith stood alongside Ethelbert and the other nobles. Bishop Eahlstan held aloft a cross.

"Good people, we celebrate this day the anointing of your most noble King, Athelbald, eldest surviving son of our late and most merciful King Athelwulf. Pray with me this day for his reign to be a long and prosperous one."

Judith bowed her head with the rest, only lifting it when she was bidden. The Bishop held a dish of oil in his hand and used it to mark a cross on Athelbald's forehead.

"In the name of our most heavenly Father, I anoint you, Athelbald, son of Athelwulf, King of Wessex."

The bishop raised aloft a golden circlet, very similar to the one on Judith's head and placed it on Athelbald's dark hair.

"Arise my Lord King."

Athelbald got to his feet and looked over the assembled nobles. Judith restrained a proud smile, as she saw how noble his appearance had become. "Good people of Wessex, I vow to rule over you with wisdom and mercy. I implore our heavenly Father to send his guidance so I may make our fair land ever prosperous. I swear to always do my duty as I shall be judged on the day of judgement by our Lord God and his most blessed son, Jesus Christ. Serve me well, my people."

"All hail the King," the Bishop proclaimed and the call was taken up by everyone present.

Athelbald took the few steps towards the throne and sat down. "I shall receive you, my people."

Judith was the first to kneel before him and once she had been raised up, she took her place next to him. They smiled at each other as Ethelbert, Ethelred and Alfred each came forward in turn. Only when the last man present had sworn loyalty did Athelbald rise to his feet to lead Judith from the church.

A grand feast followed. Athelbald's spirits had soared and with her husband so contented, Judith too was able to enjoy the occasion more than she had enjoyed any since Athelwulf's death.

∞ ∞ ∞

"What are your plans now, Brother," Ethelbert asked the next morning.

"I shall return to Sherborne," Athelbald replied.

"Sherborne?" Judith asked. "Are we not returning to Winchester?"

"No," Athelbald replied. "I have never particularly cared for it."

"It seems, my lady, that you won't be getting your own way in everything anymore," Ethelbert said with a smirk. "You won't manipulate Athelbald as you did my father."

Athelbald frowned. "Be quiet, Brother. You will not speak to Judith in that fashion."

"I will speak how I see fit," Ethelbert snapped. "I suspect you two will not remain wed for long. The bishops will not accept your marriage."

Athelbald scowled. "What is your issue, Brother? Did you think I would always remain unwed?"

"I did not expect you to marry her."

"What difference does it make to you?"

"My God, Brother. Your disloyalty astounds me. Does it truly not bother you that Father did not honour our mother as he honoured her?"

Athelbald shrugged. "I do not think the matter was ever raised when Mother was alive."

"Your father did not plan to grant me this honour," Judith put in. "My father insisted on it. No insult to your mother was intended."

Ethelbert's eyes narrowed. "You know nothing about my mother, my lady. Do not presume to comment on why my mother was not honoured as you."

"He honoured your mother in a way he never honoured me. He gave her his whole heart," Judith said. "If he seemed over-indulgent of me, it is because he could never love me as he loved her."

Ethelbert raised his eyebrows. "And I suppose you were so in love with him that you married again before he was gone three months."

Judith looked at Athelbald for support, but he was watching the exchange with a grin. The mischievous glint in his eyes suggested he was enjoying it immensely. Judith frowned, upset he had not come to her aid.

"I did not intend to disrespect your father," she said, knowing how weak that sounded.

"But you did," Ethelbert replied. "If the bishops demand an annulment, I shall support them."

"Are you rebelling against me, Brother?" Athelbald asked.

"It is what you did when our father married her," Ethelbert retorted. "I shall be advised by the bishops."

Athelbald glared at his brother. "Then get yourself back to Canterbury. I do not want you in Wessex."

"I have no intention of remaining," Ethelbert replied. "What of our brothers?"

"I am not letting you control the Athelings," Athelbald said. "Ethelred and Alfred will come to Sherborne."

"Could Alfred not return to Winchester?" Judith put in. "He has his lessons with Bishop Swithun."

"Don't be foolish, Judith," Athelbald said. "We do not want Father Swithun influencing him too much."

"But he is doing so well," Judith protested.

"I don't care," Athelbald snapped. "Damn it, Judith, there are learned men at Sherborne. Father Eahlstan can give him his lessons. The boy remains with us, which I think is what my father would have wanted."

Ethelbert smirked. "You see, my lady, you will not have everything your own way anymore."

Chapter four

Life at Sherborne was very different to life at Winchester. "I don't want you bringing too many damned monks here," was the first thing Athelbald said to her as they arrived.

Judith had liked the look of Sherborne. It was far to the west, nestled among green, rolling hills. Although not as large as the Palace of Winchester, the residence was a fine one with an abbey nearby. Judith was certain there would be many learned men at the abbey, but Athelbald had no interest in encouraging any to come to court other than Bishop Eahlstan, a man Judith continued to detest.

"I don't mind the musicians and storytellers," Athelbald continued. "And bring over as much of that Frankish wine as you want."

Judith forced a smile and bowed her head. However the lively atmosphere of Sherborne was enjoyable. The evenings were raucous and full of laughter. Often as the meal ended, musicians would strike up a tune in the courtyard and abandoning all formality, Athelbald would pull her outside to join in the dancing. Flushed from both the drinking and the dancing, Judith found she did not miss the intellectual stimulation of the court she had presided over at Winchester.

Unfortunately the dislike Judith felt for Bishop Eahlstan was shared by Alfred. "I'll not do lessons with him," he announced.

"Why not?" Athelbald asked. "He's a learned man. He will teach you well."

"I hate him," Alfred replied. "He rebelled against Father. Father trusted him and he betrayed him. I will have nothing to do with him."

"Please yourself," Athelbald shrugged.

"There must be someone else we could engage," Judith said. "Is there someone else from the abbey who could teach him?"

"I have already said I don't want a load of monks at court," Athelbald said with a frown. "Father Eahlstan will teach Alfred."

"No." Alfred glared at his brother.

"It doesn't bother me." Athelbald folded his arms, looking down with amused affection at his defiant young brother. "I thought you wanted to learn. Perhaps you won't get to be pope after all."

"Athelbald, please let us find someone for Alfred," Judith begged. "Your father would want him to continue his education."

"And I have made a perfectly good provision for this," Athelbald said. "It is not my fault the boy won't accept it."

"But surely you can understand why he doesn't want Father Eahlstan."

"Be silent, Judith," Athelbald snapped. "It is not appropriate for you to defy me. Instead try to persuade the boy to continue his lessons as I have decided."

As Athelbald flounced from the chamber, Judith looked at Alfred. "I understand why you don't want to study with Father Eahlstan," she said. "But your father would want you to learn."

"No. I will have nothing to do with him."

Judith shook her head in dismay. In his own way Alfred could be as stubborn as Athelbald.

∞∞∞

Judith made one last attempt to persuade Athelbald. In her guilt at remarrying so soon after Athelwulf's death, she felt she owed it to him to do the best she could for his youngest son. She entered the hall that evening and curtseyed deeply before her husband.

"What do you want, Judith?" he asked, turning away from the companion he had been talking to.

"I want you to listen to me about Alfred. The child is still grieving for his father as I know you also are. Could you not accede to his request for another teacher?"

Athelbald snatched his hand away from hers. "I will not have you continue to defy me," he said, raising his voice. "I expect obedience from my wife."

"But, my lord-" Judith started.

"This matter is closed," Athelbald almost shouted. "Do not speak of it again."

Judith went scarlet and took her seat miserably beside him. Everyone was looking at her except Alfred who was staring at the table, his lip quivering.

"Start to dine, my people," Athelbald cried jovially, picking up a leg of roasted fowl and biting into it.

The meal seemed to go on forever. Around the table conversations started up again, but Judith struggled to eat, the lump in her throat making it almost impossible to swallow. Athelbald regained his spirits, laughing in his usual fashion with those seated closest to him. He did not say a word to Judith the entire meal and she retired before the musicians started up their joyful tunes.

∞∞∞

Athelbald was whistling to himself as he came to their chamber where Judith lay tensely waiting for him. He said nothing as he undressed, but climbed into bed in his usual fashion and took her in his arms, his mouth seeking hers.

Judith was annoyed with herself for feeling pleasure at his touch and forced herself not to respond. After a few moments

Athelbald lifted his head and looked down at her.

"What is wrong?" he asked.

Judith prevented the angry retort. "Nothing, my lord."

Athelbald kissed her again, but again Judith was unresponsive. He stopped, frowning at her. "I expect you to carry out your duty, unless there is a good reason why you cannot."

Judith looked up at him. "I have not refused you, my lord. I am quite willing to carry out my duties."

"By God, Judith, stop this nonsense." The frown creased his face once again. "This is not how it is between us."

Judith arched her eyebrows. "Is it not? I am being as obedient as I know how."

Athelbald scowled and pulled away his arms. "Fine. I will bid you good night, my lady." He rolled over, turning his back on her.

Judith let out her breath, feeling a childish pleasure in annoying him. Firmly she quashed the longing she felt to reach out to him and accept the passionate night she could have enjoyed.

∞∞∞

"How long do you plan to keep this up?" Athelbald asked three nights later, after Judith had again sat silently beside him at dinner and received him into bed without pleasure.

"Keep what up, my lord?" Judith enquired innocently. "I am merely endeavouring to be the obedient wife you desire. I will do whatever you command."

Athelbald gave a reluctant grin. "You know damn well I desire you. So stop this nonsense and welcome me to your bed."

Judith gave him a small, submissive smile. Athelbald folded his arms across his muscular chest. His hair was tousled and Judith felt a rush of desire of her own. It had been hard to lie next to him these past few days without feeling his body pressed against hers.

"I am not going to back down over the matter of Alfred's education," Athelbald informed her. "My decision has been made."

"Of course, my lord. I have not raised the matter again."

"I know that," Athelbald said in exasperation. "So why are you being like this?"

"Like what, my lord?"

"Damn it, Judith, I have never hit a woman. My mother raised me better than that. But if you call me my lord one more time, I think I will hit you. Now stop this nonsense and tell me what is wrong. That is an order."

"I did not like how you spoke to me the other night," Judith said. "I am a princess of West Francia as well as Queen of Wessex. I expect to be treated with respect.

Athelbald's eyes narrowed. "You still think you are better than me."

Judith shrugged. "I am descended from Charles the Great. I consider my rank to be far higher than any West Saxon."

Athelbald went crimson in his rage and Judith shrank back against the pillows, her stomach churning with fear. For a moment she thought he really would hit her, whatever his upbringing. He gave a short laugh as he saw her fear, a flash of triumph dancing in his eyes.

"Yes, I probably should beat you," he said, flinging himself down on his back next to her and staring upwards. "But I won't."

For a long time they lay in silence as the candles flickered, before Judith slipped her hand into his. "I don't mean to make you angry," she whispered. "I used to think before I spoke."

Athelbald turned his head. "And I don't mean to disrespect you. I never did learn to control my temper."

Judith gave a shaky laugh. "I've noticed."

Athelbald squeezed her hand and gave a rueful grin. "I don't suppose I've convinced you to like me yet, have I?"

Judith smiled back. "You could keep trying to convince me," she said, reaching out to him.

Athelbald grin widened as he pulled her into his arms. "I was hoping you would say that."

Chapter five

The year wore on into a warm summer. Both Judith and Athelbald tried to control their tempers, although Judith was far more successful in this than her husband. Often she felt she was continually on edge to avoid annoying him. Annoying him generally resulted in a lively argument, although Athelbald bore no grudge for the words spoken in anger and the matter once settled was never referred to again. Judith suspected he enjoyed their quarrels and even more so if they were in public, but as she detested them, she did her best to keep quiet whatever he did to provoke her.

Alfred continued to refuse his lessons with Bishop Eahlstan. Instead he and Ethelred went hunting and hawking with Athelbald in the countryside around Sherborne or practised weapons skills with the men in the courtyard. Athelbald and Ethelred had always been firm friends despite the gap in their ages, but that summer the bonds strengthened with Alfred. It became increasingly common for Athelbald to return to their residence at the end of the day with an arm flung around each of his younger brothers.

"These two will be the finest warriors one day," Athelbald said with a proud smile one evening.

Judith smiled at the two red-cheeked boys. "I am sure they will." She looked at her husband. "They have a fine example to follow."

Athelbald swept Judith into his arms and gave her an exuberant kiss, pleased by her words. "My father was an accomplished warrior," he said with uncharacteristic modesty.

"So I have heard," Judith replied. "And I think you have all inherited his skill. He told me once of the day you and he fought together against the Norsemen at Aclea. He said he did not think he would have secured the victory without you at his side."

Nothing could have put Athelbald in a better mood and the evening was a merry one. But at the end he became thoughtful.

"I suppose one day those two will fight alongside me, as I fought alongside my father." He looked at his younger brothers. "I wonder if I could name one of them as my heir, rather than Ethelbert."

They had heard little beyond the occasional charter from Ethelbert and Athelbald continued to feel angered by his brother's stance.

"Although of course what I truly want is our son to follow me," Athelbald went on. "We have been wed some months now. Are there any signs you will soon present me with a child?"

"Not yet," Judith said with regret. She had been so certain during her marriage to Athelwulf that he was the reason she had not presented him with a child. His age, combined with his lack of desire for her had meant that conception was always unlikely. But Athelbald was a young man and their marriage was a passionate one. She had hoped she would quickly conceive. "These matters take time."

Athelbald shrugged. "I know little of these things," he said. "But I know many men who are presented with their first child within a year of marriage. I do not think that will happen for us."

"No," Judith said sadly. "But I hope within a year we will at least know that such a happy event is imminent. I pray every day to be blessed."

Athelbald squeezed her hand. "I know you do, sweetheart," he said. "Don't distress yourself. We shall keep trying. It is sure to happen soon."

Judith nodded, trying not to feel too much of a failure. But an unwelcome thought took root in her mind. Perhaps the fault had not lain with Athelwulf. Perhaps it lay with her and she would never present Athelbald with the son he desired.

∞∞∞

As the summer merged into autumn they received alarming news from West Francia. The fragile peace between Charles and his brother Louis, King of East Francia, had broken down. Usually Charles was the stronger of the two, but his support had dwindled and Louis had taken full advantage. Charles had fled to the South, with Ermentrude and their children, leaving his kingdom much diminished.

"I suppose this means we can no longer count on his help against the Norsemen." Athelbald frowned.

"My father will return to his realm," Judith said confidently. She could not imagine her father accepting defeat for long.

"I am not so sure," Athelbald replied. "I have heard that King Louis is a formidable warrior. He will not relinquish the territories of West Francia easily."

"Should you not aid my father?" Judith asked. "In my marriage treaty, your father and mine swore to aid each other."

"I didn't have a marriage treaty," Athelbald said. "And in any case, I'll not intervene in Frankish matters. I'll only help him against the Norse."

She shook her head.

"Don't frown like that," Athelbald said. "I don't suppose your father would intervene in internal Wessex disputes, would he?"

Reluctantly Judith shrugged.

"Exactly. Now, I wonder if King Louis would be willing to help us against the Norse invaders. I must contact him."

"You plan on allying yourself with my father's enemy?" Judith exclaimed.

"I will do what I must for Wessex," Athelbald snapped. "Don't meddle, Judith. I will not stand for it."

"I am not meddling," Judith replied. "I am merely reminding you of your obligations. Please do as you wish."

Athelbald looked at her suspiciously. "You're not arguing?"

Judith laughed. "You forget how rarely I was in my father's company. I feel nothing more than a dutiful loyalty to him. My loyalty is to Wessex now. All I say is be careful. Do not assume that my father will not regain his realm."

"Well, we shall see what happens," Athelbald replied. "But your father's plight affects you more than you think. His diminished status reflects on you."

Judith raised her eyebrows at the satisfaction in his voice.

Athelbald smirked. "I do not think your rank is higher than mine anymore."

"Do not be so sure of that," Judith replied. "I am still descended from Charles the Great."

But Athelbald was right.

∞∞∞

Life continued as normal, until the day they were informed that Archbishop Ceolnoth of Canterbury had arrived at Sherborne. In the hall Judith was shocked to see the vast numbers of priests and abbots who made up his entourage. Alongside him was Bishop Swithun. Together the two bishops approached the King.

"My Lord King," Archbishop Ceolnoth said. "We have reached a decision. Your marriage to Queen Judith, the widow of your esteemed father, King Athelwulf of Wessex, is contrary to all laws. It is abhorrent to both God and Man. In the eyes of God, Queen Judith is your mother. We insist you put her from you."

"Nonsense," Athelbald snapped, but he looked uncomfortable as he felt the eyes of the most prominent clergy in the land upon him.

Judith shrank closer to him, wondering what would happen.

"No, my Lord King, it is not nonsense. Wessex cannot continue to accept a King who is in such a state of sin. We have summoned King Ethelbert to Sherborne. If you will not put this woman from you, we shall ask King Ethelbert to ascend the throne of Wessex."

"You cannot do this," Athelbald said, getting to his feet.

"Our decision is final," Archbishop Ceolnoth replied. "You cannot stop us. There will be conflict in Wessex if you oppose us."

"We trust you will take the wisest course, my Lord King," Swithun spoke at last. "You have disgraced your father's marriage bed for long enough."

The clergy filed from the hall, leaving Athelbald and Judith staring at each other.

"What can we do?" Judith whispered.

Athelbald looked grim. "Are you with child yet?" he asked.

Judith shook her head, tears coming to her eyes. She felt such a failure each time her monthly bleeding started, but never had she regretted it more than this moment.

"It seems God is judging our union," Athelbald said softly.

"Don't say that," Judith begged. "We just need more time."

"They are not going to give us time," Athelbald snapped. "If you were with child I could claim God's blessing. But I cannot."

"You cannot put me from you," Judith cried. "You cannot say I have been merely your concubine all these months. I would be forever disgraced. My father will not stand for it."

Athelbald gave a mirthless laugh. "There is not much your father can do about this," he said. "Those men have chosen their moment well. There will be no reprisals from West Francia. Your father is too busy with other matters and his power is much diminished."

Judith stared at Athelbald in horror. Never had she felt so alone. Her dismissive comments about where her loyalties lay had come back to haunt her. Wessex, it seemed, had no loyalty to her.

Chapter six

Judith clung onto Athelbald's hand. "Please do not do this. If you send me away my life will be finished."

Athelbald pulled his hand away, suddenly appearing older. "I do not want to send you away, sweetheart," he said, with a tone of genuine affection she had never heard from him before. "But the bishops are not going to back down."

"You're going to just give up?" Judith asked, unable to believe this nightmare was happening.

"I don't know what I'm going to do," Athelbald replied slowly. "I need to think. Father Eahlstan is away on business in Exeter at the moment. He is the most powerful bishop in Wessex. After me, he is probably the most powerful man in Wessex. I shall request his immediate return."

"Will he side with us?" Judith asked.

"I don't know," Athelbald admitted. "But he has no great love for Ethelbert."

"I do not think he cares for me either," Judith said. She had only even been icily courteous to Eahlstan, never forgiving him for his betrayal of Athelwulf. It seemed her loyalty to her former husband too would be turned against her.

"You were a fool to treat him so coldly," Athelbald said brutally. "You should never insult powerful men."

"I am ruined," she whispered, looking around the empty hall in bewilderment.

"Not yet." Athelbald took her hands in his and raised them to his lips. "Do not give up. I will try to fight this, but we must not lie together until the matter is settled."

Judith stared disbelievingly at him. Her one hope that maybe the matter could be drawn out until she conceived a child had vanished.

∞∞∞

The next morning she sought out Bishop Swithun in the abbey church. She flung herself on her knees before him.

"I beg you, Father, to give my marriage your blessing," she cried.

Swithun's expression was stern but there was a hint of sympathy in his eyes. "I cannot, my Lady Queen. Even the heathens do not permit such incestuous marriages. I cannot bless the marriage between a mother and her son."

"But I am not his mother," Judith cried. "How can I be?"

"I think in your heart you know that you are. Tell me, my daughter, would you ever have considered marrying Prince Alfred if he were older?" Swithun's eyes bored into her.

"No," Judith exclaimed. "Of course not."

"Why not?"

"Because he…" Judith's face fell. "He is like a son to me."

"Yet his relationship with you is the same as the Lord King's. They are both the late King's sons and your sons in the eyes of God."

Judith shook her head. "I do not have your wisdom and logic, Father. But my heart knows that my relationships with Athelbald and Alfred are very different. I could never have considered marrying Alfred, even if he were older. But Athelbald is my husband. He was never my son."

"The heart is a foolish guide, my lady. This is why you must obey God's laws."

"But if Athelbald repudiates me, I shall have no choice but to enter a nunnery," Judith protested.

"I think that would be for the best," Swithun said gravely.

THREE TIMES THE LADY

"My lady, I am not unsympathetic. During the late King's last years I admired you greatly, but this illegal union with King Athelbald is one I cannot condone. You have committed a grievous sin and must atone. Enter a nunnery. You are young and were easily led astray. I am sure in following a religious life you will receive God's mercy."

Judith fled the church in tears. Running to her chamber she lay on her bed and sobbed in despair. It seemed no matter what she did, her destiny lay in a nun's vows.

∞∞∞

For several days Judith refused to leave her chamber, seeing only her serving women. Meals were brought to her, but she only picked at them. Sometimes she went down on her knees and prayed for her marriage to be accepted, but more often she lay on her bed, desperately trying to think of a plan to resolve the situation.

"This is not like you, Judith," Athelbald said as he came to her chamber one afternoon.

Judith looked around, startled at his voice. It was the first time in those days that he had been near her. She sat up, staring searchingly at his face, but there was no sign of hope in it. Athelbald looked back, shocked by how pale and thin she had become.

Athelbald sat down on the bed. "Father Eahlstan has returned," he said.

"And?" Judith asked breathlessly. "Is he supporting us?"

"He is not condemning us," Athelbald replied. "But he is not yet supporting us."

Judith sank back down, shaking her head in despair.

"Ethelbert will arrive tomorrow," Athelbald said. "No doubt Eahlstan is waiting to see what deal he might strike with him. Everything depends on whether I can persuade those two to support us."

149

"Eahlstan always was a traitor," Judith said, unable to keep the bitterness from her voice. "He betrayed your father and now he will betray you."

"Perhaps," Athelbald said. He looked at his wife with a sadness that frightened Judith more than ever. "Will you not take your place next to me this night?" he asked.

"Go to the hall and face what everyone is saying about me?" Judith asked with scorn. "No, I cannot."

"It is not easy for me either," Athelbald retorted.

"It is easier," Judith replied. "If you repudiate me, you will remain King. You can marry again and have children. I will be the one who loses everything. I shall be a queen no more. I will be a nun, remaining chaste for the rest of my days with no hope of ever bearing a child."

"I know," Athelbald said. "I am sorry. I wish there was more I could do."

Judith shook her head. She had longed for him to say that he would keep her at his side even if it did mean losing the crown, but she knew it was a foolish thought. However much desire there was in their marriage, it was nothing compared to his desire for the crown. She glared at him through narrowed eyes as he walked slowly towards the door.

"Your father would have stood by me," she cried. "Your father refused to ever compromise on my rank and the honour due to me. He would never have given up. You are less of a man than your father was and will be less of a king."

Athelbald turned to stare at her. Judith stared back, knowing she had just said the most hurtful words she could ever have said to him. She expected him to be angry, to shout, and to perhaps even hit her, despite the upbringing his mother had instilled in him. But he did none of those things. He simply looked at her for a long time.

"You are wrong," he said at last. "Yes, he insisted on you being honoured, but if you think he would have given up his throne for you, you are a fool."

Judith collapsed, weeping on her bed, knowing she had

probably just antagonised the only man who could help her.

Chapter seven

After a night of weeping Judith awoke with fresh purpose in her mind. Athelwulf was dead, her father was weakened and no doubt Athelbald now detested her. She could depend only on herself. One of her women informed her that Ethelbert had arrived and a council would be convened at noon. She had not been asked to attend, but she was determined none would keep her away. After all, these deliberations concerned her more than anyone.

Calling for water to wash away all traces of tears, she dressed in a tunic of the finest cream coloured wool. Over it she wore the embroidered red dress she had last worn for Athelbald's crowning. A serving woman bound up her dark hair, half covering it with a mantle of red cloth and brought out a coffer containing her finest jewels. The woman placed a belt of golden links around her waist, exclaiming how much thinner she had become and fastened it with a jewelled buckle, to match the gems in her necklace and intricate gold bangles. On her fingers sparkled the betrothal and wedding rings from both her husbands. Lastly Judith took out the gold diadem of Wessex. She stared at it for a moment or two before placing it on her head.

The serving women all murmured compliments as Judith studied herself critically in her mirror. She looked pale, but regal. Judith gave a wry smile. If this was to be her last day as Queen, she certainly still looked the part.

"My lady." A serving lad had come to the door of her chamber.

"King Athelbald is convening the council. All are present."

Judith inclined her head graciously. "Thank you." She waited a little longer so everyone would have time to assemble, determined to make an entrance into the hall.

As she walked slowly along the passageway, she could hear Athelbald already making his opening address to the men. But Judith did not increase her pace. The timing was perfect.

"My lords, reverend fathers, the Queen and I were wed before a priest at the Minster of Winchester in the proper manner. During our marriage the Queen has been a loyal and dutiful partner, whose conduct is beyond reproach. She is the daughter of King Charles of West Francia and the granddaughter of the late Emperor of the Romans, King Louis. It is unthinkable that so great a lady could be cast aside."

Judith paused at the entrance, surprised and touched by Athelbald's words. Her heart rose at the realisation that she still had one ally.

"We do not doubt that you consider yourself married, my son," Swithun said. "But the priest was wrong to condone it."

"The priest was in the wrong, but it is the Queen and I who will be punished?" Athelbald replied.

"This is not about punishment, my lord," Swithun said. "It is about atonement. You and the Queen have committed a most grievous sin. You must both atone for this to be sure of God's mercy."

"If the Queen enters a nunnery for her atonement, what must I do?" Athelbald asked in a sarcastic tone. "Donate large parts of my wealth to the church?"

Judith wanted to cheer this comment, but made her entrance into the hall in a stately manner. As she looked at the men gathered around the table, she tried to calculate how much support she could count on. There had been some hostility from the nobles on their marriage, but it was likely they could be persuaded or bribed easily enough to accept it. It was the holy men, particularly Swithun of Winchester, Eahlstan of Sherborne and Ceolnoth of Canterbury whose opinions would count. She spotted Ethelbert sitting next to Athelbald. His manner too had been hostile, but Judith was not sure if he was hostile enough to oppose his father's will and depose his brother. Next to Ethelbert she was surprised to see Ethelred and Alfred. She had thought them too young to be part of such a discussion, but they were the Athelings and anything which affected the succession would affect them.

As the men noticed her, they rose to their feet. There was surprise on the faces of the bishops and some disapproval. Judith kept her eyes focused on Athelbald. His manner was uncharacteristically serious as he addressed the men, but his words came to an abrupt stop as Judith came through the hall and sank into a deep curtsey before him.

"My Lord King and husband, I ask you most humbly to forgive me for the cruel words I spoke to you yesterday. They were spoken out of fear and do not reflect my very sincere desire to honour you as my husband and king for the rest of my days."

Athelbald raised her up, obviously shocked by her public apology, but his eyes were filled with admiration. He kissed her hands, a slight smile on his lips. "My lady, you have my wholehearted forgiveness. Indeed, I would say you were not wrong to remind me of my obligation to protect you."

Judith's dark eyes gazed into Athelbald's blue ones. For once there was no arrogance or mockery in them. Instead he looked gravely respectful and Judith's heart rose further in the knowledge that they would stand together.

"My Lady Queen," Eahlstan said. "I do not think it proper that you are at this discussion. There will be much which is beyond your understanding."

Judith raised her eyebrows in a haughty manner. "I am a consecrated queen of Wessex. It is my right to be present at this deliberation."

The bishops muttered among themselves, but Athelbald nodded. "You do most certainly have the right, my lady. I did not invite you out my wish to protect you from distress, but if you desire to be present, no man should contest it."

Judith graciously inclined her head. "Thank you, my lord. May I be seated?"

She braced herself to be ordered to sit with the Athelings, but Athelbald kept hold of her hand to seat her next to him on the throne, thus openly stating his intention to keep her as his queen. Judith gave no sign of relief as she sat down and looked gravely at the assembled men. As the men all sat once again she noticed the respect on the faces of the nobles. Her regal manner had impressed them as she had hoped it would. Judith drew strength from this, as well as the touch of Athelbald's body next to hers on the throne.

"Shall we continue, my lords, reverend fathers?" Athelbald asked. "I believe before the Queen honoured us with her presence we were discussing what form my atonement might take if we are agreed that I have indeed committed a grievous sin. No doubt so grievous a sin would require a large portion of my wealth to fully atone?"

"Well, my Lord King, we have not yet considered this matter," Archbishop Ceolnoth said cautiously.

"But it would have to be a large amount would it not?" Athelbald said, sounding surprised. "If the sin is so great it requires the Lady Queen to retire to a nunnery, it must surely require a very great portion of my wealth to ensure God's mercy."

The bishops looked bewildered and Judith too wondered what point Athelbald was trying to make.

"And since the Minster at Winchester was where I committed this grievous sin," Athelbald continued. "I feel it would be only proper that this wealth should be bestowed upon the diocese of Winchester."

Judith looked wonderingly at Athelbald, unsure how he had kept his voice so penitent. She was struggling to hide her pleasure at the look of horror on Eahlstan's face. He was used to being the most powerful bishop in the land, but at a stroke Athelbald had threatened to transfer that power to Winchester. Cracks visibly appeared in the three bishops' united front.

"My Lord King, we have not yet decided whether a sin has taken place," Eahlstan said.

"Have we not, Father?" Athelbald said. "My sincerest apologies. I thought the Church had decided that a marriage between a man and his stepmother could not ever be legal."

"I am still considering the implications, my son," Eahlstan said.

"But the marriage is not legal," Swithun protested. "As I have told you, my Lord King, from the morning after the ceremony. I am most grieved you have persisted in this sin."

"Indeed, Father," Athelbald replied. "No doubt the compensation I must pay Winchester is even greater than if I had immediately realised my error."

There was an uncomfortable silence as Swithun realised he had just been portrayed as grasping. It had been skilfully done, but Judith could feel no triumph in this. Of the three holy men, Swithun was the least mercenary.

"Could not one of you grant my brother a dispensation to marry our stepmother," Alfred suddenly piped up. "When I was in Rome I heard occasional discussions on such things."

"Be silent, Brother," Ethelbert snapped. "You are too young to know anything of these matters."

"No, Brother," Athelbald reproved. "As an Atheling, Alfred has the right to contribute to this discussion. And his time in Rome has undoubtedly given him a wisdom that eludes many of us around this table." He kept his eyes on Ethelbert who scowled at the implication it was he who lacked wisdom.

Judith smiled at Alfred, warmed by his comments. Of the brothers, Alfred was the one who had most inherited Athelwulf's deep religious beliefs. She had not been sure of his support. If only the boy had been a little older, he would have been a powerful voice at that table. There was silence for a moment as everyone looked expectantly at the bishops.

"Well," Athelbald said sharply. "What of Prince Alfred's

suggestion? Would one or more of you be prepared to give me a dispensation? I would be very… grateful."

Silence reigned again as everyone tried to work out which of the dioceses would be eager to secure the King's gratitude.

"I will not," Swithun maintained. "Alfred, I am surprised at your support for your brother. Your father would not have approved of this marriage. King Athelbald was ever a worry to him."

Alfred's face fell and Judith felt Athelbald flinch. She reflected miserably on the cruel words she had uttered the day before.

"You are mistaken, Father," she said. "The late King Athelwulf was proud of Athelbald as he was proud of all his sons. The differences between them are well known, but these were resolved. While they did not always agree, King Athelwulf always respected his son."

"That is not how it appeared to me, my Lady Queen," Swithun said solemnly.

"I think, Father, your view was clouded by the fact that the late King sought your guidance in times of strife. He spoke to me more on general, family matters. His love and pride in his eldest surviving son always shone through."

Under the table Athelbald squeezed Judith's hand in gratitude, but he addressed everyone present. "Whether I was the most dutiful son imaginable or the worst of renegades is irrelevant to this discussion," he said. "The question is the legality of my marriage. My esteemed brother raised the question of a dispensation. I am still waiting to hear whether any of you will grant me one."

"I have said I will not," Swithun maintained. "I was merely expressing my surprise that young Alfred should stand against what his father would want."

Alfred looked up at that, his grey eyes suddenly as sharp as a knife. "I don't know if Father would have wanted Athelbald to marry Judith," Alfred maintained. "But I do know that having married her, Father would expect Athelbald to protect her always. He would not want Wessex to cast her into shame."

Judith felt tears come to her eyes and she longed to run around the table to give the valiant little boy a hug. To her surprise Athelbald did exactly that.

"You Wessex men should be ashamed it has taken a nine-year-old boy to point out our duty towards this noble lady," Athelbald cried as he released his brother, giving him a hearty kiss on the top of his head. "I do not know if Father was right to be proud of me, but he was most certainly right to be proud of you."

"This is irrelevant," Ethelbert snapped back. "We must consider the legality."

"It was Father Swithun who raised the matter of Father's wishes," Athelbald said as he took his seat again next to Judith. "And there is more for us to consider, Brother. What of the alliance with West Francia which Father worked so hard to secure?"

"It is worthless," Ethelbert said with a laugh. "King Charles has been defeated."

"He is defeated, not dead," Athelbald replied. "I have heard he is making efforts to regain his territories. If he succeeds and again controls the lands just over the sea, how do you think he will react if he hears his daughter has been so dishonoured?"

Again there was an uncomfortable silence. The threat of the Norsemen was serious enough. These men did not want war with West Francia as well. Privately Judith did not think her father would be particularly bothered by her plight, but these Wessex men did not know that.

Athelbald fixed his eyes on Archbishop Ceolnoth. "West Francia has proved to be a true ally in our struggles against the Norsemen. How has Canterbury fared these last years, Father, since the alliance with West Francia? How has it fared since coming under the protection of Wessex?"

Archbishop Ceolnoth got to his feet. "My Lord King of Kent," he said to Ethelbert. "I wonder if we might discuss a few matters in private."

Ethelbert threw Judith a black look as he followed Father Ceolnoth from the hall. Athelbald gave a slight grin as he refilled their wine cups before passing the flagon around. Judith sipped at her drink, filled with unexpected hope. Athelbald reached out for a tray of honeyed cakes and passed one to her.

"Eat this, sweetheart," he whispered in her ear. "You may want some energy this night!"

Judith bit back a smile and gestured to her two younger brothers-in-law to also take a cake. Ethelred looked bored by the whole proceedings, but Alfred was visibly buoyed up by the reverence he had been shown. Suddenly he looked ridiculously like his father.

Eahlstan too reached a decision. "I require a few moments to pray for guidance, my Lord King," he said, as he got to his feet. "But I may be able to grant you my blessing."

Athelbald and Judith did not bother to hide their triumph. Athelbald openly put his arm around Judith's shoulders, a smug grin spreading across his face. Judith pulled Alfred into her arms, feeling more love than ever for her little brother-in-law. Swithun regarded them all sternly from the other side of the table, but there was a look of admiration on his kindly face.

"I cannot grant you a dispensation, my Lord King," he said. "But if either of my esteemed brothers do, I will raise no objections."

Chapter eight

Athelbald and Judith were still laughing when they reached their chamber that night, following the promise from both Eahlstan and Ceolnoth for a dispensation.

"How did we do it?" Judith asked, looking up at her husband.

Athelbald removed her gold circlet and tossed the red mantle to the floor. He picked her up in his arms and spun her around so her dark hair flew. "Playing bishops off against each other," he said with a grin. "The easiest thing on Earth."

He set Judith down on the floor, watching her with a smile as she combed her hair.

"You sweeping in, as if you were the great Emperor of the Romans himself, helped as well," he continued. "I don't think the nobles could contemplate you not being a Queen after that."

Judith smiled and Athelbald took her into his arms for a long kiss. Judith responded eagerly. She had missed him these past days. He loosened the ties at the neck of her over-dress. "Hurry up and get that thing off," he whispered, starting to unbuckle his belt.

Judith removed the dress, but paused to glance at Athelbald. "Alfred helped too," she commented. "Who would have thought he would speak up like that?"

"He's always so quiet, but when he speaks everyone listens. Damn it, he can't enter the church. What a waste that would be. The boy was born for leadership. Not Wessex. That is for our son, but if we expand our lands he could have a sub-kingdom one day as Ethelbert rules Kent."

Judith reflected that if Alfred was to be a king it was more important than ever for him to continue his education, but she had no wish to reignite that argument. Not this night of all nights. She looked at Athelbald, his clothes already strewn around him. Judith was still in her tunic.

He grinned. "What is taking you so long?"

"Help me with this lacing," Judith said, turning around, excitement darting through her as he lifted her hair to pull at the ties at the back of the tunic. She was sure he was doing it deliberately slowly, for it seemed an age before he finally pushed it from her shoulders. She turned to face him, winding her arms around his neck and standing on tiptoes to press her lips against his. He picked her up and carried her to the bed, their lips not leaving each other for a moment

"You've got to admit, sweetheart," he murmured. "You like me a bit more than a nunnery."

Judith gave a joyful laugh as she felt his hands caressing her. She buried her face in the dark hair that flowed almost to his shoulders. "I like you a lot more than a nunnery."

∞ ∞ ∞

The run up to Christmas that year was the happiest time of their marriage as both were contented and had discovered a new respect for each other. Ethelbert remained at Sherborne until the festivities ended and although Judith was sure she would never be close to him, he had unbent towards her. The Christmas celebrations were merry, but as she made her way to her chamber that night she felt a flicker of sadness as she realised it was exactly a year since Athelwulf had first gently tried to tell her he was dying.

In the weeks after Christmas Alfred and Ethelred too were subdued as the anniversary of their father's death approached and even Athelbald was reflective as he looked back on the first year of his reign. Judith felt he had managed well, but she knew not everyone would agree. Athelwulf had been well known for his charitable generosity, but this spending had been reduced by Athelbald. The clergy, who had already been angered by the scandal of their marriage, condemned him still further.

There was better news from West Francia as Judith heard her father had not only regained his supremacy in the North, but was aiming to expand his territories to the West. Judith felt very distant from such events, but she knew they made her own status higher.

Primroses and daffodils heralded the spring at Sherborne, which marked a year of their marriage and prompted further reflection from them both.

"Is there still no sign of a child?" Athelbald asked Judith one morning.

Judith bowed her head. "No, not yet," she said in a low voice. She glanced up to see Athelbald frowning.

"Why not?" he asked. "It has been a year now."

"How can I know?" Judith asked.

Athelbald shrugged. "You should have conceived by now. If you had conceived, but lost the child I would not reproach you, but to not even conceive…"

"What else can I do?" Judith demanded. "Are you accusing me of being undutiful?"

Athelbald gave a reluctant grin. "No, I know damn well you are not undutiful. So, why have you not conceived?"

"Do you think I don't also long for a child?" Judith cried. "How can you be so sure the fault lies with me?"

"You did not bear my father any children either," he replied soberly.

Judith clenched her jaw, feeling completely useless. "What do you suggest I do?

"I don't know. I have made considerable effort to sire a child on you since our marriage." Athelbald shrugged. "I want a child, Judith and you do not seem to be able to give me one."

Judith looked at him through narrowed eyes. "Then I see no point to continuing to perform my duties and putting you through such hardship. I shall receive you no longer."

"Don't be foolish," Athelbald said.

Judith turned away, tears in her eyes. "If I am barren there is no point to us lying together. Stay away from me from now on."

Athelbald shook his head. "Little fool. You will be begging me to come back to your bed before the week is out."

Judith stared after him as he left the room. He was wrong. She had endured enough. The waiting each month, praying to have conceived was becoming too hard. Those months that the bleeding was delayed a day or two were the worst. A day of hope that perhaps she had at last conceived, only for it to be dashed. She had no intention of refusing him her bed forever, but to take a break from all that seemed preferable.

∞∞∞

For the first few weeks Athelbald continued to ask her to receive him, but Judith was resolute in her refusal. Soon he gave up and his manner towards her became colder. Even the noisy quarrels stopped. As the spring was so warm, Athelbald took the opportunity to make a progression around his realm taking the Athelings with him. He did not ask Judith to accompany him and she did not request it, feeling glad of the chance to spend some quiet weeks at Sherborne.

The first days were pleasant enough. The endless rounds of arguments and passionate reconciliations were exhausting and she was glad of the rest. But soon the quiet became dull and she missed the lively energy of the Athelings. Unwillingly she admitted to herself that she was also deeply missing her husband. When she received a message announcing their return, she threw herself into planning a grand feast to welcome them back, resolving to also welcome Athelbald back into her bed.

She was waiting in the courtyard as Athelbald rode in on his black horse, Ethelred and Alfred on either side of him. Their entourage, all in crimson tunics, followed behind. As Athelbald dismounted, Judith swept into a deep curtsey, looking up at him flirtatiously through her lashes. He stretched out his hand to raise her and bowed over it. "Greetings to you, my lady," he said with a smile. "It is good to return. I bring greetings from Father Swithun."

"Welcome back, my lord," she said holding up her face expectantly for a kiss, but he simply nodded and moved on to greet Eahlstan. Alfred and Ethelred embraced her, both boys talking excitedly over each other of their journey, but Judith only half listened. Athelbald appeared to be in good spirits, so she wondered why his greeting had been so formal.

The feast was a merry one. To Judith's relief Athelbald's formal manner quickly dissipated and he was full of laughter as he told her of his progression. Judith laughed with him, but she was eager for the evening to come to an end. At last the women and children began to retire for the night. Alfred and Ethelred too wandered yawning to their chamber and Judith got up, smiling at Athelbald.

"I shall retire now. Do not sit up too long," she said.

"No, the hour grows late," he replied. "I shall retire shortly."

Judith glanced back at the door to see him still talking to his men, but she ran to their chamber, determined to be ready for when he came.

The hour grew later and the candles had almost burnt down before Judith accepted he was not coming. Wondering if she had missed him, she checked the adjoining chamber, where he slept when she was unable to receive him. It was empty. Frowning, Judith returned to her bed, puzzled as to where he was sleeping.

∞ ∞ ∞

This continued for several more nights. Finally there came a night when Athelbald came to their chambers, but still he did not come to Judith's bed. He went straight to the adjoining chamber without so much as a word. Despite the warmth of the summer night, Judith shivered. Her bed felt lonely and her body ached for the man who was lying just a short distance away. But Frankish pride prevented her from going to him. He had said she would beg for him to come back, but she was determined she would not. If he wanted her, he knew where she was.

Chapter nine

As the harvest was gathered, the abbey church prepared for a festival to celebrate and give thanks. Judith personally supervised the decorating of the church, as well as planning a feast for their own celebration.

"It looks most fine, my Lady Queen," Bishop Eahlstan said. "I heartily thank you for your efforts."

Judith inclined her head and smiled. She would never like this man, but she knew better now than to antagonise him. "Oh, I have embroidered some fresh cloths for the altar," she said. "They are in my chamber. I shall get them immediately."

"You are most kind, my Lady Queen."

With most people helping with the harvest, their residence was almost deserted. Judith hurried through the hall and up the narrow stairs to her chamber. The cloths were in a coffer by the window, but as she opened the box, she was startled by the sound of a woman's laugh.

Judith glanced around. No one should have been in her chamber at this time. Her room was empty and the door to the adjoining one was closed. For a moment she thought a sound had simply carried up from the hall. She smoothed out the fine cloths, admiring her handiwork, when she heard a gasp, followed by a deeper laugh. It had definitely come from nearby. Judith stared disbelievingly at the door to Athelbald's chamber, before a vicious rage descended on her. He was in that chamber and he was not alone. Judith flew to the door and pushed it open.

The couple on the bed were so wrapped up in each other they did not notice her straight away. For Judith it was as if time froze as she stared at them. A woman was lying in Athelbald's arms, her fair hair spilling over his chest. His hands were gently stroking the creamy skin of her body and on his face was the look of excitement she knew so well. It vanished as he saw Judith gaping at them.

He half sat up. "Judith!"

The young woman in his arms turned as well. She was stunningly pretty, her blue eyes wide in shock as she registered the Queen standing in the room.

"Get that slut out of our chamber," Judith snapped.

"This is my chamber," Athelbald blustered, but he looked uncomfortable.

"Get her out," Judith repeated between clenched teeth. "Now."

Judith turned away, unable to bear looking at them any longer. She left the altar cloths abandoned on the floor as she returned to the hall in a daze. A few more people had gathered to start the preparations for the evening meal, but Judith ignored them all. She sat down on the throne at the head of the table, oblivious to the curious stares of all who wondered why she was there at this time. A serving woman filled a cup with some wine and placed it near her hand. Judith stared at it, but in her mind all she could see was the pretty blond woman, her lips on Athelbald's and her legs entwined with his.

It was not long before the woman scurried through the hall, her head bowed. She did not even glance at Judith. A few minutes later Athelbald strode in. He hesitated as he saw Judith sitting at the table, but came determinedly towards her.

"Judith," he said. "Come to our chamber. We must talk."

Judith looked up. He was neatly dressed with his hair combed. If she had not observed the scene upstairs, she would never have guessed how he had spent the afternoon. She felt a sudden rush of hatred that he could look so composed.

"No, we will talk here."

Athelbald's composure slipped. He glanced at the people. A few were watching them with interest. "Don't be foolish. Come to our chamber."

Judith looked him firmly in the eye. "I will not. Say whatever you have to say here."

Athelbald frowned. "Go to our chamber, Judith. That is an order." His voice rose and by this time everyone in the hall was staring at them.

Judith got to her feet and folded her arms. "No. I will never go anywhere with you, ever again."

"Stop this foolishness."

"I will not," Judith almost screamed at him. "Say everything here. Let everyone know the manner of man they have for their king."

"You are the most disobedient wife any man ever had," Athelbald shouted back. "Get to our chamber this instant."

"No!" Judith cried. "Explain yourself here. What was that slut doing in our chamber?"

There was a faint gasp from the watchers. Athelbald's cheeks flushed a dull red and his eyes narrowed. He seized Judith around the waist and tried to drag her towards the door. Judith dug in her heels, pulling back.

"Get your hands off me, Athelbald," she cried breathlessly.

Athelbald did not answer, but picked her up. Judith struck out with her fists and feet, but this only tightened his arms around her. It was a perilous ascent of the stairs, but somehow Athelbald managed to place his struggling wife on the floor of their chamber without any accident. For a moment they glared at each other.

"That scene was most uncalled for," Athelbald said, folding his arms. "How dare you behave with so little grace."

Judith was speechless with fury. She raised her hand to strike him, but Athelbald caught it around her wrist. Judith flushed with shame at her action, but her anger did not abate. "How dare you berate me, Athelbald," she hissed. "You are the one in the wrong."

Athelbald looked guilty. "I am sorry I brought her to my chamber," he said. "I had expected you to be longer at the church and thought I would take a woman in comfort for once."

"What do you mean by that?" Judith cried. "Do you often take women?" She thought back to those first nights after his return to Sherborne when he had not come to their chamber. She had assumed, naively she now realised, he was drinking all night with his friends.

Athelbald shrugged. "What am I supposed to do? You have been refusing me your bed for months."

Judith swallowed over the lump in her throat. "Have you spent many nights with that slut since you returned?"

"Yes."

"And were there women while you were on progression?"

"A few," Athelbald said, not without a touch of smugness.

Judith bowed her head, her fingers again itching to slap him. She looked up at him. "But when I was receiving you, were you faithful to me?" She hated herself for the pleading note in her voice.

Athelbald hesitated. "There were not many," he said eventually. "Damn it, Judith, men in marriages such as ours are not often completely faithful. But these matters are quite unimportant. Do you think your father is always faithful to your mother?"

Judith held back the tears with difficulty. "How am I supposed to know? I barely know my father. What of your father?"

Athelbald shrugged. "I expect he was faithful to you, but he was old."

"I don't mean to me," Judith cried. "Was he faithful to your mother?"

Athelbald looked thoughtful. "I don't know. He might have been. I certainly never heard of any women, but he loved my mother very much."

Judith couldn't help the flare of jealousy which went through her towards the gentle Osburh. She had known Athelwulf as a young and handsome man and had received a devotion Judith never had either from him or his son.

"It is clear you do not love me at all," she said quietly.

Athelbald frowned again. "Don't play these games, Judith. You know damn well why I married you. I married you for the alliance with West Francia and because it enhances my prestige to have a Frankish princess at my side." He looked in dismay at Judith's distressed face. "And don't pretend it was different for you. You married me because the alternative was a nunnery and because you like being Queen of Wessex."

Judith struggled again to keep back the tears, as she stared dumbfounded at Athelbald. She could not deny his words, but the passion between them had been so great. "So I mean nothing to you?"

"Don't be silly," he replied more gently. "You mean a lot to me. You know how much I desire you. I never pretended that. I do care about you, but you should never have expected me to be faithful. I know I was wrong to bring that girl here and I am sorry for that. It will not happen like that again."

Judith bowed her head to hide the few tears she could not stop overflowing.

"I want to be in your bed," he continued. "But you have refused me. I was not going to keep begging and I was not going to force you. Are you willing to receive me yet?"

Judith shuddered. "Not this night." She looked at him, furious with herself that she could still feel any desire for him. "But soon. After the harvest celebrations."

Athelbald nodded and took her hands. "Thank you," he said. "I will give you some time to compose yourself before we dine."

"I cannot dine in the hall this night," Judith exclaimed.

"You will. I am commanding that."

"I cannot face what everyone is saying."

"I don't care. It is your fault they are saying anything at all. If you hadn't made that scene in the hall, no one would know anything about it."

"I'm sorry," she whispered.

Athelbald did not look particularly pleased by her apology. Guilt flickered across his face. "Come on, Judith. We will face everyone together, just as we always do."

Judith gave a half smile and nodded. Athelbald turned to go, but as he reached the door, Judith took a deep breath. "Athelbald, have any of these women borne you a child?"

Judith saw the answer in the pity which sprang to his eyes. "I cannot be certain with such women," he said gently. "But I believe so. I have made provision for three children who I accept are mine."

"I see," Judith said, forcing a smile. "So the fault lies with me."

Athelbald came back and put his arms around her. "I don't know, sweetheart. I don't know why it hasn't happened yet for us. You are still so young. Receive me into your bed again. We may yet be blessed."

Chapter ten

Somehow Judith's Frankish reserve carried her through that evening. She was able to smile graciously at the curious faces gazing at her as Athelbald escorted her into the hall. Those who sat near her were treated to the usual polite conversation, unaware the Queen was struggling to behave with her accustomed composure. Alfred and Ethelred were oblivious to any tension and Judith took comfort in listening to their innocent talk of the day's exploits. Athelbald maintained his usual cheer, although Judith felt it was somewhat overdone and he was not nearly as composed as he was pretending to be.

At the evening's end he got to his feet to bow politely before her, as she left the hall. Calmly Judith bade him a good night and escaped to her chamber. She lay staring into the darkness, feeling a dull sense of relief when she heard Athelbald go to the adjoining chamber.

The matter was not referred to again and a few days later came the celebration of the harvest. The solemn service in the church was followed by a feast where the wine flowed freely. Musicians played and after taking more wine than she usually did, Judith joined in the dancing with abandonment. At the end of the night, still merry from the wine and dancing, she received Athelbald into her bed. She had wondered whether she would find the experience changed, but she needn't have worried. From the moment Athelbald took her into his arms, she was able to blot out the memories and focus only on the pleasures she experienced. She responded as passionately as ever and Athelbald seemed content.

As the autumn wore into winter, their relationship slipped back into its old patterns of passionate nights and vocal disagreements, with occasional bouts of casual affection. Athelbald kept his promise. If there were other women, and Judith assumed there were, he kept them hidden from her knowledge.

Judith made the usual preparations for the Christmas celebrations, but she was not as happy as she had been the previous year. She maintained her merry manner, but listening to the story tellers, she felt a sense of misery. She glanced at her husband, his cheeks flushed with drink, engaged in a raucous conversation with his men. He was as handsome and brave as the heroes of the stories, but there was so much missing from their relationship. She found it impossible to avoid the arguments she hated so much and knowing he enjoyed them, made it worse. She realised now that he was right. Despite the passion in their relationship, she did not love him. Perhaps if she had a child, this would not matter. She could have buried herself in that relationship, but the prospect of a child seemed as distant as ever.

The sense of failure sweeping through her every time her bleeding returned, became more intense with each month. Athelbald, although undoubtedly sharing her disappointment, was impatient with her tears and Judith mostly wept alone.

However she noticed Athelbald appeared to be taking a greater interest in his younger brothers and she wondered if he might decide to make one of them his heir, ignoring the right of Ethelbert. But when she asked him about this, he was dismissive, saying such matters were too far into the future to worry about. Yet even so, the status of the two Athelings rose at Sherborne. Athelbald was closer to Ethelred, which was not surprising. They were so similar, sharing the same lively humour. He seemed fond too of Alfred, even admiring his intelligence. But as Alfred became more like his father every day, Judith wondered whether they might clash in the future.

Judith had always tried to give a mother's care to her two orphaned brothers-in-law. She loved them both, although Alfred remained her favourite. But as she forced herself to accept she was unable to bear a child, her feelings for them intensified. They could not replace the child she feared she would never bear, but she took an ever greater interest in their upbringing. If this was to be the closest she got to motherhood, she was determined to make a success of it.

The winter of that year was a cold one. Snow lay thickly on the ground well beyond Candlemas. Even when they reached the time when the flowers might be expected to grow, there was still a dusting of snow. At Sherborne they managed well enough with huge fires in the hall and often sleeping there rather than in their chambers. But away from the grand residences people were not so fortunate. The minsters and abbeys did what they could, but many died.

As the weather improved later in the spring, Athelbald announced he would spend the summer at Winchester to meet with Ethelbert. He asked Judith to accompany him and glad of the change of scene, Judith agreed. Winchester had been her first home in Wessex and she had grown to love it. Although she enjoyed life in Sherborne, she had been sorry not to have returned to Winchester since the crowning.

Athelbald summoned the Athelings to him and informed them of his intentions. "You two rascals will be in charge here," he announced, flinging his arms around the boys with a grin. "I am sure a couple of brave warriors like you can repel the Heathen Army if necessary, can you not?"

They stared at him. "We're in charge?" Alfred asked, sounding overwhelmed.

Athelbald laughed, ruffling his hair. "Well, not completely. You're both a bit young for that. Eahlstan will be here to guide you, but it will be good for you to start receiving petitioners, check over the land and such matters."

"I see," Alfred replied, a resentful look on his face.

"Alfred, I know you do not like Father Eahlstan and I understand why," Judith put in. "But sometimes it is necessary to work with people we do not like. In truth, I do not care for him myself, but he is a fine administrator and will guide you well if you let him."

"True," Athelbald said. "Alfred, if you are ever to be a king, you will need to find ways to work with all, even those you do not care for."

"Are we to be kings?" Ethelred cried. "How can that be? Surely Ethelbert will come next and both of you could have sons."

"That is correct," Athelbald said. "Although our father's will is clear that you two are both considered worthy of rule. But I intend to make Wessex ever greater. If I am successful I will need strong, loyal men to rule over parts. Of course, you are both too young for that at the moment, but you're thirteen now, Ethelred. It is time to start learning these responsibilities."

The boys nodded and Judith added, "You should both also return to your lessons. Such knowledge is valuable for kings."

Ethelred made a face and Athelbald laughed. "I know you consider such things dull, Brother, but Judith is right. I wish I had paid more attention to my lessons when I was a boy. I can read only a little and write hardly at all. Alfred, I think you could be as wise as our father if you put your mind to it."

The boys agreed, Alfred looking far happier than Ethelred.

"Well, we shall speak more of this when I return in the autumn," Athelbald said. "The summer is no time for lessons, but in the winter you will be glad to have matters to occupy yourselves."

∞∞∞

They made a leisurely journey to Winchester, Athelbald taking the time to attend to state matters along the way.

They were warmly welcomed everywhere and it was clear that although the clergy did not totally approve of Athelbald, the people liked him.

Judith was pleased to arrive in Winchester late one afternoon. It looked much the same, the Minster and palace nestling peacefully together in the sunshine. Ethelbert was already in residence. He and Athelbald greeted each other exuberantly and he gave Judith a friendly kiss on the cheek. To Judith's delight, Father Swithun too welcomed them with pleasure. He did not refer to his disapproval over their marriage, but instead seemed content to discuss various church matters with them and receive them to mass in the Minster. At the end Athelbald stared thoughtfully at the tomb of his grandfather, King Egbert.

"I must make arrangements to move my father here," he said. "Perhaps next summer we will all come to Winchester. It would not be right to do such a thing without the boys here."

Judith nodded her agreement, ashamed of herself that this matter had slipped her mind. She should have reminded Athelbald of it long ago. Touched that he was still thinking of his father, she felt more affectionate towards him than she had in a long time.

The days at Winchester slipped pleasantly by. Athelbald and Ethelbert managed their business amicably, frequently becoming most light-hearted during their discussions. Judith was asked to join them and although her opinions were not often sought, both kings required her approval in witnessing the charters, her name coming only after those two and before all other Wessex nobles and clergy.

∞∞∞

One night Judith woke with a start in the King's chamber. She lay for a moment, not certain what had woken her. It was not Athelbald. He still lay next to her, his arm resting heavily around her waist. The sky was just starting to lighten, but it was too early to rise. For some reason Judith felt uneasy as she lay still, her body tense. Just as she was assuming it had been a dream which had disturbed her, she heard the howl of a dog echoing desolately across the town. Unsure why the single howl was bothering her so much, Judith sat up, causing a sleepy protest from Athelbald. Other dogs were joining in, snarling and barking. The agitation increased and to Judith's horror, she was certain that mingling with the noise of the dogs were human shouts and screams.

"What is up with those dogs?" Athelbald muttered, sitting up next to her.

"I don't know, but can you hear shouting?" Judith asked.

Athelbald rose from the bed and lit some candles from the glowing embers of the fire. The dogs were barking more than ever. In the candle light she saw Athelbald frown. He pulled on his tunic and breeches.

"I need to see what's happening," Athelbald said, as he dressed. "Get back to sleep if you can."

Judith shook her head. "I don't think I can." She pulled a loose tunic over her head. "Wait a moment. I will come with you."

She left her hair unbound, her eyes widening as she realised Athelbald had taken up his sword. "Is that necessary?"

"I hope not," he said grimly.

In the hall other people were gathering, having also been woken by the noise. Ethelbert burst into the room just a few moments later. He too was armed. The brothers looked at each other as the shouting got louder.

"Stay back, Judith," Athelbald said. "I'm opening the door."

The sky was lighter now and a smell of smoke hit them as the great wooden doors swung open. Athelbald and Ethelbert led men into the courtyard just as the Minster bell began to toll. The sound went on far too many times for it to be simply marking an hour of prayer. Judith's heart thumped as she recognised a warning. Loud as the bell was, it could not block out the heartrending screams which still filled the grey morning air. Cautiously Judith followed the men into the courtyard. Beyond the courtyard walls, an eerie glow filled the sky and smoke billowed overhead

"Norsemen," Athelbald snapped. "It has to be."

"At Winchester?" Ethelbert cried. "How can this be?"

The shouting got louder still, and when the gate was opened, a group of town's people burst into the courtyard. "It is the heathens," they cried. "They are coming this way!"

Chapter eleven

It took some time for Athelbald to get any sense from the frightened people, but the news was terrifying. The walls had been breached and Norsemen were looting dwellings. It was a large invading force, and a sizable group were headed towards them. One sector of the town was already in flames.

"We need to muster the men," Ethelbert said urgently. "God be praised we are both here. We have a good force between us. We must get to the men before the Norsemen cut us off from our army."

Athelbald looked around. Monks had come from the Minster and were stood in the courtyard. Swithun looked calm, but these holy men would be defenceless in the face of the heathen army. "You get to the army, Brother," he said. "I will stay here to defend the palace and the Minster. Once they are secure, we will fight our way towards you."

"Agreed, Brother."

Ethelbert ran for his horse, while Athelbald shouted orders to the men who remained at the palace. All began to arm themselves.

"Take refuge in the palace, Father," Athelbald called to Swithun as he pulled on a mail shirt. "It is better defended than the Minster."

Judith ran to him. Athelbald seemed startled to see her outside, but he caught her up in his arms. "Don't be frightened, sweetheart," he said. "I'll keep them away."

Judith clung to him, taking comfort from the strength of his arms. It wasn't the first time he'd fought against the Norsemen and he'd beaten them before. "Be careful," she whispered.

Athelbald kissed her. "You know, you actually sound as if you like me," he said, with a determined grin.

Judith shook her head, trying to match his light-hearted attitude. "I do, but don't tell anyone!"

"Get inside and keep the door locked," he said.

"Is there anything I can do?" she asked, hating the thought of sitting idly inside, waiting for disaster.

"Get some food prepared and try to keep everyone calm." The sound of fighting was coming closer. Athelbald planted a last kiss on her and pushed her towards the door. Judith could still hear him shouting orders as the door slammed behind her.

The hall was crowded with monks, women, children and men too elderly to fight. Many of the women were weeping and she could see the fear on their faces. At that moment Judith wanted nothing more than to join them but she took a deep breath to steady herself. If her husband could face these fiends so bravely, the least she could do was keep everyone calm inside.

"Start preparing food," she called. "Some porridge and stew, I think. The men will be hungry once they have finished beating back the Norsemen."

Several of the women wiped their eyes and hurried to carry out Judith's orders. Judith glanced at another group. "You, take up that linen and tear it into strips. We may need bandages."

Father Swithun came to her side. "Well done, my Lady Queen," he said.

Judith gave him a trembly smile. "Thank you, Father. Will you pray for the Kings and their men?"

"Of course, my lady," he said.

The chanting of the monks and the clatter of preparations almost masked the sound of the fighting taking place outside. Almost, but not quite. Judith was unable to stop her ears straining for every sound from outside, desperately hoping for signs that Athelbald was still alive and the Norsemen

THREE TIMES THE LADY

were being beaten back. But it was impossible to distinguish individual voices in the roar of clashing metal and agonised cries. A smell of smoke filtered into the hall, much stronger than the usual smells of the fire. Judith guessed that some of the outbuildings and storage rooms had been set ablaze. The palace was mostly made from stone, so Judith prayed the fire would not spread to them.

Gradually the sounds ceased and there was a banging on the door. Everyone in the hall tensed.

"Grant us entry," came a voice.

There was a long sigh as they released their breaths at the sound of a Wessex voice and the bolts on the great door were drawn back. Judith ran anxiously over. A sweaty and dishevelled group of men were gathered there, many bloodied and bruised. Judith scanned them, a panic rising in her.

"Where is the King?" she cried.

The men looked around. "We are not sure, my lady. We thought perhaps he had already returned."

"You fools, you know the King would not return here before the Norsemen had been driven away," Judith cried. "Find him!"

One of the men took charge. "Check the Minster," he said. "Wounded men were taken in there."

Judith took a deep breath to calm herself. "We can care for men in here if they can be moved," she said. "But please, find the King."

The wearier, injured men filed into the hall, but the others returned to the courtyard. Judith followed them, horrified by what she saw. The storerooms on one side of the courtyard were still ablaze, with smoke billowing across. Straw and other debris were strewn across the stones. It was only when she stumbled on a leg that she realised that some of the debris was the bodies of men, lying where they had dropped. She ran to each one she saw, not caring that her dress was bloodied. Her heart pounded in terror as she checked them, but none were Athelbald. Many were Norsemen which would have pleased her at any other time, but all she wanted at that moment was to find her husband.

"Careful, my lady," shouted a man, as Judith ran to yet another body.

It was a Norseman, but Judith did not understand the warning until the man's hand reached up to grab her skirt. She screamed, pulling the fabric swiftly from his grasp. Briefly she looked into the man's blue eyes, filled with pain as blood flowed from the wound in his side. Judith hardened her heart against the brief flicker of sympathy she had felt for the wounded man. The heathen had got exactly what he had deserved, she thought, as she continued her search for Athelbald.

"He's over here," a voice cried from the far corner of the courtyard, near to the smoking buildings.

Judith weaved her way through the debris, her eyes stinging with the smoke. As she got closer she could make out a shape lying on the ground. Her throat burnt as she flung herself to her knees next to the body, coughs searing through her chest. It was Athelbald, a post from the burning building lying across his leg, holding him to the ground. As the men removed his helmet, Judith saw his face was deathly white and for a terrifying instant she thought he was dead. She bit back a scream, as his eyelids fluttered open. He heaved in a rasping breath, the cough tearing through his body.

"Help me get the post from his leg," the man cried.

With several men there, it was an easy matter to remove the post. Athelbald was silent apart from the tortured breaths, but Judith could see from his face the pain he was in. Gently she stroked his hair, until the men were able to lift him from the smoky corner.

Still coughing, Judith followed them back to the hall. Swithun greeted them, his face anxious as he saw the injured king.

"Take the King to his chamber," the Bishop said.

"No," Athelbald coughed. "I... must... be... here."

His voice was unrecognisable, but Judith gave a small smile of relief. His manner at least was unchanged.

"Fetch pillows and blankets," she called. "We can make the King comfortable here."

Making Athelbald comfortable proved to be a hard task. Swithun examined his leg and decided that although the swelling was severe and the bruising would no doubt be terrible, the bones did not appear to be broken.

Judith wrapped blankets around him and wiped the soot from his face. She held a cup of mead to his lips, hoping the honey would soothe his throat.

"Don't... fuss... Judith," he rasped.

Judith sighed. She might have known he would be a difficult patient. "Try to rest," she begged. "You have kept the palace and Minster safe. You can't do anything more. Ethelbert will handle the rest."

Athelbald gave a half cough, half grunt, but he allowed himself to be pushed back on the pillows. He shut his eyes and lay unmoving. All she could hear was the laboured breathing.

"Will he recover?" she whispered to Swithun once she was sure Athelbald was sleeping.

"I am not sure," Swithun said. "I hope so."

"But you said the wound to his leg was not serious." Judith clutched fearfully to Swithun's hand.

"It is not the leg which concerns me, my lady. That should heal quickly," Swithun replied gravely. "I fear he lay too long in the smoke. He is struggling for breath."

Judith looked at her husband, his chest heaving with the effort. His face was paler even than his father's had been near the end. Judith shuddered. "Pray for him, Father," she begged.

"I will, my lady."

Judith sat anxiously beside her husband, almost forgetting the danger had not yet passed. Somewhere on the edge of the town, Ethelbert was still fighting the Norsemen. At least she hoped he was still fighting them. For all she knew he could already have been defeated and the Norsemen might yet return to the palace.

The day passed very slowly. When Athelbald awoke, he was

irritable and demanded news they did not have. Judith gave him some broth, feeling a touch of hope as he swallowed.

It was late afternoon before Ethelbert returned. He was smiling triumphantly. The fight had been hard, but he had prevailed. It was the first occasion he had led the army in a full battle, but he had proved to be more than worthy of it. However his smile quickly faded as he saw his brother lying in the hall.

"My God, what happened to him?" he exclaimed.

"He drove the Norsemen away from the palace, but was trapped in the smoke," Judith said.

Athelbald's eyes shot open. "What... news... Brother?" he asked.

"The heathen scum are gone back to their boats," Ethelbert replied, kneeling down beside his brother. "Winchester is safe."

Chapter twelve

Athelbald lay in the hall for several days. Eventually he was able to hobble across the hall to his place on the dais where he slumped on his throne, his body trembling and gasping for breath. Judith quickly filled a cup of wine and held it to his lips. Impatiently Athelbald pushed it away, sending the drink splashing over Judith's arm.

"You can... stop... your fussing now... Judith," he snapped between breaths.

Judith's eyes filled with tears. She had not slept well since the night of the raid. The first nights she had insisted on sleeping in the hall with Athelbald and had lain tensely, listening to his laboured breathing, unsure how he had the strength to keep breathing like that and terrified it would fail at any moment. After two nights of this, Athelbald ordered her to sleep in her chamber. His breathing had improved a little by then and, feeling exhausted, Judith agreed. But she did not sleep much better there. She woke several times a night, her heart pounding and her ears straining for the sounds of returning Norsemen.

"My Lord King, the devoted attention of your wife is a blessing," Father Swithun said reprovingly. "Do not speak harshly towards her."

Athelbald shook his head, but he patted Judith's hand and took the cup from her. Judith met Ethelbert's concerned eyes. He gave a half smile and, to her relief, diverted attention from them by talking of the efforts already underway to repair the damage the town had sustained in the raid.

As Father Swithun had predicted, Athelbald's leg healed quickly, but he continued to be short of breath. Gradually he improved to the state where if he was sitting down it would be hard to realise anything was wrong. It was only when he climbed the stairs to their chamber afterwards to collapse panting on the bed, that Judith could see how badly the smoke had affected him.

∞∞∞

One morning in the early autumn Athelbald announced that they should soon return to Sherborne. Ethelbert had already returned to Canterbury and so Judith was not surprised Athelbald had become restless.

"Are you sure you are well enough?" Judith asked. He always seemed well in the mornings, but by noon she was aware he was tiring.

Athelbald frowned before relaxing into one of his old smiles. "A night with you leaves me well enough for anything!"

Judith smiled back, although she knew their nights too left him breathless. Not that this lessened his desires one bit. He reached out and took her hands. "We need to get back. I can't leave those two scamps alone there any longer."

Judith laughed. "I had thought of summoning Ethelred and Alfred here."

But Athelbald shook his head. "No, I want to get back to Sherborne. I can manage a ride."

"We will need to take it slowly," Judith said.

Athelbald scowled, hating being reminded of his weakness.

"Are there not many places on the way you should visit?" Judith said quickly. "There is plenty of time before the cold weather sets in."

Athelbald's face cleared. "I suppose so. Very well, how soon can we leave?"

"A few days, I suppose. Will you at least rest until we have to leave?" Judith looked in dismay as Athelbald started to scowl again. "Please, Athelbald, indulge a foolish wife."

Athelbald grimaced, but pulled her hand to his lips. Judith knew this was the closest to agreement as she was going to get.

∞∞∞

Athelbald would never admit it, but he was glad to take the journey slowly. From the moment they received Father Swithun's blessing on their departure, Judith hated every moment of that ride and had to restrain herself from staring anxiously at him the whole way. She wished she could persuade him to travel in one of the carts carrying their belongings, but knew such a suggestion would be greeted with scorn.

The excited greeting of Ethelred and Alfred as they clamoured to hear every detail of the fight with the Norsemen, cheered him considerably. Judith was glad to have arrived safely back at Sherborne, but even there she could not relax. Athelbald was determined not to let anything stop him. He continued to hunt and ride around the area as if he were still a fit man. Often he would return to their residence white and breathless, yet insisting he was recovering well. Judith had no idea if there were still other women, but she feared there were. He was as keen as ever with her, so it seemed likely. Judith hated the thought with a terror which had nothing to do with jealousy. She found ways of managing him. Sometimes she would tell him she was too tired, if she feared he had already overexerted himself that day. She doubted whether any other women would have the confidence to deal with him in this way.

The wet weather drawing in as the year was near its end was a relief as it prevented Athelbald from riding out so much, yet this did little for his health. He caught a severe cold, making his breathing more tortured than ever.

Nonetheless Judith started her plans for Christmas. It was always her favourite time of year and as ever storytellers and musicians had gathered.

"I wish you would stay in bed today," she told Athelbald a few days before Christmas. "You would feel so much better for our festivities if you did."

Athelbald rolled over to look at her, the old glint of mischief appearing in his eyes. "I would if you stayed in bed with me."

Judith laughed. "I have much to do. Besides, you would not rest at all if I stayed in bed with you."

"You have a high opinion of yourself, do you not, my lady?" Athelbald commented.

"Really? Am I wrong?" Judith demanded.

A cough shook Athelbald's body before he could reply. "Probably not."

Judith shook her head, but made no comment as Athelbald slowly began to dress. She was still fastening her hair when he walked towards the door. He had barely got there when he swayed slightly and put his hand out against the doorpost to steady himself.

"Athelbald," Judith called. "Please go back to bed. You're not well."

He turned and Judith almost cried out at the pallor of his face. Even his lips had a blue tinge. But stubbornly he shook his head as Judith ran to him.

"Please," she begged. "I know you hate me fussing, yet I cannot help but worry."

"No, Judith, I am going down," he said. "But I have little to do today. I will sit all day in my chair and listen to your damned storytellers. Will that make you happy?"

Reluctantly Judith smiled. His colour was returning. "Very well."

"And then tonight," he continued, "I expect you to make such a boring day up to me. Is that understood, sweetheart?" He put his arms around Judith and pressed his lips against hers.

Judith returned the kiss. "Obey me all day and I shall be delighted to obey you all night," she said with a smile.

Athelbald gave a laugh as he left the chamber and Judith returned to arranging her hair. Her mind was full of the busy days ahead as she descended the stairs herself. She was almost at the door to the hall when she heard a sudden crash. Her first thought was one of annoyance, as she wondered what had been dropped. But this was quickly replaced by fear as cries of shock and alarm echoed through the hall.

"Brother!" she heard Ethelred shout.

Judith picked up her skirts and ran the last steps into the hall. A crowd had gathered near the top of the table. Judith pushed through them and froze. Athelbald was lying motionless on the floor, Ethelred and Alfred kneeling at his side, their expressions terrified.

"Help him," Alfred begged.

Bishop Eahlstan was rubbing his hands while another monk had his ear to Athelbald's chest.

"What happened?" Judith whispered.

Alfred stood up, his grey eyes gravely meeting Judith's. He was sitting here," he said, gesturing to the throne. "He was talking to us, when he suddenly fell forward. I don't know what's wrong."

Judith dropped to her knees next to her husband. "Athelbald, Athelbald," she begged. "Wake up, please."

The monk lifted his head from Athelbald's chest and shook his head. Eahlstan dropped his hands and rose to his feet.

"Athelbald." Judith tried to rouse him. "Athelbald, get up. Please don't lie here."

She looked up at the solemn face of Eahlstan. "Why aren't you doing anything?" she demanded. "Get some hot ale and a pillow. Hurry."

"My Lady Queen–" Eahlstan started.

"Do something!" Judith screamed. "Help him! Why are you all standing here?"

Alfred and Ethelred both knelt down next to her and put

their arms around her. Tears were already streaming down their cheeks.

"No!" Judith cried. "No! Athelbald, Athelbald. Please wake up."

Judith flung herself forward, burying her face in Athelbald's chest, stroking his hair. "No, no no," she whispered. But he remained quite still.

Judith sat up and stared disbelievingly at his white face. She sunk her head into her hands, sobs shaking her entire body. For the second time in her short life, she was a widow.

Part Four: Year of our Lord 861

The Widow

Chapter one

The next few days passed in a complete blur. It was impossible to comprehend that Athelbald, so young and strong, was dead. Judith expected him to stride in at any moment, filling the hall with his noisy presence. But instead the great throne at the head of the table remained empty. Judith stared at it, knowing she would never sit there again.

She did not even know which day was Christmas. The celebrations Judith had planned were forgotten, as the sadness and shock enveloped Sherborne. Bishop Eahlstan conducted the funeral rites and Athelbald was laid to rest before the high altar. Afterwards Judith returned to the hall with her two bewildered brothers-in-law and the three sat in silence with no comfort to offer each other.

Ethelbert arrived some days later. He embraced Alfred and Ethelred and took Judith by the hands.

"I was never so shocked to get your message," he said. "I saw he was not well after the attack in Winchester, but I never expected this."

"He never recovered from it," Judith said sadly. "He wanted to be. I urged him to rest more, but he never would."

Ethelbert gave a faint smile. "That sounds like Athelbald. He never was good at resting or taking advice."

Judith bowed her head, smiling through her tears. "True."

"If he had rested more, he might have lived longer," Ethelbert said. "But he would have hated it."

"It was so sudden," Judith burst out. "We were laughing together in our chamber before he went down to the hall. He was just talking to his brothers when…"

Judith could not finish and Ethelbert put an arm around her, as she laid her head in her hands. "It does not sound a bad way to go," he said gently. "No fear or pain and his last moments were happy ones."

Judith composed herself with an effort. "Forgive me, Brother, we have offered you no refreshment after your ride. Shall we sit?"

Ethelbert strode toward the table, but cast a hesitant glance at Judith and his brothers. "Father Ceolnoth proclaimed me King of Wessex before I left Canterbury."

"Of course," Judith said. "That chair is yours now."

It hurt with an almost physical pain to see Ethelbert sit in the throne she had shared with Athelbald, but she knew it was his right.

Ethelbert sipped his drink, while summoning up the courage to ask Judith a question he knew she would find hard. "Is it possible you could be with child, Sister?"

Judith bowed her head. "I cannot say for certain," she replied. "But it seems unlikely."

She got confirmation she was not with child two days later and although it had been expected, it was still a bitter blow to see her last hopes dashed. For a long time she wept in her chamber, before seeking out Ethelbert.

"I am not with child," she told him. "I failed Athelbald as I failed your father."

Ethelbert shook his head. "You should not think like that," he said. "You were a good wife to them both and gave them both much happiness."

Judith gave a faint smile. Perhaps it was true, but it was a poor comfort.

"I informed your father of Athelbald's death before I left Canterbury," he said. "You will need to think of your future plans, although it is surely likely your father will want you to return."

Ethelbert was right. The message from West Francia a few weeks later stated exactly that.

"I don't want Judith to leave," Alfred cried. "She belongs here with us."

Ethelbert put his hand on his brother's shoulder. "I know, Alfred, but it is not that simple. Judith, what do you want? You have property here. If you want to stay, I shall try negotiating with your father, but… you are a consecrated queen of Wessex. I cannot allow you to remarry here. I am sorry, but such a marriage would give an ambitious man ideas beyond his station."

Judith nodded her understanding. Although remarriage was the last thing on her mind, she knew she had to think clearly. She was only eighteen years old and it was possible she might want it one day. It would not be an option in Wessex, yet she could not be certain that it would be an option in West Francia.

"My father wanted you to have the option of staying here," Ethelbert continued. "And I think Athelbald would want it as well. I know your father will not like it, but I will let you stay. Wessex would be honoured by your presence."

Judith gave a smile, grateful that Ethelbert was giving no sign of the reluctance she knew he must be feeling. The last thing he needed was to start his reign at loggerheads with West Francia. She looked at Ethelred and Alfred. At fourteen, Ethelred was a young man. Alfred was nearly twelve and while he might be glad of her for now, he would not need her for much longer. She had made Wessex her home, but with both her husbands dead, she was an outsider there. Forcing the tears back, she smiled at them.

"I shall miss you all most grievously," she said. "But I think I should return to West Francia. I shall be glad of my mother at this time."

This was not a complete lie. To weep in her mother's arms seemed most appealing.

"I think it is a wise decision, but you will be much missed,"

Ethelbert said. "We shall always consider you our kin."

"Thank you, Brother," Judith replied. "I shall have no further need of my Wessex properties. Will you oblige me by helping me to sell them?" It hurt to rid herself of the generous gifts Athelwulf and Athelbald had given her, but cutting all ties was the only way. Besides, if she ever did remarry, it would be best for Ethelbert if such a man had no claim to Wessex soil.

"Of course. You shall return to West Francia a most wealthy widow," Ethelbert said. "I know you have often feared you would be forced into a nunnery if you return, but surely possessing such wealth, you will have some say in your destiny."

"Of course." Judith smiled, not bothering to tell them how matters were in West Francia. Whether she was able to marry again would depend on her father, whatever her wealth.

Alfred looked up for the first time and Judith saw that his eyes were wet. "Brother, when it is time for Judith to depart, may I escort her to Dover? She has been as a mother to me almost as long as our true mother. I would protect her while she is in Wessex."

"Oh, Alfred." Judith's composure broke. She reflected on how little time she had spent with her parents and siblings in West Francia. These people had become a true family to her and her heart broke afresh that she would soon be leaving them.

∞∞∞

Before she left Judith was determined to fulfil her last duty to Athelwulf and speak to Ethelbert about Alfred.

"Athelbald would never relent over the choice of teacher," Judith said. "But he is nearly twelve now and still can only read a little. Please, Brother, it is my last request to you that you find someone acceptable for him."

Ethelbert nodded thoughtfully. "You are right. I will find someone from the abbey while I am at Sherborne, although

I may spend some time in Winchester after my crowning. Perhaps Father Swithun will take up his pupil again."

Judith gave her first real smile since Athelbald had died. "Thank you. That is exactly what your father would want and Alfred too."

The morning of her departure Judith walked slowly through the hall. On the day she had arrived as a newlywed with Athelbald at her side, she had expected to spend much of her life there. She had imagined her children growing up around her. Determinedly she kept her tears back as she left the hall, avoiding looking at the spot where Athelbald had died. That hall had also been the scene for so much merriment and those were the memories she wanted to treasure. Ethelbert and Ethelred hugged her warmly, both brothers looking emotional.

"I know I didn't welcome you to Wessex, Judith," Ethelbert said. "But I am grieved to see you depart. If you ever need it, you will always have a home here."

"Thank you both. Farewell, my brothers," Judith said.

"Farewell, Sister," Ethelred said. "You will be much missed."

Alfred was already on his horse and Ethelbert helped her onto hers. He stood back, his arm around Ethelred. Unable to say more Judith gave a wave of her hand as the horses trotted briskly from the courtyard. It was hard, but she knew it was for the best if she did not look back.

Chapter two

It was a long, but quiet ride to Dover which took several days. At Judith's request they stopped one night at Steyning, so she could pay her respects at Athelwulf's grave. She and Alfred knelt a long time in silence. It was the first time either of them had been back.

"Just before the Norsemen raided Winchester, Athelbald spoke of moving his body to the Minster," Judith said, laying her hand against the stone in farewell. "He planned to do it this summer."

"I thought he had forgotten about that," Alfred replied. "I never knew if he truly loved Father, but I think perhaps he did."

"Yes, he did and your father loved him. Don't doubt that. I hope one day your father's body can be moved as we planned. Perhaps you will see to it."

"I will," Alfred said.

Judith smiled sadly at the boy, who had been forced to grow up quickly, seeing he would soon be a man. He was no longer so sickly and Judith reflected that Athelbald had been right to focus on his martial training. The combination of wisdom and strength would make him a powerful leader if he ever got the chance.

"Your father was very proud of you, Alfred," she said. "Return to your studies. You have become so like him, I know you will be as wise as he was one day."

∞∞∞

Their farewell at Dover a few days later was long and emotional as neither of them wanted to say goodbye. Along with Athelwulf, Alfred had been her first tie to Wessex. Now he would be the last.

"Will we ever meet again?" Alfred asked shakily as she reluctantly released him from her embrace.

"I don't know," Judith said, glancing at the sea that was soon to separate them. "I hope so. West Francia is not so far away and you visited it once before. Perhaps you will again."

"I would like to or to see you back here," Alfred replied.

As Judith kissed the boy who had been the nearest thing she had to a son, she felt a curious feeling stir in her. "I don't know if we will meet again, but for some reason I have a sense the links between us will not be severed and may even be strengthened one day."

"I pray that you are right," Alfred said fervently. "Farewell. I shall keep you often in my prayers."

Tears cascading down her cheeks, Judith gave him a last hug. "And you will always be in mine. Farewell, Alfred."

With no further words to say Judith boarded the boat. She looked back at the shore where Alfred was still standing bareheaded, as the sailors prepared to cast off. Soon she would be away and Alfred would ride to Kingston to witness Ethelbert's crowning. Life in Wessex would go on without her. To many it would be as if she had never been there at all.

As the boat glided out of the harbour Judith put her head in her hands and wept all the way to West Francia.

∞∞∞

It was odd to arrive back at Verberie. So much had happened

since she had left just a few years before. In spite of her entourage she felt very alone. Looking back at the nervous, but excited girl who had left Verberie with Athelwulf and Alfred, she felt like weeping afresh. She had neither expected nor wanted to come back.

As on the occasion of her first arrival at Verberie, she was taken to her mother's chamber, where her mother looked much the same. She got to her feet as Judith was shown in and stared for a moment at her grey-clad daughter.

"Please inform the Lord King that the Queen of Wessex has arrived," she said to Judith's escort.

Only once the man had left the chamber did Ermentrude step forward and take Judith's hands. "Oh, Judith, so young and already a widow. Already twice widowed. My poor child."

Judith's lip trembled. "Thank you, Mother. It has been most hard."

"Your father should never have married you to that old man. It was wrong of them both to arrange such a thing."

Judith raised her head. "Mother, please do not cast aspersions on my late lord, Athelwulf. He was a truly good man who showed me nothing but kindness."

"I am sure he was, my child, but… oh, your father will be here soon. He will speak more on this matter with you. Sit down and refresh yourself at least."

Judith sat awkwardly, taking the wine cup from her mother. This was not what she had hoped for. She had thought her mother would welcome her with an embrace and allow her to sob awhile on her shoulder. Instead Ermentrude seemed ill at ease and the two sat in silence as she sipped at her drink.

Charles entered without knocking before Judith had even finished her wine. She looked pleadingly up at him, longing for some sign of affection.

"Your father is here, Judith," Ermentrude whispered.

Judith glanced at her, wondering why she was stating the obvious. Then she realised that Ermentrude had just risen from her curtsey and that both her parents were waiting for her to do the same. Judith sighed as she sank into a curtsey. She had forgotten how rigidly formal Frankish life was. Neither Athelwulf nor Athelbald would ever have expected her to curtsey to them when they were alone and even when they were not alone, the manner in Wessex had always been more relaxed. She had to blink back tears as she remembered the embrace Ethelred had received when he had seen his father for the first time after returning from Rome.

"Sit down, Judith," her father snapped with no hint of pleasure at seeing her. "It is about time I spoke to you. Your behaviour has been appalling."

Judith sucked in a shocked breath. "But Father-"

"Do not interrupt me, Judith. What were you thinking of, marrying your son?"

"He… he was not my son. He was more than a decade older than me. We were wed in the Minster."

"Do not try to justify your behaviour. You threw yourself into an incestuous relationship when your husband was scarce cold in his grave."

"I did not mean to disrespect him," Judith cried. "Father, please do not condemn me."

Charles folded his arms and looked at Judith with distaste. "This Wessex marriage was a complete mistake. Those barbarians are useful in the fight against the Heathens, but they are not good for much else."

"No, Father, this is not true. Wessex men are no barbarians. They are good men."

"Stop contradicting me, Judith. That Athelwulf. He seemed to be a sensible man. I thought he would be a good husband for you and provide you with the strong guidance you need. But as soon as he got you into Wessex, I heard that all he did was indulge you shockingly."

"No, Father," Judith protested. It was true that he had been kind and indulgent, but Judith found it impossible to consider it a fault.

"And then within weeks of his death, you jump into a union

with his son. An incestuous union. What sort of harlot are you?"

Judith bowed her head, feeling the tears come to her eyes. Remembering the lustful thoughts which had often struck her during her marriage to Athelwulf, she had no defence to his accusations. She longed bitterly for Athelbald to stand at her side to defend her, but she was completely alone.

"Do you have any idea of the efforts I had to go to, to ensure the bishops here did not condemn you? You had no right to wed anywhere without my permission."

Judith looked at her mother, hoping for some support. She had remained silent during this tirade, but Ermentrude was looking at the floor.

"I am sorry I wed without your permission, Father," Judith said quietly. "But please do not condemn my marriage. It was a true one and I am still grieving his loss."

"You have greatly disappointed me. Do not make yourself comfortable here at Verberie. I have made arrangements for you to be transported to the monastery at Senlis in the morn. Perhaps there you will be able to remain chaste, something which seems very hard for you."

"No, Father," Judith cried. "Please let me stay here at least a little while."

"I will not," Charles snapped. "You have caused me a great deal of bother and I do not wish to be troubled further. You will do as I have instructed."

"How long must I remain there?" Judith asked, almost afraid to move her lips in case they let out the sobs building up inside her. "Will I one day be permitted to marry again?"

Charles arched his eyebrows. "You see, Ermentrude, what a slut your daughter has become. Already she is thinking of the next man."

"No, Father, that is not the case. I shall be glad of some time to most sincerely grieve, but one day…"

An expression of intense dislike passed over Charles's face. "I want you to remain chaste from this day. I hope you will take your vows. But if you truly find it impossible to contain your lusts, it is possible I may find a husband for you one day if it is advantageous to me to do so. Although, I don't know why you think any man would be eager to marry you."

"I have wealth," Judith stammered.

"But you are barren, are you not? Barren and a slut. No Judith, for all your wealth, no man of high rank will want to marry you. Your wealth will endow the abbey I choose for you."

Her father's insults made Judith want to sink away. Never had she felt so ashamed.

"Now, get from my sight."

Judith raised her head, flinching at the disgust she saw on his face. Suddenly some spirit returned to her. She was the Queen of Wessex and she would not be spoken to in such a way, not even by the grandson of Charles the Great. She rose to her feet, looking in icy fury at her father.

"The West Saxons are no barbarians, my Lord King," she said, allowing the contempt to drip from her voice. "They are kind, god-fearing people. In Wessex I received kindness and comfort upon the deaths of both my lords. In Wessex I saw how kindly fathers could treat their sons. I am proud to have lived among them and that two finer kings than you will ever be, honoured me by making me their queen."

Ermentrude let out a low moan. "Oh, Judith, do not speak to your father in such a way."

"You lived among them for too long," Charles said. "You have become a Wessex barbarian yourself."

This time Judith did not flinch. Instead she favoured her father with a regal smile. "I consider that a compliment, Father. I am proud to be Judith of Wessex."

∞∞∞

Neither of her parents came to bid her farewell the next

morning, when a serving lad informed her that her escort was waiting. With hatred in her heart towards them both, Judith mounted her horse and prepared to ride to Senlis.

She took no notice of the Frankish countryside, now showing the first signs of spring. Her mind was too full of resentment at her father's accusations. Certainly she had enjoyed her marriage bed with Athelbald, but that was no sin. Despite the attraction she had always felt for Athelbald, she had not lain with any man who was not her husband. Her body at least was free from the sin of adultery. She was angered too by her father's accusation that Athelwulf had over indulged her. It was a harsh judgment on a kind and generous man. She had worked hard to repay his kindness, caring for his children and nursing them when they were ill. She had nursed him too in his final days.

The one insult which truly hurt was that she was barren. She had no defence against that. After two husbands, one of them a strong, young man, she should not be childless. She clung desperately onto Ethelbert's words that she had been a good wife to them both. It was poor comfort, but poor comfort was better than none.

It was unfair her parents had so many children, when they cared so little for them. She remembered Athelwulf sending greetings and inquiries of her health to his married daughter in Mercia. It occurred to her that her father had not communicated with her once in the years she had been in Wessex.

Judith's anger mounted as she thought of her mother. Ermentrude had just sat by the previous day, offering no words of comfort or support. Judith remembered holding her sobbing stepsons after the death of their father, as well as the rare occasions she had clashed with both her husbands over what was best for Alfred and the boy was not even her own child. She felt bitterly hurt that her mother had not even attempted to stand up for her.

"I was a better mother to Alfred, than you are to any of your true children," she muttered to herself.

Strangely the only insult that did not hurt was that she had become a Wessex barbarian. She wondered whether it was true. The comfortable family life she had enjoyed with Athelwulf, combined with the wilder years with Athelbald had undoubtedly changed her. She had cast off many of her rigid Frankish mannerisms and was now willing to display the emotions of both love and anger. Perhaps it was dangerous to behave that way in West Francia. She had been able to speak her mind with Athelbald, knowing he would never bear a grudge. Her father was a very different matter. She doubted whether her he would ever forgive or forget her outburst.

But as she dismounted her horse at Senlis, Judith found she didn't care. She was proud to have stood her ground against one of the most formidable men in Christendom. It was fitting behaviour for the Queen of Wessex. Judith put on her most regal manner as Bishop Herpoin of Senlis came out to greet her, but she could not repress her shiver as she was escorted into the monastery.

The thud of the door shutting behind her seemed to echo on in her ears. She had entered a prison and wondered whether she would ever leave.

Chapter three

The spring at Senlis was not so bad. Judith found she needed the peace and quiet of the monastery to grieve for her husband. To grieve for both of her husbands. She had tumbled into marriage with Athelbald so quickly, she had not fully grieved for Athelwulf and it gave her a sense of peace to finally do this.

She spent much time in the monastery church praying for their souls and often walked in the herb garden thinking on them both. She tried to focus on the happier days of both marriages. She realised now there had been many of those and it was best not to dwell on her failure to give either man a son. It was harder to come to terms with the days she had felt dissatisfaction with them. How she regretted that feeling now. Her marriages had not been made for love and she had been foolish to dream otherwise. Both men had, in their different ways, treated her with affection and respect. It was only now she had lost both those things that she realised how fortunate she had been. She missed the two young Athelings intensely, particularly Alfred. Often she wondered what they were doing and remembered all three of her brothers-in-law in her prayers.

By the summer Judith's grief had eased enough for her to feel restless. The monastery at Senlis was not unpleasant. She was still regarded as a guest, rather than a resident, so she occupied one of the small guest chambers instead of a nun's cell. In size and adornment there was not much difference, but at least she had a proper bed and was treated with the honour due to a queen. But she was bored. In Wessex her days had been so full. Those days had never been long enough to fit everything in. There had been fine tapestries and clothes to stitch, feasts to arrange, petitioners to greet, charters to sign and, best of all, the long evenings when she had presided over the hall, listening to musicians and storytellers or talking with members of the family and favoured guests. At Winchester there had been learned discussions, while at Sherborne there had often been dancing before the warm and passionate nights with Athelbald in their chamber. Judith was unused to having so little to do. She no longer even resented the cloister bell, as the summons to prayers did at least break up her day.

One summer's day she was summoned by Bishop Herpoin. "My lady, it is necessary for you to consider your future."

"I was not aware I had one," Judith said with a note of sarcasm she instantly regretted. The Bishop was a kindly man. Her incarceration was not his fault.

He looked flummoxed by her comment and wet his lips nervously. "My lady, I think it unlikely that the King will allow you to wed. In his last communication he expressed his wish for you to accept a religious life."

Judith felt like screaming, but she remained calm. "My dear lord, King Athelbald of Wessex has not yet been dead a year. I consider it most inappropriate for me to be thinking about my future while I am still in the deepest mourning."

"The King of Wessex died around Christmas tide, did he not, my lady?"

Judith inclined her head. "That is so."

"I shall inform the King that you will take your vows after Christmas."

Judith's eyes shot up. "I did not say I would take my vows after Christmas. I said I would consider my future then."

"But, my lady, your father's wishes are very clear. He wants you to take your vows."

"He cannot force me."

"He will not let you leave here, unless it is to take up a post at another abbey."

Judith gave a half smile. "So I am a prisoner here. I wish I had never returned to West Francia. I might not have been allowed to remarry in Wessex, but I would never have been imprisoned."

"It is not imprisonment to obey your father, Lady Judith."

Judith got to her feet. "You should address me as my Lady Queen," she snapped. "I expect my title to be respected."

"My Lady Queen, it is inappropriate for you to speak to me in that fashion."

Judith bowed her head. "Forgive me, Father. I do not mean to be impertinent. But I consider it too great an insult to my two husbands, who both honoured me with the title of queen, for it to be ignored." The Bishop looked unappeased. "And it was Archbishop Hincmar who conferred the title on me," Judith continued. "I feel it is disrespectful to him as well."

Judith had the satisfaction of seeing Father Herpoin look discomfited at that. In her head she heard Athelbald's voice. "Playing bishops off against each other. It's the easiest thing on Earth." She hid her smile at the memory. Athelbald had not been well educated, but he had been no fool.

But it was a petty triumph and afterwards Judith walked around the herb garden, wondering what she had gained by her refusal to consider her future at this time. It seemed she was just delaying the inevitable. She stared at the medicinal herbs. Once she had taken her vows, life would be busy again. If she became an abbess she would be as busy as she had been as a queen, only without the fine clothes, the feasting and the warm arms of a husband. Judith sighed. This was not what she wanted, but there seemed no choice, but to become a nun.

Again she heard Athelbald's voice. "What a waste!" Considering how different the two men had been, it was strange his father had shared his sentiments. He had once told her she was born to adorn a court.

Judith made her way to the church, her mind still on

Athelbald. She bitterly regretted now those months she had refused him her bed. If she had known they would have such a short time together, she never would have done it. She knew she had been wrong to ever be dissatisfied with him. He had never promised to love her, but he had promised her a lot of fun and that was exactly what she had got. In the church she knelt down before the altar.

"Please, Heavenly Father, grant me another chance at life. I will not squander it again," Judith prayed, staring at the figure on the crucifix. But the church remained still and Judith had no sense of any hope.

∞ ∞ ∞

The summer drew to a close and the autumn too slipped by. As Christmas came closer, Judith felt a deep sense of dread. It seemed strange to think that once she had looked forward to Christmas. It was true that some of her happiest times in Wessex had been the Christmases, but Christmas night was also the night Athelwulf had tried to tell her he was dying. And then the last Christmas… Judith's mind could not avoid the vision of Athelbald lying so suddenly dead on the floor of the hall. Now this Christmas would be the one where she would have to give up all hope of the life she longed for.

A month before Christmas came a welcome distraction. Judith was sitting, as she so often did, with some stitching, when Bishop Herpoin approached her.

"My Lady Queen," he said. "Your most noble brother is in residence at the palace. He has asked to see you."

Judith looked up in surprise. "My brother, Louis? The King of Neustria?" she exclaimed.

"Yes, my lady," Herpoin replied.

Judith's heart leapt in joy that she had not been completely forgotten by her family. "Please give me a few moments, Father," Judith said. "Let me prepare myself."

Judith straightened her hair and pulled a grey dress over her tunic. She glanced in a mirror. Last time she had seen Louis, she had been pretty young bride, finely dressed. She was far prettier now or would have been, if she were not dressed in such dull colours.

The Bishop escorted her to the doorway of the hall. "The King has asked to be alone with you, so I will leave you here, my lady."

Judith thanked the Bishop and walked into the hall. She had not been permitted there since her arrival at Senlis, but felt instantly happier to be in this secular spot away from the monastery. Louis was sitting at the head of the table talking to another man. They both rose to their feet as she entered. Judith hesitated, wondering if she should curtsey to him. But Louis grinned and opened up his arms.

"Judith!" he cried.

Judith's face broke into an answering smile and she flung herself into his arms. "Louis! Oh, it is good to see you."

Louis let her go and the siblings stared at each other. Louis was tall and thin. He was not quite seventeen, but he towered over her.

"I am so sorry about your husbands," Louis said gently. "I wanted to see you before but I have been away in the south."

Judith looked at him, trying to work out what was different. Suddenly she realised it was his voice. He spoke slowly, but there was no sign of the stammer which had once marred his words. "It doesn't matter. I am glad you are here now."

Louis gestured to the man standing behind him. "Judith, let me introduce you to my companion, Count Baldwin. He fought in our father's army, before being assigned to serve me. Baldwin, my sister, the Queen of Wessex."

Judith stretched out her hand to the man almost without looking at him. She knew exactly who this man was. Now Louis was older, he had to be given some genuine responsibilities in Neustria, but these made him a potential threat to Charles' authority. This count would be the man assigned to ensure Louis remained loyal and report back to Charles on everything. Judith hid her regret at his presence. She wanted to be able to speak freely to her brother, but now everything she said would undoubtedly be repeated to her father.

Baldwin had taken her hand and bowed over it. "It is an honour to meet you, my Lady Queen."

Judith glanced at him as he straightened himself and her heart started to thud. He was a fair-haired man, some years older than Louis, although not as tall. At the sight of his warm, natural smile, Judith's suspicions of him died on the spot. His blue eyes met hers and neither of them looked away.

Chapter four

Baldwin seemed to suddenly realise he was still holding Judith's hand. He looked somewhat startled and let it go. Judith stared at her hand for a moment. Away from the young man's warm grasp it felt cold and she longed to take his hand once again.

Louis had not noticed anything amiss, as he turned to the table. He looked over his shoulder. "Sit down, Sister. Let us drink together."

Baldwin gave Judith a slight smile which made her heart race even faster. She took a seat next to Louis and accepted the cup of wine he had poured.

"Oh, Judith, I felt so sorry for you, having to ride away to a strange land with that old man. But was he kind to you? Were you happy in Wessex?"

Judith nodded. "Yes, I was happy. Athelwulf was ever kind to me and always insisted I was accorded the highest respect from all." Judith shrugged. "According to Father he shockingly indulged me and turned me into a Wessex barbarian."

"That sounds like Father," Louis said wryly. "The only person he thinks should be treated with respect is himself. And possibly the Pope," he added.

Judith smiled, but glanced swiftly at Baldwin. She was surprised to find his eyes still fixed on her. Louis noticed her glance. "Oh, don't worry about Baldwin. He and I came to an arrangement long ago. He knows I'm not going to rebel against Father, so he doesn't feel the need to repeat every detail to him."

Baldwin grinned. "I find in your father's presence my memory becomes terrible, my lady, and the details escape me. So when I next see him, I shall undoubtedly be able to report that the King of Neustria paid a visit to his fair sister at Senlis, but you can be sure I will not recollect much more."

Judith was entranced by Baldwin's open smile and could say nothing. Louis clapped Baldwin on the shoulder. "He's not the spy you think he is, Judith, so don't worry. Tell me everything."

Judith described her years in Wessex as well as she could. Speaking of either of her husbands was too hard, so she said little on them. But she told Louis about the Norse raid, reminded him of Alfred, who Louis had met at Verberie all those years before and told him of her other brothers-in-law. "And what has been happening here?" she asked as homesickness for her adopted land threatened to overwhelm her. "I heard how Father was almost driven out."

"Mother and I fled down to Burgundy and we did not know if we would be able to return. Baldwin helped in Father's fight back."

Baldwin nodded. "It was during that campaign I first came to your father's attention, my lady, although I had been in his service some years. He honoured me then with a command position."

The afternoon swiftly passed as Louis filled Judith in on the events of the last years, including an attack by the Heathens on Paris itself. As the hour drew later, he ordered a meal to be brought to the table, but the Bishop also came to inform them it was time for Judith to return to the monastery. Judith started regretfully to rise, but Louis caught hold of her hand.

"Father, my sister will dine with me this night. I shall escort her back later."

Herpoin frowned. "My lord, your father's instructions were most clear. He wishes his daughter to remain for her own safety in the monastery. In truth I am not certain I should have allowed her to come here this day."

Louis gave a laugh. "She is only in the palace. It is no different to the monastery. What harm can possibly come to her here?"

"I know not, my lord. But this is not what the King would want."

Louis got to his feet. "I w...want my s...sister t...to dine w... with me th... this night."

Judith stared at Louis in dismay, realising his stammer had not after all completely gone away. Evidently it returned when agitated. She got up, understanding that for her brother's sake she would need to return to the monastery. But Baldwin too had risen.

"Forgive me, Father," he said. "But I have spoken with the Lord King on this matter more recently than you. Perhaps we could talk a moment."

Judith watched Baldwin and Father Herpoin in quiet conversation at the other end of the hall. The Bishop returned in a more subdued fashion.

"Forgive the interruption, my Lord King," Herpoin said to Louis. "Naturally I will entrust the guardianship of the Queen of Wessex to you as often as you wish while you are at Senlis."

Louis and Judith sat in stunned silence as Herpoin left and Baldwin took his seat back at the table, his face expressionless.

"W...what did you say to him?" Louis demanded.

"Your father did not place any restrictions on how much you could see your sister when we spoke on the matter. Indeed he seemed most unconcerned by it."

Judith looked at him suspiciously. "What exactly did my father say, my Lord Count?"

Baldwin gave an awkward smile. "I would prefer not to repeat his exact words to you, my lady."

Judith blushed and looked down, guessing what insults her father had applied. No doubt Baldwin already had a poor impression of her. But as she looked up, she saw his gaze was sympathetic.

"I may also have told Father Herpoin your father was in a delicate state of health," Baldwin continued.

Louis stared. "You lied to a bishop?" he exclaimed.

Baldwin raised his eyebrows. "It is no lie. Why he was most unwell the last time we saw him."

"But that was because of the amount of wine he drank," Louis protested.

"Was it?" Baldwin asked, giving a sorrowful shake of his head. "Alas, my lord, your medical knowledge far outstrips mine. It seemed to me your father was most grievously suffering."

"Wasn't he just," Louis muttered.

"I fear I have given the Bishop the wrong impression that your father may not be long for this world," Baldwin said solemnly, but with a mischievous gleam in his eye. "That was most unfortunate."

Judith burst out laughing, the first time she had truly laughed in nearly a year. It felt good and she had no idea how the laughter suddenly lit up her face. Baldwin looked at her in undisguised admiration, before recollecting himself and giving a sideways look at Louis. But Louis was laughing too and had not noticed.

"How long will you stay at Senlis, Brother?" Judith asked.

"I am not sure," Louis replied hesitantly, glancing at Baldwin.

"We are not due to meet your father for two months yet, my lord," Baldwin replied. "You had planned to spend Christmas tide with your mother at Verberie, but those plans can be changed. There is no reason why you cannot make a long visit with your sister."

Louis seemed astonished. "Well, you have changed your tune. You have done nothing but complain at having to visit here."

Baldwin looked embarrassed and Judith smiled warmly at him. "I do not blame you, my Lord Count. Senlis is a dull place indeed. You are fortunate to be just visiting."

Baldwin smiled sympathetically at her again. "My lord, the decision lies with you, but it seems to me it would be a kindness to spend some time with your sister."

"Agreed," Louis replied. "Let us dine."

As Judith helped herself to slices of meat stewed in a rich vegetable broth she looked again at Baldwin. "Where are you from, Lord Baldwin?" she asked.

"Flanders, my lady," Baldwin replied. "A small place named Bruges. I doubt very much if you have heard of it."

"I fear I have not," Judith replied, wondering if Baldwin were married. "Your family must miss you grievously while you are in my brother's service."

"I have no family there now, my lady," Baldwin replied. "My sisters have been long wed and my parents are no longer on this earth."

Judith inclined her head, trying to look uninterested in the fact that he was clearly still an unmarried man. The evening was a merry one and passed far too quickly. Eventually Louis got to his feet, picking up a flaming torch.

"Come, Sister, I will escort you back," he said.

Baldwin bowed before Judith and she stretched out her hand to him. He took it with a warm smile and raised it for the customary salute. Judith felt her whole hand tingle at the touch of his lips against it. It seemed they lingered a little longer than was the custom.

"It has been an honour to meet you, my lady," he said formally, but his eyes looked into hers.

Judith smiled. "It has been most pleasant. I hope we will meet again while you are at Senlis."

Judith must have uttered those polite words a thousand times in her life, but never had she meant it as she did at that moment. The sincerity seemed to come across to Baldwin because his smile widened as he nodded.

She and Louis crossed the courtyard to the monastery in silence. Just before they reached the door, he turned to her. "You said little about your husbands. Are you sure they treated you well?"

Judith nodded. "Yes, Brother. I spoke little on them because the loss still pains me. They were very different, but both gave me much happiness."

"I am glad you had that."

"Are you, Brother? I am not so sure." She looked up at the monastery with bitterness. "To have experienced such happiness will make my incarceration here or in another such establishment all the harder."

"Judith…" Louis said pleadingly.

"Oh, Louis, I know it is not your fault. But please make a long visit here. Let me have one last happy Christmas tide."

Louis hugged her. "Of course I will."

Judith entered the monastery and climbed the stairs to the guest chamber, feeling a sudden burst of happiness at the thought of the month ahead. As she lay on her narrow bed, her thoughts kept drifting to Baldwin. She well remembered her instant rush of attraction for Athelbald, but this was different. The attraction was certainly present, but there was more to it than that. Judith could not remember ever having felt so instantly comfortable with anyone. There had been such understanding in the man's eyes. Judith rolled onto her back. Staring upwards into the darkness, she wondered if she had imagined there had been more than understanding in Baldwin's eyes. She smiled as she reflected that she was unlikely to have imagined it. She was no naive girl. She had been twice married. Surely she would not mistake desire in a man's eyes.

Chapter five

Over the next few days Judith was frequently summoned to the palace. Sometimes Louis received her alone, but often Baldwin was also there for at least some of the time. For Judith these were the happiest days since she had returned to West Francia. The occasions Baldwin was present were both a joy and torture. Their polite conversation had naturally eased into a friendlier manner as the three laughed together. But Judith longed for more than friendship from this man and it was hard not to spill the words in her heart.

An occasion presented itself just two weeks before Christmas. She was making her way back to the monastery early one evening, having spent some time alone with Louis. Although she had missed Baldwin that day, it had been a most enjoyable afternoon. Judith's childhood had been cut abruptly short when she had been sent away from her brothers and sisters to the Abbey of Hasnon, but now aged nineteen, she was able to laugh again with her brother just as she had as a young girl.

She was still laughing as she returned. The winter's night was already drawing in and the courtyard was in shadows, but despite the chill, Judith did not hurry to the monastery. The levity she was feeling would be most inappropriate once she was there.

As she reached the courtyard gateway, she turned back to look again at the palace. It was not the grandest of Frankish palaces, but it was far more to her taste than the monastery. Concealed by the shadows of the gateway, the man hurrying in did not notice her until they collided, nearly knocking her to the ground. Strong arms caught her before she fell and she found herself looking up into Baldwin's face. He drew in a sharp breath and his arms quickly fell away.

"Forgive me, my lady," he said, bowing before her. "I did not see you there."

Judith looked longingly at him. She could still feel the pressure of his arms around her. "It is no matter. I am unharmed."

"Shall I escort you back, my lady?"

"My name is Judith," she said.

Baldwin swallowed. "I know, but I do not think it is proper that I address you in such a way."

Judith took a step towards him so her body was almost touching his. She looked up. The torch burning over the gateway, made his fair hair sparkle. "I do not care what is proper," she said quietly.

For a heart-stopping moment Judith thought she had misjudged his interest and expected Baldwin to push her away. But he gazed at her with a smile and took hold of both her hands. "I don't think I do either."

Judith entwined her fingers in his, waiting for him to move even closer. His smile enchanted her more than ever. She lifted her face, hoping he would kiss her.

Baldwin looked around. "Someone will see us here." He pulled her swiftly to where storage rooms lined the side of the courtyard. As he pushed open the door, a smell of clean hay greeted her.

"No one will come in here at this time," he said, lighting a small oil lamp.

"Baldwin," Judith said stretching out her hands once again to him, but to her dismay he did not move.

"We should not be alone together." In the dim light she could see the worry on his face. "I have so wanted to be alone with you, but this is wrong. I have no right to touch you."

Judith edged towards him. This time she did allow her body to brush against his. Baldwin gave a reluctant grin. "I grant you the right," she whispered.

Baldwin put his arms around her and pulled her even closer. Judith rested her head against his shoulder, her arms slipping around his waist. Never had she felt as warm and comfortable as she did wrapped in his strong arms. She lifted her face, her eyes sparkling with joy. He smiled tenderly back at her, lowering his head as Judith stood on tiptoes. Their lips met gently, almost tentatively at first, but slowly became more passionate. Judith forgot everything else. Both the happy days in Wessex and the miserable days awaiting her in the monastery were banished from her mind. All she was aware of was the sensation of his strong body against hers and the pleasure his lips were sending through her.

Reluctantly Baldwin pulled slightly away. "Oh, Judith, you are so beautiful and I want you so much. But we must stop now."

"I want you too," Judith said quietly.

"We mustn't," Baldwin replied. "I could never forgive myself for disgracing you."

"No one would know." Judith looked pleadingly at him. "Please, Baldwin."

"There is a way it could become obvious." He gave a gentle smile to remove the sting from his rejection. "I am sorry, but we must not go further."

Judith shook her head. "I am barren. I am unable to bear a child."

Baldwin heard the hurt in her voice and pulled her close to him once again. "I am sorry to hear that," he said. "Your child would be a fine one indeed. But if it means we could lie together without repercussions…" He shook his head. "No, I must not do this to you."

"Please, Baldwin." Judith's voice broke. "In a few weeks I am going to have to take religious vows. I shall never know these feelings again. Do not lie with me if you do not want me, but do not reject me because you consider it the right thing to do."

"I do want you," Baldwin said. "Judith, are you sure?"

"I am not some untouched girl, who knows not what she asks." Judith pressed her face against his chest, her cheeks burning in embarrassment at her boldness. "I have been twice wed. Baldwin, I want you."

Without any further words Baldwin unfastened his cloak. He spread it out on the hay before taking her back in his arms and kissing her once again.

Judith tossed away her mantle and began to struggle with the ties at the back of her tunic. One part of Judith was outraged at herself. As Baldwin helped her with the ties, she realised this was exactly the sort of behaviour her father expected of her. But when his hands slipped inside her clothes to caress the bare skin underneath, she no longer cared. Impatiently she pushed the tunic from her shoulders and unfastened her hair.

Baldwin stared at her, transfixed by the sight of this beautiful young woman. Judith blushed at the longing she saw in his eyes. He grinned, hastily pulling off his own clothes, before turning to where Judith was already curled up on his cloak.

"Oh, Judith," he whispered, entwining his body with hers. "Beautiful, beautiful Judith."

Judith had no words as her lips were drawn back to his and his hands gently stroked her body. Never had she realised this act could be so gentle and loving, yet still arouse in her a passion greater than any she had known.

∞∞∞

Afterwards she lay in his arms, her head resting against his chest, their bodies curled around each other. Judith nestled even closer, loving the way they seemed to fit so well together.

Baldwin was gently stroking her hair and Judith wished she could lie there forever.

Baldwin kissed the top of her head. "I suppose I should apologise for this," he said slowly. "But I don't want to."

Judith raised her head to smile radiantly at him. "Do not," she said.

Baldwin smiled back. "I should at least apologise for making you lie here on the hay. Next time I shall find somewhere more comfortable for you."

Next time. Judith lay her head back against him, overjoyed to hear there would be a next time.

Baldwin suddenly realised what he had said. "I'm sorry. I am not presuming there will be a next time. But if there is-"

Judith stopped further words with a long kiss. "I want there to be a next time. I want it more than anything."

"So do I," he said. He ran his fingers through her hair. "My beautiful Judith, I could lie here forever with you, but you will be missed soon."

Reluctantly Judith got up. "I know. I must go."

She pulled the crumpled tunic over her head and fastened the ties. It was hard, especially as away from Baldwin she quickly felt cold. He dressed far quicker than her and helped her with the last of the ties. Judith leant against him, feeling touched by the gesture. Never before had a man helped her to dress and it made her feel unbelievably cherished. Baldwin turned her around, looking dubiously at her tousled hair. He lifted a few strands.

"I think your hair might be beyond me," he said.

Judith laughed, covering it with her mantle. "I will fasten it in my chamber."

Baldwin put his arm around her shoulders as he opened the door and peered out. The courtyard was deserted.

"You go first," he said. "I will wait a moment. Until next time, my dearest."

Judith gave him a last quick kiss and a dazzling smile before darting swiftly across the courtyard. It was hard to enter the monastery slowly. She wanted to sing and dance her way to her chamber, but she kept her head bowed as if in deep contemplation and no one took any notice of her. Once in her chamber she threw off her mantle and spun around, letting her hair fly. Her happiness in that moment knew no bounds.

Chapter six

The next few times Judith saw Baldwin, it was always in the presence of her brother. She found it hard to talk to him with her usual friendly politeness, although Baldwin's manner was ever correct and impersonal. Almost Judith could believe she had dreamt the whole encounter, until she met his eyes. The tender expression in them made her heart skip with joy. Occasionally, and only when they were certain it was safe, they exchanged secret smiles, as both anticipated the moment they could be alone again.

That opportunity came a few days later when both Louis and Baldwin were in the church for Terce. While Louis was talking to the Bishop, Baldwin took the chance to say in a low voice to Judith, "Your brother is riding out this day. If you can, come to the palace."

Judith simply bowed her head to show she had understood. Over the previous weeks it had become commonplace for Judith to visit the palace, so no one questioned her as she left. She lurked near the gateway until she saw Louis galloping away.

Baldwin was waiting just inside the doorway of the deserted hall. "I have kept everyone busy. No one is around. Come."

He led Judith along a stone passageway to his chamber. The room was small and dim, with only a little light filtering in from the high window. A few faded tapestries lined the wall and with the space taken up by a bed and a low table, there was little room to move around.

Judith felt awkward. The previous occasion had been so spontaneous, she had no idea how to behave on this planned meeting. While Baldwin was engaged in lighting some candles, Judith hesitantly took the mantle from her head and unbound her hair. Baldwin smiled as he took her in his arms, stroking the silky length of her hair. He kissed her lightly on the lips and poured two cups of wine. He sat down on the bed and patted it to indicate that she should sit next to him.

"Shall we talk awhile?" he said, putting an arm around her shoulders.

Gratefully Judith nodded, giving him a shy smile. "Will Louis be away for long," she asked.

"It should take all day," Baldwin replied. "It is good for him to handle some matters on his own. In truth he does not need me as much as he thinks he does. I am not sure his father does him any favours in employing someone to be his guard dog and nursemaid."

"Is that why you do not report everything to my father?" Judith asked.

"No, that is because I like him. I don't know what your father expected. Did he really think I could be always in the King's company, hunting and hawking and not form a genuine bond?" Baldwin shrugged. "Perhaps he did. After all, I hunted with your father often enough without any friendship growing. Oh, I respect your father, but I find his mistrust so strange. Your brother is loyal enough. A father should know that about his own son. My own father, Count Audacer, Controller of the Forests of Flanders, died when I was an infant but I like to think if he had lived, we would have been closer."

"My father thinks everyone is scheming for his crown."

"He is not completely wrong. He has plenty of enemies, many of which he has brought upon himself. Your brother is not one of them, yet your father does little to earn his loyalty or to help him make a success of ruling Neustria. If King Louis is to learn anything, surely his father would be the best guide. But instead he entrusts the matter to me." Baldwin took a long drink from his cup, hesitating before further criticising Charles. "There is much that is fine in your brother, but your father struggles to see more than his ill health and poor speech. He often displays a contempt no man should display towards a son."

Judith nodded her head, thinking of Alfred, who also suffered poor health. Yet Athelwulf had loved him all the more. Baldwin was still frowning, lost in his own thoughts. "I do not understand your father at all. Why, when I think what he said about you... If I had a daughter as beautiful and charming as you, I would be the proudest man on earth."

"What did he say about me?" Judith asked quietly.

Baldwin muttered a curse. "I should not have said that. Forget it."

"I cannot," she said. "Please, Baldwin, I will only try to imagine his words."

Baldwin pulled her closer. "He did not say much. Louis was pestering him to be allowed to visit you. Eventually he agreed and said... oh, Judith, you do not want to hear this."

"Go on."

"He said, 'Tell Louis he can see his slut of a sister as much as he likes if only he stops bothering me.' I did not want to repeat that to you."

Judith leant her head against him, her cheeks burning with shame. "I am surprised you do not concur with his assessment of my character."

"I do not," Baldwin said firmly. "Before me, had you lain with any man who was not your husband?"

Judith shook her head.

"Then no man has any right to say such a thing about you."

Judith tried to smile. "Before I went to Wessex I thought it was normal for parents to be so distant from their children. But there I saw how affectionate Athelwulf, my first husband, was with his sons. Alfred and Ethelred were so informal in his company and he never hesitated to display his pride in them. It was grievous for Alfred to lose his mother when he was little more than five and his father aged not quite nine, but at least he had their love for those years. I did not even have that."

"My mother died nearly ten years ago, when I was barely fifteen," Baldwin said. "I still miss her, but as you say, I was lucky to have had her loving care for as long as I did."

"I do not think I would miss my parents at all." Judith was unable to keep the bitterness from her voice. "I am a tool for them, nothing more. I came back to West Francia a widow. My husband had been dead just a few weeks and it had all been so sudden. My father only allowed me to stay one night with them at Verberie and even there just saw me long enough to give his opinion on my character. I did not want much." Judith looked up at Baldwin, tears forming in her eyes. "I just wanted my mother's arms around me as I wept. But I did not even get that."

Judith's voice broke and she struggled to compose herself. Baldwin pulled her even closer, cupping her head with his hand. "Weep now if you want, my dearest. There is no shame in it."

Judith's sobs shook her entire body as she wept for both Athelbald and Athelwulf. She let out the grief she felt for the loss of her life in Wessex and the family she had come to love, but had to leave behind. She cried too for the parent's love she had never experienced and for the future she longed for, yet feared she would never find.

Throughout all this Baldwin said nothing, but simply held her close and stroked her hair. She clung onto him as her sobs gradually subsided, wishing she could remain forever safely in his arms.

"Drink this," Baldwin said gently. He had filled another cup of wine and put it to her lips. "You will feel a little better."

Judith managed a shaky smile, as she took it. "I must look terrible."

Baldwin looked at her, seeing the swollen red-rimmed eyes and blotchy face. "You always look beautiful to me," he said, smiling tenderly back.

"I am sorry." Judith wiped her eyes. "I should not have done that to you. I know that was not why you asked me here."

A strange expression flickered over Baldwin's face. "Oh, my beautiful Judith, do not think that of me. It is not just desire I feel for you. It is so, so much more. I hate that anything has caused you so much grief, but I am glad and honoured you were able to take comfort in my arms."

Judith clung tighter to him, unable to speak. It was so much more than desire for her as well. He was the man she had always dreamt of. Strong and brave, yet gentle and loving, just like the heroes of the fables of old. Although even they, Judith felt, might have seemed dull in their perfection compared to Baldwin. Setting her cup down she brought her lips to his in a long kiss and allowed her hands to drift over his body.

"But you do desire me as well, don't you?" she whispered, sliding down.

Baldwin moved his body on top of her, pulling at her clothing. "Oh yes, I do. Very, very much."

∞∞∞

For a long time afterwards neither of them felt any inclination to move. With their arms tightly around each other they even dozed. It was just past noon when Judith propped herself up, looking longingly on his handsome face. Briefly she wondered how she was ever supposed to make her religious vows now she had known such feelings, but swiftly pushed the thought from her mind. She knew if she allowed her thoughts to go beyond that day she would likely weep again.

Baldwin reached for her. "Come back here," he said. "I'm cold."

Judith leant over him, planting gentle kisses all over his face, welcoming the feel of his arms encircling her waist. Neither of them heard the door open.

"Baldwin, are you there?" Louis called. He gave a laugh. "Oh, I see. A woman. No wonder, you did not want to come with me this day."

Judith and Baldwin froze for an instant. Swiftly Baldwin pulled up the blankets to cover Judith's naked shoulders. She turned in horror, shrinking back against Baldwin as he half sat up. Louis stared at them, his mouth wide open.

"J...J...Judith!" he gasped.

"Louis..." Judith stopped, not sure what she would say to him.

"My lord, let me explain," Baldwin said, his voice suddenly pleading.

The look of utter disgust spreading across her brother's face filled Judith with shame. "Our f...father was r...r...right," Louis spat. "You are a slut."

"No, Louis. Please don't say that."

"My lord, this was not your sister's fault," Baldwin put in.

Louis went crimson, his face contorting into a rage she had never previously seen on her beloved brother. "B...be s...s... silent... b...both of y...y...you," he cried, struggling more than ever with the effort of the words. "G...get... dr...dr...dressed. I...I...I w...will s...see you i...in the .... c...council...ch...ch..."

Louis was unable to finish his sentence as he backed away. Judith and Baldwin looked at each other in horror as the door slammed behind him.

Chapter seven

With shaking hands, Judith dressed and tried to bind up her hair. Baldwin cursed as he pulled his tunic over his head.

"What is he doing back here? He should have been gone all day." He turned to Judith. "Oh, my dearest love, I am so sorry. I should never have touched you."

"Don't say that," Judith begged. "Please."

Baldwin looked at her with anguish obvious in his eyes. "But my actions may have cost you the only member of your family who cared for you."

"I shall never regret what we have shared," Judith said, taking hold of his arms. "And if we are now to be parted, I shall never forget it. The memories of our brief, happy time will sustain me for the rest of my life."

Baldwin looked almost as if he would cry, as he pulled Judith into his arms and kissed the top of her head. "I don't want this to be just memories," he said. "We must entreat your brother not to betray us."

The palace was still deserted as they made their way along the corridor to the council chamber. Louis turned to glare at them as they entered, his face white and his lips tight.

Judith took a step towards him. "Please, Louis, listen to us," she begged.

Louis did not answer but delivered a stinging slap across her face. Judith cried out, clutching her hand to her cheek. Baldwin stood swiftly in front of her.

"Do not do that," he cried. "There is no need for it."

Louis' fist shot out, catching Baldwin just below his eye. Baldwin flinched, but did not retaliate.

"My lord, do not be angry with your sister. Please let us explain."

"No. You will say n…nothing," Louis said, desperately trying to control his stammer. "I am dis…disgusted with you b…both. J…Judith you will t…take your v…vows with no further de…delay."

"You cannot make me," Judith replied, holding her head high.

A look of malicious triumph flashed onto Louis' face. "If you do n…not I shall ride to F…Father this day and t…tell him what I saw. What do you th…think he w…will do to B…Baldwin when he hears he r…raped his daughter?"

"I wasn't forced," Judith cried. "I was willing. Please, Louis, do not do this."

"H…he w…will kill Baldwin." Louis carried on, as if Judith hadn't spoken. "So, w…will you take your v…vows?"

"My love, do not do anything you do not want to do," Baldwin said. "My life could have ended at any time in the last few years in the battles I have fought. I am willing to pay the price for this. It is right that I should do so."

Judith looked into his eyes, tears shimmering in her own. "No, if you are dead, I shall not care what happens to me. I know I will never be permitted to leave Senlis now. I must accept a nun's life and take comfort from knowing you are alive. Be happy, my love."

Baldwin shook his head. "I cannot be," he said. "Please, Judith, don't give up."

Defiantly Judith pressed her lips against Baldwin's, knowing there would be nothing he could do. She rounded on Louis who was still looking at them with contempt. "I hate you, Louis. You condemned our father for marrying me to an old man, but what you have done to me this day is many times worse. I shall take my vows and I will become an abbess. But do not ever look for support from my abbey, Louis. Quite the opposite. I shall give succour to your enemies. I shall aid them in whatever way I can. I shall not rest until I have destroyed you. You will regret the day you ruined the life of Queen Judith of Wessex!" Her voice rose until she was almost shrieking the last words.

Judith turned away and ran to the door, slamming it behind her, not seeing how both men stared after her with open mouths.

∞∞∞

Throughout the long night which followed, Judith lay on her bed staring upward into the darkness in a despair beyond tears. Every ally she had ever had, was gone. Her husbands were dead, Louis was disgusted with her and Baldwin, for all his strength and bravery, was powerless. A minor count from Flanders could do nothing against the Frankish powers who would decide her destiny. She thought longingly of her Wessex family, but knew an appeal to them would be hopeless. By the time a message reached them, there would be nothing they could do even they wanted to, which too was unlikely. Ethelbert would have been King for a year, but he would be in no position to meddle in the affairs of West Francia.

The next morning Judith rose from her bed like a sleepwalker. Somehow she went through the motions of the morning, attending first Matins and then eating the simple breakfast. She nodded greetings to all she met with the accustomed politeness and exchanged a few words. To all around her she seemed as normal, none guessing she wanted to scream and throw the breads and porridge bowls across the room.

By the time the bell tolled for Terce, Judith had made a decision. Holding her head high and with no sign of reluctance, she approached the Bishop at the end of the prayers.

"Might I speak with you, Father?" she asked with a polite smile.

"Of course, my Lady Queen. Shall we be seated?"

Judith sat in the chair indicated, keeping her hands clasped firmly in her lap so they would not betray her agitation. She took a deep breath to utter the words which would seal her destiny. "I have considered my future, Father. I am ready to take my vows."

The Bishop beamed. "That is excellent news, my Lady Queen. I think it is a wise decision."

"Indeed," Judith replied, quashing the longing to run from the church.

"Your father will be most proud of you, my lady. I shall inform him today of your decision."

"Thank you," she replied. "I would like to take my vows soon. How early can they be arranged?"

"Why, in a week it will be the Mass of Christ's birth. What better day to affirm your new life? You will not be alone in taking your vows on that day."

Christmas, Judith reflected wearily. The festivity which had twice before seen the death of her hopes. How ironic that a day to celebrate a birth had brought her such grief.

"I shall make some time over the next days to speak further with you on your vows. You understand you will be swearing a vow of poverty, chastity and obedience, do you not?"

"Of course, Father," Judith said. She had always tried to be obedient, she thought bitterly, and it had got her nowhere. And poverty? All those gifts Athelwulf and Athelbald had bestowed upon her would now endow an abbey. For all Athelwulf's devotion to the church, Judith felt even he would not be happy about that. If there was one thing in which her two husbands had been alike, it had been in their understanding she had no wish for a religious life. And chastity? A memory of how her body had come alive in Baldwin's arms hit her harder than Louis' slap. She would not forget it, she promised herself. They could force her body to be chaste, but they would not force her mind. Some spark of Judith of Wessex would remain.

Father Herpoin gave her a kindly pat on the hand. "Spend whatever time you need in your devotions, my Lady Queen. It is essential you are well prepared for the ceremony."

Judith nodded her head. "Thank you, Father. I am grateful for your guidance."

As she followed the Bishop from the church, a messenger from the palace approached. He bowed before her. "Please excuse the interruption, my Lady Queen," the boy said. "But the King of Neustria has been summoned most unexpectedly away. He requests your presence so he may take his leave of you."

Judith's face hardened. The last person she wished to face was Louis. If she had still been in her chamber, she would have claimed an illness, but in front of the Bishop she had no choice but to bow her head and thank the boy.

"Excuse me, Father. I must take leave of my brother."

She walked slowly across the courtyard, trying not to look at the hay store where she had spent such a rapturous evening. She could see the horses already being made ready and felt relieved this would not be a long talk.

She straightened her back as she reached the doorway, muttering a quick prayer that she would keep her composure and take leave of her brother with the icy contempt he deserved.

Chapter eight

As she entered the hall she saw Louis straight away, dressed for travelling. To her consternation, Baldwin was standing just behind him. She had assumed Baldwin would have been immediately sent away. Judith's normally warm brown eyes settled on Louis in hard dark slits. She hadn't thought she could hate him more than she already did, but now she realised he meant to punish her by making her watch Baldwin ride out of her life. Judith felt panic sweep over her as she wondered whether she would be strong enough to do that. She felt faint at the thought. She stopped a few steps from her brother, forcing her head to remain high.

"I hear you are departing, my lord," she said, formally. "I wish you a most… pleasant journey."

Louis looked steadily at her. "I am sorry I hit you, Judith."

The apology confused Judith. It was the last thing she had expected, but she remained unmoved. The hit was the least of the hurt.

"Indeed," she said, her gaze not softening at all.

Louis frowned. "You c…cannot expect me to condone what I saw yesterday," he said. "It was wrong."

Judith pressed her lips angrily together, bitterly resenting another lecture.

"I spoke at great length to B…Baldwin after you left yesterday. He has accepted his actions were misguided."

A wave of betrayal crashed over her. She had given herself body and soul to Baldwin and had thought he felt the same way. But it seemed he had quickly sacrificed her to retain his position with Louis. She sent a sharp look at him, noticing the bruise on his cheek. His blue eyes were fixed on her, but Judith did not dare meet them.

"He has agreed that since he has seduced you, he must make amends. Or was it you who s...seduced him? B...Baldwin was really not clear on this matter."

Judith's chest heaved in indignation. Her eyes narrowed suspiciously. Louis' face was stern, but she was sure she had detected a touch of humour in his voice. Her fury at both men deepened, as Baldwin stood by while Louis mocked her.

"Anyway, it is of no matter. You must b...both make this matter right. You must be wed."

Judith's mouth dropped. She stared at her brother, certain she could not have heard him properly, that the sleepless night had caused her to imagine such utterances. It seemed impossible the punishment Louis was suggesting could be something she so deeply longed for.

"I do not know if Baldwin wants to marry me," she said, clenching her fists. "I will not marry him if he has been forced."

Baldwin had not yet spoken, but he stepped forward to take hold of Judith's hands. "As you can see, Judith, he has a knife to my throat," he said cheerfully. He looked down at her, the tender light in his eyes bringing a lump to her throat. "Silly girl, surely you know this is what I want more than anything in the world?"

Judith swallowed the lump with difficulty, afraid to give in to the hope being offered. "You know I will likely never bear you a child?"

Baldwin gently stroked her cheek. "I want to marry you. Oh, I won't deny it would be the proudest moment of my life to one day take your child in my arms, but I will be content to remain childless if I can call you my wife."

"Oh, Baldwin." Tears came to Judith's eyes and she flung her arms around his neck.

Baldwin held her tightly for a moment, but then he held her

slightly away from him. Looking searchingly into her face, he said, "But what of you? Your two husbands made you into a queen. I am a mere count. Is this truly what you want?"

Judith gave in to the radiant smile bursting from her. "To be the wife of Count Baldwin is the proudest title I could ever bear."

"Then it is settled," Baldwin said, his smile even wider than Judith's.

Judith looked from him to Louis, who was also smiling. "Will we be allowed?"

"It won't be easy," Louis said. "B...Baldwin and I spent a long time discussing the plan last night. It is why we did not come to you sooner."

"Father will never agree to this."

"No, the w...wedding will need to be a secret. You will likely have to flee."

"Your brother and I will leave today as we have said," Baldwin told her. "But we are going to find a priest. Louis and I think it best if a priest witnesses the marriage, so no one can cast it into doubt. There are also some other matters we need to arrange. We shall return unexpectedly in a few days. Perhaps a riding accident on our way to Verberie or some such incident. We will not see you on that day, but pack your belongings."

Judith nodded, an excited smile spreading across her face as she imagined herself escaping the monastery.

"The next day," Baldwin continued, "you must linger in the church after each service. As soon as we can, we will come to you."

"How long will you be?" Judith asked, panic striking her. "I have agreed to make religious vows on Christmas Day."

Louis and Baldwin looked at each other. "I think we can make it back by then," Baldwin said.

"What if a snowfall delays you?" Judith asked, clutching onto his hand.

"If we are not back, p...pretend a sickness," Louis suggested.

"My love, I will be back for you," Baldwin said. "I swear it."

"After the wedding I will ride to F...Father to break the news," Louis said. "You two must be away before then."

Judith let go of Baldwin's hands and turned to her brother. "You will do this for me?"

"I want you to be happy," Louis said solemnly, but a smile twitched his lips. "Besides, I c...cannot let you become an abbess, not when you have already declared war on me!"

Judith blushed and embraced her brother. "Oh, Louis, I should never have said such words to you. You are the best of brothers."

Baldwin put an arm around each of them. "You are indeed. I do not know what will happen to us, but as long as I am able, I will ever be your most loyal supporter. We must be away now, but before we go, Judith, give me your hand."

Judith slipped her hand into his, almost bursting with joy as Baldwin placed a ring on her finger. "I pledge myself to wed you."

Judith pulled a ring from her finger. "I have nothing that will fit you," she said. "But take this as a token of my love and as a symbol of my pledge to wed you."

Baldwin used a pin to fasten the ring to the front of his tunic. "I shall wear it close to my heart."

Louis folded his arms sternly, but his eyes were twinkling. "You two may have a moment to say goodbye," he said as he turned his back on them.

Baldwin grinned and took Judith into his arms for a long kiss. "It will not be long, my beautiful Judith," he whispered.

Louis shook his head when he turned back to them, casting a jaundiced eye over his sister's ecstatic face. "You need to get your face back into that icy m...mask you wore when you c...came in," he muttered. "Or everyone will know." He stretched his hand out to Judith. They walked out together with Baldwin a proper couple of steps behind them.

While it was impossible to return to the cold fury she had felt earlier, Judith did at least manage to keep her features solemn as they emerged into the courtyard where the Bishop was waiting to take his leave of Louis.

"It has been good to see you, Brother," she said. "A safe journey to you."

She was unable to keep the sparkle from her eyes as she extended her hand to Baldwin. "It has been most pleasant to meet you, my Lord Count," she said as calmly as she could.

"It was an honour to meet you, my Lady Queen," Baldwin replied, somehow managing to give the impression he was more concerned with the horses than his future bride.

Judith stood beside the Bishop as Louis and his entourage trotted away, a mixture of hope and fear filling her heart.

∞∞∞

The days passed slowly and Judith felt guilty the Bishop was giving up so much of his time to prepare her for vows she planned never to take. It was an effort to listen attentively to him, when her thoughts kept drifting to another set of vows. Ones she could not wait to make. She took to lingering in the church to kneel before the altar after every service, so this habit would not be associated with her brother's return, but her prayers for forgiveness were genuine.

It was just two days before Christmas when Judith got the news she had been waiting for.

"My Lady Queen," the Bishop said. "It seems your brother is again in residence at the palace. He fell from his horse as he was passing not far from here."

"Is he badly hurt?" Judith asked, her voice sounding alarmed.

"I do not think so. His companion said they would be likely to ride on in the morn, but that he thought it would be good for the King to rest a while today."

"I pray all will be well," Judith said. "May I see him before he leaves?"

"He will send for you if he wishes to see you," the Bishop said. "His companion said he was sleeping at present."

Judith shook her head, maintaining a concerned air. "That does not sound so good, Father. Please excuse me, I must pray for his recovery."

In her chamber Judith sank down onto her bed with relief. She had begun to fear they would not return in time. Joyfully she packed her clothes and her jewels in stout leather packs. That evening, on the way to the church, she glanced at the palace walls. There was no sign of anyone, but even though much could still go wrong, she felt safer knowing her brother and her lover were so close.

Chapter nine

At every service the next day, Judith lingered a while in the church as she had been instructed, but the day wore on with no sign of Baldwin or Louis. She had not expected them at Matins or even Terce, but by the time Sext and None were over, she began to worry. It was just starting to get dark when she made her way to the church for Vespers. Again at the end she remained kneeling before the altar.

"Please, Heavenly Father, let them come soon," she prayed.

"Is anything amiss, my daughter?" the Bishop asked. "I have noticed you have been much in the church this day."

Judith cursed herself for drawing attention to her presence. "Nothing is amiss, Father. I have felt the need of much quiet contemplation this day and it brings me peace to be alone here."

"Of course, my child. It is good you are preparing yourself for tomorrow. I shall leave you now."

Judith watched him leave from under her lowered lids, glad to see him taking a monk, the only other to have remained in the church, with him. Firmly she quashed the guilt at deceiving him. Quite alone she lifted her head. The candles were flickering and the smell of incense lingered on.

"J...Judith," Louis called softly as he entered.

Judith turned, her heart crashing in relief. "I am glad you are here. I was starting to worry."

"It has been so hard t...to come here without being seen." Louis took Judith's hands and smiled nervously. "Are you sure this is what you want, Sister?"

"More than anything," Judith replied.

Louis smiled again. "H...he is a good man, I know. But I am afraid for y...you."

"I have to do this." Judith blushed. "Not because we lay together, but because I can never know happiness any other way." She looked concerned. "Where is Baldwin? And the priest?"

"Th...they are coming. We came in separately. D...don't worry, Judith. You have my blessing."

A dark robed man entered at that moment. "Greetings to you, my Lady Queen."

"Greetings, Father," she replied, wondering what the priest was thinking of her. She sighed. It was the second time she had needed such a secretive marriage.

But these thoughts vanished as Baldwin entered and Judith's face burst into a radiant smile. They had been apart just a few days, but it felt like an age. Baldwin grinned back, taking hold of Judith's hands. She clung to them in a manner that suggested she would never let them go.

"W...we should start," Louis commanded.

"Agreed, my Lord King," the priest replied. "My Lady Queen, Count Baldwin please kneel before the altar."

Judith sank to her knees, preparing herself to wed for the third time. As the priest prayed over them, she and Baldwin exchanged nervous smiles. This was a far cry from the pomp of her first wedding at Verberie and was even more furtive than her second at Winchester.

"I, Baldwin, son of Audacer, Count in the region of Flanders, take you, Judith, Queen of Wessex as my wife from this day. I swear before God our Father to honour you for the rest of my days." Baldwin placed a ring on her finger.

Judith smiled. "I, Judith, Queen of Wessex willingly take you, Count Baldwin, son of Audacer, as my husband. I swear before God, our Heavenly Father, to honour you until death takes me." Louis passed one of his rings to her so Baldwin might have one that fitted. As she pushed it onto his finger, it was as if a great weight had lifted from her. She turned sparkling eyes to the priest, eager to hear his final words.

"In the name of God our Father, his son Lord Jesus Christ and the Divine Spirit, I declare Count Baldwin and Queen Judith wed. May no man tear you apart."

Baldwin put his arms around Judith and gently kissed her. A sense of overwhelming happiness flowed through her. She was wed to a man she loved with her whole heart and yet again she had escaped the cloister.

∞∞∞

The four did not linger long in the church. They moved swiftly along the passageway towards the outer courtyard which separated them from the palace, their footsteps sounding deafening to their ears as they tried to leave without being seen. It was dimly lit by a few flickering torches, the grey twilight beyond the doorway barely visible.

"What is the meaning of this?" The Bishop was standing outside. He stared in shock at Judith's hand clasped firmly in Baldwin's.

"M…my sister i…is l…leaving. Sh…she is now w…wed to C… Count Baldwin."

Judith's heart went out to Louis as his stammer betrayed the agitation he was trying to conceal. Her gaze dropped in shame before the shock in the Bishop's eyes.

"The Queen of Wessex was placed into my guardianship," the Bishop said. "I cannot allow this."

Judith's happy mood plummeted. Father Herpoin had only ever been kind to her and now she had caused him to be placed in a terrible position. She prayed her father would not be too angry with him, when his only fault had been to be too trusting of her and Louis.

"Forgive me, Father," Baldwin said. "But I am abducting the

Queen. There is nothing you can do."

The Bishop looked at Baldwin, whose eyes remained unflinching. "I see. She looks most content for someone being abducted. Can I assume a rescue would not be appreciated?"

To Judith's amazement a slight twinkle had appeared in the Bishop's kindly eyes. She gave a shamefaced smile. "Yes, Father."

"And this matter has your blessing, my Lord King?" he asked.

"It does," Louis said firmly.

"I think if God has joined you together, there is no action I can take. Except..." He gave Judith an apologetic glance. "I will have to inform King Charles."

"It is almost dark now, Father," Louis said. "C...can you wait until morn. I t...too will be riding to my father."

"I think perhaps I will not discover the Queen's abduction until the morn in any case," the Bishop replied.

"Please forgive me, Father, for deceiving you over the matter of my vows," Judith begged.

Bishop Herpoin smiled and placed his hand on her head. "You never deceived me, my daughter. I always knew you had no heart for religious vows although I earnestly prayed you would find contentment in your new life. It seems my prayers were answered, just not in the way I had expected. I will not question God's plan. You have my blessing, my child."

∞∞∞

In the palace Judith was amazed to see a celebratory feast had been made ready. Slabs of roasted beef, breads and honeyed fruits, far more than they could possibly eat, were spread over the table. Baldwin let go of her hand to pour out three cups of fine wine.

"Sit down, Sister," Louis said, as Judith could only stare. "Tonight is for celebration."

Judith could see men bringing her leather packs into the

palace. She gave her brother a hug. "Wait a moment," she said, running after the men.

It was just over a year since Athelbald had died and it was not improper for her to cast off her mourning. When she returned to the hall she was clad in a pale blue tunic, with an overdress of rose pink. She had combed out her dark hair and left the mass to flow over her shoulders as befitted a bride. Baldwin's eyes widened when he saw her and he caught her up in his arms.

"How," he demanded, "have you managed to appear even more beautiful this night, when you were already the most beautiful woman I have ever seen?"

Judith laughed, pleased by his reaction. "Do not be foolish."

Laughter rang out at the table that night. All three knew there might be difficult days ahead, but they allowed nothing to intrude on their joy. At length Judith rose from the table, informing Baldwin, with a flirtatious glance, that she was retiring for the night.

Baldwin was not long in following her. He quickly tore off his clothes, before sitting on the bed and gazing on his new wife.

"Are you not coming into bed?" Judith asked.

"Let me look at you a moment," Baldwin replied with a smile. "Unlike certain people I intend to only have one wedding night. I must make the most of it."

Judith laughed and propped herself up on the pillows. "This wedding night feels very different to my others," she said.

"Were you very frightened on the first one?" Baldwin asked, reaching out to stroke her hair.

Judith thought back. "A little, but not much. I always knew he would be kind and he never gave me any cause to fear. Everyone pitied me for marrying such an old man, but I never felt sorry for myself. We had an odd kind of marriage, but in a strange way we were happy together. Perhaps if he had lived longer the lack of passion might have caused problems, I don't know."

"What of your next husband?"

"Athelbald?" Judith could not repress a smile at the memories. "Oh, there was most certainly passion there. Too much passion perhaps. We spent half our time arguing."

"And the other half?"

"We were in bed," Judith said dryly.

Baldwin laughed, but then looked sober. "I am sorry, it sounds difficult. Did he ever hurt you?"

"Oh no, there was more of his father in him than that. They weren't the easiest of years, but I never regretted my marriage to him. They were exciting times. Athelbald was so vital. Even when he was dying, he was so full of life that no one realised it until he was gone."

"It sounds like you cared very much for them both," Baldwin said, unable to keep a wistful note from his voice.

"I did," Judith replied, thinking of the father and son who had both been her husbands. "Athelwulf took the most unsatisfactory of girls from the nunnery and made her into a queen everyone respected. And Athelbald introduced me to pleasures I had never dreamt existed. I was so alive during those years in Wessex, not like this last year in the monastery. In their different ways, they gave me so much and I will keep them both always in my heart." She reached out to take Baldwin's hands in hers. "But I did not know what love truly was until the day I was summoned here to see my brother and standing behind him was the most handsome man I had ever seen."

Baldwin grinned and shook his head.

"And the moment I looked into your eyes, I started to live again."

Baldwin twisted his fingers around hers. "You were so different to what I had expected. Your father had given me one impression, but Louis gave me quite another. I was expecting an older, most mournful lady. And then you entered and you were just a young girl. Just a very beautiful young girl. I couldn't take my eyes off you."

This time it was Judith's turn to blush and disclaim. She

knelt up, putting her arms around his neck. "Do you think maybe you've looked at me for long enough now?" she whispered.

Baldwin brought his lips against hers as his body pressed her into the mattress. "I will never tire of looking at you," he replied softly.

As Judith lay back in the circle of his arms she reflected that she had never felt as beautiful as she did that night.

Part Five: The Year of our Lord 862-4

Baldwin's Countess

Chapter one

"Farewell, Brother," Judith said, hugging Louis in the courtyard the next morning as they prepared for a hasty departure. "There are no words to thank you for everything."

"Just stay as happy as you are now," Louis said, smiling at his sister's radiant face. He embraced Baldwin. "I know you'll look after my sister, just as you looked after me."

Baldwin clapped Louis on the back. "You don't need looking after anymore, Louis," he said. "You're a capable leader. Don't let your father dominate you. And remember, if you ever need my aid, just send word."

As they trotted briskly away from Senlis, Judith asked, "How did Louis come to agree to our marriage?"

Baldwin grinned. "Well, after your little outburst left him speechless, I took the chance to tell him everything. I did agree it was wrong to take you to my bed that day. Can you blame him for being shocked by what he saw? I would not be happy if I found one of my sisters in such a position."

"I know," she replied.

"While I have been serving Louis, there have been other women." Baldwin gave a sideways glance at Judith, who simply laughed. "Quite a few women. He feared that I considered you merely another one of my conquests. But I assured him of how much I love you and how I wanted to make matters right. He knew how unhappy you were, so he was glad to give us his blessing. He cares very much for you."

Judith was silent. It had never occurred to her even a month ago that Louis would be able to help her. It seemed she had more allies than she had realised.

"So, where are we going?" she asked.

"North," Baldwin replied. "We will make for my lands near Bruges. Although it is part of West Francia, so if your father is very angry, we may need to flee further. There is a man named Rurik who controls lands beyond Flanders. I have already sent word to him that we may need to make a lengthy visit. He is no friend of your father's, so he will give us sanctuary if necessary."

"Rurik? Is he a heathen?" Judith asked.

"I believe he has recently accepted baptism, but my dearest, we cannot afford to be too choosy in our friends. You know how your father can be."

"And will Rurik accept us?" Judith asked.

Baldwin nodded. "I am known as a fine fighter. He would be glad to accept me."

"You would fight on the side of the Norsemen against West Francia?"

Baldwin reined in his horse. "It is not what I want, Judith, but we may have no choice."

"What of Wessex? Ethelbert said he would always welcome me back," Judith said.

"It is a possibility," Baldwin replied. "But would he really go against your father? At the moment I have no such assurances from Wessex and I do have an offer from Rurik. My love, we will have to take our chances where we can. If you cannot accept this..." He glanced back the way they had come. "Do you want to go back there?"

"No," Judith exclaimed. "You are right. If I have to live among heathens to be with you, I will."

∞∞∞

Baldwin and Louis had been busy in the days they were away from Senlis, and the residences where they stayed overnight were expecting them and most welcoming. They could easily have lingered many days at each one, but Baldwin was determined to keep heading north. He wanted to put as much distance as possible between them and Charles. The rides each day were exhausting, but Judith did not complain. Every time she felt she was flagging, she looked at the handsome face of the man on the horse next to her, still unable to believe he was her husband. She should have been a nun by this time, spending her days in prayer and her nights on a pallet. But instead she was with the man she loved and her nights were in his arms.

Poor weather made their journey slow and uncomfortable. They rode on one afternoon through a rain so heavy it left Judith soaked to the skin. They did not make it to their intended destination that night, but instead begged for refuge at a much humbler dwelling. The people there had no idea who they were, Baldwin simply saying he was travelling home with his new wife. The woman of the household fussed over Judith, drying her clothes and urging cups of hot ale on her.

"I know these standards are not what you are used to," Baldwin said, looking anxiously at his wife. She was sat by the fire, her cheeks red and her hair in bedraggled strands.

Judith took his hand, smiling at the woman who was busying herself with some broth. "No, for me to receive so warm a welcome in West Francia is almost unheard of."

They slept that night on the floor of the dwelling and departed the next day full of thanks to their kind hosts. The skies were still grey, but at least the rain had stopped. It was not too far until their next destination and they arrived soon after noon. However, the welcome was very different.

"Please forgive me," their intended host said, wringing his hands. "But messengers have come from the King. All are forbidden from offering you refuge. I shall give you some refreshment, but I must beg that you are then quickly on your way. In truth I should be apprehending you and I fear the repercussions if the King learns I have harboured you."

Disheartened by this news, they and their entourage made a quick meal. Barely had they finished when a messenger from Louis arrived.

"I bring you greetings from the King of Neustria," the messenger said. "He says King Charles is most angry. He has vowed to kill Count Baldwin for the abduction of his daughter and will ensure the Queen of Wessex is returned to the most secure abbey he can find. King Louis urges you to be away with all speed. Men are looking for you and everyone has been forbidden from offering you refuge. Even Rurik may not be able to help."

Judith watched Baldwin anxiously as he frowned for a moment before gesturing to one of his men. "Ride ahead at all speed to Rurik. I must know if we are still welcome in his realm. Tell him we are on our way to him."

"Will he stand against my father?" Judith asked, as the man scrambled to his horse and rode away.

"I think so," Baldwin replied. "Oh my dearest love, the next days are not going to be easy. We must ride faster and I do not know where we will sleep. We cannot put good people in danger by residing with them."

"I can give you tents," their host said. "I wish I could do more for you, but at least you will be dry."

Baldwin thanked him and put his arms around Judith. "Are you sure this is what you want?" he asked. "If there is any part of you which felt pressured into marrying me, please say. I will hand myself over to your father's men and you can be returned to comfort."

Judith clung tightly onto him. "Returned to imprisonment, you mean. No, my love, you know I wanted to marry you more than anything. I can tolerate the ride. I can tolerate the rain and the cold nights. The one thing I cannot tolerate is being apart from you."

Baldwin smiled and kissed her. "We will stay together,

somehow." He turned to face his men. "My friends, I am now a fugitive from the justice of King Charles. I am charged with the most grievous crime of abducting his fair daughter. Anyone who rides with us risks being charged alongside me. I will judge no man harshly if he would prefer to part ways."

Baldwin looked at his men, but they were men who had been well chosen. No one said a word until one of their number stepped forward.

"My lord, I speak for us all when I say it will be an honour to continue to serve you and your lady. We all stand with you."

Judith and Baldwin smiled on the men. "Then finish your meal quickly and let us ride on. The sooner I can bring my lady to safety and comfort the better."

Their host provided them with not just tents, but also provisions. Baldwin was concerned the laden horses would not go as fast as he wished them to, but he was aware of the risks of bartering for food. With such quantities, they could go a long way before needing to draw attention to themselves.

∞∞∞

Despite Baldwin's best efforts to care for his wife, the ride and the nights were as uncomfortable as he had feared. Their progress was slower than he hoped, and he took to sending scouts ahead to ensure they would evade the King's men. The messenger he sent to Rurik returned, assuring them they were still welcome there. Judith had never seen Baldwin look so relieved.

"Soon we shall be safe, my love," he said. "I thank God I now have somewhere to take you."

They rode on, hoping just a few more days would bring them to safety. But their efforts were to be in vain.

"My lord," came the shout of one of the scouts Baldwin had sent ahead. "The King's men are ahead of us. I do not think we can make it."

Baldwin cursed, looking frantically around him.

"Wessex," Judith urged. "If we head west we can get to one of the ports along the coast. I know the sea journey will be more perilous than the one from Boulogne or Calais, but do we have any choice?"

"Heading west takes us even deeper into your father's realm, my love. I do not think we would make it to the coast." He looked agitated. "We need to head east. It should not take so long to be out of West Francia."

"What lands will we come to?"

"East will bring us to Middle Francia."

"King Lothair is my kinsman," Judith said. "We can beg for refuge."

"He is your father's nephew," Baldwin said slowly. "But there is no love between them. Ride ahead to the border," he said to his scout. "Beg him to grant us sanctuary. Tell him we are coming at all speed."

Chapter two

The ride to the border with Middle Francia was hard and frightening. They scarcely dared to stop even for meals. They rode until darkness fell and rose before dawn. Scouts were continually sent out in all directions to check if pursuit was closer than they thought. Riding through every settlement was a terrifying ordeal, as they wondered if the King's men might be lying in wait. And even as they passed safely through, they could not resist looking back, fearing a message might even then be making its way to their pursuers, informing them of their whereabouts.

"The border is not far now, my dearest," Baldwin said one afternoon, when they had stopped for a furtive break. He looked anxiously at Judith's face.

Judith tried to smile. She had never felt so exhausted. She took another swig of ale, hoping the drink would revive her a little. Baldwin gently enclosed her in his arms and stroked her hair. He was worried about her. He and the other men were used to such fast and desperate rides, but she was not. Judith shut her eyes as she leant against him, longing for a few minutes of oblivion.

"My lord," came the frantic voice of one of the scouts, jarring Judith from her brief respite. "The King's men are behind us. They know we are here."

Baldwin and Judith scrambled to their feet. "Everyone to your horses, now," Baldwin cried. "Ride for the border. Do not worry about staying together. We shall regroup on the other side. It will be harder to pursue us if we are not in a group."

He lifted Judith onto her horse and swiftly mounted his own. "Ready?" he asked her.

Judith nodded fearfully. "Baldwin, are we going to stay together?"

Baldwin gave a half smile. "Always," he replied.

He kicked his horse into action and they sped away. The ride had already been fast, but now it raced to terrifying speeds. The green countryside passed in a blur. Judith was an accomplished horsewoman, accustomed to riding her whole life. But never had she needed to ride like that.

They sped through meadows and woods, not daring to slow their tired horses for an instant. Shouts came from the other side of the valley, startling them into even greater speeds. But it didn't seem to matter what they did. The King's men were gaining on them.

"Faster, my love," Baldwin called.

Judith urged her exhausted horse on, ignoring the sweat on the animal's neck. She was terrified it would collapse from the strain. A longer stretch of wood gave her some hope they might lose their pursuers and she would have liked to linger on in the shelter of the trees. But soon the woods thinned and as they emerged to an open stretch of land, she kicked her horse sharply into a gallop once again. Together they raced across the open land, but Judith felt vulnerable knowing how easy they would be to spot.

However they had made it some way across before they heard the shouts of men emerging from the woodland. Judith glanced back, crying out in fear. Her shout startled her horse, causing it to stumble. "Baldwin!" she cried, clinging desperately onto the reins, but it was in vain. She slid sideways from the saddle, hitting the ground hard. The horse reared, its hoofs narrowly missing Judith as it came back down and galloped away. Judith lay shocked on the ground, pain sweeping through her body.

"Judith!" Baldwin reined in his horse and slid to the ground.

Judith tried to rise, her whole body screaming in agony. "Ride on. They are coming," she managed to say through gritted teeth.

"I'm not leaving you," Baldwin cried. He helped her to her feet, but she cried out again, as pain coursed through her leg. Baldwin cast an agonised look at the men careering towards them.

"I can't ride," Judith exclaimed, tears streaking from her eyes. She clung onto Baldwin as her leg threatened to give way. "My arm hurts too much and my horse has gone."

Baldwin nodded. "I know," he said, lifting her so she was seated sideways on his horse.

"What are you doing?" Judith exclaimed, as Baldwin mounted behind her. "The horse will be too slow with us both."

"He will have to manage," Baldwin said grimly. "Hold on as best you can, my love."

Judith clasped her good arm as tightly around his waist as she could as Baldwin spurred his horse on. She tried to ignore the pain as she was jolted around, although every hoof thud was agony. She bit her lip to stop herself from shrieking. She knew both Baldwin and the horse needed every scrap of concentration.

"Stop in the name of the King!" came a shout from excruciatingly nearby.

Baldwin ignored it, his eyes fixed firmly ahead. Judith looked up at him, trying to take comfort from the determination on his face and the strength in his arms.

A flurry of arrows whipped through the air, striking the ground close to them, but Baldwin did not even seem to see them as his horse left them behind. He made for another wooded tract, plunging into the thick trees. Instead of making straight through he veered sharply to the right, hoping to lose the King's men. It seemed to have worked. As they emerged again onto open land there was no sign of pursuit.

Baldwin did not slacken his pace, although he breathed a sigh of relief as they came upon a river. He galloped along the bank looking for a ford or a bridge. Distant voices told them they had again been spotted by the King's men, but the pursuit was not as close as it had been. However Judith felt no relief. She knew they could not keep this up for much longer. The horse was surely on the brink of collapse. She clung ever tighter to Baldwin, terrified they would soon be dragged apart. The horrifying possibility she might witness Baldwin killed before her eyes by those men, who imagined they were rescuing her, came into her mind. And try as she might, she could not get the image to fade.

Baldwin gave an exclamation of satisfaction as they came upon a bridge. It was narrow, but Baldwin urged the horse briskly over it. Judith reflected that such a bridge could not possibly allow horses to ride abreast and felt a faint glimmer of hope that this would help them.

As they reached the far bank, Baldwin steered his horse away from the river. Again he went into some woods. As well as providing cover, the dense trees forced Baldwin to slow the pace of his exhausted horse.

"How are you faring, my love?" he asked.

Judith's head was slumped against his chest, but she looked up at this. Her face was white and the pain evident in her eyes. "Well enough," she replied, forcing a faint smile.

Baldwin smiled back, dropping a quick kiss on her forehead, but his eyes were anxious as he looked at the arm which was not gripping him tightly. It hung limply across Judith's lap.

As the trees thinned, Baldwin encouraged his horse to pick up speed, causing Judith to again hide her winces of pain. But as they came out of the trees, Baldwin cried out in shock, sharply reining in his horse. Judith lifted her head to see what had startled Baldwin and cried out herself. A group of armed men were gathered there, all eyes fixed on them. They were mounted on horses which looked fresh, in a stark contrast to their own quivering animal. Baldwin glanced helplessly back into the woods, knowing more armed men were somewhere the other side. He let go of the reins with one hand and clasped it protectively around Judith's shoulders. She bit her lip, trying frantically to think of some way of escape. Her arm clung even tighter to Baldwin's waist, wanting to make it impossible for any man to tear them apart.

"Stay where you are," the leader of the men called, bringing his horse towards them.

"There is nowhere we can go," Baldwin said desolately in a low voice to Judith. "Be strong, my love."

The man pulled his horse up in front of them. He was a young man about the same age as Baldwin, with dark brown hair and hazel eyes. He looked curiously at them, his eyes eventually settling on Judith.

"You must be my kinswoman, Queen Judith of Wessex," the man said, a touch of amusement in his voice. "Allow me to present myself, my lady. I am King Lothair of Middle Francia." His eyes moved to Baldwin and became harder. "And you must be Count Baldwin, son of Audacer."

Judith slid shakily down from the horse, ignoring the pain surging through her as her leg touched the ground. She limped forward a few paces to kneel stiffly on the grass in front of King Lothair. As Baldwin knelt beside her, she looked beseechingly up at her kinsman.

"My Lord King, I and my husband beg for refuge in your land."

Chapter three

The look of amusement returned to Lothair's face. "Well, well, a daughter of King Charles of West Francia kneeling before me. How I wish my dear uncle could see this."

Judith bowed her head, but said nothing. Baldwin reached for her hand. Lothair observed the action and noticed too the exhausted droop of Judith's head. He dismounted and strode towards them.

"My dear kinswoman, please forgive me. This is a poor welcome I am giving you." He stretched out his hand. "Please rise, my dear lady. I most willingly grant you refuge."

Judith gave a smile as she rose painfully to her feet, leaning on her cousin's arm. But she had not missed the emphasis Lothair had placed on the word 'you'.

"And my husband?" she asked.

Lothair's gaze flickered over Baldwin who continued to kneel. "From what I have heard he does not deserve my protection. Abduction of a young woman from the security of a monastery is a most serious crime."

Baldwin looked up. "It is indeed, my Lord King. I am grateful for the protection you are willing to grant my wife. There are armed men from West Francia in pursuit of us. They crossed the river a little after us and cannot be far away."

Lothair raised his eyebrows and gestured to some of his men. "Intercept them," he instructed. "Inform them that if they advance any further into Middle Francia, I shall consider them in breach of the Treaty of Verdun. It will be an act of war and I shall retaliate accordingly."

Baldwin gave a relieved sigh as the men set off. "My Lord King, all I ask for myself is that you listen to our account of events before deciding my fate."

Lothair stared at him, considering his words. "Very well. Please rise, Count Baldwin." He looked again at Judith. "I am being a poor host. Come sit yourself a moment and we shall have some refreshment before bringing you to shelter."

Lothair's men had spread out thick blankets and Lothair poured cups of ale for them all. Judith sipped at hers, too weary even to speak. Both Baldwin and Lothair looked anxiously at her, as she sat with her head bowed, her hair falling forward to conceal her face.

"Are you ready to ride on?" Lothair asked, as Judith set down her cup.

She nodded, but Baldwin put his arm around her. "She is injured and very tired. I do not think she has the strength to go far, even on my horse."

"I have a residence close by. We shall head there," Lothair replied.

"Thank you, cousin," Judith replied, leaning against Baldwin. He picked her up and carried her to his horse, which was looking much better for the rest.

"You are safe now, my love," he whispered to Judith as they set off at a gentle pace.

Lothair apologised for the poor size of the residence they arrived at, clearly just a hunting lodge, but neither Judith nor Baldwin cared as they sat in the hall with a jug of wine and some hot food at last. Their entourage, including their pack horses, began to join them and Lothair accepted with increased amusement these fugitives from his much-hated uncle.

"The hour is late," Lothair said as they ate their fill. "I shall speak with you both in the morning. For now get some rest."

In their chamber Judith was almost unable to keep her

eyes open, as she awkwardly pulled off her clothes. Baldwin watched her, concerned she was still barely using her right arm. Bruises were beginning to appear all down her side, but it was clear her shoulder had borne the brunt of the impact.

"You should hate me now for putting you in such danger," he said in an anguished tone.

Judith shook her head, smiling at him. Very gently he ran his hand down her arm, still distressed she had been hurt. "Baldwin, I am so tired."

Baldwin nodded. "I know," he said, pulling back the covers. He patted the pillow. "Put your head there, my dearest."

Judith lay down, the softness of the mattress feeling unbelievably luxurious after their last nights on the ground. It was ironic that on this first night for an age in a comfortable bed, she had no energy. She gazed up at Baldwin who was smiling tenderly at her. "I am sorry," she whispered.

Baldwin pressed his lips to her forehead. "Shh, my love. You need not be sorry. We will have a lifetime of nights together. For now you must sleep."

Gratefully Judith closed her eyes, relaxing her aching body as Baldwin stroked her hair. She smiled as she savoured the feeling of security he always brought her, even in the most dangerous of times.

∞ ∞ ∞

When Judith awoke she was alone. She had slept long and deeply and had no idea if Baldwin had simply arisen earlier or had not shared the chamber with her. The light coming through the tiny window told her the hour was already advanced. Judith quickly threw back the covers. She felt considerably better for her deep sleep, although her body was still stiff and painful. Her pack had been brought in and she pulled on a simple blue tunic. After an attempt at binding up her hair brought a searing reminder of her injuries, she left it tied loosely around her shoulders.

She found Baldwin and Lothair in deep conversation in the hall. Both men got to their feet as she entered.

"I had no idea how late it was. Please forgive me," she exclaimed.

Baldwin smiled at her. "You needed that sleep," he said, taking her in his arms. "And you look so much better for it."

Judith felt somewhat ashamed of how weak she must have appeared the night before. She turned calmly to her cousin.

"Forgive me, my lord. I am sure I did not adequately convey my gratitude to you last night. Your hospitality was very much appreciated," she said with a regal smile.

Lothair nodded, looking far more impressed than he had the previous day. "You thanked me many times, my dear cousin," he said, kissing her hand. "I am delighted to have the pleasure of hosting you. I trust you will remain in my realm, for now at least."

"I would be most glad to remain," Judith replied. "But only if the protection is extended to my husband. If no refuge is granted to him, there is no place for me."

"I may be able to grant him refuge as long as..."

Judith raised her eyebrows, but Baldwin gave a slight bow. "I shall let you two talk," he said and made his way to the door.

"Sit down, cousin," Lothair said, pulling back a chair. "Break your fast." He gestured to a platter of smoked meat and bread and poured Judith a cup of ale.

Judith helped herself to the food, but did not immediately eat. She sipped impatiently at her drink. "Why can you not offer my husband sanctuary?" she asked.

"Perhaps I can," Lothair said slowly. "But the information I received was that he had abducted you from the security of a monastery. And when you arrived in my realm, you were restrained on his horse and in obvious pain."

"You think Baldwin did that?" Judith said.

"My dearest cousin, if you were abducted from the monastery and if he has forced certain acts upon you, please tell me. You need not see him again. No shame will be on you. No one would have anything but contempt for a man who snatches a defenceless young woman from the monastery where she was placed for protection. You are safe now and can be protected from him."

Judith looked steadily back at her cousin. "I was injured in a fall from my horse, while trying to escape my father's men. Tell me, if you were taken to a monastery and told you had to stay there to take holy vows, would you consider yourself protected?"

Lothair shook his head. "No, I would consider myself imprisoned."

"That is exactly how I felt," Judith replied. "I left Senlis of my own will. I do not consider myself to have been abducted. I believe Baldwin rescued me. My brother, Louis, was at our wedding."

"I do not like to think that a man would collude in the abduction and rape of his own sister," Lothair commented. "But nothing would surprise me about the son of Charles of West Francia."

"Louis is nothing like my father," Judith exclaimed indignantly. "He is kind and gentle."

"I see. And your injuries are all from the fall? Baldwin has not hurt you at all?"

"No. I do not know what I can say to convince you. When Baldwin asked me to be his wife, it was the happiest moment of my life."

"You do not need to say anything, cousin." He smiled, observing how radiant Judith's face had become when speaking of that moment. "Have you eaten enough? Shall we join him?"

Judith leant on her cousin as they made their way to the courtyard where Baldwin was sitting.

"My dear Count Baldwin," Lothair said formally. "I am most happy to grant sanctuary to both you and your fair wife."

"I thank you," Baldwin replied. "I hope I can one day repay

your kindness."

"A new friendship is always an advantage," Lothair said noncommittally. "Now, I would like to return to Aachen at the earliest opportunity. But perhaps we should rest here a few days."

"I agree," Baldwin replied. "I don't think Judith should ride for a day or two at least."

"I am fine," protested Judith, unable to help smiling as she met the incredulous stare of both men. "But it would be good not to have to sit on a horse for a few days."

"Excellent. I shall send word to Aachen to prepare a welcome for you."

"Will we meet your lady wife there?" Judith asked.

"No," Lothair replied. "Please make yourselves comfortable here. I have much to do."

Judith stared at him as he strode away, puzzled by his abrupt reply.

"He has problems in his own marriage," Baldwin told her. "He does not wish to remain married to his wife, but your father and Archbishop Hincmar are opposing his efforts to annul it. Why do you think he is so sympathetic to us?"

"I don't know. I hadn't thought about it," Judith replied.

"Aachen is his main residence, but he lives there with his concubine and their son." Baldwin put his arms around Judith and looked ruefully down at her. "I am not sure I should be taking you to such a place."

Judith laughed. "You forget you are talking to the woman who once married her own son! I think I shall fit in very well."

Chapter four

Accustomed to the fine palaces of West Francia and Wessex, both Judith and Baldwin were nonetheless stunned when they arrived at the Palace of Aachen. Judith was fascinated by this residence which had been the main home of her ancestor, Charles the Great, the first in her family to be crowned emperor. The hall was the grandest Judith had ever seen, and beyond it were endless galleries and council chambers. The library was said to rival the papal library in Rome and Lothair told her how much their powerful ancestor had enjoyed listening to poems and stories. Judith smiled, wondering if this was where she had inherited her own love of such stories.

Beyond huge bronze doors was a chapel, so magnificent that Judith doubted there was anywhere in Christendom to rival it. Mosaics covered the walls, illuminated by the winters light streaming through the windows, as well as what seemed to be a thousand lamps. Lothair pointed out the white marble throne of Charles the Great and confessed that he continued to be awed when he sat on it himself.

The feast laid on to welcome them was lavish to an excess which took Judith's breath away and left Baldwin embarrassed.

"Nonsense, my friends," Lothair cried to the protests of them both. "You have not yet had a proper wedding celebration. This should be it."

Judith suspected the celebration was more about sending a message to her father. He would not be pleased to hear his undutiful daughter and the fugitive Baldwin had been so honoured.

"My dear cousin, please meet Lady Waldrada, she who I hope will soon be the Queen of Middle Francia," Lothair said, presenting his concubine.

"Welcome to Aachen, my lady." Waldrada was an attractive blonde woman. Her greeting was somewhat uncomfortable, but eventually she dropped into a curtsey, deciding that Judith's rank as Queen of Wessex meant she outranked any other woman, even if in future she held a higher title.

Judith, who had no idea if the rank she now held was that of princess, queen or countess, simply smiled back, hoping to put the young woman at her ease. It was obvious Waldrada and Lothair were very much in love and Judith could not help but feel sympathy for them.

"What has happened to Lothair's wife?" Judith asked Baldwin that night after they had been conducted to a luxurious chamber. Sumptuous fur covers were spread over the bed and bright tapestries accentuated with golden threads adorned the walls. They began to realise why Lothair had been so apologetic about the first residence.

"Queen Teutburga is at Metz," Baldwin replied. "Lothair has been trying to annul his marriage for years. It was forced on him by his father, who died the following year. Your uncle, Louis of East Francia, is sympathetic to Lothair's wish for an annulment, but your father won't hear of it. According to Lothair, Teutburga is an immoral woman, who committed incest with her brother."

"Did she?" Judith asked, looking shocked at this story.

"She proved her innocence," Baldwin said. "The truth is, Lothair wants rid of her because she cannot have children and Waldrada can. That is also the reason why your father does not want the annulment. He is sensing lands available if Lothair should die without legitimate issue." Baldwin was still looking around the chamber in wonder. "I have never seen anywhere so fine, have you?"

"I wonder what will happen to Teutburga," Judith said. "She cannot win. If Lothair is forced to keep her, she will have a husband who hates her. But if she is repudiated, her life is over." Judith's memories of how the bishops had once condemned her for incest forced a note of bitter sadness into her voice.

"Judith?" Baldwin asked, sitting down beside her. Suddenly he realised what he had said. "Oh, my dearest, this has no relevance to us."

"Has it not? I am barren and I too was once accused of incest. You must feel you have a poor wife."

"My love, I want to be married to you. If I cannot have children with you, I do not want them with anyone," Baldwin said. "I consider myself the most fortunate of men to have you by my side."

As Judith allowed Baldwin to comfort her, she realised she was not sure what to make of her cousin following this revelation. He was an excellent host. He had been solicitous towards her following her injuries and although she had been indignant at his initial accusations of Baldwin, she now realised it had been a sign of his genuine concern for her. Yet she couldn't help but sympathise with his wife. Teutburga's fate could so easily have been her own. She thought back with affection of Athelbald. Their marriage had not been ideal, but for all his faults, he had always stood by her, even as she failed to give him a child.

"Do you think we can trust my cousin?" Judith asked.

"For now we have to," Baldwin replied. "I think he is genuinely sympathetic towards us, but his support is mainly motivated by a desire to avenge himself on your father. He would undoubtedly hand us over if your father made it worth his while."

"I thought we would be safe here," Judith sighed.

"We are for the time being. This will be a refuge for us over the winter. If your father has not relented by the spring, we will need to think more."

"I knew my father would be angry, but I hoped once the deed was done he would accept us and perhaps even bestow some lands upon you. He accepted my marriage to Athelbald, although that too was without his permission."

"He was a King," Baldwin replied. "If you had eloped with a man of power, he would have accepted it. But I am a nobody."

"No, no, my love. Don't say that," Judith cried.

Baldwin held her tightly. "What a pair we are. You wish you could give me a child and I wish I could give you a home. Both seem beyond our reach at the moment."

"We have each other," Judith said. "As long as I have that, I can bear the rest."

∞∞∞

Baldwin was determined to be of use to his host while he was a guest in his realm, leaving Judith in the company of Waldrada. Now Waldrada realised Judith was no arrogant Frankish princess, the two were becoming friends. Although they did not speak of it, their shared desire to have their unions with the men they loved recognised, created a bond between them. Lothair took Baldwin with him on daily rides in the area around Aachen and he bathed with Lothair and his entourage in the hot springs. When they returned, Lothair suggested with a wink that Baldwin might like to show the bath house to Judith. Baldwin grinned and the next day did exactly that.

Judith had never before experienced such quantities of warm water. Being unable to swim, she sat in the shallows, enjoying the feeling of hot water on her body and reflecting on what a pleasant way it was to spend a winters day. As the warmth of the water eased the remaining aches from her riding accident, she understood why her great-grandfather had made Aachen his winter residence. With a laugh Baldwin pulled her into the deeper water, supporting her as she floated. For a brief time they forgot to worry about the reprisals of King

Charles, as they laughed and splashed each other in the warm waters of the spa.

It was just as they sat down to dine one evening that the first messenger from Charles arrived. They were unsurprised to hear from him. The tales of Lothair's hospitality had undoubtedly reached him and had probably made him even angrier than he already was.

"Lord King Lothair of Middle Francia," the messenger said. "King Charles of West Francia demands that you deliver the criminal Baldwin to his justice and return the Queen of Wessex to his protection. Under the terms of the Treaty of Verdun, you should not be harbouring such a criminal and enemy of West Francia."

The Treaty of Verdun had been signed by King Charles with his brothers, Louis of East Francia and Lothair of Middle Francia, their host's father, when Judith was a baby. It had divided the empire of Judith's grandfather, the Emperor Louis, among the brothers and made an agreement that the three would not harbour each other's enemies.

Lothair got to his feet, a look of surprise on his face. "The Treaty of Verdun? My dear man, please take some refreshment while I compose my reply to my most noble uncle. I had no idea he would raise the matter of the Treaty of Verdun."

Judith slipped her hand in Baldwin's under the table, fearing what would come next.

"But I do not think such a treaty is relevant," Lothair continued. "I can understand my dear uncle's ambitions for his fair daughter, but it is no crime for her to have no inclination for a religious life. And while it is indeed most bold of Baldwin to aspire to the hand of a Princess of West Francia, such an aspiration does not render him an enemy."

Judith relaxed, knowing they were still safe for the moment.

"Please assure my uncle I have no intention of harbouring criminals. This charming couple are simply making a visit to my realm. I am sure my fair cousin and her husband will be delighted to return to West Francia as soon as they receive assurances from King Charles that he will give their union his blessing." Lothair grinned and it was obvious this reply was giving him no end of pleasure.

Once the messenger had departed again for West Francia, they slipped back into their routines and Lothair continued to treat them as his honoured guests. But it did not take long for the next messenger to arrive.

"My Lord King," the messenger said, bowing before Lothair. "Your noble uncle and King of West Francia is most disappointed by your refusal to deliver his enemy to his justice and your insistence on leaving his fair daughter, the Queen of Wessex, in the hands of her abductor. But he will not at this time declare war with you over this matter and hopes your conscience will soon see the duty you owe to your cousin."

Judith and Baldwin looked at each other and smiled, relieved they were still safe in Middle Francia. However the messenger had not come alone. A priest was with him. He approached Baldwin, holding aloft a cross.

"My Lord Count, I am here as the representative of Archbishop Hincmar of Rheims and the bishops of West Francia. Your crimes against the noble daughter of the King of West Francia have been judged in your absence. On the charge of abduction, you have been judged to be guilty."

"Don't be ridiculous," Judith exclaimed. "I have not been abducted."

"My Lady Queen, you are a woman who has been led astray by this man. Your heart has been greatly misled and Archbishop Hincmar wishes nothing more than for you to return from the life of sin this man has dragged you into."

"My father would put me in an abbey," Judith protested.

"It is necessary, my lady, for you to repent for the sins this man has forced upon you."

"Never mind that, Father," Baldwin said, seeing how indignant his wife was becoming. "What judgement has been passed upon me?"

The priest looked sternly at him. "My Lord Count, in the

name of Archbishop Hincmar of Rheims and the bishops of West Francia, with the support of the most merciful and noble King Charles of West Francia, I pass upon you the sentence of excommunication. May God have mercy on your soul."

Chapter five

Baldwin went white and stumbled from the hall. Everyone else was stunned into silence.

"You can't do this," Judith almost shrieked at the priest. "My husband has done nothing wrong."

"This is the judgement of Archbishop Hincmar. It is not appropriate for a young woman such as yourself to question it," the priest replied calmly. "And the will of Father Hincmar and indeed your own father is that you share in the punishment of excommunication. Archbishop Hincmar is particularly distressed at your sin, as it was he who once consecrated you a queen. He little knew he was conferring the role on one so unworthy. Queen Judith of Wessex, I pronounce on you the sentence of excommunication to remain until you return to your father as an obedient daughter should."

The people of the court sucked in their breath at this, but Judith looked at the priest in scorn. It was not the first time she had clashed with the clergy over a marriage.

"I thought I had been abducted," Judith said in a scathing tone. "How kind of my father to punish me for that."

"Your father is aware it is a fault in your character which allowed you to be abducted. A woman's mind is not strong. It is very easily influenced by the wiles of an evil man such as Count Baldwin."

"Oh, be quiet," Judith snapped. The surrounding people gasped upon hearing her speak in such fashion to the priest, but Judith did not hear them. She had already followed

Baldwin from the hall.

She found him in their chamber, sitting on the floor with his head in his hands. Judith knelt down next to him, shocked to see him so dejected. Ever since they had left Senlis, Baldwin had been the more optimistic of them. She put her arm around him and he looked up.

"I've been excommunicated, Judith," he said. "Cast out of the church. What am I going to do?"

"So have I, but we're still free," Judith replied. "We have not been sent back to West Francia."

"I can never again attend church and receive the sacraments." Baldwin seemed to have barely heard her. "I am damned."

"We are still together," Judith said. "That is all that matters."

Baldwin shook his head. "I shall have to go back."

"What?" Judith stared at him. "You can't. Don't be foolish. I know this is a harsh judgement, but there is no need for us to go back. We can still be together."

"Our souls are at stake," Baldwin said. "There is no choice."

"No, my love, don't," Judith cried, clutching even tighter to his arm. "They will kill you and send me to a nunnery. You can't leave me."

Baldwin shook her off and got to his feet. "This is my eternal soul, Judith. If I am excommunicated I could be damned for all time."

"But, Baldwin-"

Baldwin shook his head, his eyes narrowing. "Your family are all the same. None of you care about others. Everyone hates your father, but he does not care. All he cares for is the power. People are just there for him to use. And your cousin, Lothair. He is as bad. He does not want to be married to Teutburga, so he accused her of the most grievous of crimes. Do you know what she had to do to prove her innocence?"

Silently Judith shook her head.

"She had to undertake the trial by boiling water. She had to retrieve a stone from the bottom of a pail of scalding water.

Can you imagine how that hurt? She was fortunate her burns healed, for it proved her innocence."

"I am not like my family," Judith protested.

"Yes, you are," Baldwin snapped. "You were just fourteen when you were betrothed to the Wessex king. You should have been horrified at marrying an old man and being sent to a foreign land. But not you. All you cared was that he was a king. All you cared about was your position."

"I am married to you now, Baldwin," Judith cried. "Position means nothing to me."

"I am facing eternal damnation. But that doesn't bother you, does it? All you care is that I am here to cater for your pleasures. You use people, Judith. Just like your father."

"No, my love. I do not."

"Your own soul is also at stake, but you do not even care for that. Perhaps it is because, like so many of your family, you do not have one."

Baldwin stormed from the room and Judith collapsed weeping on the bed. She wept for herself and Baldwin, so soon to be torn apart. She wept for Lothair and Waldrada, who longed to marry, but also for poor scarred Teutburga, desperately clinging onto her position. Those three were caught up in the schemes of Lothair's father. A man who had died the year after he had hatched them. These Frankish power games were bringing no end of misery.

When Baldwin returned some time later, Judith had dried her tears and was still lying on the bed, staring at the ceiling. She sat up as he came in.

"Baldwin, did I abduct you?" she asked.

Baldwin stared, his brow creasing as if he was not certain he had properly heard her words. "What?"

"Did you feel you had to marry me and flee West Francia because I had thrown myself at you?"

"No! Oh, my beautiful Judith, I never felt that. You know I fell in love with you. Louis never put any pressure on me to marry you. Quite the opposite. I went down on my knees to beg him to give us his blessing."

Judith flung her arms tightly around him and buried her head in his shoulder, relieved to feel him return her embrace.

"I am sorry I said such things to you, my dearest. You are nothing like your father."

Judith gave him a shaky smile. "You were not wrong. I was little more than a child, but I willingly accepted the hand of a man old enough to be my grandfather, just because he was a king. I had just about enough sense to be relieved he was a kind man, but I would have put up with a worse one if he had made me a queen and offered me a life away from the cloister. You were right. I do use people. I used Athelbald to remain a queen."

"I know you cared for him as well," Baldwin protested.

"Yes, I did, but I still used him. He used me too, to enhance his prestige. We were two of a kind really," Judith replied sadly. "I learnt so much during those years in Wessex. I thought granting me a crown was the greatest gift Athelwulf could give me, but I was wrong. The greatest gift he gave me was to place me at the heart of his family. He loved his boys so much. Athelbald rebelled against him. I think my father would kill any son of his who tried to take his crown, but Athelwulf forgave him and shared his power. He loved being a king, but he loved his sons more."

Baldwin smiled gently and took her hands.

"I was never in love with either of them, but they were part of my Wessex family who I came to love so much. When I came back here, I won't deny I missed being a queen with all the prestige and riches such a position gave me. But what I missed intolerably was my family. Ethelred and Alfred had been almost like sons to me. Alfred was just a little boy when I met him. I thought I would see him grow into a man, but I had to leave him behind. I had to leave them all behind."

"And me?" Baldwin asked.

"I didn't use you just to get away from the monastery, I swear it. I fell in love with you. As a princess of West Francia, I should have buried my feelings and considered a mere count beneath my notice. But I did not fall in love with a count. I fell in love with a man. I fell in love with you, Baldwin and I will do whatever you want. If you feel you have to go back, I will go with you. I know my father will send me to a nunnery, but I won't care. If he has you executed, there will be nothing more in this life for me." Judith tried to smile, but the thought of the punishment her father might inflict on Baldwin made it impossible to stop the tears from spilling over.

"I don't know what to do. There is not much that scares me, but excommunication does. Why does it not scare you?"

"My fear is being trapped in the church, not being cast out of it. Besides, this is not the first time the church has condemned a marriage of mine." Judith gave a rueful smile. "I am still the daughter of Charles of West Francia. My family are used to not caring what anyone thinks. Even God, it seems."

Baldwin pulled her close and rested his cheek on the top of her head.

Her eyes brimming with tears, Judith looked up at him. "Whatever happens, we must not regret these months. They have been desperate and dangerous, but they have been the happiest of my life."

"Mine too," Baldwin replied. "My love, I am going away for a day or two to think about what we should do next. I do not think we will be welcome at Lothair's court for much longer."

"You will come back, won't you?" Judith said. "Even if it is just to say goodbye."

"Of course I will. Why wouldn't I?"

"Going back to West Francia alone and leaving me in the protection of my cousin is just the sort of stupidly noble thing you would do."

Baldwin smiled. "Even now you can make me laugh! I promise, my love, I will be back in a few days."

∞∞∞

Judith missed Baldwin intensely while he was away. If he decided to return to West Francia she wondered how she would bear it. Waldrada was kind to her, inviting her to bathe in the warm springs with her and her ladies, but nothing could ease Judith's mood. Lothair was as charming as ever, but beneath the smiles, Judith could see Baldwin was right. They were starting to outstay their welcome. Worry kept her awake at night, lonely and cold in the luxurious bedchamber.

She found the cheerful bustle of Lothair's court hard to deal with and took to walking around Aachen, lost in her own thoughts. On one afternoon she even rode a little way out into the countryside. She tethered her horse and sent back her escort just wanting to be alone. For a long time she sat on the low hill, staring to the south. The realm of Mid Francia stretched away before her, forever it seemed. Somewhere way beyond the horizon were the high mountains Alfred and Athelwulf had once crossed on their journey from Rome. Athelwulf had crossed those and made his way through West Francia, never imagining that by the time he got back to Wessex he would have a new wife. Or had he? Judith realised she had no idea whether it was he or Charles who had first suggested the match. Without Athelwulf she might well have remained in the Abbey at Hasnon and would never have experienced the joys of the years in Wessex or her marriage to Baldwin. But she would never have experienced the pain of loss either. She decided that if Baldwin did return to his death in West Francia, she would return to Wessex. She could enter a nunnery there, so her wealth would endow a Wessex establishment, not a Frankish one. Judith sank her head into her hands, knowing what a hollow victory that would be.

"I was told I would find you here," a voice said, startling Judith from her brooding.

"Baldwin!" Judith leapt up, staring searchingly at him. His face was drawn and he looked older than he had done just a few days before.

"Shall we sit down," Baldwin said. "We need to talk."

"My dearest love, I shall support whatever you think best," Judith said, hoping she could get through this talk without crying. "For myself I just want us to be together, but you should not face eternal damnation for my sake. I am not worth it."

"Excommunication scares me more than almost anything," Baldwin said. "But there's something which scares me more: Being without you."

Judith's endeavours to keep the tears back failed, as she realised just how much this man loved her.

Baldwin put his arm around her. "I know I would not be without you for long. Your father would undoubtedly kill me. But even a few days, knowing I would never see you again, is unbearable. So, if you still want me-"

Judith kissed him before he could finish. "You fool, of course, I still want you."

"I may never be able to give you a home," Baldwin warned. "Thanks to the bishops I may not be able to give you much at all."

"Playing bishops off against each other," Judith said softly. "It's the easiest thing on Earth."

"What?" Baldwin looked puzzled.

Judith shook her head, although a thought was stirring in her. "It's just something Athelbald said once."

"Well, we've got no chance playing off the bishops," Baldwin said. "They're all going to do what your father wants. They're all under his control."

Judith nodded, staring thoughtfully to the south, thinking once again of the stories Alfred and Athelwulf had told her.

"I don't know what we will do now. Rurik has been warned against harbouring us, so I am not sure if we can even go there. With the stain of excommunication on me, I do not know who would welcome us. But if you truly still want me, we will stay together, although I don't know where we will go."

Judith was silent for a moment, before turning to Baldwin, her eyes shining. "I do," she said. "We are going to Rome."

"Rome?" Baldwin exclaimed. "My love, do you know how far

it is? Why would we go there?"

Judith flung her arms around his neck. "Think, Baldwin. Who is the one bishop my father cannot control?"

Baldwin's eyes widened and he stared at his determined looking wife. "You can't be serious."

"I have never been more serious," Judith replied. "We are going to petition the Pope."

Chapter six

Baldwin needed some convincing. "It's a very long way. Are you sure you can cope with such a journey?"

"Athelwulf managed it when he had seen more than fifty years and Alfred did the journey twice before he was seven years old. He was not the strongest of children. We are young and healthy. If they could do it, I am sure we can."

"Will the Pope even be willing to see us?" Baldwin asked.

"I think so," Judith replied. "Athelwulf gave many fine gifts to the Pope when he was there. I know it was a previous Pope in office, but it was only seven years ago. I am sure there will be many there who remember him. I am still his widow and Queen of Wessex."

"It is a long way to go, with no assurances of success. The Pope might side with your father."

"But if we have nowhere else to go, what do we have to lose?"

Baldwin looked down into Judith's eyes, her dark hair blowing around her face in the breeze. He gave a rueful shake of his head. "I am starting to realise that when you get that look on your face, your course of action is fixed in your mind and there will be no dissuading you."

Judith laughed. "My dearest, I do not wish to force any course of action that is abhorrent on you. But you should not face excommunication for my sake. You have said yourself we cannot stay here, so why not go to Rome? If the Pope supports us my father will have to back down. Or if he will not allow us back into West Francia, we can still be welcomed elsewhere.

Once you are free from the stain of excommunication another ruler would surely be pleased to gain a man such as yourself. We could come back here, or go to Rurik or Wessex even. Ethelbert would be glad of your experience against the Norsemen."

"Stop, Judith," Baldwin said with a laugh. "One plan at a time. If we go to Rome we will need money for the journey. I have very little, since I have no access to my lands."

"We will sell my jewels," Judith replied.

Baldwin frowned. "I don't like that. What sort of man takes his wife's jewels to live?"

"They are just jewels," Judith said. "I would rather not sell my betrothal and wedding rings, but the others are unimportant. We shall sell the jewels from my father first." Judith thought of the gifts he had lavished on her when she married Athelwulf. She would get a certain satisfaction in selling those to fund their journey. It irritated her that Charles had held on to much of her wealth, planning on using it to endow an abbey. She resolved that once her marriage to Baldwin had been recognised, she would retrieve it as a dowry. Realising Baldwin was still looking downcast, she gently stroked his cheek. "Once everything is settled, you can buy me many more and I will treasure them because they will be from you."

Baldwin smiled reluctantly. "Very well. I shall pray that one day I can provide everything you deserve. I am a poor husband at present."

"If I have your love, you have already given me the most precious of gifts. Truly everything else is unimportant."

Baldwin took her into his arms, giving her a lingering kiss. "And your love makes me the richest and most fortunate of men. This plan is madness itself, but no madder than our elopement. With you all things are possible. Even the Pope himself will helpless in the face of your determination."

∞∞∞

Lothair applauded their plan, concealing any relief he felt at ridding himself of his guests. For the remainder of their stay he hosted lavish feasts and presented them with some generous gifts which would greatly ease their finances on the journey.

Judith turned into a whirlwind of activity, bartering mercilessly with her jewels to gain the highest prices from the nobles of Middle Francia. She even sold many of her fine dresses. She ignored Baldwin's protests, saying it would be far easier to travel light and only the plainest of tunics would be needed on the journey.

Eventually they were ready and Judith took her leave of Waldrada. Lothair had announced that he would accompany them to the south of his realm and so it was with a huge entourage that they left Aachen in the spring. For some time Judith had been impatient to start their journey, but Baldwin had said there was no point. The snow would make the mountains impassable.

The journey south was a merry one, with all of the Middle Franks in a mischievous mood as they reflected gleefully on the foiled plans of the West Frankish king.

After nearly three weeks they arrived at Besancon, where they could join what the people of Wessex called the Via Francigena. It was a route which started in Canterbury and brought pilgrims through West Francia, over the mountains and into the Kingdom of Italy. It would take them all the way to Rome. At Besancon Lothair took his leave of them.

"I wish you every success, my dear cousin," Lothair said, kissing Judith on the cheek.

"Thank you for your hospitality," Judith replied. "We were in a desperate state indeed when we arrived. Your kindness will never be forgotten."

"I only hope one day I shall be in a position to repay you for your support," Baldwin said with a bow.

"My dear friend, I was honoured to receive you both and have greatly enjoyed your company these past months. I shall be eager to hear of your progress. If all goes well for you, I would be tempted to follow your example to sort my own marital issues."

Judith again felt a flicker of sympathy for Queen Teutburga, but it was not her place to comment.

"It is easy to find guides along the route and everyone is most welcoming to pilgrims," Lothair continued. "In any case, I have written a deposition for you." He handed Baldwin a scroll. "It instructs any in my realm or in the realm of my brother, the Emperor Louis to grant you whatever assistance or hospitality you need."

Judith and Baldwin thanked him again and with the cries of farewell echoing around them, they started their horses along the Via Francigena. They rode in silence to start with, Judith's thoughts often going to Athelwulf and Alfred, trying to imagine them riding along this very path. She knew it had been different for them. They had been accompanied by a huge entourage, while Judith and Baldwin were on their own, with only one extra horse to carry their belongings.

Much as Judith had enjoyed her days in Aachen, it was wonderful to be alone with Baldwin. They made the most of being able to travel at their own pace, stopping whenever the fancy took them. Upon arrival at Antifern, they found thermal spas, almost as impressive as the ones at Aachen.

"I think a few days rest would do us good," Baldwin said with a smile.

Judith flung her arms around his neck, already anticipating the chance to wash the grime of the journey from her body. As Lothair had promised, they found the people hospitable. They had decided not to reveal their rank unless it was necessary and at the spas Judith found it liberating to be an ordinary pilgrim, relaxing in the simple hospitality on offer.

Two days after leaving the spa they came early one evening to Losanna on the shores of a lake so huge that Judith was sure it must be the sea.

"No, the sea is a long way to the south," Baldwin told her. "I have seen it and we are nowhere near. This is Lake Lausanne."

They dismounted and let their horses drink from the lake. Baldwin put his arm around Judith, smiling at the look of amazement on her face, as the dark, still waters stretched out before them.

"There are the mountains we must cross," he said, pointing to the far side of the lake.

Judith's eyes had already been wide with wonder, but at the sight of the Alps she could only stare silently, as she took in the rocky crags rising before them. She had been aware that their way had been growing steadily hillier and had fancied herself already in the mountains. But as she looked at the towering pinnacles, she realised their climb had scarcely begun. They stretched into the dusky sky, seemingly endless. Her gaze moved upwards until she could make out the peaks, white against the deep blue sky.

"Is that snow?" she asked.

"Yes, they say it is always cold enough for snow on the tops, although the valleys should be clear by now."

Judith had grown up in the north of West Francia, where there were few hills to speak of. In Wessex she had become familiar with the rolling hills of that land, but nothing had prepared her for the sight of these mountains.

"Alfred tried to tell me of these once," she said. "But I had no idea how big they would be."

"The biggest in Christendom," Baldwin said.

"And we have to go over them?" Judith asked. "How will we do it?" The summits of the mountains looked treacherous with their combination of rock and ice. She wondered how Alfred had coped.

Baldwin laughed. "Don't worry, we don't have to go right over the top. There are valleys and passes to take us through. We shall employ a guide at the other side of the lake."

The horses finished their drink and Baldwin tethered them to a tree on a patch of grass. Judith wandered down to the water's edge, dipping her hand in the water. She gasped at how cold it was and looked again at the icy peaks of the mountains, now turning pink in the evening light. Baldwin stood behind her, his arms around her waist. She leant her head back against him.

"Oh, Baldwin, I have never seen anything so amazing in my life."

Baldwin kissed the top of her head. "You never cease to surprise me, my love. I feared you would find this journey so hard. All this travel, no comforts and yet still you can find wonders. I have seen these mountains before, but never have they looked as spectacular as they do now I am seeing them with you."

"So we are really going over?" Judith said, her eyes sparkling with excitement.

"We really are," Baldwin replied. "And on the other side is the Kingdom of Italy and the road to Rome."

Chapter seven

They spent a few nights on the far side of the lake, ensuring they had provisions for the long trek over the Alps. A local boy agreed to be their guide, an agreement he was all the more enthusiastic about when he saw the reward on offer.

"You are sure the passes are safe?" Baldwin asked. "I want no harm coming to my lady."

"Yes, my lord," the boy replied. "The King's messengers have already passed through a few weeks back, as have the Holy Father's and the Emperor's coming the other way."

"Which King?" Judith asked anxiously, wondering if her father's messengers were already proceeding them to Rome with her father's views on their marriage."

But the boy shrugged. The King could mean her father or Lothair. It could even mean Louis or another of Judith's brothers, Charles, both of whom held kingships.

There was a chill in the air as the next day Judith, Baldwin and their guide started up into the mountains. Both Judith and Baldwin were wrapped in their warmest cloaks and hoods, as they passed through meadows strewn with flowers, but the higher they climbed the more the crisp air seeped through.

But the heights they scaled and the clear air gave them stunning views back over Francia, making Judith exclaim in delight every time she turned. They were now further than Baldwin had ever been and were glad of their cheerful guide. It was a certainty that on their own, they would have been lost in the valleys.

The steep ways made progress slow and the further they went into the mountains, the fewer people they saw. Soon came the first night when they had to stop with no dwelling in sight. Baldwin and their guide set up a tent in a sheltered spot and built a fire to heat food and ale. The memories of that evening, snuggled in Baldwin's arms while the flames danced up into the black sky would be ones that Judith would always cherish. Even the cold night in the tent, covered with every cloak she owned, could not dampen her spirits. Baldwin stopped looking anxiously at her, but instead became increasingly proud. It was clear his wife was not to be daunted by anything.

The pass took them between the snow covered peaks, where it seemed that new sights awaited them all the time. Judith was fascinated by strange goat-like creatures they saw jumping from rock to rock, never once losing their footing. They noticed the tracks of both wolves and bears, but to everyone's relief, they had no encounters with the more dangerous wildlife. Their guide pointed at one of the peaks. "They say that is the highest mountain in the world."

Judith and Baldwin, staring at the white rocks disappearing into the clouds, could well believe him.

Despite the rocky terrain, the path was mostly good and followed a road which had been there since the days of the Romans. Some days after they started their climb into the mountains they came upon a tiny monastery and the Abbot came out to welcome them, bidding them stay the night. Their guide accepted eagerly, but Baldwin and Judith hesitated.

"We have been excommunicated, Father," Baldwin said. "I would be most glad for my wife to sleep in shelter this night, but we should not disgrace your order."

The Abbot looked at them in a puzzled fashion. "And what is your crime?" he asked.

"The crime I was accused of is the abduction and forced marriage of the widowed daughter of the King of West Francia.

We are journeying to Rome to ask the Holy Father to bless our union."

The Abbot was startled and bowed to Judith. "You are a Princess of West Francia? I bid you welcome, my lady. Who was your husband?"

"My first husband was King Athelwulf of Wessex," Judith replied.

The Abbot looked even more shocked. "Why, I believe I met him once, my lady. Did he not pass through these mountains on holy pilgrimage to Rome?"

"That is so," Judith replied. "It was before our marriage."

The Abbot looked up. Dark clouds were amassing in the sky and it was obvious a rainstorm was brewing. Baldwin tried not to look anxious as he followed the Abbot's gaze.

"Your late husband was a most god fearing man. I enjoyed my talks with him immensely," he said. "I cannot allow his wife to spend a night in the open, particularly when the night promises to be as wild as this. I appreciate your honesty, but I still bid you most welcome."

With the first huge drops of rain starting to fall, Judith and Baldwin accepted his offer with relief. They were taken to the tiny guest chamber, their guide assuring them he would be happy to sleep before the fire in the refectory.

"I fear it is poor accommodation for a Queen," the Abbot said. "But the holy mother of God once slept in poorer."

Judith looked at the pallet, guessing it would be as lumpy as the one she had slept on as a girl before her marriage, but she smiled warmly at the Abbot. "Father, I have slept in many places since fleeing my father's realm. I have learnt that if the welcome is warm, the accommodation is fine indeed. I heartily thank you for your hospitality."

The rain hung over the mountains for several days and the Abbot insisted they remain. "Many a traveller has fallen grievously ill after trying to journey in such treacherous conditions."

Although they were eager to continue with their journey,

both Judith and Baldwin were glad of a few days rest and gladder still they were not out in the torrential rain. When Baldwin ventured out to see to their horses, he reported that the path was treacherous with mud and there might well be a risk of landslides.

∞∞∞

As the skies cleared, the guide announced it would be safe to resume their journey. They left behind a generous gift for the monastery and bade farewell to the Abbot and the monks.

"I shall keep you both in my prayers," the Abbot said. "I hope your pilgrimage proves successful. Marriage is a most holy sacrament, but it does not seem to be one you have entered lightly. I believe your union should be respected by all."

As they continued on their journey, they had never been so glad of their guide. He often went ahead of them to check the path was safe, before allowing them to proceed. They did not pass any further settlements and again Baldwin and the boy erected a tent for the next few nights. The snowy peaks still loomed over them, but Judith felt it was not as cold as it had been.

"We are starting to come down now," Baldwin told her.

Sure enough the next day brought them to Agusta, a town of ancient walls. The people welcomed the travellers and they spent a merry night with music under the starry sky. Their guide was well known in the town and was easily able to command accommodation for them. Despite the warm welcome, Baldwin was wary of revealing who they were. If their rank was guessed at, they could easily become a target for thieves. So Judith was able to mingle freely with the womenfolk of the town, enjoying the informal conversation and when the musicians started to play, she happily allowed Baldwin to pull her into a dance, not caring that her tunic was old or her hair tousled.

The next morning their guide took his leave of them. "Follow the stream," he told them. "It will bring you down from the mountains. I have no further knowledge of the road ahead, but you will find guides at Saint Martin's bridge in Pubei if you should need one."

Baldwin handed over the agreed payment. "Thank you, my friend," he said. "Your guidance has been much appreciated. I wish you a safe journey back."

"Thank you." Judith smiled, impulsively flinging her arms around the boy and kissing him on both cheeks. The boy went scarlet and mumbled his farewells, as he started his way back over the mountains.

The boy proved to be right. Although steep in places, it was an easy matter to follow the stream down. They camped near to an abbey the next night, gladly accepting food from the monks. But as the weather was fine, they decided not to try the conscience of the abbot by demanding entry to his foundation.

It was on the next day that the stream rounded a ridge and Baldwin reined in his horse, a grin of triumph on his face.

"There, Judith," he cried pointing ahead of him. "That is the Kingdom of Italy."

Judith cast one look back at the rugged mountains behind them. "We have crossed the Alps," she said in wonder. "I can scarce believe it." Looking at the lofty pinnacles, the ice glinting in the sunshine, it seemed impossible anyone could pass through. "And that is the Kingdom of Italy." Judith's eyes sparkled. "Oh my love, we are nearly at our journey's end."

Baldwin grinned and shook his head. "I am afraid we are nowhere near our journey's end," he said. "We have made good progress and the road should be easier from now on, but we still have a long way to go."

Chapter eight

They spent a few days at Pubei before crossing the river to start again on their way. Out of the mountains the early summer was warm and Judith found she did not mind the long ride, as the weather was so pleasant.

The ride took them along rivers and old roads. They mostly slept in a tent by the roadside, only venturing into dwellings if they were invited. A few weeks after coming down from the mountains they arrived in Pavia. By this time heartily tired of the dust from the road, Judith suggested they present their credentials at the imperial residence. As Judith's cousin, the Emperor Louis, was not there, they were welcomed by the Marquis of Lombardy who did not seem surprised to see them.

"The King's messengers passed through a month back," he said. "I heard of your marriage and your plans to go to Rome."

Judith looked anxiously at Baldwin. "My father will already have blackened our name to the Pope," she said. "Is our case hopeless, do you think?"

"Not necessarily," Baldwin replied. "His Holiness will need to hear from your father in any case. If he is as wise as I have heard, it will not matter whose version he hears first."

Judith couldn't help but smile at Baldwin's optimism. "It just seems my father is always one step ahead of us."

"My love, the fact that I am still alive and you are not in a nun's cell is proof we are one step ahead of him."

"His Holiness is indeed a most wise man," the Marquis said. "I cannot say if your petition will be successful, but the Pope will not be influenced by the will of the King of West Francia. He will judge your marriage according to God's laws."

Although welcoming, their host mostly left them to themselves. Serving women were provided to wash their travel-stained clothes and they were allowed to sleep in the Emperor's own chamber. Judith could easily have enjoyed the luxury longer, but the thought of her father's messengers already close to Rome made them both restless. After a few days they informed their host they would need to move on.

"I wish you both godspeed and good fortune with your mission," the man replied. "I shall order provisions to be packed for your journey."

"We heartily thank you for your generosity," Baldwin said, overwhelmed by the amount of food and flagons of wine being loaded onto their pack horse.

"The Emperor would be most eager to provide for his kinswoman. It has been an honour to receive you."

With such an overburdened horse, their progress for the next few days was slower. But Baldwin's spirits were high.

"I thought you would be more concerned by the thought of my father's messengers," Judith commented.

"We received a warm welcome in Pavia," Baldwin said. "That was interesting, was it not?"

"Why should a representative of my cousin not welcome me warmly?" Judith said. "Perhaps some of my family are kinder than you think."

"Some, perhaps," Baldwin said with a smile. "But not the Emperor. The Emperor, like his brother, Lothair, does not care for your father. By showing his support for us, he is sending a message of defiance to King Charles. If the Pope has been influenced, by your father's messengers, the support of the Emperor will counterbalance this."

Judith looked doubtful, but when they received a similar welcome in Piacenza, she began to think that Baldwin was right. Her own spirits rose, as they left that town with even more provisions and a generous gift from the Emperor.

∞∞∞

Now they were away from the mountains, there were more dwellings around for shelter. On their arrival in Aulla they were stunned to find a castle catering solely for pilgrims. There were other guests there, mostly those who had wintered in Rome and were now returning. They were happy to pass on many tips for the journey ahead. It was a joyous, informal atmosphere with a mixture of religious men and women, common people and nobles. To Judith's delight there was even a Wessex man present, who, once he got over his awe at meeting the Queen, was pleased to give news from his land, reporting that King Ethelbert and his brothers were all prospering.

The further south they went, the hotter the weather became. They took to rising early and finding a shady spot as the sun rose higher. Even though it greatly slowed their progress, those afternoons were pleasant, as they dozed under the tree or talked matters over while sharing a flagon of ale.

One afternoon Judith reined in her horse and stared into the distance. The sun was sparkling on a huge body of water. "Is that the sea?" she asked.

Baldwin looked in the direction she was pointing. "It looks like it. One of the men at Aulla said the road runs close to the coast for a short time."

Judith was stunned by the crystal clear waters at Luni, but what should have been a picturesque harbour was marred by the remains of charred buildings. Even the church was open to the sky.

"Was that a heathen attack?" Baldwin asked one of the fishermen, an olive skinned, dark haired man.

The man spat and nodded. "Last year they came with no warning. Burnt half the town and robbed our church."

Baldwin shook his head. "I have fought against them in West

Francia. Flanders, where I was raised, was often attacked. But we are near their homeland there. It is terrible indeed that they are coming so far south."

"They'll be attacking Rome itself next," the man said gloomily.

As Baldwin started describing some of the tactics he had used to fight off the Norsemen in the North, Judith wandered down to the water's edge. Even with the breeze off the sea, the day was becoming sweltering, the sun blazing out of a cloudless sky. She took off her mantle, lifting her hair to allow some air underneath. Kicking off her shoes she dipped her toes dubiously in the water. She was shocked. The seas she had seen off West Francia and Wessex were always cold. This sea felt pleasant. Lifting up the skirt of the tunic, she waded out to cool herself.

"What are you doing, Judith?"

She turned to see Baldwin watching her with amusement. He was finding it hard to believe that this bareheaded girl, her skirts lifted to her knee was the dignified daughter of a King of West Francia and one of the highest ranking women in Christendom.

"Have you ever felt a sea so warm?" she asked, oblivious to how she looked.

"I have seen this sea," Baldwin replied. "The Mediterranean makes up the south coast of West Francia."

He took off his own shoes and waded out to join her. Judith put her arms around him, not caring if the bottom of her tunic was trailing in the water and they stood together looking out over the sparkling sea. It seemed impossible to imagine that this tranquil scene had not so long ago been the site of a Norse raid.

∞∞∞

As the summer wore on, the amount of travelling they

were able to do by day became less. Desperate to reach their journey's end they tried once to ride on through the middle of the day. But the sun beating down on them made it unbearable. Judith felt light headed, her heart pounding in her ears.

"Baldwin, I am feeling faint," she said.

Baldwin reined in his horse and passed her a flagon of ale. He scanned the dusty road ahead. "Can you ride on a little way, my dearest? There is a settlement ahead."

The settlement turned out to be a small town named Lucca. They stopped at the first residence. It was an impressive villa with a columned façade, where they were greeted by a dark haired man.

"I am glad to welcome you here a while, or even to stay a night or two if you wish," the man said. "But you are pilgrims, I believe. You are most welcome, but I am not of your faith. My name is Moses ben Meshullan. I am a Jew. I will not be offended if you prefer to ride on to the church of San Giulia or San Frediano."

Judith's eyes widened. She did not think she had ever spoken to any who were not of her faith and wasn't sure how to respond. But Baldwin took Moses' hands. "If you are willing to offer us a bed for this night, my wife and I will be honoured to accept. Since you are not of our faith, I do not mind telling you we have been excommunicated. This lady is the daughter of the King of West Francia and we wed without his permission."

Over drinks and food provided by their kind host, Baldwin and Judith told Moses their story. He was delighted to be hosting a Frankish princess and when they departed the next day, they were overwhelmed by the gifts he urged on them.

"We are told other faiths are wrong, but Moses was so kind and welcoming," Judith remarked to Baldwin as they rode on.

"The faith may be wrong, but the man is not," Baldwin replied. "I have met many of other faiths. I have met other Jews. I have met heathen Norsemen. I have even once ridden on an envoy to the Moors, far to the south beyond the Kingdom of Aquitaine. I have found both good and bad men in all, just as in our own faith."

∞∞∞

From that point they avoided any further rides in the middle of the day, instead choosing to ride on late into the evening whenever the moon was bright enough. They were relieved when their route took them through a heavily forested area. They made good ground that day, spending the night in the walled village of San Gimignano.

Once they had passed Siena it became increasingly common for them to encounter other pilgrims. Occasionally they dismounted to walk alongside, enjoying the camaraderie of shared food and stories along the way. Baldwin even gave up his horse to an old man who was struggling in the heat as they rounded Lake Bolsena and brought him to the safety of an abbey where he could rest himself for a few days.

The summer was well advanced when they came to Sutri. Baldwin pointed out the liveried soldiers at one of the grander residences. "That is the Papal livery," he said. "This land must belong to the Pope."

"Does that mean that we will soon be there?" Judith asked. Never had she realised the journey would be so long. It occurred to her that if she had realised it, she would likely not have suggested such a venture.

"I believe so," Baldwin said. "A few more days I hope."

He was right. On the morning of the third day they came upon a small group of pilgrims chattering excitedly and pointing into the distance. They reined in their horses to see what was so interesting. A city was before them. In the haze they could see the shimmering shape of a basilica, bigger than any they had ever seen and near it, an obelisk rising into the sky, reaching it seemed almost to Heaven.

"Baldwin, is that… can that be…" Judith had tears in her eyes, and was unable to get the words out.

Baldwin too was silent for a long time. "Yes, my dearest," he breathed eventually. "That is Rome."

Judith shook her head in wonder. Of all the sights she had seen on their journey, none had been as awe-inspiring as the one they saw before them. "God be praised. We have made it."

Chapter nine

Entering the City of Rome was an exciting experience. The streets were filled with more people than Judith had ever seen. It was far busier than Winchester or even Paris. The city was crammed with churches and abbeys, yet Judith also saw many older building, including crumbling heathen temples and it seemed strange to her that these still existed in the most Christian of cities. The majority of the pilgrims entering Rome headed straight for the Basilica of Saint Peter to pray at the holy shrine. Many removed their shoes to make the final steps barefoot. Judith and Baldwin cast longing glances at the facade they had glimpsed from so far away, but they did not follow the other pilgrims. Until the sentence of excommunication had been lifted, they did not dare enter such a holy space.

"We need somewhere to stay," Baldwin said. "The Emperor has a residence here. We should go there."

"No," Judith said with a firm shake of her head. "I do not want to be here as a Princess of West Francia. I am the Queen of Wessex. We should stay in the Saxon Quarter."

"Is there such a thing?" Baldwin asked.

"There is," Judith replied. "It is known as the Schola Saxonum. Athelwulf stayed there when he was in Rome. Indeed he restored it after a fire had almost destroyed it. I am still his widow, so they can repay his generosity by granting us refuge."

Baldwin frowned. "I think the Emperor's accommodation

would be better. It will appear more prestigious."

"We will also be more likely to run into my father's messengers. I am not going there." She looked stubbornly at Baldwin. "Are you accompanying me to the Schola Saxonum or not?"

Baldwin did not look happy, but he whistled at a young boy who was stood nearby. "Can you bring myself and this lady to the Schola Saxonum?" he asked. "There will be a coin in it for you."

The boy was happy to oblige and led them to an area not far from the Basilica of Saint Peter, in the shadows of a huge castle. "That is the Castle of Sant Angelo," the boy told them. "Here the blessed Pope Gregory saw an angel on the roof."

"Does the Pope live there?" Judith asked, astounded by the sheer size of the castle.

"Not usually," the boy replied. "He would go there if Rome was under attack. And here is the Schola Saxonum."

The boy indicated a small church with a cluster of buildings around it. Baldwin thanked the boy and tossed him the promised coin. He looked at the buildings. It was still out of the question for them to enter the church. The other buildings seemed to be mostly houses, stables and stores, but one was clearly an ale house. They tethered their horses to a post and pushed open the door.

"If you need accommodation, you are out of luck," a voice called. "We are full."

In spite of the words, Judith smiled at the sound of a Wessex voice. She nodded at the man, obviously the host of the ale house, feeling instantly at home.

"I think you will find room for me and my husband," Judith announced. "I am the Queen of Wessex."

The man stared at her and grinned. "And I am his Holiness the Pope, Lady."

Judith gave the man a stern look. "No, my man. I am the Queen of Wessex. I was the wife of the great King Athelwulf, as well as his most noble son, King Athelbald. I am not accustomed to lack of belief."

Listen, Lady, I do not have time for this nonsense."

Judith extended her hand to display the fine rings she wore. "This was a betrothal ring from King Athelwulf and this was the ring he gave me on the day I became his wife," she said. "These ones are from King Athelbald."

The man shuffled, starting to look uncomfortable. Baldwin tugged on Judith's arm. "What is he saying?"

For a moment Judith was surprised. It had been so natural to slip back into the West Saxon tongue, she had forgotten she was speaking a foreign language.

"Where are the credentials from Lothair," Judith asked.

Baldwin passed them to her and she waved them airily in front of the man. "Perhaps you were not aware that the noble King Athelwulf married me on his way back from Rome. Before our marriage I was titled Princess Judith of West Francia. This is a deposition from my kinsman the King of Middle Francia. The Emperor Louis is another of my cousins."

The man's mouth dropped open and he fell to his knees. "My Lady Queen, please forgive me."

"Forgiveness is granted," Judith replied with a benevolent smile. She had forgotten how much she enjoyed being a queen. "I present to you my new husband, Count Baldwin, son of Audacer. I trust there will be no further problem finding us accommodation. After all, were it not for my late husband's generosity and patience, you would not have any space to offer anyone."

"That is so, my Lady Queen," the man stammered. "We all remember King Athelwulf with great reverence and affection. Naturally I will have quarters prepared immediately. Please, allow me to offer you and your husband some refreshment."

Graciously Judith inclined her head. "I thank you. Some food would be most welcome. Our horses are tethered outside. See to their stabling and take our packs to our quarters."

"Of course, my Lady Queen." The man hastily cleared a table where he set out a jug of ale and flat discs of bread and cheese.

"Will this be sufficient, my lady? Is there anything more you require?"

"No, that will be all for now," Judith replied, taking a seat.

"Lose the act, Judith," Baldwin said with a slight frown. "You have scared the man half to death."

"We needed somewhere to stay and now we have it," Judith said serenely.

Baldwin said nothing more and when the man returned, he appeared to have recovered from his fear. "Your quarters are ready, My Lady Queen," he said with a deep bow.

The chamber they were shown to was small, but comfortably furnished. "I hope this is adequate for you, my lady," the man said. "King Athelwulf slept here with his son, Prince Alfred."

Judith smiled, easily able to picture the two of them there. "Thank you, this is most pleasant."

The man backed out of the room. "Anything you need, my Lady Queen, my lord, just ask."

"I see why you wanted to come here," Baldwin commented. "You could not have lorded it over everyone in the emperor's palace."

Judith smiled, flinging herself down on the bed. She stretched out her arms to him and in spite of his disapproval, Baldwin was unable to resist going into them. "So this is it, my love. Journey's end," she said. "What now?"

Baldwin kissed her tenderly. "The hour draws late. We can do nothing more this night. In the morning we shall find out how to gain an audience with the Holy Father."

∞∞∞

When Judith had first announced that they should head to Rome, she had assumed it would be an easy matter to see the Pope when they arrived. But now they were there, they had no idea how to achieve such a thing. The Wessex priest at the Schola Saxonum suggested they present themselves at one of the Papal churches and make their intentions known, forcing Judith to confess that they had been excommunicated. The priest was taken aback but promised he would make some enquiries.

They spent a few days waiting, passing the time by exploring Rome. Of all the cities Judith had seen, none was so fascinating. On their fifth day in the city they were visited by a papal priest, who introduced himself as Father Benedetto. His manner was not encouraging, as he implied that the Pope had far more important matters to deal with.

"My husband, King Athelwulf, gave most generously to His Holiness, when he was in Rome," Judith commented. "It seems a poor repayment to give his widow so little welcome."

"I was not aware ties were attached to those gifts, my lady," the priest replied.

"There were not," Judith said with the queenliest dignity she could manage. "My husband gave those gifts freely, because of his great faith and generosity. But he was the finest of men, who always listened to petitioners, however humble. He spoke most favourably of his time in Rome and of his admiration for all he saw. It pains me greatly to think he was misled into believing the Holy Father's mercy and good judgement is available to all. If he had realised it, I believe he would have bestowed his gifts on a more deserving cause."

Father Benedetto shuffled, obviously realising it would not impress the West Saxons to find out that after their King's generosity, his widow had been shabbily treated. "Your late husband is held in high esteem here," he said. "I will honour his memory by speaking of you to my patron, Cardinal Giovanni. He may intercede for you with His Holiness."

Judith smiled with triumph as the priest left and flung herself into Baldwin's arms. "My dearest, we are one step closer to our aim," she cried. "I knew invoking Athelwulf's name would help us."

"You were correct," Baldwin replied.

Judith did not notice Baldwin's lack of enthusiasm, as she chattered on. "Athelbald was not happy at the cost of the gifts, Athelwulf gave the Pope. But they were worth it, were they not? I think without his generosity we would not stand a chance."

Baldwin shrugged, looking miserable.

"It is strange, I feel so close to him and Alfred here. Almost I can see them."

"Stop it, Judith," Baldwin cried suddenly.

Judith stared at him in shock.

"I have had enough," he snapped. "Since we got here, you have not stopped talking about your noble husband. How sorry I am that you now merely have me."

Chapter ten

Baldwin stormed from the room and after a few shocked moments Judith followed him. He was striding from the Schola Saxonum, making her run to keep him in sight. Eventually he stopped to sit on a low wall. As she paused to catch her breath, Judith stared at him. He cut a lonely figure, as he gazed longingly at the columns of Saint Peter's Basilica, which was so close yet as inaccessible to them as ever. Judith sat down next to him, reaching out to take his hand, but he stiffened and pulled it away.

"Baldwin, what have I done wrong?" Judith begged. "Please talk to me."

"I never thought to marry a widow," Baldwin said, almost as if he were speaking to himself rather than her. "I always assumed I would wed a maid. A woman who had known no man, but me."

Judith looked bewildered. "But you always knew I was a widow, even before we met. Why is this suddenly a problem now?"

"It did not seem to matter before. Oh, Judith, I know you have done nothing wrong. I have done everything wrong. King Athelwulf was a great man who was able to do so much for you. I should have buried my feelings for you back at Senlis. I had no right to touch you."

Judith was frightened by this speech. "You have done nothing wrong, my love. You rescued me from the life I hated."

"King Athelwulf and King Athelbald gave you the life and

position you wanted. The life you longed for. The life you still long for. I have been able to give you only disgrace and danger."

"That is not true. You have given me your love and protection. You have no idea how important that is for me."

"What has my protection done for you? I love you, Judith. I love you more than any man ever could, but I have not been able to give you all the things you deserve. I have given you no gifts, no title, no position."

"No, this is not true," Judith cried. "You gave me the sunset over the dark waters of Lake Lausanne, starry nights among snowy mountain peaks and the blazing sun sparkling off the Mediterranean Sea. If my father had approved our marriage we would have stayed in West Francia and I know we would have been happy, but I would never have seen these wonders."

"You paid for that journey by selling your jewels. I gave you nothing."

"But I could not have made such a journey without you." Judith reached for his hand once again. He allowed it to remain in hers, but his expression was still downcast.

"I can see how much you enjoy reigning over the Schola Saxonum," Baldwin said with a sad smile. "You were born to be a queen. With me you will never again know that respect. Even if our marriage is approved, our best hope is that you become a mere courtier at whatever court we attach ourselves to. I do not think you can ever be contented."

"If we are together, I will not care," Judith whispered. "Please, Baldwin. Do not speak this way."

As he looked at Judith, she could see the tears simmering in his eyes. "Even here King Athelwulf is more use to you than I am. It is only in his name that we can secure accommodation. He is the one who will gain you the audience with the Pope. Yet again, I am useless."

Judith gently put her arms around him, a lump coming to her throat. She felt thoroughly ashamed of herself. She had been so enjoying her reminiscences and the prestige which came with being Athelwulf's queen that she had not stopped to consider how Baldwin was feeling. She was a poor wife to not even notice how disheartened he was.

"You are right," she said. "I am enjoying being a queen again. But that is not why I came to Rome. If we see the Pope it will be to implore him to grant me the one title I truly want – your wife. My love, I am so sorry that I have not noticed your feelings. The love and care you have given me has been matched by no man and I have not repaid it at all. Tell me what you want us to do. We do not have to stay at the Schola Saxonum if you are not comfortable there."

Baldwin shrugged. "I am not uncomfortable. I just wish I was not so beholden to your first husband. I hate that he was able to give you everything you deserve and I cannot. I hate that even if our marriage is blessed by the Pope, it will only be because of him. Even dead, he is of more use to you than I am alive."

Judith considered his words. "Please do not begrudge Athelwulf his ability to do this," she said. "Looking back, I realise Athelwulf often felt guilty about our marriage. When he married a princess of West Francia he did not care about me. It was an arrangement for an alliance to benefit the two lands. Nothing more. But once we were wed, he got to know me and he started to like me."

"Of course he liked you," Baldwin replied. "Who could help it?"

"My own father does not like me," Judith retorted with a smile, but her mood quickly became serious again. "I was mostly contented enough, for I did not know then how a marriage could be. I did not truly know that until I married you. But Athelwulf knew how it should be between a man and a woman. The love we have, he shared with the Lady Osburh, his first wife. He came to care for me, but he was never in love with me. I believe he felt guilty that in arranging our marriage, he had taken from me the chance to enjoy a love such as ours."

Baldwin put his arm around Judith, understanding dawning on his face.

"I do not know if he would have approved of my marriage to

his son, but I know he would have liked you. He would be glad I had known true love and I think he would be proud that he has been able to help me here. I am sorry if this hurts you, but I cannot help but feel close to him here. It means so much to me to feel I have his blessing."

Baldwin looked at her. "Can you truly be happy just to be my wife? You will have to give up so much."

Judith smiled back. "Truly. Besides, I gave up nothing, but a miserable life in a monastery. You were happy in my brother's service. It is you who have given up everything to be with me."

"I do not regret it. I never believed it was possible to love a woman as I love you. But I fear I will always live in the shadow of those two kings who knew you first. How can you not find me lacking?"

"I understand you find it hard to love a widow." Tears came to Judith's eyes as she tried to find a way to reassure him. "I am sorry I was no untouched maid for you. It is true I gave Athelwulf and Athelbald my body, my affection and my respect, but I never gave them my heart. You are the only man who has had that and the only man who will ever have it. Oh, Baldwin, you are the man I have dreamt of my whole life. How could I find you lacking?" Judith looked up at him, relieved to see him smile. "Now, please tell me if you want us to find new accommodation. I like staying at the Schola Saxonum, but I will not stay there if it makes you unhappy. Whatever you decide, I promise I will not speak of my two husbands again."

"No, it would be foolish to move," Baldwin said, holding her closer. "Forgive me for my jealousy, my love. I did not mean to make you feel wrong for marrying before. Please do not feel that you cannot talk of them. Those two marriages are part of you. You should never have to keep any part of yourself from me."

Judith gave him a gentle smile. "I have one more reason to be grateful to Athelwulf and Athelbald. I do not think you would have much liked the arrogant Frankish princess who left Verberie with Athelwulf, but my marriages and the life they gave me in Wessex, changed me. Those two men helped me become a woman you could love. Of all the gifts they gave me, that one must surely rank among the greatest."

"Six years ago I too was very different. I was just a minor member of your father's entourage who had not yet even reached his notice. I do not think I was ready to love any woman back then. Judith, please speak of your husbands whenever you wish. I hope you can be contented in the life I give you, but whatever happens, it is right that you never forget them. I know that."

"As long as you also know that you are the man I love more than life itself, more even than my immortal soul."

Baldwin kissed her long and tenderly. "I am an undeserving fool, but you have my whole heart, always."

Chapter eleven

They received a message later that day to present themselves at the residence of Cardinal Giovanni. They set off hopefully hand in hand to make the short walk to his home, a sprawling one storey building just a stone's throw from the Basilica of Saint Peter. They were welcomed in by Father Benedetto and introduced to the Cardinal.

Judith disliked him on sight. He was a tall, thin man with cropped dark hair and eyes like tiny black pebbles. He looked them up and down, making a bored gesture to bid them both to rise. He did not ask them to be seated.

"I have spoken at great length on this matter with the messengers of the noble King Charles, as has His Holiness," the Cardinal said. "I do not see why I need to discuss this any further with you."

"We beg you most humbly for a short period of your time," Baldwin said.

"You are a mere count," the Cardinal snapped. "Why do you presume to know better than King Charles? You have abducted his daughter and forced her into a sinful life of licentiousness."

"Your Eminence, my wife and I do not see it as an abduction."

"Do not refer to that woman as your wife," Cardinal Giovanni said with a frown. "Your ceremony was illegal."

"Forgive me, Your Eminence, but I must disagree," Baldwin said desperately. "The union was witnessed by a priest and held in the presence of my w… the Queen's brother."

"You had no permission."

"But it was no abduction, Your Eminence," Judith said. "I attended the ceremony of my free choice."

"I do not wish to speak to you, Lady Queen." The Cardinal glared at Judith. "Your father's message made it plain what manner of a woman you have become. I do not doubt you are revelling in this life of sin."

Judith's face burnt, but she did not flinch before the man's eyes. "I was twice honourably married and now am honourably married a third time."

"I said be quiet." The Cardinal's voice rose. "It is most unsuitable for a widow to need to marry again. What of the vows you made to your first husband? You are an adulterer."

"It is not illegal for a widow to remarry," Baldwin pleaded. "And I want nothing more than to receive her father's blessing."

"She needs to be returned to her father, so she can take her place in an abbey as befits a widowed woman. Until you carry out this honourable act, your sentence of excommunication will remain. You are abhorrent to both God and man."

"Please, Father," Judith begged. "Listen to us. I mean no disrespect to my late husbands."

"I have ordered you to be silent," the Cardinal spat. "You have heard my decision."

"No," Judith cried. "You do not understand. I was married to my first husband when I was little more than a child, yet I ever tried to be a good wife. Why is it so terrible to marry again for love?"

"For lust," the Cardinal said. "Your father's assessment of your character was correct."

"No, for love," Judith retorted, ignoring Baldwin's tug on her arm. "Please permit us to speak with the Holy Father. He is the one who must make the final decision. That is all we ask."

"I shall not let you disgrace the presence of His Holiness. He is already aware of your father's will and needs no further discussion." The Cardinal got to his feet. "Now remove yourselves from my residence. Your presence disgusts me.

Return to face the justice of King Charles and may God have mercy on your souls."

"My father is a cruel man and so are you," Judith cried. "May God have mercy on yours."

"Judith," Baldwin broke in. "You cannot speak to the cardinal in this way."

Judith stopped, aghast at herself. "Forgive me, Your Eminence. I did not mean-"

"You, my lady, are a disgrace to West Francia and all Christendom. Go back to your father. And you," he turned to Baldwin, "try to keep your concubine under control while she remains in your protection."

As the Cardinal swept away from them Judith burst into tears. Baldwin took her into his arms and held her very tightly.

"I am sorry," she sobbed. "I have ruined everything."

"No, my love. He had already decided against us."

"I never learnt to control my temper. You must despise me."

"Of course I don't. I would never despise you. You should not have spoken in that way, but it made no difference. He condemned us the moment he heard from your father. He does not think widows should remarry."

"It is unfair. Widows and widowers remarry all the time. Athelwulf was a widower when he married me, but no one condemned him. Why is everyone against us?"

"I don't know," Baldwin said, stroking Judith's hair.

"What do we do now?" Judith asked.

"I have no idea." Baldwin bit his lip. "Our funds are running short. I don't know where to turn next."

Judith looked desolately at Baldwin, terrified of the future.

"My lord, my lady," said a soft voice.

They had forgotten Father Benedetto was still there. He was clearly waiting for them to leave.

"Thank you for your help, Father," Baldwin said.

"I am sorry matters did not go as you wished," the man replied.

Unable to speak further, Baldwin nodded to him. With

his arm around Judith they walked slowly along the ancient street. Neither said a word and neither looked back, but Father Benedetto stared thoughtfully after them.

∞∞∞

It was a miserable night. Both Judith and Baldwin merely picked at their meal that evening. When they retired to their chamber they put their arms tightly around each other and lay without talking. Judith slept intermittently, occasionally drifting into troubled dreams.

The next morning there was none of their usual light-hearted conversation. They remained silently in their chamber, having no idea of what to do or where to go. Judith struggled to even look at Baldwin, knowing that looking into his eyes would destroy her composure. She was sure if she started weeping that day, she would be unable ever to stop.

A firm knock on their chamber door made them both start. Wearily Baldwin got to his feet to pull open the door.

"Father Benedetto?" The Priest was the last man he had expected. "Welcome, Father. What brings you this way?"

Judith had been sitting downcast on the bed, but as the Priest entered she got up, forcing a smile of welcome to her face.

"I bring you commands from His Holiness, Pope Nicholas," Benedetto said.

Judith and Baldwin both waited for the order to leave Rome, but the man smiled at their anxious faces.

"His Holiness requests you attend mass in Saint Peter's Basilica at noon this day. Afterwards he will talk to you both."

"But Cardinal Giovanni said he would not admit us to the presence of the Holy Father," Baldwin exclaimed.

"Cardinal Giovanni is not the only man who can talk to His Holiness," Father Benedetto said. "He sent me to an audience with the Pope on some other matters. I took it upon myself to tell the Holy Father you were here. He remembers your first husband, King Athelwulf, very fondly, my lady. He would be most interested to meet you."

"And we can attend mass?" Judith let out a trembling breath. When she had been ruled by the cloister bell in the abbey, she would never have believed she would miss attending mass as much as she did.

"That was His Holiness' command."

Baldwin and Judith looked at each other, hope coming to their eyes. "Thank you, Father, for your intercession." Baldwin withdrew some coins from his pouch. "Please take these for your charities. I wish I could give you more."

"Speak to the Holy Father first, my son," Father Benedetto said. "If your petition is successful I will be glad to use such monies for the poor. But if it is not, I think you will need your funds for yourselves."

The Priest turned his eyes sternly to Judith. "And you, my daughter, should watch your tongue when you speak to the Holy Father. Such an outburst as you made yesterday would not be appropriate."

Judith blushed, while Baldwin failed to stifle his snort of laughter. The Priest kept his eyes fixed disapprovingly on her, but there was a tremor at the corner of his mouth and Judith realised he disliked the odious cardinal as much as she had.

Chapter twelve

When Judith joined Baldwin in the ale house late that morning, he almost burst out laughing at the sight of her. There was no sign of the wild haired, pink cheeked creature who had crossed the Alps with him in this demure, grey-clad young woman, her dark hair concealed under a mantle. He took her by the shoulders. "You look-"

"If you tell me I look beautiful, I shall never again believe you when you compliment me," Judith warned.

"Proper," Baldwin finished with a smile.

Judith ground her teeth, profoundly irritated by how well the subdued colours suited Baldwin. His hair had been bleached even blonder by the scorching sun and it gleamed against his dark tunic, while his blue eyes sparkled in his tanned face. "Damn you, Baldwin, how do you manage to be more handsome than ever in such drabbery?"

Baldwin grinned, his decidedly smug look making Judith laugh in spite of her irritation. But Baldwin's smile faded and he looked seriously at his wife. "You will be careful how you talk to the Pope, won't you?"

Judith nodded. "Yes, I swear it. I won't say a word unless he speaks to me first. I won't disgrace you."

"Judith, one of the things I love most about you, is the way you have no fear of speaking your mind. If circumstances had been different yesterday, I would have been applauding you. But not today."

"I got into the habit of speaking my mind so freely when I

married Athelbald," Judith said wryly. "Believe it or not, before I married him I was beautifully mannered and exceptionally well behaved."

"I struggle to imagine you as well behaved," Baldwin said, ignoring the indignant look Judith flung him. "Come, we should go."

They left the gate of the Schola Saxonum, looking to where the columns of Saint Peter's Basilica rose before them. Judith stopped. "Wait, Baldwin. This is truly journey's end. We should complete it barefoot, as pilgrims."

Judith tugged off her shoes, the stones feeling pleasantly warm under her bare feet. Baldwin had done the same and they made their way solemnly towards the Basilica. As they entered the gateway to the square before it, Judith felt as if a weight had been lifted from her. At last she was being accepted back into the church. However she also felt a surge of nerves at the task awaiting them. She looked up at the towering obelisk they had viewed from afar, knowing the success of those months of travel rested on this visit.

The bell began to toll as they crossed the square and the people milling around the fountain headed to the columned atrium of the basilica. Judith and Baldwin joined them, mingling among the other pilgrims. Inside it was cool and it took a few moments for Judith's eyes to adapt to the dim light. The interior was lit by candles, which would illuminate the church on a cloudy day, but seemed almost feeble after the blazing sun outside. In a quick glance she took in rows of columns and walls lined with statues, frescos and mosaics. She would have liked to look at those for longer, but they needed to keep moving as scores of people entered the basilica behind them. There seemed no end to the numbers of pilgrims, yet still it was not even half full. Judith remembered the stories she had heard of the crowds of people who had attended the crowning of her great-grandfather in this very place. She had not believed them until that moment. At the end of the Basilica was a raised altar, richly adorned, and Judith and Baldwin were not alone in staring at it in awe. It was the tomb of Saint Peter himself and the place all these pilgrims had come to see. In that instant Judith forgot their own mission as the ancient tomb held her gaze, overwhelmed to be in the presence of the holiest of relics.

Judith's rank meant they could take places close to the altar, but with unspoken agreement they simply filed into place with the other pilgrims and stood with their heads bowed, waiting for the mass to begin.

A smell of incense heralded the arrival of the pontiff. He led a procession of priests and monks, swinging his censer as he walked. Judith stole a swift look as he walked close to where they were standing. He was clean shaven, with the papal crown over a fringe of wavy, grey hair. His embroidered white robes swept along the floor as he walked and his face was serene. Behind him, she was relieved to see Father Benedetto and even more relieved there was no sign of Cardinal Giovanni. She bowed her head again as the Pope reached the altar and lifted the cross. Everyone fell to their knees.

"Te Deum laudamus," he started the mass, his voice echoing powerfully throughout the basilica.

Like all the other pilgrims, Judith gazed adoringly at him. The words of the mass were so familiar she could have recited them herself, yet here in this sacred spot they seemed to take on a new meaning.

When it was time to receive the host, Judith and Baldwin joined the long line of worshippers kneeling before the Pope. As the wafer was put into her mouth and she took a sip of the wine, Judith felt more at peace than she had in years. Whatever happened now, her soul belonged once more to God. Father Benedetto was assisting in the mass, but there was no sign of recognition on his face as he performed his duties. The Pope laid his hand on her head in blessing and then she followed Baldwin back to their space.

After the Pope had pronounced his final Benedictus, it seemed that everyone moved at once. Some made for the doorway, while others surged forward to kneel on the steps before the shrine. For a long time Judith and Baldwin stood still, not sure where to go. There was no sign of the Pope or Father Benedetto. As the throng around the altar cleared a little, they pressed forward to kneel before it. There Judith prayed with more earnestness than she ever had before.

"Blessed Saint Peter, look favourably on my marriage. Grant me the right to stay with my husband for as long as life keeps us here."

Both she and Baldwin were so intent on their prayers they did not notice the faint gasp of the other pilgrims. Even as they filed out, Judith and Baldwin remained oblivious to all. When they did raise their heads, they were startled to find all the worshippers had left, and even more surprised to see the Pope standing behind the altar. Up close they realised he was a diminutive man, but in his white robes and papal regalia he managed an air of indescribable majesty.

"Queen Judith and Count Baldwin, I believe," The Pope said with a gentle smile. "Allow me to present myself. I am Pope Nicholas."

Judith and Baldwin remained on their knees. "Please forgive us, Holy Father, for not noticing your presence," Baldwin exclaimed.

"You were intent on your devotions," the Pope replied. "I am not surprised. I am here on an almost daily basis and yet still this sacred shrine awes me. I believe this is the first time you have seen it and of course, this is the first time you have entered a church in some months."

"Yes, Father," Baldwin said.

"Please rise and come this way," Pope Nicholas said. "We have some weighty matters to discuss."

Judith cast an anxious glance at Baldwin as they followed the man who had the power to decide their future once and for all. He tried to give her a reassuring smile, but in truth Baldwin was as nervous as she was. They entered a small chamber, where the Pope took a seat in an elaborately carved chair and gestured to two other chairs.

"Please be seated," he said. "And take a drink."

Judith took a mouthful of wine, hoping it would calm her nerves. Not daring to meet the Pope's eyes her gaze settled on one of the fine rings he was wearing. One of her rare childhood memories of her father stirred, as she remembered him sending a chest of costly gifts to the Pope then in office. Nervously she wondered how she could ever hope to compete with the influence of a man who could bestow such riches.

Chapter thirteen

"I met your husband, King Athelwulf, many times when he was in Rome," Pope Nicholas said. "He was a godfearing and learned man."

"Yes, Holy Father," Judith replied. "I missed him most terribly when he died."

"No doubt you knew his son, young Prince Alfred," the Pope continued. "He was much admired here for his intelligence, despite his tender years. My predecessor considered him the closest he would get to a son of his own."

"Alfred was that to me too, Father." Judith kept her voice even, but the Pope gave her a sympathetic smile, as if he realised how hard it had been for Judith to leave him.

"I always expected to see him back here one day. Do you think that will happen?"

"I am not sure, Father," Judith said. "I believe he is being prepared for leadership in Wessex, although his brother, my late husband, King Athelbald, often used to joke that Alfred might one day…" It occurred rather late to Judith that the present incumbent might not be the best person to share Athelbald's joke. "Reach high episcopal office," she finished lamely, not daring to look at Baldwin.

"Was the word King Athelbald used, 'pope'?" the pontiff inquired.

"Forgive me, Father, he meant no offence." Judith stole a frightened look upwards, surprised to see the Pope's eyes twinkling.

"No forgiveness is needed, my daughter. No man lives forever and I most certainly shall not. Somewhere, out in Christendom, there are indeed intelligent young boys who will one day grace this office. It may have been a jest, but it would not surprise me in the slightest if Alfred proved to be such a one, although of course it may be that Wessex will need him more."

Judith gave a nervous smile and sipped some more of her wine.

"Now, to the matter in hand. Your father communicated to me the most grievous news that his widowed daughter had been abducted by a ruthless young count. He was indeed saddened when Archbishop Hincmar was forced to excommunicate you, but he hoped such an act would bring you to your senses and encourage you to extricate yourself from such a sinful union. I believe you do not see it that way."

"No, Father. I attended the church at Senlis of my own volition where I was most honourably bound to Count Baldwin in marriage."

"But you did not have your father's permission."

"It is true that I am guilty of deceiving my father. I am willing to do penance for it, but I still hold that my marriage is a true one."

"It is not illegal for widows to remarry, but it is not something we encourage. It does appear to be wrong in light of the vows you made to your first husband," Pope Nicholas said. "Of course your first marriage was to a man of advanced years and was very brief. I sympathise with your wish to marry again. But your second was to a young man. A third marriage does seem excessive."

"My second marriage was not much longer than my first, Father," Judith said quietly.

"But a nunnery would have been more appropriate after his death, my daughter. I must question why you are so unwilling to carry out God's work."

"I am not unwilling, Father," Judith said, trying not to weep.

"But I can carry out God's work as a wife. I have ever striven to bring a god-fearing nature to my household. I worked closely in Winchester with my husband and Bishop Swithun to achieve that aim." Prudently she decided not to mention the more lax atmosphere of Sherborne.

The Pope nodded and smiled at her in a kindly fashion, but as he turned to Baldwin, she was not certain whether he was agreeing with her.

"You are an exceptionally bold young man to be eloping with a daughter of the King of West Francia," he commented.

"I know," Baldwin said with a wry smile. "And I hope one day to most heartily beg his pardon. Queen Judith is worthy of better, I know. But I did not abduct her. We both made our vows willingly and before God.

"What were you doing before your union with Queen Judith?"

"I was in the household of her most noble brother, King Louis of Neustria. We were much occupied in securing the coast against the heathen raiders. Before that, I was attached to King Charles himself and often engaged in a similar task."

The Pope shook his head, his face becoming more solemn than ever. "These heathen raiders are becoming more threatening with each passing year. They have even raided the coast a little north of here."

"On our journey we saw the signs of such attacks," Baldwin said. "It is terrible indeed to think they have come so close to this holy city. I grew up in Flanders, where we suffered most grievously. I was engaged in fighting them from an early age."

It seemed to Judith the Pope had forgotten about the question of their marriage as he discussed the Norse problem at great length with Baldwin.

"Your suggestions as to how to deal with this threat are very interesting," the Pope said eventually. "They are ideas I should discuss with the Emperor. If I was to approve your marriage, what would your plans be?"

"I would hope we could return to West Francia and that

King Charles will forgive us. I would like my lands restored so I may provide adequately for my wife and would also wish to continue to serve King Charles as both his loyal subject and his son by marriage," Baldwin replied. "But if he does not wish to welcome us into West Francia, I will offer my service to any other good Christian king. I believe my experiences could make me valuable to any who are suffering from the heathen attacks."

"And if I do not approve your marriage?"

Baldwin was silent for a long time, but he fixed his blue eyes determinedly on the Pope. Suddenly there was nothing nervous about him. "Father, it will grieve me greatly to go against your wishes, but there is nothing you can say to convince me my marriage is not a true one. In marriage I took on a sacred obligation to provide for my wife and it is one I must fulfil. If no Christian king is willing to accept us, I must take my services elsewhere."

"You would live and fight among heathens?" the Pope asked after a stunned silence.

"If Christendom casts us out, I shall have no choice."

Pope Nicholas stared at them both, while Judith tried surreptitiously to wipe her eyes. Baldwin reached for her hand, but he met the Pope's gaze without a hint of apology.

"Well, I have some thinking to do," the Pope said at last. "Please excuse me a moment, while I seek guidance. Help yourselves to some more refreshment. Those honey-cakes are very fine."

"I don't know why you worried about me speaking too forcefully," Judith said once the Pope had left the chamber. "You have practically declared war on him."

"You suggested setting a child onto his throne," Baldwin retorted.

"That was a jest," Judith replied. "He thought it amusing. He was not amused by you."

Baldwin shrugged. "I simply spoke the truth."

Judith leant her head against his shoulder, feeling incredibly proud that Baldwin had no fear of anyone, not even the Pope. She tried to nibble on one of the cakes, but although it undoubtedly was fine, she could not stomach it.

Pope Nicholas returned a while later bearing a vellum scroll. "No, no, don't get up," he said as he bustled into the room. He sat back down on his carved chair. "I have written a missive to King Charles, informing him that your marriage has my blessing and strongly advising him to accept it. In any case, you are now under my protection."

"Y...you are giving us your blessing?" Judith asked in surprise.

"I am, my daughter." He directed a kind smile at them. "I do not condone your actions. I consider it wrong that you wed without your father's permission and I hope you will both beg his forgiveness."

"We will," breathed Judith.

"However I believe strongly that once the marriage vows have been made, they should not be set aside. You are married in the eyes of the Heavenly Father. Your earthly father will have to accept this."

"Father, your blessing means more to us than I could possibly express," Baldwin said.

"I can see you two did not make your vows lightly, in spite of the covert nature. They should be upheld by both God and man." He frowned slightly at Baldwin. "And you, young man, can convey your gratitude by continuing to defend Christendom against the heathen scourge."

Baldwin grinned. "I will."

"If you do not want to return to West Francia, I can arrange for you to enter the Emperor's service. Our coast could most certainly use a warrior of your calibre."

"Thank you, Father, but I think my first duty should be to support my father by marriage. I hope in loyally serving him, I can atone for marrying his daughter without permission. If he has no need of my services, I would be honoured indeed to serve the Emperor."

"I think you are wise, my son," the Pope said. "This missive will be sent to West Francia at all speed. I understand you are short of funds, so please accept this." He placed a heavy bag of coins on the table.

"Father, that is too generous," Judith exclaimed.

"Your husband, King Athelwulf, gave most generously when he was here. This is a small repayment."

"I cannot accept a repayment," Judith said. "My husband gave his gifts freely, Father."

"And so do I, my child," the Pope smiled.

Baldwin took the coins. "Thank you, Father. It will greatly ease our return journey. But I shall consider this a loan. Once we are settled, I shall donate the repayments to the poor."

"You are indeed a most wise young man," the Pope said, getting to his feet. "I believe you are truly worthy of marriage into the House of West Francia and I hope King Charles appreciates his good fortune in gaining such a son. Take care of your wife."

Judith prepared to drop into a curtsey, but the Pope took her hands and kissed her on both cheeks. "And you, my Lady Countess, should consider this marriage your last."

Overjoyed to hear her rightful title, Judith abandoned her proper manner to fling her arms around the old Pope's neck. "Thank you, Father. It will be."

The Pope smiled and laid his hand on their heads in blessing. Judith and Baldwin walked slowly through the Basilica, pausing before the Shrine of Saint Peter to give their heartfelt thanks. Once out in the square they looked at each other, triumphant smiles bursting onto their faces as the realisation of what they had achieved dawned on them.

"We have done it," Judith cried. "No one can deny our marriage now, not even my father."

Baldwin swept Judith into his arms and spun her around, not caring how her mantle fell from her head and her hair flew wildly. The pilgrims and clergy who had lingered on by the fountain looked curiously at the jubilant pair. Setting Judith down, Baldwin grinned at them all. "This beautiful lady," he announced proudly, "is my wife!"

Chapter fourteen

With the year now advancing towards the autumn, Judith and Baldwin lingered on in Rome, while they waited to hear how Charles would respond to the papal command. As news of the Pope's blessing spread, many nobles and visiting dignitaries were eager to host them. The first to do this were the men of the Schola Saxonum, who threw a grand feast for them that very night. Many had sympathy for their young queen, who had been twice widowed and were overjoyed to see her happiness.

It was not until the spring, after the mountains cleared of snow, that they received word from Charles agreeing to forgive Baldwin and commanding them to return to West Francia. Remembering how long the journey had taken, Judith's heart almost failed her at the thought of the long trip back. But it turned out to be not so bad. Just as the people of Rome had celebrated their marriage, so too did the various abbeys and nobles whose domains they journeyed through.

In Lucca they were hosted again by Moses, the Jewish man who had welcomed them on their outward journey. He was delighted to hear of their success and invited many from the Jewish community for a celebration of their own. Judith was not sure if the Pope would have approved such a festivity, but for herself she joined in with joy. If she had learnt one thing since fleeing the monastery at Senlis, it was that welcome could come in many forms. Judith vowed that once she and Baldwin had a household of their own she would not forget this and would welcome any, so long as they came in peace.

It was well past midsummer before they started their climb to Agusta. As Baldwin consulted with the villagers, Judith looked back towards the Kingdom of Italy. It had been an incredible journey with sights she knew would linger on in her memories for the rest of her life.

The cool of the mountains was pleasant after their ride along the hot and dusty roads of the Kingdom of Italy and on the nights they were unable to find a shelter, Judith was glad to snuggle next to Baldwin in their tent.

"Look," their guide said pointing ahead after several days in the mountains. Beneath them the rocky mountainside met with a dark body of water stretching out to the horizon.

"Is it Lake Lausanne?" she asked.

The guide nodded.

"God be praised, we are through the Alps again," Baldwin said.

After showing them the correct path, their guide took his leave of them and it was with a mixture of relief and fear that Judith and Baldwin descended into Francia.

∞∞∞

Lake Lausanne was in Middle Francia and Baldwin, who was still nervous about his father-in-law's reaction, suggested they stay there, while they waited to hear the latest orders from King Charles. The Abbey was pleased to welcome them and a messenger was dispatched. Anxiously Judith waited to hear what her father had to say.

"Count Baldwin," the messenger announced on his return. "King Charles of West Francia commands you and Queen Judith to travel with all speed to the Abbey of Saint Germaine at Auxerre. There King Charles will assure himself you are married in the way the apostle has said is legal and suitable."

Judith frowned. "We are married. This has been affirmed by

the Pope. Why does my father require another ceremony?"

"These are the King's orders, my lady."

"Judith, it is fine," Baldwin replied.

"He is still denying our marriage."

"No, he isn't. With this ceremony, he is giving our union both his royal and paternal approval. Naturally we will do as he has said. The Abbot of Saint Germaine is your brother. There is no more fitting place to bestow his blessing."

"He is a brother I barely remember," Judith said. "He was sent away to a monastery as soon as my father realised he was crippled. I do not suppose he cares anything for me."

Judith could not hide her fears that this was a trap, but they put together an entourage and journeyed as they had been instructed to Auxerre. The abbey was a new building, lying close to the ancient cathedral. Judith's brother, the Abbot of Saint Germaine welcomed them formally and without recognition, introducing a group of the King's representatives who had been summoned to witness the ceremony.

The faces of the representatives were stern, leaving them in no doubt their actions were still considered disgraceful. Not to be daunted, Baldwin greeted each one with apparent pleasure, while Judith assumed her most regal manner as she extended her hand for each to kiss. All took her hand with polite formality, until she reached the last in the line.

"W...welcome back, Judith."

"Louis?" Judith gasped, overjoyed to see a friendly face. Her fears this might all be a trap vanished.

Louis hugged her and Baldwin, before looking in awe at them both. "Well, you two have caused a stir," he said. "Cousin Lothair? Rome? H...his Holiness himself?"

"Oh dear, was Father very angry with you?" she asked guiltily.

"F...furious." Louis grinned. "The B...bishop's messenger caught up with him as he was returning from his Christmas celebrations. I have never heard him yell so much! I kept my distance and m...made my escape to Neustria the next day. I didn't see him again for some time."

"Sounds sensible," Baldwin said.

"M...mind you, that was n...nothing compared to his rage when he got the message from His Holiness." Louis was almost choking with laughter. "I thought he was going to b...become a heathen on the spot!"

Judith too dissolved into giggles as she tried to picture the scene, tears of laughter streaming down her face.

Louis wiped his eyes and controlled himself, as the King's representatives looked disapprovingly at them. "F...Father Hincmar calmed him and convinced Father to accept the Pope's will, although he was not happy himself at having his sentence overturned." Louis looked at his brother-in-law. "R...really, Baldwin, the Pope? That was a bold step even for you."

Baldwin grinned. "Don't blame me for that one. That was all your sister's fault. Once she gets an idea in her head..."

"T...taken on more than you can handle, have you, Brother?" Louis asked with a sly look at Judith.

Baldwin laughed. "Absolutely!"

Judith gave him a look of mock fury, but was unable to withhold her smile. It was good to be home.

The Abbot coughed. "I wonder if you might keep the reunion for later, my brother," he said. "Our noble father is eager for the ceremony to take place."

Louis nodded, gesturing for Baldwin to go ahead of them into the church.

"Is Father here?" Judith asked nervously.

"Yes," Louis replied. "H...he will see you later as he is not coming to the ceremony. He said he had n...no stomach for it."

Judith almost collapsed back into laughter at that comment. With difficulty she restrained herself as Louis took her arm and led her towards the altar where Baldwin was already kneeling. She met his eyes as she knelt down beside him and nearly lost her composure again at the mischievous gleam in them. She sighed as she forced her mouth to remain solemn. Four weddings were excessive enough, but to have two of them to the same man was beyond ridiculous.

∞∞∞

After the ceremony a feast was served in the refectory. Of all the feasts held to celebrate their marriage, this was by far the most meagre. It was clear to Judith that her father's blessing was through gritted teeth. This was also the least enjoyable celebration. She was unable to relax over the meal, as she waited to be summoned to his presence.

"Do you know what Father's plans are?" Judith asked Louis.

"I think he p…plans to put Baldwin in charge of one of the Marches."

Baldwin set down his cup. "Really?" He looked delighted. "I shall be able to give you a home at last, my love," he said. "And although you are no longer a queen, a margravine is not so different."

"I don't care about that, Baldwin, really," Judith protested. "You know all I care about is being your wife."

"R…rubbish," Louis said. "You will love presiding over a court once again. You know you will."

Judith opened her mouth to protest, but Baldwin took her hand. "My love, if your father does such a thing it will be good for us both. I shall enjoy having lands again, so why should you not enjoy your role? I know you will fulfil it to perfection."

When the King's man summoned them, Judith and Baldwin went hand in hand. Charles was magnificently dressed, but his face as he stared at them was frozen. They knelt penitently down on the floor, with their heads bowed. Charles did not speak, but looked down at them out of eyes narrowed in fury.

"My Lord King," Baldwin said. "I humbly beg your forgiveness for my audacity in secretly marrying your fair daughter. I wish to affirm my most heartfelt desire to ever serve you in whatever capacity I can."

"Get up," Charles snapped. "Not you," he added as Judith

started to rise. She bit her lip and sank back down to the floor.

Baldwin frowned, but stood with his head bowed before the King.

"You both disgust me," Charles said. "I already knew of her character, but I thought you, Baldwin, had more sense. You have married a harlot. Even in a monastery she had no difficulty in finding a man. What does that tell you of her morals? If you leave her alone for more than a day or two, you can be sure that little slut will find another man to fill her bed."

Baldwin looked his father-in-law firmly in the eye. "My Lord King, I do most earnestly wish to serve you, but I will allow no man to say such things about my wife. Not even you."

Charles snorted. "Then let us quickly conclude our business. From this day, you, Baldwin, son of Audacer are titled Margrave of Flanders. You will have control of the March of Flanders, including but not limited to your existing lands, under my overlordship."

Baldwin's face lit up. He bowed deeply. "My Lord King, you do me a great honour. I shall endeavour always to fulfil my role to the best of my abilities."

Charles' lips set into a grim smile. "I wonder if you will consider it an honour when you are slaughtered by the Norsemen. You have not been in Flanders for some time and have no idea of the state it has fallen into. This is no honour. I fully expect the heathens to swiftly dispatch you." His eyes drifted down to where Judith was still kneeling on the floor. "When that happens, you will enter a nunnery and that will be the end of the trouble you cause."

"I still consider defending Flanders to be a great honour, my lord," Baldwin said quietly.

"Well, enjoy your honour, Baldwin. I shall have the charters sent to you as soon as is possible." Charles shook his head, the narrowed eyes making his distaste in his son-in-law obvious. "You are a fool. Your future in my service was bright, but you have thrown it away for a life with a barren slut of a wife. I trust she did tell you she is barren. She has already failed to give two husbands an heir. I have no idea why a man of your experience wanted to be the third. Until the Norsemen kill you, you will undoubtedly spend your days cursing your misfortune."

Without another word, Charles stalked away. Looking stunned, Baldwin pulled Judith back to her feet. "I shall prove him wrong," Baldwin maintained. "I will defeat the Norsemen and make Flanders prosperous once again."

Judith nodded and tried to smile despite the lump in her throat.

Baldwin looked at her in concern. "My dearest love, forget his words. This is wonderful news. I shall take you to Bruges. I have long wanted to show it to you. At last I shall be able to give you the home you deserve."

"You will give me a home, but he is right. I shall never give you a child." A tear trickled down Judith's cheek.

Baldwin put his arms around her. "We will be happy in Flanders. That is all that matters. Your father was wrong. I shall consider myself ever fortunate to have you at my side." Judith began to smile, as ever buoyed up by Baldwin's optimism. Baldwin's smile widened and he brought his lips to hers. "I am truly the most fortunate of men. After all, how many men do you know who get to enjoy not just one, but two wedding nights with the most beautiful lady in West Francia?"

Chapter fifteen

It was not until Christmas that Judith and Baldwin arrived in Flanders. They did not see Charles again, but Louis joined them for some of their journey north, until it was time for him to branch off for Neustria.

"Do you think Father will ever forgive me?" she asked Louis, as they prepared to go their separate ways.

"No," Louis replied. "He hates disobedience."

Judith gave a sad smile. She had been expecting Louis' answer, but it still hurt. "All I did was get married. Athelbald rebelled against Athelwulf. He tried to take his kingdom, but Athelwulf forgave him and always continued to love him."

"Those W…Wessex men were different to Father. You were fortunate to live among them." Louis smiled and gave his sister a hug. Baldwin was coming towards them. "I think you will find Flanders men to your liking too."

Judith's face brightened. "I think I will as well," she said, slipping an arm around her husband's waist.

"Take care of my sister," Louis said.

"Always," Baldwin replied. "Farewell, Louis. It has been good to see you again."

"We must meet again soon, p…perhaps in the autumn, to talk about the defence of the coast," Louis said, mounting his horse. "Farewell to you both."

Judith waved to her brother, before continuing their own journey. They made their way slowly, lingering often along the way until the King's messengers brought charters granting

Baldwin the rights to the March of Flanders. Baldwin was overjoyed at the extent of the lands which had been bestowed upon him. "Well, Countess of the March, it is truly time for us to go home."

"Indeed, my Lord Margrave, it most certainly is," Judith replied.

They were warmly received when they arrived in Flanders, but the most rapturous welcome of all came when they eventually made their entry into Bruges, a little settlement of boats and waterways which enchanted Judith from her first glimpse. The cheers of the people rang out on all sides. They had long petitioned King Charles to grant them a leader of their own, rather than being under the direct rule of West Francia and were delighted their wishes had finally been granted. The fact that the man chosen was Count Baldwin, one of their own people, ensured their joy was complete.

There were loud cheers too for his pretty Frankish countess. The story of everything Baldwin and Judith had gone through to be together had proceeded them and touched many hearts. Judith couldn't help but laugh as she realised she had become the heroine of a romantic tale, similar to the ones she had once listened to.

There was a small castle in the centre of the town which would be their main residence. As they dismounted, the chief burghers bowed to them and the Abbot delivered the formal welcome.

"Lord Baldwin, Count of the March of Flanders, on behalf of the abbeys, burghers and people of Flanders, I bid you and your noble countess welcome." The Abbot's face relaxed into a smile. "Son of Audacer, we are overjoyed by your return. Welcome home!"

"Thank you for your welcome, Father," Baldwin replied. "My Countess and I are delighted to be here."

One of the burghers bowed before Judith and presented her with the keys to the castle. Judith thanked the man and with a smile at Baldwin, she turned them in the lock. Never had she been so excited to arrive at a new home. Returning the smile, Baldwin pushed open the door. He took Judith by the hand and led her inside. The hall was small and dominated by a long wooden table upon which food and wine were laid out to welcome them. The chairs on the dais were covered in costly, but plain cloths and the walls were unadorned.

"I know this is not as grand as Verberie or Winchester," Baldwin said anxiously. "But we shall improve it."

Judith turned to look at him, her eyes sparkling. To the delight of the watching burghers, she flung herself into Baldwin's arms. "Baldwin, this is our home. It is the finest place in Christendom."

∞∞∞

They spent an idyllic spring in Bruges. As ever Judith threw herself into stamping her own mark on her new home. As she wove and stitched fine hangings for the walls she prayed that this time it would be a home she could enjoy for the rest of her life. Their journey provided plenty of inspiration for the tapestries and soon scenes of lakes and mountains filled the walls. Judith planned next to create one of the Holy City itself, while wondering if she could possibly do it justice. She enjoyed her memories as she worked but she did not wish herself back. After nearly two years of travelling, she was glad to be settled.

It was strange after so many months of being always in each other's company to now have their separate duties to carry out. Baldwin was busy dealing with the business of the March, but Judith could see how easily he grew into his role. She realised she had been naïve to think they could have continued indefinitely to be everything to each other. This life suited them well. Her days were full with the management of her household and she often received petitioners of her own. Reluctantly she admitted to herself that although she would have gone anywhere to be with Baldwin, she was glad not to be a courtier watching another woman reign over the household. As Athelwulf had once told her, she was born to adorn a court.

At the end of every day Baldwin returned and they presided over the meal in the hall, talking to visitors while musicians played. Each evening they retired to their chamber more happily than the last, still exchanging news from their day but as eager as ever for the night ahead.

Judith remembered her vow to repay the hospitality they had enjoyed on their journey and they welcomed many travellers and traders from the channel ports. Baldwin was especially pleased to welcome the first trader and after some amicable bargaining, he purchased a jewelled necklace which he ceremoniously presented to Judith, as the first of the replacements he was determined to bestow upon her.

But the idyll was brought to an abrupt end when news reached them of visitors of the most unwelcome kind - the Norsemen had attacked their coast. Baldwin summoned his men and prepared for defence. Judith watched him dressing on the morning of his departure, her heart breaking at the thought she might never see him again. His manner was calm and confident, but she knew how worried he was about the coastal settlements.

The prediction of her father rang in her ears. The thought that he would take Baldwin from her after all, filled her with an unspeakable terror.

"I suppose it is useless to tell you not to worry." Baldwin crouched down, taking hold of her hands.

"Yes," Judith replied, gripping them tightly.

Baldwin half smiled and kissed her forehead. "My love, we are not far from the coast here. If I cannot halt the heathens, you must flee inland. Promise me, Judith. I need to know you are safe."

"I promise, but..." Judith flung her arms around his neck. "Please be careful. Please come safely back to me."

"I shall do my best."

He stood up, stretching his hand out to her. Judith had

brought a relaxed manner to her household, but on that day she returned her bearing to the distantly regal manner of a princess of West Francia. Only with such a mask would she be able to bid Baldwin farewell without collapsing in tears. As the Countess of Flanders, she needed to display her total confidence in victory, just as Baldwin must not betray any fear. She looked at him, wondering if he felt any.

"Are you afraid, Baldwin?" she asked, just as they reached the door.

"Only a fool would not be," Baldwin replied. "I am not afraid to fight. I am not even much afraid to die, but I am terrified of what will happen to Flanders and to you if I fail. Such fear is not a weakness. It is a strength that will ever drive me on."

Putting a bright smile on her face as she bade farewell to Baldwin was one of the hardest things Judith had ever had to do. Accepting a brief kiss, when what she wanted to do was cling to him and never let him go, was almost impossible.

"Farewell, my lord husband," she said as he mounted his horse. "May God send you victory."

There was a slight tremor in her voice despite her best efforts and they stared at each other for a few moments, trying to put a lifetime of love into their gaze, before Baldwin urged his horse into a steady trot. The following men quickly obscured him from view and Judith's fists clenched as she made herself return calmly to the castle, trying very hard not to weep.

∞∞∞

The next weeks were difficult. The summer was warm, but for Judith an endless chill filled her heart. She managed to move around the castle by day with her usual assurance, but at night she gave up and cried herself to a sleep full of foreboding dreams. She awoke each morning terrified of what the day would bring.

Baldwin's messengers came back regularly. Judith received

each one with a feeling of sickness in her stomach and her heart thumping so loudly she could scarcely hear the man speak. She feared that the message would be to flee inland or worse, that Baldwin had been slain. But always the messages were positive, Baldwin's confidence ever shining through. Shortly before midsummer came one final message from him.

"My Lady Countess of the March of Flanders, I bring you greetings from your most noble husband the Margrave."

Judith relaxed her grip on the arms of the chair as the relief flowed through her once again.

"He bids you be of good cheer. The heathens have been driven back and have departed our coast."

The hall erupted into cheers and Judith felt tears welling in her eyes.

"He requests you prepare a celebration for three days hence when he and the men will return."

Judith gave up the attempt to remain composed. With tears and smiles she embraced the messenger, her mind already going to the grandest of celebrations.

∞∞∞

Three days later, bubbling with excitement, Judith dressed in a fine green dress and adorned herself with jewels as she prepared to welcome back her triumphant husband. The smells of a lavish banquet wafted through the castle as Judith waited for the day to pass in agonising slowness.

The sounds of faint cheers heralded the return long before there was any sign of the men. As the cheers got louder she took a jug of the costliest wine to the head of the table and began to pour it into cups.

When the cheers became deafening, Judith was unable to bear it any longer. She abandoned her task and ran to the doorway, just as Baldwin was striding in. The smile on the face of the victorious margrave was dazzling and Judith flung herself into his arms, her lips meeting his in a passionate kiss. For a long time they clung together.

"Welcome back, my love," she said. "I have so missed you."

"And I you, my dearest," Baldwin replied, kissing her again. "But I have done it. I kept Flanders safe."

"I am so proud of you," Judith said, her face radiant with joy. "Words cannot express how proud."

She took his hand to lead him to the table. Baldwin was still describing some of the battles they had fought, too buoyed up even to sit down, as Judith handed him a drink.

"I knew I would succeed in Flanders," Baldwin said, his smile wider than ever. "The Norsemen did not kill me. Your father was wrong about me."

Judith smiled back. "My father was wrong about me too."

Baldwin took a mouthful of his drink. "What do you mean, my love?"

Judith gazed at him, hardly able to believe the words she was about to utter. She had spent weeks denying the signs even to herself. "It seems," she said softly, "that I am not barren after all."

Baldwin set his cup back on the table, staring open-mouthed at Judith, all thoughts of his victories clearly going straight out of his head. "Judith, do you mean…"

Judith smoothed her dress so he could see how her stomach was just starting to swell. "I am with child, my love. We are going to have a child."

Baldwin gave a cry of joy and swept her up in his arms once again. "Oh Judith, my beautiful, beautiful Judith. I am truly the most fortunate man alive."

Judith laughed with him, feeling as if her heart would burst with happiness. She would never know why she had not conceived in her first two marriages or why it had taken two years with Baldwin. All she knew was that at last she had everything she had ever wanted.

Postscript – Year of our Lord 871

Lady of Flanders

Baldwin watched Judith with a slight smile as she darted around the hall, checking on the final preparations for the visit of her father. She was as elegantly dressed as ever in a blue over-dress, embroidered on the wide sleeves and hem with silver thread. The seven years since they had arrived in Bruges, combined with the rigours of childbearing, had brought subtle changes to both her face and body, but the opinion of all who came to Bruges was that the Countess of Flanders was an exceptionally attractive woman. The people of Flanders, who adored their countess, went further. They had taken to calling her Judith the Beautiful, a title which had Baldwin's wholehearted agreement.

As Baldwin's fortunes had increased over the years, the castle had been improved and the hall was considerably larger. He had managed to keep the Norsemen away from the coast and had been rewarded with more land by his father-in-law. The years had not been all kind to them. Their first child, a boy Judith named Charles in an effort to appease her father, had been sickly almost from birth and to their great sorrow had not lived to see out his third year. But they had been more fortunate in their subsequent children, resulting now in a family of three. Their two handsome sons, Baldwin aged five and Raoul aged three, dressed in blue tunics, waited impatiently to meet their grandfather. Both boys had inherited Judith's fine dark eyes, unlike their little sister Guinhilde. The dark haired, blue eyed little girl had been born in the autumn of the previous year and many were already saying she would be as fair as her mother one day. Perhaps there would be more children in the future, but even if there were not, Judith reflected proudly, these three lively children were a never ending source of joy for a woman who had once been sure she would remain childless.

The faint sounds of cheers reached them and Judith glanced at Baldwin with a touch of anxiety. She had not seen her father since her wedding in Auxerre and had no idea how he would greet her. It was surely impossible he could still consider her a slut. She and Baldwin were as devoted to each other as ever and there had not been one hint of a scandal about either of them in their days in Flanders. Baldwin had met Charles on several occasions. His loyal support of his father-in-law had won him much admiration and ironically he had become one of Charles' firm favourites. However Baldwin reported that although Charles enquired occasionally about their children, he had not once mentioned Judith.

"Everything is perfect, Judith," Baldwin said, putting his arms around her.

"It needs to be to impress my father," Judith muttered, still looking around the hall. It was smaller than those of the palaces of West Francia, but it emulated much of their elegance. Frescos and tapestries adorned the walls, while Baldwin's banners hung from the high ceiling.

"You know your father is not an easy man to please," Baldwin said gently. "Do not take it to heart if he is not. Just remember how proud I am of my beautiful wife."

A sound of horns alerted them to the arrival. Baldwin took Judith by the arm and followed by their two sons and a nurse carrying their daughter, they left the castle to greet him.

Charles was now a grey haired man, but there seemed to have been no diminishment of his strength. He continued to reign West Francia with a firm hand, riding regularly to the various parts of his realm. The realm had increased in size. Judith's cousin, Lothair, had died shortly after securing his much longed for divorce and Charles had wasted no time in declaring his children by Waldrada illegitimate. Much of Middle Francia had been annexed to West Francia and Archbishop Hincmar had crowned Charles at Metz. Ermentrude had also died a few years previously, leaving Charles free to marry a woman a little younger than Judith. Unsurprisingly she had already presented Charles with a daughter.

Judith had become reconciled with her mother shortly before she died. Ermentrude had been living in an abbey for her last few years, having finally turned against Charles when he executed her brother. Judith could never forget the pain of the day she had arrived at Verberie as a grieving widow, but she had forgiven it. She recognised that marriage to Charles of West Francia was a very different prospect to any of her own marriages. Her husbands had, in their different ways, all been strong-willed men, but none had wanted to break her own will. Even Athelbald, the most overbearing of the three, had much preferred a wife whose spirit was intact.

As Charles dismounted, Baldwin bowed and Judith sank into her deepest curtsey.

"Welcome to Bruges, my lord," Baldwin said.

"Thank you, my boy," Charles said jovially, taking Baldwin's hands. "I am delighted to be here. Are these your children?"

Charles had not even glanced at Judith. She stood awkwardly as Baldwin beckoned the boys forward and took his daughter from the arms of her nurse. "My lord, may I present my sons, Baldwin and Raoul and my daughter Guinhilde."

The two boys did them credit as they bowed before their grandfather, but to Judith's consternation, the baby simply removed her fist from her mouth and blew bubbles at him.

"That one is like her mother," Charles muttered darkly.

Baldwin grinned. "I hope so," he said, returning the baby to her nurse.

Charles patted the two boys on the head. "Fine children, my boy. Most fine. Shall we enter?"

Baldwin gave an anxious look at Judith, who had still not

been acknowledged. She gave a slight smile, trying not to show how this treatment was hurting her. As Charles took Baldwin's arm, she trailed uncertainly behind them. In the hall Charles looked around, obviously impressed by what he saw.

"You have done very well," he said to Baldwin. "I was shown the new town defences on my entry. It is all most impressive."

"Thank you, my lord," Baldwin replied. "But I have not achieved this alone. As you know there has been one at my side whose support has been beyond compare."

At this Charles could not avoid looking at Judith. His eyes were cold as she sank down into a deep curtsey once again and remained down, looking pleadingly up at her father. Baldwin frowned, hating the look of desperation on the face of his normally feisty and self-assured wife. His fists clenched and he was not sure what he would do if the King treated her with contempt. But Judith's humble attitude had a different effect on Charles. His face softened and he stretched out his hands to raise up his daughter.

"My dear Judith," he said, kissing her on each cheek. "It is indeed good to see you. Yes, you have both managed excellently here."

"Thank you, Father," Judith murmured, the warmth of this greeting beyond her wildest hopes.

"I have received many guests in West Francia who have come on from here," Charles continued. "All have been full of praise for the hospitality they have received from the fair Countess of Flanders. It makes me most proud."

Judith's face lit up and she was unable to speak. Baldwin came to her rescue. "You are rightfully proud, my lord and we are delighted you can now experience this hospitality for yourself. Would you care for some sustenance after your journey?" Baldwin gestured to the table. "There will be a feast in your honour this night, but Judith thought you might be in need of some refreshment now."

"Thank you, my dear child," Charles said. "That would certainly be most welcome."

Charles kept Judith's arm in his, while they made their way to the table. As Baldwin pulled out a chair, Charles looked at them. "Sit down with me," he ordered. "And send those children away. They are most fine, but they do not need to watch me eat."

Judith hid her smile as she gestured to the nurse to remove the children. She reflected that for a man who did not particularly care for children, Charles had sired rather a lot.

As they ate, Charles gave them news on Louis. In the early years he had been a frequent visitor to Bruges, but five years before he had been given the kingdom of Aquitaine in addition to Neustria and visits had become less common. Louis had married the same year as Judith and Baldwin's official wedding. He too had not sought permission from his father, but Charles had clearly understood that having another child petition the Pope would be ridiculous and so the union had been allowed to stand. He had several children, yet Charles continued to hint that the marriage should be put aside.

Charles drained his cup and set it down on the table. "Judith, do you remember that boy, who came with King Athelwulf to Verberie all those years ago? Alfred."

"Alfred?" Judith asked. "Of course I remember him." She realised Charles had never really understood the Wessex court if he thought Alfred had been a mere passing acquaintance. She had thought often of him over the years and always tried to get news from any Wessex visitors who passed through their land.

"It seems he is King of Wessex now," Charles said.

Judith's mouth opened in shock. She had been sorry to hear of Ethelbert's death a few years previously. And now Ethelred was also gone. She thought sadly of those four fine sons Athelwulf had been so proud of. Now only the youngest and frailest was left. Although as he must be in his early twenties, it seemed he was not as frail as she and Athelwulf had once feared.

"I think Alfred will rule well," she said. "Even as a boy, he was most wise."

"I hear he is a fine warrior," Charles added. "He has already had some success against the heathens during his brother's reign. Well, my boy, I think I would like to retire to my chamber now a while," he said to Baldwin.

Judith also got to her feet as Charles tucked his hand under Baldwin's arm. "Is Alfred wed yet?" she asked, hoping Alfred had gained a new family as he lost the last of his brothers.

"I believe so," Charles said, not looking particularly interested. "I heard he married a Mercian lady a few years back. I think they only have a daughter so far, but I expect there will be more."

Charles kissed Judith's cheek again before leaving the hall with Baldwin. Judith blinked back a few tears, feeling unexpectedly emotional at the show of affection. With their formidable grandfather gone, the children came to pick at the remains of the food. Judith watched them with a smile, as Baldwin returned to the hall, encircling her with his strong arms. She leant back against his chest, turning her head for a kiss.

"I never thought he would say he was proud of me," she said. "The only time he ever said that was when I married Athelwulf and that was only because I was doing what he wanted."

Baldwin tightened his arms around her. "The news from Wessex must bring back some memories."

Judith nodded. "In my mind Ethelred and Alfred are still young boys. But of course, Ethelred was a man with sons of his own. And Alfred? I can scarce believe he is a warrior and a king, a husband and a father…" Judith's voice trailed off, and she stared speculatively at her own children.

Baldwin grinned as he watched the familiar determined look spread over her face. "What are you planning, Judith?" he asked.

The look faded as Judith laughed. "Oh, I know such matters are years off yet, but would it really be so bad? Let me tell you, Baldwin, that a marriage with the House of Wessex can be an excellent prospect."

Baldwin smiled. "I am sure it is. And what would the House of Wessex say to this? Would they be happy for a marriage into Flanders?"

Judith put her arms around her husband and looked up into his sparkling blue eyes, her smile growing radiant. "As a Queen of Wessex, I can assure you there can be no finer destiny than marriage into the House of Flanders."

Some notes on names

It is a certainty that when King Æthelwulf of Wessex named his four oldest sons Æthelstan, Æthelbald, Æthelbert and Æthelred he was not considering the problems it would cause for the historical novelists of the future! As the A and E can be used interchangeably I decided to use the A for Athelwulf and Athelbald and the E for Ethelred and Ethelbert in this book to avoid confusion for both my readers and myself. In reality all of these kings had the same start to their names.

Every named character in this book really existed and took part in the events of this story. Records are not always complete and are particularly poor for Athelbald's reign, but as much as possible the characters here acted as the chronicles describe.

The one exception to this is the unsympathetic Cardinal Giovanni, who is fictional. There were several Cardinal Giovanni's around at that time, but this character is not meant to cast aspersions on any one of those. I am aware that in my books the ecclesiastical figures tend to be sympathetic characters – the tolerant Frank priest in 'The Girl from Brittia' and the kindly Abbot of Iona in 'Kenneth's Queen'. This book contains many ecclesiastical figures, who cover the whole range of beliefs and attitudes - The unworldly Saint Swithun, the more pragmatic Bishop Eahlstan, the strict theologian Archbishop Hincmar, the fair minded Pope Nicholas as well the intolerant Cardinal Giovanni. The character is fictional, but the beliefs he expressed are not.

Father Benedetto is the future Pope Benedict IV, who would have been a young man in Rome at this time. However the idea of him being the intermediary for Judith and Baldwin is my own invention.

Baldwin – a romantic hero or a cold hearted abductor?

The description of Judith's escape from Senlis in the Annals of St Bertin presents her as an active participant, but later Baldwin is described as her abductor. It is debated whether Baldwin was motivated by romance or ambition.

However while marriage into the Frank royal family may seem like an act of ambition, there was a high probability that such an act would result not in high office, but in execution. Charles the Bald was a remarkable king, but he was not an easy man. By the end of his life, he had quarrelled with most of those closest to him, including his sons, his first wife and even his great supporter, Archbishop Hincmar. Baldwin appears in his later life to be politically astute as well as a capable leader. He could undoubtedly have found better ways to gain favour with King Charles than abducting his daughter.

Charles' lack of tolerance for disobedience can most notably be seen in his treatment of his son Carlomann. A treatment which stands in stark contrast to Athelwulf's conciliatory actions following his son's rebellion. Carlomann was from an early age destined for the church, but like his sister, he appears to have had no liking for this role. His attempts to escape led to him being imprisoned, like Judith, at Senlis. Also like Judith he escaped, but his rebellion was short lived. He was tried and sentenced to death with his sentence commuted to being blinded. It seems Judith and Baldwin got off lightly. What would their fate have been if they had been apprehended before arriving at Lothair's court? His marriage to Judith could easily have ended in disaster.

Baldwin was a young man, probably no more than twenty-five when he met Judith. This young widowed princess must have appeared to him as a tragically romantic figure. There was no immediate political gain to the elopement, so it seems reasonable to believe the act was a romantic one. As Margrave of Flanders, Baldwin was a strong supporter of both Charles the Bald and later Louis the Stammerer and his sons were strong supporters of Louis' sons, although as grandsons of Charles the Bald they could easily have pushed their own claims. All in all, Baldwin comes across as an honourable man, willing to prove his worth to his wife's family. Not at all a ruthless, ambitious abductor.

The role of Louis in their story is interesting. Louis was little more than a boy, around 16 years old at the time of the elopement. He was never politically astute, but was a rather gentle people pleaser. It seems uncharacteristic for him to collude in the cold hearted abduction of his own sister and far easier to imagine him being swept up in the romance of the situation.

The truth will probably never be known, but given the lengths Judith and Baldwin went to in order to stay together, the probability remains that their story is a true Dark Ages love story. And it surely means that Flanders has the most romantic of all founding legends.

Some notes on dates

Judith is often described as 14 at the time of her marriage to Athelwulf, but this does not fit with the accepted date of her parent's marriage. It is possible that she was a year or even two years younger than she is presented here.

Another odd date is the Viking attack on Winchester. It is dated to the summer of 860, but to Ethelbert's reign not Athelbald's. But given that the only date I can find for Athelbald's death is December 860, this does not add up. Did Athelbald die earlier in the year? Was the year of the raid recorded wrongly? Or was there confusion over the reign because Ethelbert was already King of Kent and became King of Wessex later that year? Perhaps Athelbald was already ailing and Ethelbert had taken over many of his duties. The possibility of placing Judith at the scene of a Viking attack was too exciting for me to resist, so I included the event, but give credit to Ethelbert for defeating the Heathen Army.

Just as Judith's date of birth is not known, so too is the date of her death. There are no further records of her after the 870s, leading some historians to think she died then, but this cannot be certain. Records of women are few, so it is possible she lived on in historical obscurity. And in the 890s something interesting happened – the ties between Judith's family and the House of Wessex reasserted themselves, in the marriage of Judith's eldest son, Baldwin and Alfred's youngest daughter, Ælfthryth. The birth of their son, Arnulf, resulted at last in a common descendant for Judith and Baldwin, Alfred and Athelwulf.

This marriage raises the tantalising possibility that Judith was still alive at this point and used her Wessex connections to arrange the marriage. Whatever the truth, it is certainly nice to think that in agreeing to the match, Alfred remembered his former stepmother and sister-in-law with some affection. And that Judith was there to welcome Athelwulf's young granddaughter to her new life.

Women of the Dark Ages

More than a thousand years before today was a fabulous period where history and legend collided to form what is often known as the Dark Ages. Peering through the mists of time figures emerge, often insubstantially becoming as much legendary as historical. And if the men are hard to see, the women are even harder. Each of the books in the Women on the Dark Ages series tells the stories of the forgotten or uncelebrated, but very remarkable women who lived through these tumultuous times.

The Saxon Marriage

The story of Eadgyth of Wessex and her marriage to Otto, the young Hope of Saxony.

God's Maidservant

Treachery, tragedy and triumph – the story of Adelaide of Italy, one of the tenth century's most remarkable women.

Dawn Of The Franks

Bitter betrayal, forbidden love and the visions sent by the Gods as Queen Basina of Thuringia seeks her destiny.

Kenneth's Queen

The tale of the unknown wife of Scottish king, Kenneth Mac

Alpin.

The Girl From Brittia

The curious tale of a sixth century warrior princess, known only as The Island Girl.

Quest for New England

It is the 1070s, England is reeling from the Conquest and an epic voyage is about to begin...

1066 is probably the most famous date in English history and we all know what happened. Duke William of Normandy invaded England, winning a decisive victory at the Battle of Hastings, bringing as end to the Anglo-Saxon era.

But not all Anglo-Saxons were quietly absorbed into the regime. There were rebellions and when these failed, some preferred exile over submission. The Quest for New England trilogy is based on a true story, following a large group of Anglo-Saxons in their search for a place to call home.

Rising From The Ruins

After the defeat at Hastings, the failure of rebellions and the devastation of the North, England desperately needs a new hero. Will Siward of Gloucester be that man?

Peril & Plunder

Siward and his Anglo-Saxon exiles have escaped England, but can they escape the ghosts of the past. Can they even escape the Normans?

Courage Of The Conquered

Sinister secrets lurk beneath the splendour of a fabulous city. Will Siward's Quest for New England end in heart-breaking tragedy?

Tales of the Wasteland

The year 536 has been called the worst year to be alive, spanning a decade of cold, famine and disease. The world was a wasteland.
But like all good wastelands it is also a spiritual wasteland inhabited by disreputable and damaged kings.
These are their stories...

Tyrant Whelp

Custennin was King of Dumnonia.
Legend names him a kinsman of King Arthur.
So why did a monk write the words to damn him for all time?

Fisher King

Told around firesides, retold into legend, his anguish echoes down the centuries... The tale of the Fisher King – the man behind the myth.

About The Author

Anna Chant

Anna Chant was born and spent her childhood in Essex. She studied history at the University of Sheffield, before qualifying as a primary teacher. In her spare time she enjoys walking the coast and countryside of Devon where she lives with her husband, three sons and a rather cheeky bearded dragon. 'Three Times the Lady' is her third novel. Anna has fallen in love with the Dark Ages and in particular the part played by the often unrecorded and uncelebrated women of the time. She plans to tell the stories of as many as possible!

I hope you have enjoyed reading 'Three Times the Lady'. Writing this book has been a joy, getting to know some of the great religious and royal figures of the age. Charles the Bald, Louis the Stammerer, five Wessex kings, including Alfred the Great, Baldwin Iron Arm, Hincmar of Rheims, Pope Nicholas and Saint Swithun – it truly has a star studded cast! The locations too are spectacular – Winchester, Aachen and Rome are some of the greatest power centres of the Dark Ages. Good reviews are critical to a book's success, so please take a moment to leave your review on the platform where you bought the book. I look forward to hearing from you!

For more news, offers, upcoming releases and all things Dark Age please get in touch via

My Facebook page: https://www.facebook.com/darkagevoices/

Check out my blog: https://darkagevoices.wordpress.com/
Or follow me on Twitter: https://twitter.com/anna_chant

To find out more about Judith of West Francia and the other characters and locations of this book I have pinned many of the sites I used for research onto a Pinterest board - https://www.pinterest.co.uk/annachant/judith-of-flanders/

Printed in Great Britain
by Amazon